PRAISE FOR THE 65TH OCTAVE

*"Gary Scott is a real life Indiana Jones—world adventurer, peerless specula-
tor and raconteur extraordinaire. How could anything less than a great
work of suspense and intrigue flow from his pen..."*

BOB MEIER
SENIOR MARKET STRATEGIST
FOX INC., CHICAGO

*"High drama and mystery teachings join in this profound, fast paced and
impactful adventure thriller as compelling as the best modern fiction."*

VERNON M. SYLVEST, M.D.
MEDICAL DIRECTOR OF LABCORP AMERICA
FOUNDER OF THE INSTITUTE OF HIGHER HEALING

*"This book is a must for those awakening to their own internal guidance. A
vivid, realistic, fascinating story with a twist in every chapter—guaranteed to
keep you reading all night."*

CALIN V. POP, M.D.
AUTHOR OF *THE SYMBOLIC MESSAGE OF ILLNESS*

*"Gary Scott has crafted an indelible glimpse into the realm of the transcenden-
tal basis of higher states of consciousness, not through the world of spirit, but
through a world of high drama, global banking, cunning, treachery and espi-
onage. Intimate and gripping, The 65th Octave is an important work for spiritual
seekers and thrill seekers alike."*

JAY GLASER, M.D.
MEDICAL DIRECTOR
MAHARISHI AYURVEDIC HEALTH CENTER

*"A story about the importance of using the intellect and mysterious forces
beyond our comprehension to gain true freedom..."*

SIR MILES R. WALKER
FORMER PRIME MINISTER OF ISLE OF MAN

"The book was GREAT! I am looking forw

LORD RICHARD MACAULAY-MANNYN
MEMBER OF THE HOUSE OF LORDS

D0817134

"*The 65th Octave satisfied all I look for in a good novel: fine writing, engaging plot from the first page, suspense, intrigue, surprise, a sensitive, intelligent male character combined with beautiful, wise, strong women, travel to places I love, both far and near, believable, and high adventure. Best of all, I loved the way it combines mystery with great wisdom; and high finance with spirituality. Well done!*"

JANE KERN
AUTHOR OF *INVENTING A SCHOOL—*
EXPANDING THE BOUNDARIES OF LEARNING

"*Gary Scott has combined years of experience with international travel and investing to give us an intriguing mystery and a lesson in life and investing. He has captured both the physical and mystical uniqueness of the Everglades.*"

RALPH ARWOOD, M.D.
EVERGLADES WILDLIFE PHOTOGRAPHER

"*A captivating and action packed romp through the world of high finance and mysticism. An unlikely hero and a hard-to-resist heroine have a lot to teach the world about true power.*"

A.K. WILSON
NATIONAL INDEPENDENT REVIEW

"*Many insights and practical lessons may be gleaned from the pages of this book. Universal truths are revealed concerning the actions and interactions of people's lives, desires, and ambitions, and about how we may adopt positive responses for our own lives.*"

DR. H. L. SARGENT
ENVIRONMENTAL SPECIALIST

"*This is a wonderful double barreled read. In the first instance I read it as a great story but had to go back and read it again to delve into the provocative ideas.*"

DAVID MELNIK
OUEEN'S COUNSEL

Robert

May The spirit

of The Tortoise be with

you always!

[signature]

4-2021

Van cover BC

THE
65TH
OCTAVE

GARY A. SCOTT

Sunstar
PUBLISHING LTD.

The 65th Octave
by *Gary A. Scott*

Gary A. Scott
United States Copyright, 2000
Sunstar Publishing, Ltd.
204 South 20th Street
Fairfield, Iowa 52556

LCCN: 98-061429
ISBN: 1-887472-55-X

Photo of the Author by Ralph Arwood, MD
Text design by Irene Archer

Printed in the U.S.A.

Readers interested in obtaining further information on the subject matter of this book are invited to correspond with:

The Secretary, Sunstar Publishing, Ltd.
204 South 20th Street, Fairfield, Iowa 52556

For more Sunstar Books, please visit our website:
www.sunstarpub.com

TO MERRI

Special thanks to:
Mom, Cheri, Cinda, Jacob, Francesca and Eleanor
for their inspiration and encouragement.

CONTENTS

Foreword . . . . *ix*

CHAPTER ONE 1

CHAPTER TWO 10

CHAPTER THREE 16

CHAPTER FOUR 18

CHAPTER FIVE 23

CHAPTER SIX 30

CHAPTER SEVEN 38

CHAPTER EIGHT 47

CHAPTER NINE 53

CHAPTER TEN 57

CHAPTER ELEVEN 64

CHAPTER TWELVE 69

CHAPTER THIRTEEN 73

CHAPTER FOURTEEN 76

CHAPTER FIFTEEN 78

CHAPTER SIXTEEN 82

CHAPTER SEVENTEEN 90

CHAPTER EIGHTEEN 100

CHAPTER NINETEEN 105

CHAPTER TWENTY 110

CHAPTER TWENTY ONE 118

CHAPTER TWENTY TWO 132

CHAPTER TWENTY THREE 136

CHAPTER TWENTY FOUR 139

CHAPTER TWENTY FIVE 148

CHAPTER TWENTY SIX 155

CHAPTER TWENTY SEVEN 160

CHAPTER TWENTY EIGHT 166

CHAPTER TWENTY NINE 174

CHAPTER THIRTY 179

CHAPTER THIRTY ONE 184

CHAPTER THIRTY TWO 190

CHAPTER THIRTY THREE 202

CHAPTER THIRTY FOUR 208

CHAPTER THIRTY FIVE 217

CHAPTER THIRTY SIX 222

CHAPTER THIRTY SEVEN 227

CHAPTER THIRTY EIGHT 238

CHAPTER THIRTY NINE 242

CHAPTER FORTY 261

CHAPTER FORTY ONE 263

Excerpt from 64th Treaty 270

Author's Note 275

About Gary Scott 278

FOREWORD

After 10 years in office, I ceased to be Chief Minister in December, 1996, but retained my seat in Tynwald and have responsibility within the Treasury and travel overseas on promotional visits for the island.

Though the Isle of Man is a well known, well regulated international financial centre located in the middle of the Irish Sea, few understand the importance of its history in mystical and democratic terms. Little is known about the mystery of the Druids who made our misty isle their home. Few history books stress how this land was a meeting place for the Celts and Vikings and how this union brought the first democracy that later became a model for free men everywhere and has lasted for a continuous period exceeding 1000 years.

This makes it quite fitting that The 65th Octave, a story about the importance of using the intellect and mysterious forces beyond our comprehension to gain true freedom, unveils the secrets of our tiny island so well. It seems proper that this book about money, wealth and high finance also so clearly identifies our island's beauty, mystery, historic contribution and rustic charm.

Anyone who reads The 65th Octave and then stands at the ring of ancient Neolithic stones called Cashtal-yn-ard (Castle on the Height), at dawn will understand the spirit of The 65th Octave, a fast reading, page turning novel, that does describe real magic.

I invite anyone looking for a spiritual adventure to read The 65th Octave, then visit our fair Isle and you will feel and understand the picture that Gary Scott so accurately painted in the fast paced, mystical story.

—*Sir Miles R. Walker (former Prime Minister of Isle of Man)*

CHAPTER ONE

Robin MacAllen's stomach knotted when Usha, his executive assistant, entered the luxurious hotel suite. Dressed in silk, she was as always cool and elegant, despite Miami's sweltering air. Robin slouched in his chair, his shoes unlaced and necktie undone, wearily fingering the stubble on his chin. He was long past his limits. What now?

Robin's athletic body was well proportioned, the outcome of summers of hard work on the high seas; he appeared capable of handling anything, anytime. He was. But in the past decades he had also learned his boundaries. This last four-week business trip to Europe had pushed him far. The flight home had been tiring—an electrical storm had bucked the plane and the snarled traffic from the airport escalated the jet lag, making him feel older than his forty-five years. He had barely made his keynote speech at the Global Banking Symposium after the flight.

At these seminars, bankers paid him an abundant $725 an hour for his expert advice. At the top of a highly specialized field MacAllen identified global frauds and scams at every financial level. The more he charged, the more the bankers called.

After this trip, he had cancelled all his meetings. One financial institution had even offered to quadruple his fee but continuing this crushing weariness was not worth any amount.

Robin combed his dark hair with his fingers as he watched Usha walk silently on the polished pine floor. She ignored his obvious exhaustion. "A gentleman is here for a consultation. He says it's a matter of life or death."

Though physically strong, Robin possessed a composed and easy-going manner. He rarely lost his temper with anyone, and never showed his anger to Usha. But the choked terseness of his reply cautioned her that his patience was sparse. Robin had left his assistant explicit instructions not to be disturbed. "I asked you to cancel all consultations. I don't care what his problem is or what he'll pay. I'm beat, Usha. Ask him back tomorrow."

The old man in a rumpled tweed coat who trailed behind her reeked of trouble and grief. Any interruption was bad enough; this old man's bearing suggested something even worse. Take on more trouble? Impossible!

Usha blinked twice and stepped further into the suite. Though barely half Robin's size she replied with force. "He says he can't pay anything. I think you should listen. It's one of those feelings you pay me to get."

What she said next really didn't matter because there was a standing arrangement between them. Robin always helped those who couldn't pay. Business was thriving. The luxury suite he kept here in Miami, his ranch in the Everglades, his home in Old Naples, London and Hong Kong flats and all his global travels were paid for by men who saved millions from his advice. Rich men could afford to wait for his help. But most likely this poor man could not.

Robin always remembered. Rich as he was now, he wasn't always. His wealth had risen from talent combined with relentless focus, hard work and much luck. Had the man offered any amount of money, tonight he might have turned it down. Chances were this disheveled old man was the bearer of headaches and bad news. But since he couldn't pay a dime, Robin knew he would hear his story.

He sighed and compelled himself to walk across the room where he poured a Miami Special -black Cuban coffee thick with sugar. Robin felt trapped. "Okay, Usha, I'll see him. Keep it short. What's he want?"

He groaned as he slugged down the coffee then reached for more.

"He won't say. He just says it's a matter of utmost importance. Of life or death."

"Great." He groaned again. "A mystery man. The gods must be angry."

Her almond-shaped face was serious. "I don't know about the gods, but I do know my intuition. This man is sincere, Robin."

MacAllen raised his hand in mock surrender. "Okay. Okay. I give up. What's sleep anyway? Send in Mr. Sincere."

Warily, he watched the old man enter and approach him. "Thank yu for seein' me. Fergus Clague is ma name."

Robin caught the Scottish brogue and immediately recognized him as the man who hawked books at Miami Airport. The old man had a rugged look of strength that was out of character for his age. Robin noticed the ragged tweed coat as too well filled, and the man's bearing too straight and strong for his years. Robin's warning instinct, with the help of the second cup of coffee, pushed their way through his sleep-deprived mind.

"Yu cover yurr surprise well, young man. This is a good sign. I see yurr younger than I'd thought. Aye, I guess we can forgive an old man whose eyes er not what they ought to be. Yurr surprised I know yu from the airport? Yurr there often."

He continued in a soft yet steady voice. "I've seen and remember yu so I guess it not be strange yu'll remember me. But I'll guess yu'll find it strange I know yurr name and that yurr family er Scots. Yu'll be surprised at other things I know about yu too. I'm pleased. Yu confirm my assessments of yu."

Robin watched the old man settle into an armchair as he continued speaking. "Yu might think I'm crazy, bein' at the airport every day. I see a lot. I've seen many thousands a people in this airport but I know exactly how many times I'll have seen yu pass, Mr. MacAllen. I'll even be rememberin' the first time I saw yu, because in that minute I knew yu had the second sight, too. I've known for days we'd be speakin'. Even before yu flew back from Europe."

The hushed words quickened. "Listen to me, laddie MacAllen and listen good. We Scots are Celts and er history goes back a long way. But there is a parallel history et goes back further, much further, perhaps to the beginin' of time. I can't tell yu all there is to know. But just knowin' that history has caused more men to die than yu can tell. Caused a purge in the Highland too horrible to think. That purge is thought ta ended hundreds of years ago. It did not. The purge goes on ta this day. I'm one of the last Carriers—those who know the whole story but are not of the Controllers. I been lucky in this but now me time is near. Last week me best friend who was also a Carrier was found murdered in London. He'd been hidin' there for many years. We stayed in touch. If they found him they'll have found me. Me days are numbered. I have knowledge it's important I pass on. I have to tell yu!"

He paused, seemed to consider whether or not to continue, then straightened, as if a decision had been made. "The first time I saw yu I realized yu might not even be aware yu have the second sight. Yu aren't even hidin' it! That's a dangerous thing—so I guess yu'll be free a the Controllers.

"I wanted to tell yu but had to be sure yurr the one who should know. I'm given' yu a book. It's got the secrets that'll be givin' yu more things than yu'll want to know. Yu'll find ways to make more money than yu can count. Yu'll be able to make it in stocks, in bonds, in business, in almost anything yu'll choose. This secret's worth billions but it also can be a curse. Yurr about to receive a call from England. Yu'll be needin' this book when yu go there. And go there yu will. So I'm givin' it to yu now. It can bring yu a fortune. Might save yurr life, too."

Robin leaned back in his chair, his thoughts beginning to leap ahead to what the old man was about to say. Instinctively he began to calculate the scam. He frowned. How'd he know my name? Probably watched me book a flight. Clague could easily have surmised I was of Scottish ancestry. This could be a variation of the treasure map scam. Next he'll want a little seed money to put his secret to work. He had seen better cons.

Why has the old man picked me? I know just about every con, trick, scam, deception and fraud ever devised. Robin felt a steely anger well up at the insult of this con.

Thinking to end this now, he said, "I suppose you need some cash. How much?"

The old man's eyes turned a stony blue and he stared piercingly at Robin. "Och, Laddie, it isn't money that I'll be needin' where I'm goin'. I'll be needin' time but don't have even that now, so I'll only be needin' yu to know the secret. Yu have the sight. Yurr not bein' tracked. Maybe yu can succeed where I canno'. But watch out. There's more danger then yu'll be needin' if the Controllers discover yu know. Once yu understand the secret yu'll know what to do with it. Yurr sight tells me it is so."

Clague's eyes sparkled and brightened. "Most think the secret came from China but that's not true. The secret was born with the Celts. A long, long time ago they took it to Scotland. Yu see, Laddie, Scotland has always been a hard country. High and cold, little good ground for anything save a bit of wheat and clear water to be makin' a fine whiskey. But that's why we chose those lands. Yu'll find Celt blood all over the world, where you'd never expect. Always cold, hard places we'll be because we always be tryin' to escape the Controllers."

The man's words tumbled rapidly out while he still had Robin's attention. "But a man can't live through freezin' winters on just good whiskey. Many a Scot became a travelin' man. A few ended in the East way back when China was still a new place and white men were rare there. Marco Polo had a few hardy Scots with him. Don't get me wrong—Scots did no' go just to Asia. Went west, too. Did yu know one a the Native American chiefs was a Scot?

"It was in Asia where they used the secret. Some were bold and openly used the knowledge to help the Emperors keep the masses under control. Europe's monarchies all lost power but the Emperors in Asia stayed strong with the secret. Because the Controllers were not there!"

The old man leaned nearer to Robin, and his words sharpened. "Opium! That's the way they did it in those days. They built a big trade of it. Run it out a Canton down the Pearl River to Hong Kong. The Emperors allowed it for the secret. Then opium became forbidden but they never got caught. They used the secret, Laddie MacAllen. Knew when and where the patrol boats would be. Always knew what type of goods would be needed next.

"They kept the secret. Handed it down from one Taipan to the next. But they made their mistake by bringing it back ta Europe. That's where the Controllers were, Laddie—spotted the power right away, they did."

Clague's voice grew even stronger, its agitation penetrating Robin like shards of ice. "The Controllers been trying ta take over for five hundred years. They've been brutal and wiped out whole nations. That's what the destruction of the Toltecs, Olmecs and the Aztecs was all about. Ever wondered why Central American Indians look like Orientals? Because they started in the same place. The Scots escaped north to the mountains, others east and some sailed west takin' the secret with them. That's why there was so much gold. The secret needs gold."

Robin was only half listening to the rambling history lesson when his mind honed in on the gold. This, then, would be the lure. Soon the old Scot would be explaining how they could find a map with the gold.

"Mr. Clague," Robin snapped. "I am not interested in discovering lost treasure or learning the whereabouts of hidden gold. Let's stop wasting your time and mine."

Looking determined, the old man sank back in his chair and crossed his arms. "Mr. MacAllen, yurr suspicious nature is good. Yu'll be needin' it. I'm not here for the askin', just the tellin'. There is no treasure. Usin' the secret requires gold if yu don't have the second sight. Aren't yu listenin' to me, Laddie? That's why when the Spanish were so interested in the Aztecs and the Incas and their gold, the Controllers knew that they had the secret. It did no' take long for the Controllers to arrange to wipe out the whole nation. The Controllers did no' want anyone to have the knowledge. They annihilated whole civilizations in Central and South America, leavin' no' one soul alive—afraid even one might escape and tell of the secrets."

Robin sat forward, thinking that this account was not the first he'd heard of nations being destroyed solely for the possession of gold. Something the old man had said, or possibly the way he said it, alerted him. Intent now on hearing the rest of the tale, he leaned closer as Clague continued.

"It became clear ta the Controllers that there were some in Scotland and the East still knew the secret. The Emperors in China fell in bloody wars that brought them down. The Controllers orchestrated the Highland massacres. We Scots are clannish and tough and did no' make it easy for them. They could no' kill us all. We've learned how ta hide. And we've the second sight yu know, that feelin' at the base of the neck and in the gut that tells what we can and canno' trust. When it's important it grows so strong yurr head aches. I'm sure yu have felt it but maybe yu did no' know what it was."

Clague's voice softened and slowed. "I've had the second sight my life through. Brought me and me friends everythin' we wanted for forty years. But, Laddie, the Controllers ne'er gave up. Traced us down a few years back and started killin' us all. Me friend in London was the last, next to me. When he died I knew me days were numbered. I have to pass the secret on and now I'm passin' it on to yu. Yu, me and a few lives means nothin' ta them."

Clague reached in his pocket and pulled out a book. Holding it up in the air, he sighed. "They've annihilated nations just suspectin' some may of had this secret. This book tells all yu'll need to know. Read with care, Laddie MacAllen, for few men know its contents. This book's from a friend who'll call yu soon. Leave as soon as yu can and take the book with you. Read it and yu'll know what yu have to do."

The old man placed the book on Robin's desk and sagged wearily in the chair. "I've got to go now."

He rose with effort, straightened and said in a quiet voice, "I canno' be seen with yu. This time we spent puts yu in danger enuf."

Without another word Clague walked to the door and was gone.

A musty smell from the old cracked leather book permeated the air. Robin ran his hand along its crusted spine. His brows creased together as he tucked the book into his coat pocket and called to his assistant. "You really missed on that one, Usha. Old Clague must be crazy. Darned if I can figure out the scam and what he's after. But I'm just too tired to work it out now."

He reached for another cup of Miami Special. "What's your feeling, Usha? I can't seem to get a lock on it. Something is very wrong. I've got a strange feeling, a real sense of dread."

"I heard the whole conversation," she began. Usha stopped talking as the phone rang, went over and picked it up. Her eyes opened wide in stunned disbelief. "Ian Fletcher is calling from England. He sounds almost as crazy as Clague."

Robin clicked the conference speaker on, and Ian's voice jumped loudly into the room. "Robin!" Ian was almost crying. "I'm just outside Nailsworth and I need your help! It's extremely urgent. You must come here. Now!"

Robin and Ian had been business associates and close friends almost from the day they had met in the Philippines. If anyone was unflappable it was Ian, yet now he sounded more desperate than he could ever have imagined. He was astounded at the terror in Ian's voice.

"Fly back now?" Robin was so tired he could barely speak. "Ian, remember last week in London? How exhausted I was? I've just gotten back and I've been working the whole time. Can't this wait just a few days?"

Ian did not pause before replying. "No… I'm desperate… No. Robin this is beyond comprehension. Please come here to the Cotswolds. Nailsworth. On tonight's flight. Please!"

The thought of another flight and lengthy drive into the English countryside was overwhelming. His eyes blurred with weariness. A request like this from Ian was almost unimaginable. Robin groaned. "Isn't Nailsworth that little village just down the hill from Minchinhampton?"

Ian's rasped reply was panicky. "Yes, and for God's sake please get here quickly!"

"Okay, calm down, Ian, and let me think. There's a pub just outside Nailsworth called the White Stag. Let's meet there for dinner tomorrow. If I can get a plane out tonight, I'll reach Heathrow early, rent a car and drive down."

"No!" Ian shouted. The intensity in his voice was startling. "Do not come into Nailsworth. Especially not the White Stag. They might see you there. Drive to Minchinhampton instead. Just past the village square watch for a store called Gough's on the left and then an intersection. Go straight over and down a steep hill. About two miles on, the road forks. Take the right turning. About a mile on, you'll see a huge oak on the left. Follow the path across the road from that tree into the hills. Don't come until midnight. Whatever you do, don't let anyone know you're coming. I'll be waiting there and will signal and..."

Fletcher's voice abruptly stopped. It took Robin several seconds to realize there was no sound coming from the other line.

"Ian? You'll signal what? Ian. You there? Ian?"

He waited but there was no answer. Robin had so much to do; he had planned some fishing in the Everglades with his friend Billy Osceola, a Seminole. And yet, tired or not, he would fly to England without delay.

Robin's adrenaline surged as he moved into action.

"Usha, I'm heading for the airport. Call and make reservations. First flight available, London or Manchester, first class. I can drive to the Cotswolds from either place in a couple of hours. Also, have a rental car ready when I get there, a big one that's fast. Mercedes or an Audi. And call Billy Osceola for me in the morning and cancel our fishing trip."

MacAllen's brief meeting with Fergus Clague did not resurface in his mind until an hour later when an overworked Miami traffic cop shouted at Robin for dashing over the airport road to catch his flight. "Hey, get on the crosswalk. Can't ya see how fast those cars are going? I'm getting tired of scraping you guys off the road. Already had to clean up after that old Scot who's always hanging around here. Got killed. Stepped right in front of a car. Hit and run. If I see ya cross like that again, it's gonna cost ya."

Robin was stunned for a moment. Then he reached into his pocket, felt for the book and raced down the terminal to board his plane.

CHAPTER
TWO

Robin stepped out of the car he had rented at Heathrow, blinked back weariness and stared into the pitch dark. There was not a sound. He was alone on the path Ian had described. Since leaving the twisting country road, a feeling of danger had grown in him, a sense of someone's presence. A chill shot up Robin's spine, raising the hair at the base of his skull.

He was jet lagged and exhausted. Nine hours traveling from Miami to London and an additional five driving had left him done in. Ian should have been here by this time. Worry for his friend absorbed him. Ian Fletcher's insistence on meeting here on this windswept hill after midnight was uncharacteristic. An hour had passed since he had seen another car, a beat-up Vauxhall driven by an obviously drunken Englishman probably on his way home after the local pub had closed. Ian was nearly an hour late. Robin's intuition told him he was being observed and his gut churned. Ian wouldn't be hiding like this. MacAllen could not isolate the reasons, but he knew someone—certainly not Ian—was somehow watching him.

Feelings of danger increased, giving him goose bumps up and down his neck. Robin's senses were fully alert and straining to peel back the surrounding veil of darkness to see if anyone was there. Fear was not in Robin's nature. He forced himself to relax despite his screaming instincts cautioning him that something was wrong. In the course of his work over the years, he had been alone in foreign countries, had walked down many isolated roads in the black of night. He had been in precarious positions many times before and was capable of taking care of himself, anywhere, anytime. So why was he feeling such foreboding now?

Robin thought of the old man and his story. Why should this particular tale bother him so much? Clague was less than credible, perhaps had even been deranged. His credentials were questionable. He couldn't even pay a fee so it had to be Clague's death and Ian's frantic call for help coming so close together. Was his friend's absence the warning? Robin did not believe in coincidence; Ian's call had come exactly as the old man had predicted.

Robin's wariness grew as he slid back into the Audi and drove forward in low gear, rechecking the trail and signs Ian had said would be there. His concern increased as he recalled the fear in Ian Fletcher's voice. Ian, who had always been fearless.

Just ahead was the massive oak looming blacker than the night. Robin saw the trail Ian had described, just to the right of the tree, two damp ruts of mud cutting cross the middle of the rounded hill. Far below, lights shone from a distant village. He turned the car onto the path and let it slip slowly forward.

There was little for his senses to grasp, just the smell of burnt grass scorched by his car's overheated muffler and a tiny beam of light from the flashlight he held out the window.

MacAllen craned forward to see where the track ended. Avoiding the brake lights, he let the car roll silently to a stop. Robin turned the engine off and sat in the silence, shrouded by darkness. The only sound was the Audi's motor ticking as it cooled.

The trail was revealed intermittently when the stars and moon broke through the clouds. The countryside offered no clue that at the foot of this hill sat the village of Nailsworth. Nothing was out here. Except Robin and that presence he felt -whoever, whatever, it was. The tingling at the back of his neck intensified.

Robin eased quietly out of the car, making sure the door light did not turn on. He shook his deepening tension loose and to calm himself, did a quick meditation. Many of his business years had been spent in Asia and there he had learned different meditation and body control techniques. The one he preferred, and began to use now, was a mantra that had originated in Vietnam. "Breathing in, I calm my whole body…" he repeated again and again. Now alert but composed, he left the door ajar for a quick escape and worked his way towards the end of the path.

Again, Robin felt an ever-increasing presence. Robin did not know who might be watching or what he expected to find, he only knew that Ian was not there. His friend would never have been this late nor have remained silent when Robin arrived. The prickle on his scalp alerted MacAllen to trouble. Someone, or something else, was waiting and watching.

Where many would have fled, Robin moved slowly forward, challenging whatever lay ahead. Feeling strangely alive, his strength, born of caution and experience, grew stronger as he silently crept further up the path.

All his senses keen, Robin moved ahead. He did not expect to find his friend though he was sure this was the place on the trail Ian had described.

The base of his neck again shivered. There was someone watching him closely; he was being carefully measured. Who and why? How? MacAllen shook his head clear of this sensation and inched carefully down the path, concerned that it could end abruptly, without warning, a sheer bluff offering a deadly plunge onto the rocks below. His eyes strained and his ears tried to penetrate the space ahead. He listened for some change in the path or any movement.

The English countryside seemed tame compared to the rugged outdoors back in the States. Many had been foolishly lulled into danger by the gentleness of these hills. Robin knew this tranquility belied a real danger. He recalled rock climbing near this area and what his guide had warned.

"Danger in this land is time. Untold centuries of man have lived here. Their scars, stumps and scabs left behind are just waiting to get you. Many old mine pits they worked back then. Step into one and you're good as dead."

He shook his growing anxiety and stepped forward with care, his feet cautiously feeling each step. The trail ended suddenly at a promontory and Robin stood silently in the black night, thinking.

He shrank deeper inside his heavy wool jacket and stared into the darkness. This was a lonely, deadly place... he brushed these troublesome thoughts aside. If Ian had problems, they were not at this place. He wondered if Clague's story really was tied into Ian's call. Robin did not believe in coincidence.

Robin's eyes pierced the blanket of night surrounding him. His inner feelings would not dismiss that someone was watching him, and probing his thoughts. Who? Why don't they show themselves? The stillness and the sense of a presence magnified his anxiety. He needed very much to make something happen.

Robin had learned to be patient and calm. He crouched and waited, focusing his attention on the emptiness surrounding him. Like a predator he waited. Nothing happened. Nothing moved. His legs were sore and beginning to knot, his body trembled with fatigue. As the tingling sensation started to wane and the prickles disappeared, he knew he was alone. Whoever, whatever, had been there... was no longer watching him.

Slowly and cautiously, he stood and stretched his aching body. Robin reluctantly crept back to the Audi. If someone had been there, he had not shown himself. Ian Fletcher was not coming.

The Bear Inn at Amberly several miles away was the type of country inn that made the English countryside famous. Centuries old and steeped in tradition, it held commanding views of the valley below. But driving in the middle of this starless bitter night, Robin failed to find this comforting. Chilled and worn-out, he arrived to find the hotel locked. He had forgotten to request a night key.

Leaning heavily on the stone gate for support, he was too tired to admonish himself. Ages might pass before the innkeeper heard the buzzer and awoke to let him in. MacAllen stabbed a half-frozen finger at the dark nipple of the night bell that was only visible for its contrast against the light color of the Cotswold stone. A tingle and shudders moving up his spine made him feel once again that he was being observed. He was too tired to care. He ignored the stinging sensation on his hairline and reached again for the bell.

As his finger touched it, arms wrapped around him, crushed his body. Robin tried to whirl around to face his adversary, thinking that perhaps some drunk had grabbed him for support, but something had him locked tight. He could see nothing. The pressure on him was immense. Then the grip relaxed for a second and Robin twisted sharply, jerking himself free from the hold. Nobody, nothing was there! The pressure hit him again. Unbelievable pain increased as invisible limbs tightened around him.

He reeled back against the cold stone. Force from the vise-like grip crushed him. His head felt ready to explode. Was this a heart attack? No, the pressure was external. He forced himself to stay calm. How was this happening? MacAllen's strength was a match for any man, yet he was being crushed helplessly.

Like some invisible claw, the attack enmeshed his entire being. Air was being forced out of his constricted body. This grip could not be a man's. The instinct for survival pounded in his head. Robin would not panic. He tried to breathe in deeply but his lungs remained pinned tight. He forced his body to ignore the intense pressure and slipped into his mantra. "Breathing in, I calm my whole body…" He went limp and dropped to his knees. Hitting the pavement, his face and cheek scraped against the ice. He willed himself to relax again and let his mind drop away, absorbed by his simple mantra. He let his mind drift and looked within, releasing his pain. Quiet now, his thoughts went deeper, deep inside, as warmth rushed in. The lights from inside the hotel slowly began to fade.

Far away, through a deep fog, Robin heard a worried voice. "Sir! Sir! Are you okay? Sir?"

He was alive, and feeling the cold ice bite at his face. He strained to push himself from the harsh pavement and its numbing cold.

"Are you alright? Wake up. Sir!"

Robin blinked. "What happened?" he groggily asked the innkeeper kneeling next to him.

"I don't know. I came out to answer the bell. Found you lying here. Shall I call Dr. Chilman?"

Robin felt his strength beginning to return. "No. Ugh, no. Don't do that," he said, regaining his senses. "I-I'm fine. Must've slipped on the ice. It's dark. I-I just knocked the wind out of me, that's all. Help me up. Maybe a shot of brandy will warm me."

The innkeeper helped him to the lounge and settled him uncertainly on a short stool in front of the fireplace. Robin stared at the coals dimming in their final warm orange glow.

The innkeeper hurried around the bar with a large snifter of Armagnac. Robin inhaled its acrid fumes, took a huge gulp and coughed. "Thanks, I'm fine now."

"If you're sure then, sir. I can still call Dr. Chilman at home to come across the hill and take a look."

"No, no," Robin replied as he turned from the fire and waved the man to bed. "I'm fine and I'm really sorry about all this. Please, go on back to bed. I'll turn in soon myself."

The innkeeper padded softly across the faded floral carpet and headed back to his warm bedroom, leaving Robin alone in front of the dying coals.

Despite his long journey, the disheartening wait on the hill and this terrorizing attack, Robin knew he would not sleep. The brandy burned his throat but also soothed him. Was this a sudden medical problem or just exhaustion? Had Clague's warning come true? He had received Ian's call, returned to England, and now there had been this mysterious assault. He wondered if these unexplained events, the presence he felt and this attack were related.

Comforted by the fire, his mind puzzled over the facts. He thought about the tingling sensation that had cautioned him on the hill and just before the attack. This was the same sensation he felt in his business when he sensed a financial problem. He had always called it instinct. These goose bumps had saved him from more deceptions than he could count.

This was what Clague had called his second sight when he had told him the story about the book. "The book," he muttered. He had brought it with him, meaning to read it on the plane, but had not. He had carried it in his coat and now he reached into the pocket to confirm what his second sight already knew. His pocket was empty!

CHAPTER THREE

Robin slumped in an old cracked leather chair he had pulled in front of the fire. Orange embers winked warmly in the dim room and with the brandy they erased the chill that encompassed him. He started to doze in front of the dying coals. Jolting awake, he thought one more time about Clague's tale. Part of it must be true. Cradling the Armagnac, he walked to the lead-framed window where he could see the entrance to the inn slowly becoming visible in the cold, gray dawn. His fear for Ian grew along with the morning light.

In less than twenty-four hours, too many of Clague's predictions had come true. The old man was dead. Ian was nowhere and someone had mugged him. He had to assume his friend was in very serious trouble.

The old Scot had warned him of ruthless people called Controllers. Even if half his account was accurate, these Controllers had annihilated civilizations just to stop the knowledge that the book contained. Surely if they did all this, they would and could go further. But why hadn't they killed him when they took the book? They must have known, then, that he had not read it!

Startled by this revelation, Robin remembered the odd feelings he had had while waiting alone on the Common. "They read my mind," he said aloud to the fire. "They knew I hadn't read the book. That's why I'm still alive!"

On the flight over to England, he hadn't been able to sleep

despite his fatigue. John Thurlow, a friend and computer whiz from San Francisco had recently sent him a newly invented hand-held scanner. It was a gift with a string attached. He knew Robin had many high-tech contacts in influential places. "Give the scanner a try," John had requested. "Pass its wonders on to those who need to know."

John had developed this scanner thinking it could change the face of communications. A complete computer itself, hardly bigger than a pen, it worked on its own and could copy hundreds of pages. It could scan a whole book, store it and download everything into any personal computer.

On the plane, Robin had copied the time-worn book to see how the scanner worked. Now he hoped it had worked as well as John claimed. This manuscript, so unceremoniously and uniquely stolen, must be worth reading; must have deadly information they would kill for. Will John's scanner work with my laptop? Do they know I've copied the book? Staring out the window at the bleak icy Common that lay below the hotel, MacAllen concentrated on alternatives for helping Ian. He saw no connections except the book, and that was gone. His only hope might be the scanner.

Robin stumbled up the creaky carpeted stairs that led to his room. He entered, locked the door behind him, and turned up the clanking steam register. Settling into a faded green armchair he put his Thinkpad on his lap, plugged the scanner in and began typing codes.

The computer screen glowed faintly white in the almost colorless dawn-lit room. Then it came alive with a burst of color. Robin smiled. The scanner had worked perfectly. A title glowed brightly white against the blue background of the screen. It burned deeply into Robin's mind—"The 65th Octave."

CHAPTER FOUR

Robin shivered in the chilly room and felt his mind wander as he stared at the screen. "The 65th Octave." What does this mean? His thoughts were drawn to the words, but more to the remarkable nature of his friend's scanner. Sitting in the gloom of the ashen morning light, he realized it had copied everything exactly as it had appeared in the book. The glow spreading softly into the room showed every word, mark, note and spot, as if he were looking at the book itself.

Different people had seemingly made the notes that covered the pages. They told of experiences and incidents, referring to specific pages of the book. The book itself was ancient and well used, as if handed down from one generation to another. Notes on one page were dated 1893.

Rather than read the entire volume from the screen, he attached the computer to his small printer. With fingers still stiff from the chill that pervaded the room, Robin typed in the print command and the electronic chatter began to fill the room.

While the printer slowly proceeded in its tedious task, Robin rose and looked out the thick glass window at the dismal weather. His mind pondered the events of the day. Here he was printing an ancient text claiming to contain the wisdom of the world that had been copied onto a personal computer by a device no larger than a pencil. Yesterday he had been 4,500 miles away and had crossed the Atlantic in one night. The fantastic, incredible modern world.

Yet, here he was being forced to believe that someone, or something had read his mind and could control him with forces he couldn't see or hear, and then leave without a trace. Even worse, the only explanation might be in a book that was well over 100 years old! And what about Ian? Will this book help me find him? Robin took a long sip of his cold coffee. He stood, stretched and walked to the steaming Teasmaid that was provided with the room. The rich aroma from the Cuban espresso he always carried with him spiraled up from his cup and he winced as the hot, burnt flavor jolted him awake.

MacAllen realized the temperature had dropped and a rising dampness was seeping from the thick stone walls. The coolness nipped his feet and darkened his solemn mood even more. He walked to the steam register and fully opened the old radiators.

The printer's staccato tapping faded into the background as his thoughts once again drifted back to Ian's disappearance. No wonder Ian had called him, he thought. There had been so many impossible events. So much that I would previously have dismissed as quackery now seems real.

As he eased back down into the chair, Ian was still on his mind— a buddy since Robin had started his first business in the Philippines. He remembered the incident that had sealed their friendship forever. An event that, of course, had involved a woman.

Robin remembered fleeing the West Coast to escape his father's death. Raised without a mother, his dad had meant everything to him and then his loss… Robin stopped, pushed away the immeasurable ache and forced himself to remember Manila instead.

Manila had been booming; business had started well and he quickly became rich. Robin had everything - money, success, strength, good health and very good looks. Yet he wasn't happy; couldn't have fun, and didn't want to. He just worked, often sixteen hours a day. His father's death had pushed him into a shell; his body and mind deadened. With no desire for escape, work blotted out the grief and the pain.

Then, he had met Ian, who worked for the large accounting firm that Robin had retained. Ian's expertise in helping Robin expand his business had been brilliant. As they became friends, Ian wasted no time challenging Robin's reclusive frame of mind.

"What the hell's the matter with you, Robin? There are beautiful women all over this place. And they are drooling for you my lad. They love the dark, silent type. But you're missing out. Why don't I organize us some dates, eh?"

Robin remembered his reply. "I've never been a womanizer, Ian. Always had just one girl, someone worth spending time with. I never liked messing around. Now isn't the time for me."

Ian hadn't pressed but called Robin a few days later. "Do me a favor, mate? One of my big clients, Gloria Gartner, is having a birthday party. I'm invited and jolly well can't be there. The old biddy is going to be mad as hell. Fill in for me, would you? Charm the old girl's socks off. Apologize for me and explain you're the ogre that's making me stay in the office and work. Be there exactly at eight. Please don't let me down on this."

Robin had arrived expecting the party to be in full swing. No one was there.

The room had a typical Filipino feel: breezy fans arcing lazily above wooden parquet floors, rich hardwood trim and a huge table loaded with food. In the middle of the table was a brown bag, and Robin was unable to resist a peek. Inside was a whole roasted pig, looking so alive and so mean Robin jumped back in surprise.

His sudden retreat was greeted with immense laughter and he jumped again, shocked by the unexpected presence. A young woman, Eurasian, beautiful beyond belief, had quietly entered the room. "A big man like you? Afraid of a little cooked pig." She laughed as she extended her hand. "Melanie Chong. I'm an associate at Ian Fletcher's office. I specialize in finance."

"Not the pig, just the unexpected. Robin MacAllen. How'd you sneak in so quietly?" he asked while taking in her exotic appearance, her lustrous black hair, almond eyes and silken skin.

"Ian asked me to fill in for him at the last moment, so I'm unexpected," she smiled coyly. "Are you afraid of me too?"

"Ugh, yes. I mean no. I'm not afraid, just surprised. Where is everyone?" Robin looked about uncomfortably.

Her stunning good looks had tied Robin's tongue. They had chatted haltingly for the hour before anyone else arrived. She too was a loner. They had talked into the night, and soon after become lovers.

All his memories came flooding back. She had changed Robin's life and had helped him out of his shell. He learned later how Ian had set everything up, including making sure no one except Robin and Melanie arrived before nine.

Then, Melanie disappeared. His stomach ground as he recalled the panic, the search and the hours, weeks and months of anguish and waiting, the police, and the dozens of reports. Never knowing. He angrily pushed these recollections away. "Dammit! That's in the past. She's gone and I can't bring her back. Ian's the one who needs me now."

He jumped up suddenly to disengage his thoughts and looked out at the morning mist rising off the Common. How could Ian be in trouble? We met in London just last week. He was working on a puzzling case for an English stockbroker; a client killed by lightning who owed money. There were many irregularities and Ian had been hired to investigate.

Could this be just like Melanie? He slammed his fist against the unforgiving stone wall, letting the pain erase the memory again.

To focus his attention, he sat down and opened a new file in his computer. This is like any other scam. I have to be logical. "Got to stay organized," he mumbled under his breath, and began an orderly and disciplined listing of all of his thoughts as he typed:

Gloucestershire, England— 8:45 a.m.

Fact: Fergus Clague contacts me. He says a friend will call from England. Clague gives me a book. Clague is then killed in a hit and run.

Fact: Ian Fletcher calls and asks for help. Ian Fletcher is missing.

Fact: I have been attacked by some person or force unknown to me. The book has been stolen.

Questions: Does Clague, book or my attack have anything to do with Ian? Is Ian's disappearance connected with his latest investigation? Are all events some gigantic coincidence? Can this be an incredible con?

Need to Investigate: Has Clague really died? I didn't see his body. Was policeman at airport genuine? Could he be part of con?

Robin stopped as his computer repeatedly beeped with the burden of his typing and the printing of the book. He pondered his last point as he waited.

Con men rely on the public's acceptance of authority figures. A fraud always relies on one of four fatal attractions—greed, fear, anger or lust. People accept their good luck because phony figures of authority tell them they can. A fake banker says 100% profits are sure. Or a fake policeman could make me believe Clague's death. He returned to the keyboard.

Possible Deceptions: Did Ian really call? Is he actually missing? Was I attacked last night? Could I have been drugged instead?

Possible Motives for Events: Could Ian have stumbled on some incredible industrial con? But why me? Because of Ian's call? Because of something else? What?

MacAllen stopped typing and reviewed the logic of these points again. Nothing quite fit; there were too many unanswered questions. His stomach twisted in knots as he began typing again.

Questions: How could they know I'd return to England? How could they position a policeman in Miami to be exactly at the right place at the right time? How could they follow me to the Inn? How could they read my mind?

Robin shook his head. Things are too loose for a good scam. He stared at the screen and waited for the computer. And if this is a confidence trick, it's definitely big.

Discouraged, his mood plunged. A raw sleet had moved in from the north and had turned everything even darker and grayer. The room was suddenly punctuated by silence as the printer stopped.

Slumping back into his chair, Robin picked up the printed pages.

CHAPTER FIVE

Robin forgot the chill as he scanned the printout. "This is perfect, better than the book," he whispered under his breath. "Now maybe I can get some facts." His heart raced, he was exhilarated, excited, as he saw how the mini-scanner had picked up every smudge and spot. The pages' many notes were as clear as the book itself. The scanner's image enhancement had actually filled the faded spots and dirty areas with a reproduction that was uncanny.

The 65th Octave

In the beginning, we were one. In one place and at peace. Here was anywhere we wanted to be. Things were anything we desired. Time was only imagination. Life was perfection. All was harmony and balance.

There were no Controllers. There were no thoughts or concepts of domination or control. We were all part of our universe, tiny reflections, each a part of the whole.

We each did our part, no more and no less, because there was no sloth and thus no need for ambition. By this, we were eternally bathed in nature's harmonious light. Joy was our nature. It was with us always and want was not.

Robin stopped reading as he noticed a lighter pattern over the words. Scrutinizing faint shadows that traced across the page, he saw that the book had been used by someone as a back pad. The pressure had left an indentation on the pages. The scanner was so sensitive it had recorded even the shadows cast by these slight markings on the paper.

As he adjusted the light to read the shadows better, the handwriting became more distinctive. Small and tight, it was the neat orderly script he knew and had seen hundreds of times before. The handwriting belonged to Ian Fletcher!

Quickly, he put down the printout and returned to his computer to see if he could enhance, decipher and clarify the text.

The damp morning draft grudgingly gave way to a wan winter sun, but Robin did not notice. His body tensed in concentration as the original text from the book slowly faded from the screen. What had been shadows became clearer, rose from the background and replaced words that had been the original text. The shadows became letters. With increasing tempo, new words cleared and became lines that focused. Suddenly, Ian Fletcher's notes rose brightly onto the screen, shimmered across it.

Robin leaned forward eagerly; his eyes wrinkled in intense curiosity.

This is for Robin MacAllen or anyone who might have answered my call for help in case his arrival is too late for me. When you review these notes, you may wonder if am I making some horrendous mistake or perhaps am going crazy. I cannot answer either question for certain. Since finding the attic, my life has turned upside down. All I have known to be true in twenty years of accounting and business can now be thrown out the window.

There is too much my imagination cannot explain, so I will try to record it in the hopes my writing will make more sense than my thoughts. Perhaps getting recent events on paper will highlight some pattern, so all this shows some logical order. If I am no longer around, I hope, at the least, that these notes can save everyone else from what I have found. I cannot seem to make sense of it, but I do know that what I've seen is more dangerous than anyone can imagine. The very freedom of the world may be at stake.

It began three weeks ago, January 5, when I came to Cheltenham to investigate the estate of T. Milow Smythe. Mr. Smythe's unexpected passing by an act of God had left an unresolved debt of two hundred and eight thousand pounds sterling with the brokerage firm of Howe, Puddle and Rudd. Mr. Smythe was found dead on a secluded path after being struck by lightning during the night.

For Mr. Smythe to have had such a large account with Howe, Puddle and Rudd was not necessarily unusual. The way the loans were made was abnormal, but it was the state of Mr. Smythe's account that caused the biggest concern and warranted my firm being called. According to the records, Mr. Smythe had always dealt with the firm, but account opening records for him could not be found. The firm's current records date back ten years and during that time Mr. Smythe had been a substantial client. A further investigation of the firm's microfilms showed that he had been a client clear back in 1946 when the company first started filming its records!

A cursory glance into several archive files showed that Mr. Smythe's name was there too. In fact, T. Milow Smythe appeared in an account record from 1892, which would mean that he had been with the firm for nearly one hundred years. Perhaps even further back than that, but the partners stopped looking at that time due to two other curiosities.

It seemed that although Mr. Symthe had been a client for over a hundred years (which in itself was obviously impossible), there also wasn't any record of his address or any other personal data. This was a second impossibility; clients, especially those with loans, are well documented. Even more incredible was that Mr. Smythe had never paid one single cent to the firm! Not one! Over time, Mr. Smythe had bought shares from the

*firm with interest-free credit and each month the investments he
had chosen had made profits! If the records were correct, the
stockbrokers had been paying Mr. Smythe the inflation adjusted
equivalent of fifteen thousand pounds sterling every week for
the past one hundred years!*

*What made this even odder —totally impossible— was that
no one in the firm seemed to know Mr. Smythe. The broker who
had made the last few transactions vaguely remembered placing
the order. All business had been conducted over the phone.
Other than that, no one knew Smythe, or at least no one in
Howe, Puddle and Rudd admitted knowing him.*

Robin pulled himself away from the glowing screen, stood and
stretched. His head pounded but the pain was being replaced by a
piercing sense of excitement. He now felt he knew what was happening from this bit of information he had just read. Someone
employed by the stockbrokers must have set up a phony account and
had been using it to milk the firm. As incredible as it seemed, it
appeared the theft had been going on for over one hundred years!
This was impossible, of course, but the embezzler must have been
extremely clever and had generated old records to support the false
account. A very shrewd and creative thief indeed. Robin's face
smoothed over with relief. This was the first information he had
found that made any sense to him at all.

He collapsed back in his chair, and said in a somber voice, "Ian's
in way over his head. He never deals with crimes like these, with
stakes that are so high, millions and millions of dollars a year! The
vastness of this theft is unreal. "

A foreboding hit Robin's gut like a sledgehammer. If this
swindler is as ruthless and shrewd as he seems to be, Ian could be in
terrible trouble. And then questions began pounding into his
thoughts. How did the old man, Clague, deliver that book to me in
Miami even before Ian had called? Why didn't Ian make our ren-
dezvous last night? And where is he?

Infuriated, frustrated and very worried, Robin returned to his computer. He looked once more at the glowing impressions that were Ian's notes.

T. Milow Smythe was hard to trace. My first thought was that the man did not exist. Once I examined the initial facts, I assumed that some sort of white–collar crime was involved and I wanted to investigate it in that way. I was looking for guilty stockbrokers, not Mr. Smythe.

But it quickly occurred to me that there was a body, and that body had been carrying documentation from Howe, Puddle and Rudd when found dead on the Common. Mr. Smythe had several delivery notes that indicated he had made share purchases from the firm. These were the only identifying papers on the body. No one could find any other record of T. Milow Smythe. The documents and records at the stockbrokers were all that attested to this man's existence.

We tried the telephone company and the post office but neither had any records whatsoever for a Mr. T. Milow Smythe. The police were at a loss as well. We placed advertisements in local papers; I thought such an unusual name would get some response but nothing came of it.

While placing the notices in the newspapers, I had another idea. The Financial Times is the most widely read daily investment paper in England. Anyone who invests heavily reads this paper.

I wondered if Mr. Smythe from Cheltenham or nearby was a subscriber to the Financial Times. A few quick calls found that a Mr. Smythe did indeed have the paper delivered daily, to a post office in a small village near Cheltenham called Dowdeswell.

I looked at the Ordinance Survey Map of the area and it showed that the footpath from Dowdeswell village to Cheltenham leads right to the spot where Mr. Smythe's body was found.

I was able to find Mr. Smythe's home easily. A trip to the village post office was all it required. England has a modern postal service but the village postal systems are still much as they've been for more than a hundred years. Quite often, an address has little more than a person's name and the name of the cottage and village. In Mr. Smythe's case it was "Thaxton Cottage, Dowdeswell, Gloucestershire," and the postal code.

The local postmaster had a small sweets shop and offered the postal service as an extra. He also knew everything about everyone in Dowdeswell.

Roger Quinn has been postmaster there for over thirty years. He knew Thaxton Cottage, even though it was remote. He also knew of Mr. Smythe though he could not recall seeing him for years. In fact, he couldn't remember if he had ever seen him. Thaxton Cottage was so remote there was no road leading to it. There was only a path to the cottage that was accessible by foot and the postman didn't deliver there. Smythe received only the Financial Times and mail from a stockbroker. There was not much mail but it was continuous, so an arrangement had been made to have any mail put in a milk crate behind the post office. Mr. Smythe picked it up whenever he came into the village. He had been doing this for years. Mr. Quinn stated that this arrangement had been made when he took over the post office thirty years ago. The postmaster showed me how to get to the cottage but suggested I wait for Mr. Smythe to stop by as he hadn't picked up his mail that day!

I was astounded to learn that the mail was still being picked up. Could it mean that the man found on the Common was not Smythe? Could it have been someone other than Smythe picking up mail? If so, why had no orders been placed with the stock brokers after the man's death? Had the courier's death ended the deal?

I wanted to find out more, so following the postmaster's instructions, I hiked out to Thaxton Cottage. A bleaker place at this time of year you will never want to see. It was a little two-

room up two-room down detached cottage that sits on the edge of a forest on a small foot path running between Dowdeswell and Charlton Kings Common.

The cottage is halfway up a steep hill and has a commanding view of the valley. God knows the place was never built for living in the winter. A bitter wind streaks from the valley floor. Biting cold, it numbs the very roots of your soul. But someone had been living there, that is for certain!

The place looked deserted. In retrospect it was foolish of me to go in on my own. Trespassing is the only word for what I did. A court order would have been easy to obtain and a local constable could have helped me, though now I doubt it would have mattered much at all.

I knocked loudly several times.

Robin blinked. Ian Fletcher's notes then came to an abrupt end.

CHAPTER SIX

The cursor on the computer screen blinked and flashed, taunting Robin with the end of the page.

He grabbed the printout of the book and began to read it again. Could there be more pages from Ian? Or had the notes suddenly stopped for reasons too sinister to even think about?

Then MacAllen saw faint outlines on other pages as well. Ian had written more notes, each on a different page, almost as if he had anticipated someone finding them.

Sweating despite the continued chill, Robin began deciphering again. The blue and white screen slowly focused on the precisely written shadows. His screen blinked; images formed and the notes sprang clearly into view.

After breaking the lock, I walked in and saw that Thaxton Cottage looked as dreary within as it did on the outside. The decor was so old and decrepit that the parts I could see were almost indistinguishable. Little could be seen because decades worth of neatly folded Financial Times papers were piled over everything and stacked up against the walls.

Along with all the papers, the cottage contained only an old pine table and two chairs, all gray with age. A kettle with one dirty teacup sat on a wood-burning stove in a kitchen that was also full of Financial Times. The smell of damp rotting paper was overwhelming.

I had to use all my willpower not to retch and I was about to leave when my curiosity was engaged by a most peculiar fact.

I was not cold. At first, I thought the stone walls were simply stopping the raw whipping wind, but as my numbness from being outside wore off, I realized that Thaxton Cottage was distinctly warm inside.

What made this odd was that there wasn't any source of heat -not in the kitchen, living room or the potato scuttle on the side of the house. No fire was burning, the stove was not warm and the cottage was not wired for electricity.

A cottage such as this would never have its heater upstairs. The place was little more than a big chimney anyway. But whatever the source it had to be upstairs and it had to be immensely powerful to send heat downstairs and make the cottage like a steam bath.

I decided to investigate and shouted several times up the stairs. The last thing I wanted was to shock an invalid, or even worse, an armed resident. I climbed the steps, which were nothing more than ancient crumbling stone wrapped in a circle around the chimney. There were two rooms and it was in the first that I found the files. There were hundreds of them in boxes, in meticulous order, dated and alphabetized. Dusk was falling and the fading daylight came dimly through a tiny upstairs window; what I saw was enough.

These were records of T. Milow Smythe's account at Howe, Puddle and Rudd. Thousands of orders dating back over a hundred years. Yet that was not all. Those documents were just the beginning, because all those profits had been put into other accounts and magnified many times over.

There were dozens of double-blind accounts, lent to a company formed in the Isle of Man. The shares of that firm appeared to be owned by other companies registered in tax havens and in many other parts of the world. There was the Milow Company of Hong Kong, T. Smythe Trading in Karachi, Milow and Smythe Investments in Georgetown, Cayman. There were so many in different countries I could not study them with care, but I could easily see they went back for years.

The most amazing part was the money. Every account seemed to be as profitable as Mr. Smythe's person alone. They all appeared to accrue money, week upon week, day upon day. I did not see a single purchase that had lost value. None of the investments seem to have been held long either. The shares were bought, went up and were sold. It was as if the buyer could somehow see into the future!

This trading had taken place all over the world in dozens of stock markets. The cash was taken each and every week and filtered into a large number of different company accounts, where it still appeared to be. I found the figures hard to believe because not one of those accounts had any withdrawals of the money. From a quick calculation, it appeared I was looking at the records of a conglomerate with assets in the billions of pounds. And none of these billions had been spent. They were just sitting there, mainly in cash and bonds.

Robin stooped and rubbed his forehead that was beginning to hurt fiercely. His mouth was dry and he found it hard to swallow. It appeared to be insider trading, and he wanted it to be this, or anything else he could understand. But insider trading on such scale simply couldn't have gone on for decades without notice. And surely con artists would have spent the money! Just sitting in stocks and bonds didn't make any sense.

He pushed away his doubts and returned to Ian's words.

Have I made some monstrous mistake? The implications are so horrendous I cannot even comprehend them. I was looking at what could mean the end of the whole financial world as we know it. And it was all sitting there in a tumbledown cottage in the middle of nowhere.

The records were current, up to the very day I discovered them in Thaxton Cottage. Yet no one was in the cottage. And no one had been going in or out of the cottage either. The house was surrounded by mud; nobody could have entered or left without sinking into that slime. I checked when I left. My footprints were as fresh as when I entered.

However, this mystery was nothing whatsoever compared to what I found in the second room. My time may be very short now and as I cannot explain what I found, I'll write what happened in the hopes that it adds some sense to all this.

The other room was where I found the source of the heat. In it was an orb unlike anything I had ever seen -small, about the size of a fish bowl and colored gold. In fact, it looked as if it were made of pure gold. Although I am not an expert, I do know that gold has an inner luminescence not seen in any other metal.

I cannot say how that orb was the source of heat because I did not feel any warmth radiating from it as would be expected. I put my hand close to it and still didn't feel any heat. But the closer I got the warmer I felt. I was compelled to touch it, even though I knew I should not. I wet my finger and touched it quickly to see if it was hot. It was not. But what I did experience was an improbable and astounding thrill. I put my hands on the globe once more and felt warmth coming from deep inside me. It was comforting. Until suddenly I realized I was being watched. I looked around. No one was there, but somehow they knew me, knew everything I knew, everything I had done and seen. Someone was reading my mind!

Again, MacAllen stopped reading. How could someone know what the hell Ian was thinking? And who? Maybe these notes were a joke. He wanted to laugh, but then he remembered his own experience. He quickly returned to the notes.

I cannot tell how or what they knew or even who they were. All I can write even now is that I knew. I thought I saw shadows just outside my vision staring intently at me, as if they were piercing my brain. They had focused their total attention on my thoughts, memories, and emotions. My whole being, my entire history was clear to them. I let go of the orb and ran from the room. There was an old book lying there and for some inexplicable reason I had to have it. I grabbed it and continued running. There's little else I remember that night besides the penetrating cold, splashing through mud and rain, and then catching the train. I don't know why. I can only recall I felt driven to grab that book and then hide it!

When I woke the next morning, to my astonishment I was in my London apartment. I was clean, dressed in my nightclothes and the papers in my briefcase indicated I had been working on an audit case in the City. I cannot express the bewildering feeling that stayed with me through the day. It was as if all that had happened were a dream. No one in my office knew anything about the case with the Cheltenham stockbrokers.

I called Howe, Puddle and Rudd and talked to one of the partners. He thought I had lost my sanity. He denied we had ever met. Everything that had happened seemed to be a fantasy. I started to think I was going mad.

Only two things convinced me otherwise. First, I knew I was being followed. Someone seemed to know every move I made. I tried to throw them off track by taking the Underground to places I had never been. I would jump off one train unexpectedly and get onto another. I watched and made sure that no one was trailing me.

I'm not experienced at this sort of thing, but I do know I was not being followed. Yet when I reached my destination, I knew they were there, watching and waiting. But what were they waiting for? I never knew, nor did I even know who they really were. I could never see them straight on. All I could see were fleeting glimpses spotted out of the corner of my eye, or the indistinct outlines in a mirror. When I looked, they were always gone. But I knew they were there!

The second reason was that I knew the book was still right where I had hidden it.

The next day, my seizures started. Some invisible force was grabbing me and crushing me while I slept. When I woke up, I knew they had been there looking for the book. I kept the secret where they could not see. I am not even sure I could see myself. I believe I did not want to ever lay eyes on that book again. Doing so would confirm to me that what had happened was real. I preferred to think, or at least hope, it was all a dream and soon I would wake and all would be well.

I knew they, whoever they were, had followed me, but I also knew what I had to do. I had to get this book into someone's hands without their knowing.

There was a London phone number in the journal I felt pressed to call. The man who answered was expecting me. I was absolutely flabbergasted, until he mentioned your name and said that you needed the book. I came totally undone then. How could he know you?

He told me how to write these notes and where to hide the book at the White Stag Inn in Cheltenham. He said he would get it to you. Tomorrow I'll return to the White Stag and leave it. What will happen then I can't even guess.

I feel trapped in some mystifying illusion, like I am a character in a Franz Kafka story where the world takes on nightmarish unreality. I don't know if I am sane or not, but I have written this just in case there is some logic in all these events that I can't see.

If they take me, Robin, you're my only hope. If you or anyone else gets these notes, if you get my call, for God's sake come and help me!

Putting down the manuscript, Robin stood and walked slowly to the window. How could he find Ian? Even as the thought came, his instincts told him to leave it alone. If this was white-collar crime of the highest order, he should turn it over to the police and be on his way. This was a matter for them. And it was clear that Ian had lost his mind.

Uneasily, he reviewed his options. "Best not to get involved," he said grimly into the empty room, but even as the words escaped his lips, he realized they weren't truly what he felt. He couldn't abandon anyone in need, much less a friend. The constabulary would never believe this tale. So if he didn't help Ian, who would? No one else even knew of his old friend's plight.

I have a few tricks of my own, he thought. For now, it's time to get out of sight. With these notions wavering in his mind, he slumped in his chair and caved in to utter exhaustion. He slipped into a deep sleep, with troubled dreams of golden orbs, Ian, dark shadows and piles of cash. A face appeared, of a wizened old man, wrinkled, creased and very ancient. "Follow the money. Follow the money," he bellowed, over and over in a powerful unchanging voice.

He was awakened, stiff and sore, by the ringing of the phone. The innkeeper was worried because Robin had not appeared from his room the entire day. He ordered a sandwich—a Ploughman: onions, bread and cheese. He also asked for coffee, strong and black.

When the food arrived, he ate slowly and reviewed his plan. Whoever this is, he warned himself, they're the best. I have to be thoroughly cautious if I want to come out of this alive, much less help Ian.

MacAllen finished his meal, left the tray in the hall and walked slowly down to the ancient oak registration desk, where he picked up a night key. "I won't be back until late and I'll sleep most of the day tomorrow. Don't disturb me, please." Then he left.

The evening air hit him like an ice-cold saw cutting hungrily into his flesh. Shrinking deep into his coat, Robin walked tenderly over the slick pavement. Fog had dropped again, and spotlights from the inn swirled in eerie patterns as they fought unsuccessfully to cast light onto the surroundings.

He slid into his rented Audi, thought of last night's attack and shivered, but not from the frigid air. A sound from the thick mist caught his attention. He turned the key quickly and locked the doors. What a bitch, he thought. If they're still here, I can't see them. If they follow me, I won't even know. But then, he thought, if I can't see them, they can't see me. He turned the car's heater to defrost, backed slowly out of the car park, turned right and drove into the mist.

CHAPTER SEVEN

The thick fog immediately swallowed Robin. Away from the lights of the inn, darkness and mist dropped visibility to barely a few feet. This would make it easy to lose anyone who tried to follow. For now, though, he wanted them to pursue. If they were still on his trail, Robin needed to know. MacAllen wanted very badly to throw them off kilter. He slowed his car even more, creeping so that even an amateur could not lose him. He wanted any tails to believe he was heading for a pub, and a drink or two. "Don't let them know I'm leaving," he muttered into the silence.

Moving with care, he drove up a steep hill leading away from the Bear and towards the route to Minchinhampton Common. He had guessed correctly that the clouds would be hanging low in the valley. In this fog, no one could see him. Until they suddenly broke free of its grip. Any pursuers would not know where the fog would end. Only then, too late, could they see him!

Higher on the Common, it was clear. The fog below stood like immense walls as he emerged into the thin, chilled air. The stars shone brightly, the moon a brilliant mirror of reflected glory. MacAllen stopped and waited.

He sat at the top of the hill for five minutes, enjoying the heat in the car. Yet he was still shivering, his body shaking in anticipation. If his attackers were to appear, let them come now.

After several minutes, Robin knew no one had come after him.

Good, he thought. But his gut feeling shouted that something was very wrong. Even though no one had followed, he sensed keenly that he was being watched. "Come on you idiot," he growled at himself. "Stop jumping at shadows. No one is out there. They would have emerged by now."

Night had come early. Robin drove back down the Common into the valley, banks of swirling mist slowing him once more. Inching down obscure roads, he crossed the main Stroud-Cirencester highway at the bottom and rose slowly once again up Chalford Hill—a village of pewter-stoned cottages stained charcoal by the drizzle. Only warm light straining from curtained windows suggested any life at all. MacAllen longed to be safe with a family inside one of these homes, cozy before a fire.

Sudden thoughts of his father and Melanie came, and Robin choked backed an unexpected scalding wetness that burnt his eyes. "God dammit, MacAllen. Keep your mind on what's going on now," he scolded himself. He began using his mantra to blot out the pain and restore his focus. "Breathing in, I calm my whole body…" He whispered it again and again to the night.

Halfway up Chalford Hill, the fog lifted. Robin stopped once more and waited; his breath was still. The silence was total. He stared into the haze, waiting for pursuers to appear. There was nothing, no one. Logic told him he was in the clear, but that feeling within still haunted him.

There was nothing more than a twinge on the back of his neck, growing and spreading into a dull headache. Robin respected his instincts, but he came up empty. He thought, perhaps, he was overreacting from the attack. Pausing for a moment, he relaxed letting the warmth from the heater seep through his body. For the first time since he had decided on this plan, MacAllen felt back in control of his life. He pulled the gear selector of the Audi into place and drove slowly up the rest of the hill.

Out of Chalford, he drove down Cowscombe Hill and then climbed the A419 highway. After several miles, Robin turned right and moved slowly onto a back road that would lead to a little-used

British Rail Station at Kemble. He relaxed and began to hum a tune. It was an old Russian classic. He drove on through the night, humming March Slav- a funeral dirge. Was this a tune he whistled for himself, or was it for his assailants?

The car tires crunched on the gravel drive at the station's entrance. The mist had been blown away by an icy north wind.

Caution was the key to his plan; MacAllen would take nothing for granted. He would wait, standing at this cold and deserted station because it was barely used even during peak hours. It was exactly what Robin wanted. And now it was certain to be empty, what he needed most. Anyone following would find their job very difficult without showing themselves.

Using the train made him less predictable. Robin needed to get his stalkers to make a mistake and show themselves. Until now, everything had been in their favor. They had spotted him before he was aware of it. He still didn't know how or why. Maybe they had tracked him via Ian's call. Or maybe they had picked him up through the old man or had even followed him onto the plane. Perhaps they had brought him into play when he showed up last night.

Wherever it had been, and whoever it was that had attacked him, they were good. They'd been successful only because he had not expected it. Now MacAllen knew exactly where he was going and what he was going to do. They, whoever they were, did not. If any one wanted to know, they'd have to follow him. And Robin wanted to see them in this process.

He stepped into the waiting room and moved into a shadow. The small space was dark except for an eerie orange glow cast by a dim electric fire. The heater burned weakly in defense of the intense cold. A bitter wind whipped the station with icy defiance. The room smelled like dried sweat and stale urine. Still Robin did not move. He sat and waited in the gloom.

Despite the station being deserted MacAllen still had not shaken the feeling he was being watched. He kept seeing movement in the corners, just outside his angle of vision- brief scurrying like rats in motion or snakes slithering through thick grass. Yet when he looked, there was only dark pavement swept by a harsh wind and the black-ness of night.

Robin moved from his position in the waiting room to a high bridge that crossed over the tracks. In the shadows, he found his per-fect vantage point. From there, he could spot any car sitting on the roadside or in the parking lot.

MacAllen skipped the first easterly train that dragged to a halt at the station. Anyone watching would assume he planned riding west, to Bath or Bristol. Or he could simply be waiting for someone. The rented Audi was still sitting prominently in the station car park.

Robin let the westbound train pass as well. He would catch the next one east to London's Paddington Station. Then he would travel by Underground, changing trains several times until he checked into a small bed and breakfast he knew. Then he could sleep.

Another sound caught his attention. MacAllen whirled and looked behind him. Again, nothing. Ominous thoughts now raced through his mind. What if they can read my thoughts? What if they know I've copied the book? Have I led them to the perfect place for my murder? Robin heard a very quiet sound suddenly start and then begin to grow. He stiffened in anticipation, his thick muscles coiled. A high-pitched singing, steel upon steel grew. A slight vibration becoming a sharp metallic whine. He tensed even more, and then realized it was the sound of the next train.

He boarded within minutes and sat down, shaking as he thought of what a grave mistake waiting in such an isolated place could have been. The warmth in the train comforted MacAllen and he dismissed this notion. "Nonsense," he mumbled to himself. "There's no one out there. Rein in your imagination, dammit!"

Yet, as the train pulled from the station Robin saw movement in the shadows, far to his right. He looked closer now, straining to see through the glare of the train on the window. Nothing.

Robin slipped into a short, fitful sleep, dreaming of the events of the past day. Waking up with a thick, foul taste in his mouth, he rose and walked jerkily down the aisle to the buffet and ordered deep amber Forest Brown ale. Though not much of a drinker, Robin drank vigorously, and the dark ale had an immediate effect, washing the sourness from his mouth. He looked out watching dreary village lights and lines of nude winter trees exposed by the headlights of a lone car working its way through the night.

Two hours later Robin disembarked at Paddington Station. Then, with the night before him, he descended into the Underground, switching randomly from one train to another as he worked his way to Hammersmith Station, where he would normally catch the train to Heathrow.

All the way, MacAllen watched for followers. He was good at this and knew it.

Taking his time, he backtracked again, then left the Tube at Hammersmith, switched onto the District Line and rode one more train for two stops to Turnham Green Station. Robin began walking towards a small bed and breakfast, the Benmar, just a short distance away if he had chosen to walk to it directly. Instead, he turned in the opposite direction and strode away from the hotel for several hundred yards. Then he crossed over and followed his path back, to see one last time if anyone was trailing him.

The streets were damp and cold. Dense fog swirled heavily over the pavement and the few cars still out moved slowly. Robin walked at a brisk pace down Turnham Green Terrace and then turned right to head west on Bath Road. It was faintly lit; the quiet was disturbed only by the oily diesel rattle of a taxi cruising by. Robin heard leather on concrete, the shuffle of a foot, a muffled brush of cloth.

His breath quickened and all his senses became alert as he stepped into the opaque shadows. Darkness deepened where a streetlight had been shattered.

The base of his neck tingled as a figure stepped suddenly out of the mist. "Ey mate, got a few pence for a poor fella?" a man called. More soft sounds. Others were with him, hidden in the fog. MacAllen realized he was outnumbered. There were at least six or seven of them standing near a pub, now long closed.

The one who had spoken came closer. Now Robin could see them all, counting seven. The man who approached wore a black leather coat and pants, with high topped thick-soled boots. His hair was cut in a Mohawk and bright green. As the man stepped closer, a reek of sweat and stale beer overwhelmed Robin despite the freshness of the night. The man came close and spoke again. "I asked if you got a little to share with us poor mates. Wot's the matta? You too good to talk to us lads?"

The green hair and outfit so relieved Robin that in spite of an icy wariness clutching him, he laughed. Attackers that worried him would be professional, he was sure of that much. They would be good and dressed inconspicuously. Men in plain clothes and cheap everyday suits would worry him. They would strike, as before, suddenly, without sound and without warning.

His assailants would not sport green hair or leather jackets. MacAllen was surrounded by men who had no control over his fate. He laughed again with relief. The green-haired man standing before him did not take well to Robin's reaction. The sharp click of a knife and its dull glint told Robin this. He looked quickly around at seven punks, a small gang. MacAllen started to freeze up and immediately his mantra came into his mind. His body continued to tighten but his mind cleared and became curiously detached. "Breathing in, I calm my whole body..."

Fear is important at the right time, he thought unemotionally as the man drew nearer. It was sobering that most men lived in fear all the time. What a mistake! Most people live with so much fear they don't know when they should be afraid.

The man approached and Robin's fright turned to blind rage. Blood rushed to his head and red flashes swept away any dullness he had. He stood dead still. MacAllen wanted to fight; he wanted to unleash his anger. And yet, he would not start it. Someone in the gang had to make the first move.

"I would advise you to get out of my way," he cautioned quietly.

"You lafen at me, mate?" the man sneered. "Boys, this man thinks somfink is funny. Any of you see anythink funny?" he asked his friends drunkenly.

One of the seven replied, "Yeah, Gov, I see somfink real funny.

This bloke heah. He looks funny to me. Maybe we should teach him a think or two."

Thank you, thought Robin. Now he knew the leader was in front and his number two behind. He was ready. Turning, he looked at number two and spoke. "I'm warning you, my friend, please get out of my way." He knew this last threat would be the spark and he wanted to deal with that hoodlum first. As he spoke, MacAllen prepared to strike.

As the man stepped forward, also with a knife, Robin finally gave way. The backup man, whom he now faced, swiped at him without a word.

MacAllen felt the blade catch his sleeve and bite. He felt blood rise. Moving closer, he lashed out with his foot at the man's groin with pent-up fury. The connection was sure, solid and hard.

Number two's eyes bulged, red veins popping among the whites. Shocked at first into silence, the man tried to drop his switchblade, suck in his breath and scream- all at the same time. But he could do nothing except collapse to the pavement with an agonizing groan.

Robin saw none of this; he had already started his pivot. The briefcase he carried, made of wood, weighed ten pounds or more. Swung at the full extension of his long arms, it moved like a sledgehammer in a deadly arc. The case flew a full 180° before it stopped suddenly just below the gang leader's nose, with a force greatly magnified by the man's forward thrust.

Robin's assailant probably had never studied physics, but his body understood this force of nature at once. Bones buckled, crunched and finally shattered. Veins gave way under the force and broke. The pressure sprayed blood from the punk's now flattened face and the man dropped like a stone. The remaining five stared at their fallen comrades.

In less than three seconds, two were down. An inhuman sound, part anger, part animal, ripped from Robin's throat. It sounded of death and vented his rage. MacAllen began to charge the other five, then stopped. They were gone. He heard the panicked men running and bumping in the blackness as they fled.

Robin walked quickly away without offering help to the two men now groaning on the concrete. All of his senses were heightened as blood pumped violently through his heaving chest.

Even as he walked faster down the damp pavement, he reminded himself that victory often carries a heavy price. Could he have avoided hurting those punks? Would his outburst teach them a lesson, or just make them worse? In the end, he didn't bother to answer his questions; they didn't matter all that much to him right now.

Fortunately, the Irish woman who ran the bed and breakfast had been a friend for many years and so she asked no questions when Robin arrived covered in blood. Silently, she bandaged the small gash, checked him in and showed him to his room.

Trying to sleep was a waste of time. He was restless, rising often to look out the window at the road below. He saw movement out of the corner of his eye. But nothing was there. Was someone standing outside watching the house? Shrouded in swirling mist, the poorly lit street appeared eerily full of crawling snakes. He examined the street, inch by inch, watching closely, straining to see within the dark recesses. Robin saw nothing.

Very early the next morning, he walked the short distance to Turnham Green Station where he boarded a train and headed to the airport. The station was deserted yet he watched carefully for a tail. MacAllen felt he was in the clear. Phase two was almost over.

Arriving at Heathrow, Robin changed tactics. Now, if someone was waiting to follow him, he wanted whoever it was to see him. He walked briskly to the counter, speaking in a voice louder than necessary as he booked a first class seat to Miami.

To accentuate the illusion that he was deserting his old friend, he called both Ian's home and office in London, leaving the same message on each machine. "Ian, I don't know what game you're playing, but I'm fed up. I'm going home for good!"

Robin conspicuously moved around the airport, then boarded the plane early and scrutinized everyone who came aboard. No one looked familiar, suspicious or out of place. Finally the crew locked the doors and the plane slowly began to roll from the gate.

For the second time in just two days MacAllen ordered an unaccustomed drink- a double shot of gin, straight up and cold. He drank deeply, tasting its harsh bite.

At last, Robin felt he was in the clear. This was his last conscious thought as he slid slowly into that semi-state between wakefulness and sleep. His mind drifted and headed for the comfort of darkness more profound than the night. As he sank further into oblivion, his subconscious took over and he drifted into dreams.

He sat in a small room. He was reading notes covered in gold, dripping with gold, reading words that jumped from the page and turned into tiny pools of molten gold. They floated, spinning round, black points on gold. He was reading Ian Fletcher's notes.

Robin knew he was being followed but could not see who they were. He could never see them straight on, only saw fleeting glimpses, only faint silhouettes. When he looked they were gone, though he knew they were there!

The plane buffeted briefly in unseen turbulence. Soon the metallic voice of the captain announced that they had entered U.S. airspace and were headed south over the eastern coast of the U.S., their final leg into Miami. Robin was wide awake now and his mind was speeding through everything he had to do.

Ian Fletcher was in trouble. As soon as he could, Robin needed to return to Cheltenham and pick up Ian's trail. He leaned back, refreshed, relaxed and once again planned his attack.

MacAllen would be in Miami by late afternoon. His first goal was to finish reading the book Clague had given him. Since leaving the Bear, while on the train and on this flight, he had watched and slept, purposely ignoring his printout of the book. If his pursuers had watched him, he had not wanted them to know about this copy.

Robin would put his plan into action by checking into an isolated motel, reading the book and getting a good night's sleep. The next morning, when he was reinvigorated, he would take the first step in his fight back. Robin MacAllen was going to disappear!

CHAPTER EIGHT

Robin departed the plane and saw that Miami International was in a worse than normal afternoon crush. Murder would be easy in this sea of travelers and this was a good place to commit it. Whoever had Ian would likely kill away from home if they could. Long distance deaths don't create a fuss. Robin shivered at how Clague had died here, kept a watchful eye around him and scanned the mass of voyagers.

After an hour of delay he left the airport in a forest green Dodge Durango 4x4 that he kept stored in the long term car park. The rosy glow in the west told him dusk was near, and he pushed hard through Miami's congested traffic to reach Highway 41 before dark.

The Tamiami Trail is a thin ribbon of asphalt dissecting the lower portion of South Florida from east to west. It traverses isolated parts of the Everglades and is a perfect escape route from crowds. Robin wanted to be on that road before nightfall so he could see if he was being pursued.

After twenty minutes of heavy traffic, Miami ended suddenly. The scenery shifted from busy four-lane congestion to an empty road running along a large canal cutting through a dense tangle of rotting vegetation and fetid swamp. He sped westward directly into an ominous looking squall line. When the bulky frame of his sport utility vehicle hit the bad weather several minutes later, turbulent winds and sheets of heavy rain quickly buffeted the car. The purple dusk instantly turned into coal-like darkness. He fought strong gusts and strained to see into the menacing night ahead.

Robin's destination was a small motel, The Everglades Inn, run by a local tribe on the Miccosukee Indian Reservation. Just a handful of tiny rooms, the inn catered mostly to fishermen looking for seclusion. This solitary place was exactly where he wanted to be.

As he pulled into the motel, he cursed his bad luck and glared through the downpour one more time. There was no way to know if he'd been followed in this mess; a rain-darkened night made it impossible to spot surveillance or anything else.

Checking in, he noted that he was the only guest. Good. This will uncover anyone trailing me, he thought. But still Robin didn't let his guard down and he drove his Dodge behind the motel, obscuring it from the road. Then he backed it against a clump of tall swamp grass that made it even more inconspicuous and blocked the license plate from view as well. He left the SUV slowly, looked around and went to the rear of it where he balanced a small piece of wood precariously on the inside of the vehicle's exhaust. If anyone tampered with the car, the wood would certainly fall off. He then cautiously walked around the motel twice, stopping and watching, waiting before he double-locked himself into the clean sparsely furnished room.

Without bothering to unpack, he stumbled into the shower. The previous days in England, the lengthy flight back and the strain of getting out of Miami safely had taken their toll. He leaned, exhausted, against the stall and let needles of scalding water pound his aching shoulders and neck. Then, with his tense muscles relaxed, he staggered into bed.

A sense of comfort began to envelop him. The Everglades were his favorite stomping grounds, his territory. If someone had come after him, they were on his turf now. Tomorrow was another day and he would be ready.

Letting his concerns fade, MacAllen opened the copy of the book, stretched his legs and started to read. He promptly fell into a sound sleep.

Robin awoke with a start from disturbing, bizarre dreams. His body struggled with jet lag and his empty stomach was begging for food. He was disoriented and could not remember where he was. Sweating, his head spinning, he tried to recall his whereabouts. Ian Fletcher, a crushing force, trains, flying, and being followed by shadowy people he could never see but only sense. Then he was fully awake, his breath still coming hard and his heart hammering. Could this another attack?

He took a deep breath to collect himself. No, it was just a nightmare. He leaned back against the pillow and began reciting his mantra. "Breathing in, I calm my whole body..." Breathe in. Calm. Breathe out. Calm.

He was home now and was on the offensive. If anyone was indeed chasing after him, Robin planned to become his worst nightmare. With that thought, he drifted back to sleep once more.

And again he woke suddenly. The copy of the book fell off his chest as he sat up. He looked at his watch—3:12 a.m. Remembering all the reading that lay ahead of him, got up, dressed and walked outside. He was instantly attacked by a swarm of mosquitoes. Waving them off, he breathed in the warm, moist air and let the gentle swell of crickets and the deeper bass croaking of frogs divert him for a few moments.

Huge clouds of insects formed, moving reflections over the pale yellow lights that shone weakly around the motel parking lot. He walked towards the reservation restaurant, hoping it might be open so he could satisfy the hunger he felt. All he found was a coffee dispenser. Fishing in his pocket for change, he found some coins, fed them into the machine and was rewarded with a cup of very hot, very black coffee. Breakfast would have to wait. Traveling anywhere would make it too easy for someone to follow him and he wanted to finish reading the book.

Back in his room he returned to the manuscript and started to read, forcing his mind to ignore the uncomfortable signals from his stomach.

Very soon, Robin was glad he had not eaten. His stomach was in knots! What he had just read could not be true, could never have happened. He simply could not be in the book. Yet, he was. And the narrative absolutely could not contain directions, written days or weeks ago, about where he was going now. But it did, and it also gave him a clear set of instructions about what he was to do.

MacAllen rose and pinched the bridge of his nose. His thoughts swirled madly. This is far bigger than I imagined; someone has anticipated every move I've made. And that can't be; it is totally and utterly impossible! Can they possibly see the future? Events were not unfolding logically and he got up from the bed where he'd been sitting, encompassed by great agitation. He had to clear his mind and twice had to meditate before his mind was quiet enough to think. Sweat was pouring from him despite the chill of the morning air.

He opened his computer and went back to work on his notes.

The Everglades—5:24 a.m.

Fact: The book has revealed so much. Enough for me to contemplate for the rest of my life.

Fact: On the last page are handwritten notes addressed directly to me, telling me what to do when I get to this place. The message was written before I decided to come here and the directions are coded but precise. These were written by someone other than Ian Fletcher.

Questions: How can someone I don't know write me a message like this? How could I have become involved even before Clague gave the book to me?

Questions: How is Ian involved? Were these notes in the book before Ian read it?

Fact: Ian is in...

MacAllen abruptly switched the computer off and slammed it shut as he jumped up from the bed, more disturbed than he'd ever been. Adrenaline was surging through him and his body demanded that he move. "Logic is not the answer," he swore under his breath as he stretched to relieve the stress. Action. Action is the only thing that'll help me find out what's happening. Don't think too much. I've got to match up my thinking with action. Then we'll see what happens.

It was much too early to call anyone, but with what he had just read he ignored normal courtesies. Despite his always-strong inner discipline, he could not wait.

The room did not have a phone. He stepped outside into the beginning of dawn. Slivers of orange and pink were riding the eastern horizon.

What he had just read had broadened the mystery. Once more, the book had shattered his composure and attacked his sense of safety. He felt violated. Someone he didn't know understood him completely- his secrets, his thoughts, his moves. And Robin could not imagine who it might be.

There was only one direction to take. Follow the one lead that was written in the manuscript. He had no choice but to pursue it. Fate seemed to have taken over and destiny was moving him. Even here at home he had lost control.

He found a bank of pay phones just outside his door. It would take just one call to comply with the directions in the book, but first he called his assistant, Usha. Her whispered hello gave away that she had been asleep.

"Usha, I'm so sorry about this early call but we've got to talk."

His voice brought her quickly awake. "Robin?"

"Usha, I've stumbled onto something that's really bad. I'm in way over my head. I haven't figured it out yet so I can't really explain it to you. And I don't think you should know anyway. I've got to find somebody, now. I can't say who and I don't want you involved right now. But later I'll need your help so don't go to the office. I need you to stay at home. Don't leave the phone. And don't tell anyone, Usha, not even your husband. My life and yours could depend on this."

Without another word, Robin hung up.

He planned to give her copies of the book and Ian Fletcher's notes, and would print them as he traveled in the car. Whatever was happening was seriously wrong, and it wasn't an illusion that his life could end in a heartbeat. God knows there have been enough warnings, he thought. He had friends in law enforcement and if he died or disappeared like Ian Fletcher, Usha needed to get these notes to them. "God knows if they'll believe what they read," he muttered, dialing the phone again.

Three days ago he had planned to go fishing with his friend Billy Osceola. That was before the old Scotsman had arrived at his hotel with the book. And now Robin urgently needed to see Billy. It might even save him. He wondered, as he dialed his friend's number, if this call would answer his questions and save his sanity if not his life.

In spite of the bright morning sun already warming the thick tropical air, his body shivered with a chill that the Florida weather could not soften. And then, Billy answered the phone.

CHAPTER NINE

The sun was well above the horizon as Robin sped along the Tamiami Trail. The speed signs read 55 mph, but there was little traffic this early and Robin sped; there was no one to stop him. His mind turned over Billy Osceola's reaction when Robin had called and asked him to arrange a meeting with his sister, Talking Panther.

"Hey man, no can do. For our tribe, she's the purity. Most of our people don't want a white man tainting her presence. Sorry, Robin, I can't do it."

"Billy," Robin pushed, "this is really important. You've got to let me see her, even if it's in secret. It's a matter of life and death. My life and others."

Robin's neck knotted as he recalled Billy's hesitation. Something had been bothering his friend. Robin had heard it in his voice. He wondered if Billy could be involved in the fraud. If he is, I'm really in trouble. No one needs to follow me; I'll be walking right into my own trap, deep in the Everglade swamps. Anything could happen there. And nobody even knows where I am.

I can't turn back, he thought, as he turned off the Tamiami Trail and drove north up deserted Highway 27 at an even greater speed. The road was badly in need of repair but his vehicle had heavy-duty shocks made for this type of surface and they easily absorbed the impact.

As he drove, MacAllen watched the steaming flat landscape and was reminded why this land was called the Devil's Garden. There was little beyond forsaken scrub with swamp and alligators. Only fifty miles from Miami, here was some of the wildest land in the United States. No wonder Billy's tribe hides his sister here. What is it about her secret?

Robin had little to do but ponder how the narrative directed him to contact Billy's sister. He was still absolutely astonished. A note in the book had told him to contact Billy Osceola's sister who was an unknown tribal healer and lived in the Devil's Garden reservation! The story of Billy having a sister who was a medicine woman was one he had already heard from the Seminoles but he had dismissed it.

What could the connection be between me, the book, Ian Fletcher, con men in England and the Seminole Indians? Certainly each is part of my life, but how could they all be linked? Billy and Ian don't know each other. They're thousands of miles apart.

He pushed the Durango harder and remembered the first night he and Billy had talked about the Seminole Center at Devil's Garden.

"We, the Seminole, have long understood the white man's insatiable avarice. They are stupid and greedy. The white men outnumber us and have always been better armed so the best we can do is a standoff. But we've never surrendered, man. Instead, long ago we created a secret place and hid our most valued knowledge there. We only let you see what we want you to see. Your society can't last. You don't keep the balance. You don't give back. Even our most primitive ancestors knew the laws of giving—you can't take without giving in return.

"We've been waiting a hundred and fifty years for your society to fall. We're patient, man, but we won't have to wait much longer. The real jungles aren't in the wilderness anymore. They're the cities. And when everything falls apart, we'll have the words and the secrets of how to live in perfect harmony with nature. The People will survive."

Robin was now racing towards one curious outcome of the tribe's plan—a great Seminole charade created right in the middle of the Devil's Garden. One of the largest bingo halls in the world stood far from the white man's civilization, among swamp cabbage, mangrove, palmetto ledge and fields of fennel. This hall hosted avid gambling fans from all over the state, but few knew the real reason why it had been built. That building now loomed out of the morning fog as Robin drove quickly past.

The bingo hall wasn't built just for profit. It had been put up because it provided the perfect cover for large numbers of Seminoles to congregate. They met at the hall, then melted into the swamp and carried out their mysterious rites; no one took any notice. Practicing their oracles this way unobserved but right under the white man's nose, was a great source of Seminole humor. Billy had often joked about it with Robin.

Robin did not see that humor now, and he stomped harder on the accelerator making the Durango surge ahead. His impatience was not far from being out of control.

Turning left on a dirt road, the SUV left billows of dust as it raced past the bingo hall. Ahead, surrounded by swamp and forest so thick that few humans could penetrate it lay the heart of the reservation.

He shifted into four-wheel drive, and drove a mile down a swampy mud track until he reached a small, grassy meadow with oak trees and palm hammocks. He parked and started treading down a heavily obscured trail working out his impatience with the fast pace he took.

As he hiked quickly through thick brush, Robin recalled how he had first met Billy. Years ago he had been fishing by himself in the Everglades and had stepped on a rattlesnake. The bite struck a major artery and venom had flooded his system, leaving him paralyzed and in terrible pain. He thought he was going to die alone in this swamp when Billy Osceola, who had also been fishing, stumbled upon him by chance.

Billy had known what to do. "I'll get Swamp Jimson for you, man. It's a wild plant that grows out here. It's part of the nightshade family. Our people use it for snakebites. Tradition says its leaf eats the snake poison. Scientifically, I think the alkaloids in the plant break down the venom or pull it out. Be careful not to let this get on your hands and or touch your mouth. You'll go crazy if you do. Jimson Weed is powerful stuff, man. "

Billy's natural remedy had worked and had eased Robin's pain during the time it had taken him to get help.

Years later, he repaid the favor. The Federal government had pressed charges against a Seminole tribal chairman for killing an endangered Florida panther on tribal land as part of an ancient rite.

Robin had used his government connections to help get that indictment dismissed. Even though Robin downplayed his involvement, the Seminoles accepted him as a brother and had initiated him into many of their rites. Over years of friendship, MacAllen became familiar with the tribe's secret center, their hidden way of life and their waiting game. He heard that Billy had a sister named Talking Panther, who was the tribe's secret spiritual leader and medicine woman but had rejected it as a fable. Billy had never mentioned her and had only laughed when he asked.

Now, he knew Billy actually did have a sister, and Robin needed very much to see her. This absorbed his thoughts as he worked the trail, sweating under the severe and unrelenting sun.

Without hearing a sound he was suddenly grabbed from behind. He stopped, paralyzed for a moment, and then instinctively his body began to react. Even as MacAllen tried to escape his unknown assailant, he knew it would be too late. He had been sloppy and was going to pay the price. Adrenaline coursed through him, his mind preparing for battle, his blood racing wildly.

And then, relaxing for just an instant to try to break free of the grip, he jumped back and started to swing even as he heard a man whisper.

"Hey, man, quiet down. You sound like a herd of wild pigs crashing through the brush. What do you think you're doing?"

It was Billy, and Robin turned to see the muscular hulk of his friend, checked his swing and spontaneously embraced him.

"Billy, what's an ugly goat like you doing out here with the alligators?" Billy did not produce his normal broad smile at this familiar greeting, but motioned ominously for Robin to be quiet.

Robin's voice turned serious. "Thank God you're here, Billy."

His old friend nodded, then motioned more urgently for Robin to be silent and follow him. He turned around and headed further into the dense swamp on a path Robin hadn't even seen.

CHAPTER TEN

The fire was an inviting beacon working its way through the brisk night air. It radiated peacefulness, but Robin's agitation was nonetheless growing by the minute as he fired suspicious questions at Billy. "How long are we going to have to wait, Billy? We've hiked nearly three hours and I know you were leading me in circles. We've been waiting here for over an hour. What's going on?" He shifted uncomfortably towards the fire to fight a chill in him that was not caused by the night. He waited there as Billy replied.

"Come on, man. I've done all I could. I convinced most of the elders to let you meet her, but I still can't be sure if she'll come. Two of the elders were against it. They said it was the wrong time. I had to leave it to the others to talk them into it. They all have to agree or she won't move."

Robin leaned closer to Billy and said, "Sure, but why all this hiking in circles, and why haven't you told me about Talking Panther before?"

Billy stood up and stepped into shadows that covered his face as he spoke. "Listen, you're a good friend, but this is tribal, it's sacred. Not even all the tribe knows about her. Shit, man, the council was really pissed off when I told them you knew. They think I broke my oath. They didn't buy your story either. An old man, a book that predicts the future, mysterious forces in England? You think our stories sound strange? It's a miracle they let me bring you here at all. Most

Seminole are not even allowed in this place. It's completely sacred, only for healers and elders and the most secret gatherings. They wouldn't even let me come here if Talking Panther weren't my sister. They certainly wouldn't let me just bring you straight here. That's why they said you could only come here like this, hidden by the night. If you get to meet her, it'll be pure luck. We just have to wait."

Sitting near the dimming fire, Robin's doubts escalated. Does Talking Panther even exist? Could Billy have led him here to be murdered and was just stalling? Nothing quite made sense, and there was nowhere else to go.

As he was about to ask Billy another question, MacAllen realized that a woman was sitting across from him, on the other side of the fire. She was very old, perhaps eighty, with a huge girth. She was dressed in a long ceremonial skirt in rich gold-colored hues. Her hair was long, black and oily. Her complexion was very wrinkled yet somehow smooth, almost the texture and color of golden leaves that had dried and lay on a hardened autumn ground.

She was too old to be Billy's sister, and Robin was wary of a trick. I have to be sure this is Billy's sister. The note in the book was clear. I must talk only to Billy's sister, and no one else.

His doubts stabbed at him. He had not seen or heard this woman arrive. He had watched Billy move away from the fire. And when he looked back, she was there. Did Billy move away to distract me?

She had not yet spoken a word. Billy returned, sat next to Robin and leaned close. "Don't say anything until she speaks directly to you. She may be talking with the spirits. She may even start talking to them before she speaks to you. This is a solemn ceremony and you can't interrupt."

An hour passed, and Talking Panther's eyes remained closed. Robin whispered to Billy, "Hell, how long is this going to keep up? Ian's danger is urgent. I told you how much trouble he's in. It's day-time in England already. Every hour, every minute…" He stopped whispering because at that moment Talking Panther opened her eyes.

The Seminole medicine woman focused her attention on Robin. "You are troubled, my friend. For many miles this day when you were coming, I felt your agitation. You have brought heavy burdens to me. I know this already though we have not spoken and I have not used my stone. The forces are disturbed in a way I have never experienced in my years. Is this not a problem you should take to your white brothers rather than bringing these dark forces to our people?"

MacAllen shifted before the heat of the flames. Feeling some comfort in her gentle voice, despite the harshness of her words, he replied, "I need your help, Talking Panther. I have never asked for help like this before, and ask now only because I have no other choice. If this is not a matter for you, then you know it already." Shifting away from the fire slightly, he peered towards the edge of the woods. A fleeting movement fading in the shadows caught his attention, but he saw that Talking Panther took no notice of it at all. Her attention remained only on him.

"Talking Panther, I am not actually here for help. I am not even sure why I'm here except that a note was given to me that told me to speak with you. This is the only reason I have come here. The message said you have an urgent communication for me and that you would share the Golden Words."

At his mention of the Golden Words, Robin saw Billy Osceola's face become as pale as the ivory moon that was climbing in the sky. Robin's explanation to Billy had not mentioned the Golden Words. The notes in the journal had been addressed only to him. The message had ended with "Speak these words to no one, do not even think them until you have spoken to Talking Panther." Though written in strange prose, Robin had immediately understood its meaning.

Billy moved his lips as if to speak, then swallowed and remained silent. Talking Panther, her eyes widening slightly in surprise, spoke quietly.

"That is the message I never thought I would hear in my lifetime. We of the land come from many generations and come from a place far way. That we are now in this small forsaken territory is no accident at all. We have known this would be our temporary fate since time for us began. We have also always known you would come- a white man asking for the Golden Words. I never expected that I would be the Carrier to hear you ask for them.

"Unlike the white man, we do not leave our love, our under-standing and our generations to scrawls on paper. For how can paper speak of the moon glow, or tell of the sunrise? How can the paper see when the word has passed, and when it is not clear? We are a people of words and I am the Carrier of the Words. It is I who have the words of our fathers and their fathers, as it has been passed down since the beginning of time. Some of these words we tell to all. Others are for only a few. But the Golden Words are only for the Carriers. It is only the Carriers that know to ask for them. Since in our people's time no one has ever asked, I understand now why I have felt the rifts around us. I must go and prepare."

She rose gracefully despite her bulk, and left.

Robin started to object but Billy cut him short. "Man, if you want to stay for Talking Panther, be careful. I don't know everything, but I do know there is some kind of door connected to the Golden Words. This door is supposed to be shut for everyone except the great healers we call Carriers. It's supposed to stay shut for ordinary people for our protection—not to save the words. We'd better get out of here."

Billy rose from before the fire and squatted in front of Robin as he continued. "The legends say that when you get the words you go through the door and can never return. Where you go, I don't know. But that's one reason I've never talked much about her. This is real. Don't think this is just a weird story. I've been around her enough to know it really happens. I've never seen her act like this. She's never left a sacred fire before. To prepare means she is preparing for death. I'm not waiting around. You should come with me and forget this ever happened."

"I can't go Billy. Ian is in trouble. I don't understand any of this but I can't stop, and your sister is the only lead I have."

Robin rose and took Billy by the arm, guiding him back towards the fireside. "Let me explain something I didn't tell you before. Even though part of the book was missing, there was a handwritten note in it telling me to come here. It said that the Golden Words would answer all my questions and said I'd be warned about the words but that I had to ignore the warnings. None of this makes sense, but it's all I have to go by, I have to stay and see it through."

Robin kicked at the ground. He didn't believe the manuscript was real. The story made some sense, maybe, but the message to him certainly did not. This must be a hoax, and a good one; that final note in the book had brought him here.

The handwritten prose had been clear. "Go forth, man of the mount—go forth to your friends—to the Golden Cat and to the wilderness. Go forth to the rivers of grass, for there your answers will be. For there will be your life. There you will find the Golden Message. Go forth into the wilderness and speak of your heart to the woman who does battle with spirits, sickness and snakes. Her memories are yours. Evil lurks near, and no one else is pure. Speak these words only to the Golden Cat and ask her for the Golden Words. Speak only to the Golden Cat, for to any others your words will be like a death blacker than a starless night, like a storm such as you've never seen."

Robin decided to speak candidly to his friend.

"Billy, I didn't really believe Talking Panther would shed any light on all this. I had just hoped to eliminate you from the picture. I thought you would think the story was amusing. It's a crazy scam and I've got to start excluding the people who aren't involved in this. You're acting like the Golden Words are real. It makes me think you're part of the trickery. What's happening can't be real. The sequences are wrong. You're the only connection in all of this. And I want to know what's going on."

As the night grew colder, he moved closer to the flames and gazed into the night, waiting for a reply from Billy. The roughness of his thoughts brought up memories of being observed. Maybe, he thought, it wasn't only the bitter night air that was chilling him. Billy replied, "Robin, you've got me wrong. Let's forget this, man. I don't know what you've stumbled onto, but there's a lot more danger than you can understand. Let's just get out of here."

Robin stood and balanced the strength of his suspicions against the earnestness of his friend. He saw that Billy really was afraid. Could he be scared because I caught on to him, or is his fear about something he really doesn't understand?

He stared at the flames and decided to trust his friend a little longer. He replied quietly, "Billy, I believe you, but I've got to stay. Maybe later, I'll need your help. I'll call. But go ahead and leave for now if you want. I'll be okay."

Talking Panther had returned without a sound. "We must leave," she said. "No Carrier has ever given the Golden Words more than one time in their life. It is the last thing we do when we are ready to pass and enter the Spirit Realm. We must divulge our words to a new Carrier before we make this journey. I am not ready to die but I must be ready for death. This is the only way to bring the words. Such an asking for the words like this has never taken place and I do not know what will happen. I cannot guarantee anything, even your safety, but you and I must leave. To share with the Golden Ones who deliver the Golden Words, it is necessary to be alone."

Robin followed Talking Panther through the night. The dry raspy throttle of palmetto bushes being pushed aside cracked like cannons and drowned out all other sounds of the night. They moved from clearing to clearing, into and out of small hammocks of oak, pine and palmetto. The land seemed wilder, the brush taller and the smells more ominous than any terrain he'd covered in the Everglades before.

When the two entered a large clearing, Talking Panther walked to a small hammock of palms standing on a large mound. In the middle of it was a grave decayed and half tumbled inward, with a cracked granite headstone unnaturally slanted. From the height of the mound MacAllan could see in the distance the major four-lane I-75, which ran from Naples on the western coast through to the east. They had been traveling south, away from the darkness and towards this road that bisected the southern tip of the reservation. In the pitch-black night, Robin had been turned entirely around.

Talking Panther stopped. "This is the place I have chosen to meet with the Golden Ones and with them share the Golden Words. It seems close to man but I have a reason. Others are looking for you. I can sense this. If you want the Golden Words, this is to be expected. There are some who need to stop you from knowing these secrets."

Robin stared at headlights as they sped past. He longed for something ordinary- the safety and familiarity of his Durango, or his aging but perfectly preserved Jeep with its old worn seats and vigorous hum of the engine as it flew down the highways.

"How tied we are to the known," he muttered. Talking Panther did not acknowledge him. She sat silently, leaving an awkward pause.

Maybe I should stop expecting anything and try to be flexible instead. But his mind immediately rejected the notion. Doubts pummeled his thoughts. This has to be a con, his logic argued. I'm just missing some vital clue or link. Talking Panther and Billy must be involved in it. Surely I've mentioned Ian Fletcher to Billy in passing. They could have known enough about Ian and me to set this up. This was the only rational explanation he could find.

Talking Panther pulled from her leather pouch a golden orb that pulsed with an unearthly glow and radiated peculiar warmth. She sat, holding the small globe in her hands, and without another word slipped into a trance.

Robin could not speak. He knew he was looking at the very same orb Ian had described in his note.

CHAPTER
ELEVEN

The rush of distant cars added to the eerie cacophony of the swamp– crickets, frogs and an alligator hawking in the distance. A faint wind from the south stirred and rattled the palmettos.

MacAllen finally said, very softly, "What do we do now?"

Talking Panther stared strangely at the golden orb. Robin was too stunned by the sight of it to speak again. Somehow, someway, though Robin couldn't make any sense of them, Ian's notes were real.

Rough bark from the tree behind him scratched his back as he thought through these recent events. There was too much money missing that had never been spent. There wasn't any rationale to this swindle. Whoever set me up did it perfectly. I'm definitely out of control. Taking the initiative is no longer possible. All I can do now is try to make something happen.

Talking Panther had remained silent. Robin was about to speak louder when he saw her shift slightly in the dark. She said, "I have waited for you to ask as I can only share with those who ask."

She looked directly at him and continued. "There is trouble here. I am ready but something is wrong. There is something in the vibrations I do not understand, a feeling that someone knows we are here. I have never experienced this before. It is as though they are blocking your future, or that you have no future at all. But this cannot be. It is as if the rain rises into the sky and the river flows up to the mountain. What is, is not, and what is not, is."

The scent of dog fennel caught Robin's awareness as he leaned closer to hear her last words. When he looked over at her, Talking Panther was gone. Her body was there, but in that instant, an undeniable transformation had taken place. Her posture had changed and her breath was not the same. The glint in her eye and set of her face told him he was facing someone, something, different, new. A stranger looked directly into his eyes.

The metamorphosis stunned him. His breath quickened and his body tensed. What a fool I am, he thought. I'm in over my head. It is the middle of the night. I am in a secluded part of the reservation, miles from nowhere. My plans have fallen through. I have no way to defend myself and nowhere to run. He tried to rise but something in those predator-like eyes held him.

He was drawn deeper into those eyes as a dry, raspy voice began to speak. "In the beginning, we were one. We all had the words and these words were the all. Then many left, and we were no longer one; the knowledge was lost by the Leavers. We who stayed accepted a covenant to keep these words pure. Our prophecy was that one day all would again have the words. We gave these Golden Words to only a chosen few to pass them through each generation. Until now. The prophecy has been fulfilled.

"You, an ancestor of the Leavers, have asked for the words. But something is wrong. Talking Panther cannot find the Golden Words for you. We have waited since the beginning of time to assure this duty would be fulfilled. Now, someone wants to stop you, and wants this prophecy to end. Some want these words only as their own. This cannot be. We are all of an intelligence that flows through all veins. These words belong to the universe and life's eternal quest is to exchange this ancient knowledge and treat it as new. Its search is to forever blend this knowledge among all things, so everything evolves and improves.

"Freedom is whatever we wish, but fewer freedoms are dealt with by nature as quickly as the ones that resist this urge to blend. So I will speak for Talking Panther and give you these words."

Robin pressed his back into the rough bark of the palm. Like a mouse trapped by the hypnotic gaze of a snake, he sat and watched.

"In the beginning, we were one. We were all in the middle and this was good. All knew the other and were in harmony with nature. Then there was change. Some of us wandered and left the middle. Some went east, and others went west. We lost touch.

"In the east and the west they settled, and they forgot that there was a middle. For their sons, the east and the west were the middle. To them the middle was the east or the west. This was unstable. Those who departed from the middle saw it no more, because blindness often seems an easier way. Those in the east saw our sunrise and called it sunset. Those in the west saw our sunset and called it sunrise. The difference was confusing and the confusion made the differences an issue.

"In the beginning, we were one. We were united by all that was common. We became united by all that was different. Spread so far apart, the view was truly beyond even the vision of the eagle. The distance was great and each had his daily toil. In this way, it became easier to look only within the horizon rather than beyond. One group became the left and the other the right, and each from its homeland could not see the position of the other. None could see they were part of the whole. Few saw that there was a whole.

"This was the beginning of ignorance and its son, fear. Fear made each feel less and made each want to be more. Fear blinded the truth that each was equal. Fear became the father of the desire for control. This desire for control brought deaths and pain. A few decided to leave. In those times there were many places where man was not, and we went to such places. Some went to the mountains, others crossed the great ice or the great waters of the south.

"Our people crossed the greatest waters and came to the land where time began. Order was restored for us because we had the words and knew how to use the stones.

"With the stone we could see the future. We could see where the deer would be, where the rain for our crops would fall, and where to avoid misfortune. We lived in harmony, generation after generation. For others this was not so. Many misused the power of the stone.

They forgot the sun would always rise and would always set. They forgot that nature would always provide, and they felt a need to control nature. Only a fool can hope to make the sun rise in the sky or the sun set, but fear clouds the most boundless vision, just as morning mists cloud the power of the sun. Those in fear used the stone to control rather than flow with nature. They began to conquer others.

"These conquerors understood the power of the stone and began to gather them. More stones to them meant more power. These men conquered far to the east and far to the west, and collected many stones. They called themselves Controllers."

Robin blinked when he heard the word Controllers. They were the ones the old Scotsman, Clague, had said were after him. This voice in the wilderness knows about the Controllers! Robin's interest was piqued and he leaned forward, eager to hear more.

The gravely voice continued. "Over generations, conquering became so common that the fear from which it all began was forgotten. Fear became a way of life. The more stones the Controllers gained, the more they desired. They also desired to control the Golden Words used with the stones. In many places, only the Controllers knew the words and they gave false words to confuse and weaken all others. Then the Controllers learned of us, and of our stones. And learned that we knew the words. They felt great dread and that led to great desire. And they came in large boats, wearing iron.

"When they arrived, they were few. We were many, but we were of the old ways and did not know of such things as domination, subjugation, possession and war. We did not understand hiding in the stone. The killing and the robbing began. Those who knew the Golden Words and had the stones were killed. Only a few, who learned how to hide in the vibrations, were able to escape. This was when the prophecy began that a time would come when the sons of the Leavers would arrive for the words so that all could have the words again.

"You have come, but the Controllers have come as well. They are alert and searching. Something is amiss and they want to know. Talking Panther cannot use the stone now. To do so would let them know, but I of the spirit have brought you these Golden Words."

Robin was startled as if from a trance. He thought he had been aware and comfortable but realized he had been in some form of hypnotic state. Distrust echoed in his mind. Had it been a dream? No, it was real, but obviously some type of con. He was finally about to be given the bait. Where would this all lead?

Talking Panther interrupted his thoughts, whispering to him in a frightened tone, "Robin, take these words and go! Your doubts can be seen. You must set them aside and go now, quickly. Death approaches. Death is looking for you!"

Robin froze, too stunned to move. The Seminole urgently voiced the warning again, grabbed Robin and shook him. "We must leave. Hurry!"

Unsteadily, he rose and followed the medicine woman as she rushed away from the mound and into the brush. He ran after her, still groggy because of the trance, not seeing where they went until a blinding brightness was nearby. Suddenly, the beam stopped and remained still for a moment, then changed direction and began creeping directly towards them.

CHAPTER TWELVE

The brilliant shaft of light flickered against the green brush and moved ominously closer. When her path was illuminated for just an instant MacAllen could see that Talking Panther's face was extremely pale. Neither the light nor her age seemed to slow her. Her large frame moved with such agility and speed through the underbrush that Robin could barely keep pace with her.

The woods were black and inky. Fireflies winked in the background like tiny malevolent eyes stalking the path. The thickets ripped the radiant full moon into jagged, wicked reflections. Robin's body struggled with the underbrush as he tried to keep pace with the fleeting form of the old woman as she slipped silently from shadow to shadow. Confusion and turmoil spread his frustration further, and a rush of sickness spread deep within him.

He ran even faster, crashing into the brush, oblivious of the cuts and scrapes the palmettos lashed upon him. When Talking Panther finally slowed and came to rest far inside the woods, he was exhausted and gasping for air.

MacAllen was amazed – Talking Panther was not even breathing heavily. "Who was that?" he managed to say, trying to pacify his growing anger.

"Quiet," she whispered fiercely, "now is not the time for talking. Who they are does not matter because they are Controllers. Answers will only be illusions they want us to see. Why didn't we know they were coming? I was well hidden in the vibrations. How were we unmasked? We must survive, and we must find answers."

He inhaled deeply to settle himself down. "How can they follow us in this brush?"

Talking Panther answered softly now, her tone without emotion. "These are Controllers. They have learned a technique that allows them to follow. I don't know how they do this so all we can do is run. Billy will be here any minute to help and then we must go."

Just then, Billy Osceola stepped from the shadows. His high cheekbones, accented by charcoal stripes of paint, matched the green, black and brown camouflage clothing he wore. The war paint made him melt into the darkness and a twelve-gauge Mossberg hung from the crook of his arm. It had been converted into a riot gun with a shortened barrel of stainless steel that turned the moon reflecting onto it dull metal gray.

"Billy, how'd you get here?" MacAllen asked.

His friend ignored him and spoke to Talking Panther instead. "Over here, let's go! Quick! We don't have much time before they get this far. Then we'll be screwed. Follow me, Robin," Billy whispered. "We're going into water. I don't think they'll be able to follow us through this."

They stepped off the trail into the swamp and Robin recoiled as the frigid water licked up his body. An icy chill bit at his waistline, and the nauseating sour swamp odor filled his nostrils. The slimy thickness of the swamp bed sucked the shoes off his feet. He groped blindly and forced himself to follow the dim forms that moved even more deeply into the water. Something spongy yet unforgiving touched him, pushed hard and cut, or maybe bit at the underside of one of his feet. The water was nearly to his nose now and he saw Billy raise the shotgun over his head trying to keep it dry.

Thoughts of alligators and water snakes distressed him. The fetid smell grew stronger and green slime lapped almost to his lips. He pushed onward, digging his toes into the sludge to raise himself even an inch higher. After what seemed an eternity, the water began to drop off, and in the moonlight ahead Robin saw the dim outline of Billy's pickup.

The old Toyota could not be beaten in this swamp; little else would have worked as well. Billy noiselessly signaled for them to climb into the truck. Jumping in, he fired up the engine, put the rig into gear and swung sharply away from the swamp onto a hard dirt track nearby. The truck roared into the pitch dark ahead.

Billy craned his head, attempting to pierce the utter blackness. As the Toyota growled, lurched and bumped down the road, they sat huddled, drenched and smelling like the foul swamp. The Indian turned the heater full blast to dry their clothes some and to try to alleviate the rank smell in the tiny cab.

They rocked uneasily, sandwiched one against the other in the narrow confines of the truck. In normal circumstances, Robin would have held on for life. But now, with the comforting warmth of the heater and the soft purr of its fan, utter weariness took hold. He dimly realized he was drifting in and out of sleep.

The pain, the fear, the long days and this unexpected dash through dense brush and fetid swamp had completely drained him. Unhindered by full wakefulness, the demons of unanswered mysteries rose to the surface and haunted him in his illusory world.

What was happening to Ian Fletcher? How could he have been followed? Had his friends really betrayed him? He slipped into a complex dream. There were huge piles of money —green, red, silver and gold money, everywhere. Bundles of money flowed from baskets and buckets and danced in the air, and a huge sign sat boldly over it all: DO NOT SPEND!

His mind's eye opened. He sat alone on a windswept English Common. Little cottages flew by stacked full of pink newspapers. There were incandescent orbs vibrating and pulsating, looking at him and through him. From one of these, Talking Panther grew closer, cackling, ebony and evil.

Dazed from his tormented nightmare, Robin jerked as the rusty pickup ground on along the swamp road. He turned groggily to face Billy and Talking Panther who were awake and alone in their thoughts. He saw a flash of something outside the truck and peered into the night. He saw the flashes again, not of light but spots of darkness moving within shadows. He saw them move with deadly precision. He felt them looking, observing and feeling, knowing they were near him. He realized the truck was their target as they began to close in on the pickup, moving nearer still. MacAllen recoiled as he saw indistinct forms scatter and search and move closer. Billy kept driving along, unsteadily.

Billy and Talking Panther continued to stare ahead into the night, seemingly unaware of the danger surrounding them. Robin tried to shout a warning but was frozen in his half sleep as the vague shapes moved nearer and nearer. The awakened half of his mind was aware but was immobilized in exhaustion, while another part watched, mesmerized and fascinated as the shapes bobbed and advanced.

Robin drifted into a sounder sleep, and his subconscious recalled Ian's words about the shadows. As his mind plunged again into sinister dreams, it was with the certainty that he had been pursued by murky shadows. And that they followed him still.

CHAPTER
THIRTEEN

Robin woke with a start and banged his head against the roof of the truck. "Damn!" He sat up, twisted uncomfortably, and looked around.

Morning haze hung over the waist high grass and inhibited his view. Immediately he knew this was not going to be a good day.

The silence of dawn lingered heavily in the air. A thin wedge of sunlight was just beginning to color the eastern horizon with brilliant shafts of reddish orange.

He grimaced as he looked at a gash on his face in the Toyota's rear view mirror. "Someone's going to pay for this," he cursed under his breath.

He sank back and groaned, remembering their escape from the swamp. Sitting up quickly, Robin spun around and saw that Billy and Talking Panther were gone. "Damn!"

Rubbing his throbbing temple, MacAllen dropped stiffly from the truck's cab and checked himself over. His clothes were crusted with mud and torn, his bare feet were badly gashed from last night's trek. His muscles were cramped and he stretched to alleviate their dull ache. He walked around the battered pickup that sat in a grove shrouded in mist.

Not far to his right, Robin saw a large picket fence running to a cattle feeder and disappearing into a fog-covered field that lay just beyond. An old wooden ranch house, half obscured by the haze, stood across the field.

"Dammit," he swore venomously as a cloud rolled over the Toyota and blocked his view. He could barely see the end of the truck. Robin stood shivering in the depressing gloom of the morning. What a mess I've gotten myself into. I don't know where I am. I can't even see what's around me. And I don't know what's happened to Billy and his sister. I can't rule out that they've set me up and I don't dare approach the house in case they have.

Huddled, trying to stay out of the wind, he reviewed the past day. "They tricked me at every turn. Even in my own back yard," he fumed crossly to himself.

His stomach growled loudly. A light lunch the day before had been his last food. He clenched his teeth and again spat, "Dammit." His mouth turned sour as he thought over his situation more thoroughly. I don't even know who's doing this. Billy's… I can't believe it.

Despite the coolness, Robin decided to watch and wait. He trembled harder as the morning wind rose and whipped across the field. Going back to the truck, he sought warmth that was not there. He tried to collect his thoughts.

As his anger grew, he banged the dashboard with his fist and stomped again out of the Toyota. He rubbed his bare feet in the wet grass. "I've got to clear my mind," he scolded himself, leaning against the truck's cab.

Robin began his mantra. "Breathing in, I calm my whole body…" Shivering in the damp, he found it hard to sit still. Instead, he rose and walked to the fence and began pushing until it creaked and twisted with the force. The effort worked out his anger, helped warm him up and quiet him down.

Why do con artists make me so mad anyway? It's people's own greed that lets them get fooled. If the suckers weren't trying to get something for nothing, they wouldn't be tricked. The marks are as guilty as the con men. As Robin's muscles relaxed, he stopped pushing and leaned against the fence.

But people can't always control their desires. Their minds aren't sharp, like Dad's when he was old. Am I enraged only because con artists killed Dad? Or also that they made him into a fool? Maybe that's what's getting to me now. And Melanie...? He chased away those thoughts. I'm not angry they're trying to deceive me. I'm infuriated that they know me and think I can be fooled.

He stood up rapidly, his jaw set. Enough thinking, dammit. Thinking is not the answer. Action is. Risky or not, I have to get into that house!

With hands clenched by his side, MacAllen started walking quickly towards the house. I'm going to find out what's going on now. I could not have been followed. The only one who knew where I was going was Billy. He recalled the vague shadows he had seen, then hesitated. What was that, my imagination? Get real, MacAllen, Billy could have organized everything – the journal, the old Scot and a bogus cop at Miami Airport. He's the only one who'd know I'd come to him after reading that book. And Talking Panther? What about that meeting and her voice last night? Tricks!

He clenched his fists tighter and strode more rapidly towards the house. Okay, Billy, you brought me here so I guess you want me in there. As he neared it he stopped and crouched, allowing his arms to fall loose at his sides for better balance.

Robin began to run quietly in that position towards the nearest window. No reason I have to walk right in without having a look first.

Just then, the side door exploded open and Billy Osceola stepped swiftly onto the porch. He spotted Robin and headed straight for him.

CHAPTER FOURTEEN

"Hey, Robin. Morning, man. You gave us a hell of a scare last night. Come on in. We've got a little time before we have to move again. You need to get cleaned up and hear the latest. Like some breakfast?"

Billy was dressed as a ranch hand in denims, jacket and a green baseball hat with John Deere emblazoned across the bill. Robin checked his anger. He was mad, but could not afford to be stupid. Playing the game might bring answers. Besides, breakfast sounded good.

"Billy. Am I ever glad to see you," he replied as he slowed down and moved more gingerly, remembering his bare feet.

The Seminole replied with a wave of his hand. "We've got a hot shower and a razor, some fresh clothes and shoes for you. I think we've got time for that. Let's go to the bunkroom."

They entered a small building with three bunks pushed against the far wall; two were made up. A beat-up Formica table stood in the middle of a plain, wood plank floor. A clean, pressed, blue and white plaid cotton shirt and a pair of faded jeans along with well-used leather boat shoes were lying on one of the lower beds.

"I think everything should fit. Shower's at the end of the room. I'll get some food fry'n and be right back. Hurry, we don't have much time. Can't stay here long."

As he spread the rich lather and scraped the stubble quickly from his face, Robin wondered what game Billy was going to play now His mind continued to sort through the facts.

He let the scalding water wash the grime and the blood of the previous night away. The heat and steam helped ease his doubts. He toweled fiercely and donned the fresh clothes that lay on the bed. His mood lifted. Billy was his friend. He couldn't be trying to scam me. If he was, why all this?

Then he recalled the night before, the disconcerting, very bizarre events, and how he had been drawn to the familiarity of the headlights on the road. I wanted everything normal so badly. The thought was so unexpected it startled him. I just wanted what I'm used to. I didn't want Billy's betrayal to be real. I wanted to be in control and the road and the lights were something I knew and could understand. These customary little habits–the razor, clean clothes, the hot shower–are making me feel more in control. But are they just Billy's tools? Maybe he's trying to disconcert me with the familiar.

How often do I crawl into my little habits just because I don't want to face reality? Don't be stupid, MacAllen. There is no answer except Billy. He has to be the key to this double-cross.

Billy returned and motioned Robin to follow him back to the farmhouse. Their feet crunched on gravel as they walked across the driveway. At the house, Billy hastily turned and headed towards the truck. "Gotta get somethin, man. I'll be right back. Go on in. Talking Panther and my other sister's inside."

The wooden slats thumped under Robin's feet as he crossed the porch. The screen door squeaked open and he walked into the warm room. A small black wood-burning stove crackled nearby. Despite its inviting glow, Robin slowed and cautiously scanned the room.

His eyes adjusted to the dimness and Robin saw two women. Their eyes locked. Suddenly paralyzed, his mind swirled like an unexpected dust devil, with scattered bits of chaos flying everywhere. His mouth gaped, his tongue froze and the room started to spin around him.

CHAPTER
FIFTEEN

Jimmy Ray Burnett turned suddenly right off the Immokalee Road and stamped hard on the accelerator of his large Chevy Caprice. Ignoring the slick pavement, he nearly lost control. The heavy suspension of the car was overpowered by its high-performance engine.

"Son of a bitch," he cursed as the rear end swung wildly into the wrong lane. Swerving hard left, he regained control and stomped on the pedal again. The car surged forward and the accelerator tipped rapidly past ninety. The speed limit sign, which read forty-five, was a blur by the time he raced by.

Jimmy Ray did not care. He had been sheriff of Hendry County for eleven years; his daddy had been the sheriff before. Right now he was too enraged to care about how fast he went, who saw him or what they thought. He bellowed at a driver as he roared past, "Get outta my way, asshole!"

"Idiot deputies," he grumbled. "They can't do anything right." As the words left his mouth, he winced with the pain again. He was still not sure of its source. Was it another upset stomach or chafing from his very large belt buckle encrusted with diamonds and eighteen-karat gold? The buckle was a work of art, but contained one very large flaw. It was cast in the form of an eagle, and the beak, just where it was sharpest, continually dug deeply into Jimmy Ray's flab –a constant source of irritation to him. The buckle had been a gift from the owner of a local food-processing plant who knew how much Jimmy Ray liked gold. The owner also knew how useful making the sheriff happy could be.

As he forced his squad car to lurch ahead even faster, he thought vaguely that the pain was probably the damn buckle. He had attached his custom made holster that contained his most powerful handgun to it. The fully loaded Magnum forty-four and an extra cylinder of bullets pulled heavily at his belt.

Still, the stomach pains had become more frequent and the fact that he had to be here right now, and had to carry his gun, made him suspect that his stomach was hurting from more than just the belt.

"Damned deputies," he muttered again, thinking of the girl and her inviting softness. The memory of her made his stomach churn even more. She's so damn hot! Whew! And ready to beddy, right now, dammit. I can do anything I want with her. Everything! She's there waitin' in my bed, and I'm here, doing my deputies' job. "Shit!" Yeah, she's gonna be good! He grinned and stomped even harder on the accelerator. Gotta get this done and go get me a piece o' that girl.

As he drove the rapidly accelerating car down the straight road, his mind drifted over the events that had led the girl to his bed and the ones that had brought him out of it.

She was new in town and had started working as a dispatcher at his headquarters. Divorced, a young working mother, she was trying desperately to get ahead. And she was smart. Other than that, she was just his type...small, slim, with large breasts and long blond hair. Despite her being alone, she had repelled Jimmy Ray's uncouth advances and had even talked to her attorney about filing a sexual discrimination suit when he would not stop.

"Goddamn women libbers!" He had learned about her potential lawsuit because her attorney was Mort Wilkenson, who had an expensive cocaine habit that Jimmy Ray supplied. Mort always owed him and had talked the girl out of the suit and had told Jimmy Ray about it.

He laughed under his breath as he remembered the trap he had set for the girl. Though Jimmy Ray repelled her, she was attracted to John Turner, his deputy.

John had once made a mistake when racing to answer a 911 call. He had hit a pedestrian and had panicked. Jimmy Ray covered for the deputy and then had used the cover-up to force John to help in his rackets, dope, payoffs and girls. John had to do anything Jimmy Ray said. The new dispatcher didn't know all that.

"Take her out and give her a good time, John," Jimmy Ray had told the deputy. "I'll pay! Start her with booze then try her on a little coke. Go easy, take your time, get her confidence. When she's ready, have her pick up a few ounces from our supplier. Just let me know the time she's going to make that pickup. You understand me, boy?"

The seduction had been easy. The girl had no local friends. John was good looking, amiable, smart, fun to be with and had taken a real interest in her daughter's welfare as well. But the corruption had not worked. She wouldn't touch the drugs. She had threatened to stop seeing John if he even mentioned them again.

The sheriff smiled and recalled how he had finally broken her instead with plain old beer. "Get your brother Sam drunk," he had instructed John. "Have the girl drive him home. Say you got to work and tell her that the boy's too drunk to drive. Let me know when they leave".

Jimmy Ray then had her stopped and hauled in. Sam was under-age, only nineteen, and because there was beer in the car, she was responsible. Supplying alcohol to minors was a serious crime, and Jimmy Ray remembered telling the girl's attorney what to do. "Mort, explain to her that there's no one around to look after her little girl. Tell her plain. Her daughter could end up in a foster home chosen by the local social services. She'll end up in jail. Tell her the only way out is for me to help."

He sneered as he pictured his friend Mort speaking in his slow southern country drawl. "Ma'am, this could be big trouble for y'all. Worse for your dauhta. But there might just be a way out. I could talk with the sheriff, ma'am. We could sweep this all under the rug. Jimmy Ray can be very helpful for his friends, and in this county he can make most anything happen. Yes ma'am, he can."

Jimmy Ray remembered how she had begged for his forgiveness. She agreed to all his conditions. He had very much enjoyed feeling the young woman shudder in revulsion when he had kissed her to seal the arrangement. He had taken the kiss then but he planned to take more, much more, now.

"Shit," he shouted as he thought of her waiting for him now. Just an hour ago he had been about to collect what he wanted most. Instead, he was out here in the fog searching for some son of a bitch as a result of a man he had met only once.

"Goddamn phone call." The call had come from his supplier, a man he hardly knew. But the caller was his source of the drugs that brought him a great deal of money and power. The caller was not the type who asked for help. He demanded it: the message had been abrupt and straightforward. He was to get a certain man or he would lose his drugs, his power, his money, and much more. The job was meant to be easy. The supplier had told him exactly where the man had been sitting with some Indian squaw at the edge of I-75. He had sent out three cars and six men, more than enough to do such a simple job.

"But those damn stupid deputies botched it," he bellowed, punching the steering wheel with vehemence. "Those idiots shouldn't a lost him last night. Now I gotta do the job."

He remembered his supplier's second call this morning, again telling him where the man was. This call had been short, simple and to a deadly point. "Jimmy Ray, we're watching you right now trying to screw that girl. The man we want has escaped, and we know where he is. We want him within three hours or we'll have your balls instead. Then you won't be able to screw anybody."

Horror engulfed him as he remembered the flat dispassionate fury in the man's voice. How could they a been watching me? He made a mental note to have his house and office swept for bugs upon his return. These bastards didn't play around. Sweat broke across his brow and his churning stomach growled its agitation again. Gotta get this son of a bitch.

He pushed the accelerator to the floor.

CHAPTER
SIXTEEN

Robin placed his hand against the wall to conceal a sudden wave of dizziness. Nausea slugged his gut and his mind spun. Amidst his racing thoughts came the answer to a question about Talking Panther that had nagged at him the night before. Something about her had seemed so familiar, but he hadn't been able to put his finger on it.

The two women sitting at the kitchen table were identical twins. And each one looked exactly like Melanie Chong! Last night, Robin had missed the resemblance of the old woman to Melanie because of her age and size.

"Melanie?" Robin blurted. The likeness between both these women and Melanie was striking. Both were about thirty. Their features also made them look like a young Talking Panther. Talking Panther's appearance was as Robin imagined Melanie would look when she reached eighty. If she reaches eighty, he thought. If she's alive. He tried to push back a sudden acute dismay. But the enormous remorse and pain he had stifled for years swept over him like an avalanche.

Robin's mouth remained agape and he couldn't speak a word. She is, uh, they are Melanie, he thought. No. Almost! These women are incredible lookalikes. One of them came over and spoke. "You're just in time for breakfast, Robin. Sit over here. Meet my sister, Silent Panther."

Robin's eyes were fixed on the woman who spoke. She was extraordinarily beautiful, slender and dark. Her skin was a softly shimmering golden copper. Black hair draped loosely around her neck and partially covered a white cotton T-shirt that read "Immokalee Tomato Fest" across the front. The T-shirt was tight and very well filled. The woman's smoky brown eyes were piercing, yet laughing at the same time. She wore a full handmade quilted Seminole skirt of vivid colors—orange, deep purple, white and indigo. Robin looked at Silent Panther and could see no obvious difference from the other woman except that she wore a plain, pale blue T-shirt.

Looking back at the speaker, some words finally tumbled out. "You're identical twins?" he asked. Great ice breaker, MacAllen, he thought. He closed his eyes, thought his mantra for a heartbeat, and took a deep breath. His composure came back to him and he asked calmly, "Where's Talking Panther?"

"I am Talking Panther, Robin," the woman said. His jaw locked again. He was hearing the same voice as last night but this wasn't the same woman by fifty years. His mind raced. Could they be Talking Panther's daughters? MacAllen's suspicions soared. He had come for answers and they were trying to throw him off.

What kind of game is this? Hidden treasure gambits by the old Scot had failed. Are they going to try luring me with sex instead? But Melanie, how could they know?

To gain time, Robin looked around the cabin. The room was dim and warm from the stove. Seminole art hung on the walls. Beside the wood burning stove sat a very old, well-polished round oak table surrounded by wooden chairs. This was a kitchen but had the look of a room used for more. The well scuffed, yellow pine floor told of many meetings around that table. The walls were lined with books as well as kitchen utensils. A computer sat humming on a desk next to the books. This was a place, then, where people not only ate but met, worked and thought.

Billy all of a sudden exploded into the room, slamming the screen door. He slapped Robin on the back as he walked by, ripped a piece of bread from the steaming loaf that sat in the middle of the table and stuck it in his mouth.

He looked over at Robin and choked as he let out a startled laugh. "Man, I haven't seen that look on your face since I found you in the swamp with a snake hanging onto your leg. Come sit down, man. I'll explain everything. Listen, let's eat. We don't have much time. I called your secretary this morning; I didn't want her calling the sheriff, which she was about to do. She insisted on meeting you. I said I'd rather not but she wouldn't accept no. We're supposed to meet her in an hour and we're half an hour away."

Billy pointed to the huge loaf of homemade bread. Steam and aroma rose from an old-fashioned blue enameled coffeepot. Billy made thick, heavy, black coffee the way he liked. Robin took another long breath and sat. "Okay, Billy, if it was anyone else, I'd be out of here. And I'm curious how you're going to pull this one off. But you've been a good friend. If you hadn't fixed that snakebite I guess I wouldn't even be alive. Talk away."

He took another look at the two women, sat down, helped himself to a cup of the rich coffee and tore a piece of bread off the fresh loaf. The hot bread was a Seminole specialty made of pumpkin, spiced heavily and deep fried. This and the coffee gave MacAllen a badly needed jolt of energy.

Billy chewed for a moment longer, ran his tongue along the side of his mouth and began to speak. "You're a good friend, Robin, but I haven't been able to tell you everything. Like about this house. It belongs to the tribe. Few know we own it. A friendly rancher runs the place. If anyone looks, they think he's the owner. The world thinks we're the hired help. Truth is it's the other way around. And that's the way we like to keep it. We got here last night the back way, through the swamp. You were out cold. Now that you've calmed down, they won't be able to find you so fast. I'll explain everything later but I can see from your look I'd better explain Talking Panther and Silent Panther first or you ain't gonna listen to anything."

Robin leaned back and half shut his eyes to mask the anger that was ready to explode out of him. The agony of controlling his breath made his chest burn like a hot iron cage. His hands lay in his lap clinched like vise grips. He was usually slow to anger and quick to smooth out, but Robin feared the moment his temper snapped, unleashing danger, for himself and anyone around him. He forced his hands open and laid them, palms down, on the tabletop. He pressed his palms harder on the oak surface, letting the feel of rough wood ground him. If he wanted to learn anything at all, he had to stay placid.

He silently began his mantra and his mind struggled between it and trying to assimilate what was going on. They have to have Ian if they know about Melanie, he realized. Only Ian knew Melanie. But these women resemble her so much. Why? As he continued to struggle with this tension he picked up his cup, stood and paced around the room loosening his legs. Moving closer to the heat of the cast iron stove, he turned, looked straight at Billy and said flatly, "Yeah, Billy, I think you you'd better explain."

Billy scraped his chair back and started to blink, looking like a man not sure where to start. He's about to tell me a big lie, Robin thought.

"Let me be straight, man. I've thought of you more as a brother than any other white man I know. But, you are still white. I didn't know you're what we call 'One Who Carries the Stone in his Head.' I didn't even know this yesterday when you asked to hear the Golden Words. Talking Panther and I were knocked out when you laid that one on us. We only realized who you really were late last night."

Billy's brows unfurled and his face relaxed as he plunged ahead. "But I'm getting off track. We don't let the world know much about our ways. Look at our history, we can't afford to. We do lots a things to throw people off track. That's why we hide the fact that we own several dozen large and profitable agricultural businesses like this ranch. That's also why we throw in a little hocus-pocus about our eighty year-old medicine woman."

Billy raised his cup, motioned to the two women and continued speaking. "Talking Panther is our medicine woman, but she knows more about medicine than just what she has learned of our ways. She graduated from Harvard an MD. God knows, though, she's found our medicine works better than yours, but she knows both."

His face knitted into a frown as he stopped his explanation and paused for a moment. "It's not a good idea around here to have a young, pretty medicine woman with a medical degree. That would attract attention we don't want or need, especially when she has an identical twin sister. That would really get us in the news. Making Talking Panther look eighty and making everyone think she hides in the woods, gives her a great deal of freedom. She can travel wherever she wants to. When she dresses Italian no one ever knows she isn't European. It's handy to be seen but not be seen. We can get people to talk about us genuinely that way. We can stay in touch with what people really think. If we're Indians, people treat us different."

As Robin's anger diminished, his confusion grew. Is Billy really trying to make me believe this woman is the same eighty-year old I met last night? A tremor shot up his spine as he realized that this conversation had to be heading somewhere, and he did not expect to know where. He moved closer to the stove and one step nearer the door.

Billy drank some coffee as he continued talking. "Up to last night, you were just a really good friend. But when you asked for the Golden Words, everything changed. Those words are the heart of our tribe, Robin, passed down from one generation to the next. Only our tribe knows about the words. And our traditions say we must share them with anyone who asks, but only if they ask for them first. Giving the Golden Words to someone who has not asked is like giving a child a loaded gun. But if someone does ask, it means they're connected to our destiny."

Billy bent forward casting his eyes at the floor, and became silent. Robin squirmed in that silence, but before he could say a word, Billy looked back up and shot him a question. "Are you familiar with inherited memory?"

Robin's reply was edged with irritation. "Inherited memory? You mean through DNA and things like that? That's nonsense. What does that have to do with Talking Panther? Come on, Billy, get to the point."

Billy grinned and held both hands up in mock surrender. "Bear with me, my friend. We think differently sometimes so don't close your mind quite yet, man. Our people believe that the body has intelligence far beyond that of the brain. The brain just organizes the many different types of intelligence within our body. We call these fields of intelligence 'spirits.' Your heart, for example, has great intelligence. Your heart has a great force and is a powerful spirit. If you remove the brain, but give it food, the heart knows how to keep on beating. We also believe that each force can communicate with the outside world through more than just our five senses. Each force has its own direct paths of energy – in our eyes, in our ears, in our feet and hands. So when anything happens to you, your heart knows, just as your brain does. Let's say you step on a red hot coal. Before your brain ever gets the message to your heart, it is already pumping harder and faster."

What the hell is Billy talking about? Robin almost spat out his thought. Instead, he walked over to the oak table and poured himself more coffee to help rein in his exasperation. "I've studied science, Billy," he said dryly. "What's the point?"

Billy watched and waited as Robin slowly returned to the stove and then he continued speaking. "Our body is connected through many independent pathways far deeper than the simple knowing of our brain. Our medicine men know this, and our medicine works on these pathways. Our ancestors who moved to the East took this knowledge with them, too. In China, when treating these pathways, they call it acupuncture. We Seminole use an almost identical form of treatment, except we use bee stings instead of needles. Did you know that?"

Robin's patience gave out at the question. "I didn't, Billy, but so what? This is all great theory, but what does it have to do with all this?" He waved at the room and the two women. "I want to know what the hell's going on!" he growled.

Billy leaned back in his chair and smiled. "Okay, okay. So much the white man's way, always trying to rush to the point while ignoring the big picture. Always in a hurry, but never knowing where to go. You should be in a hurry now, but you've got to see that big picture before we move on, and I'm just trying to help."

He went on with his explanation. "This process of knowing and learning goes three ways. One is the memory in our brain. We are easily aware of this memory because it is at the conscious level. The second memory, in our cells, we call the subconscious. The third memory is even deeper; it is at the root of all thought. Western medicine calls these roots DNA. We call it the Grandfathers. Our people were never aware of DNA as the white man knows it, but since time began, our medicine men understood the power of its memories. Your scientists run around spending billions of dollars trying to make new discoveries, and then they give them new names. Yet all they do is find out what we have known forever. DNA is matter in its least solid form. It is solid, but so ephemeral it changes easily and changes all the time, based on the memories it gains. The changes are subtle. They have to be, because the DNA carries the memories that bind our bodies together. Change the DNA too rapidly and our whole body falls apart. DNA is a memory that passes beyond death. If you walk on enough fiery coals, not only will your heart beat faster, you will have children whose hearts beat faster too. We call this inherited memory. Your science calls it adaptation."

At this point, Robin cut the Seminole short. "Okay, Billy, enough stalling! I don't need a science lesson; I don't want a science lesson. Maybe DNA is memory, but right now I'm standing here worn-out from spending the night in a rancid swamp and I'm wondering who the hell has tracked me clear across the Atlantic Ocean. Are you going to tell me what's going on, Billy, or not?"

The woman Billy had called Talking Panther rose and walked to him. "Compose yourself, Robin." And she gently touched his arm. Though she had barely brushed him, a spark shot right through his body.

Her voice was soft and low. "It is important for you to relax. Billy was trying to prepare you for an answer you cannot believe, but must. We don't have time to explain but it's important, so Billy tried. Knowing what he says will help you survive. I'll let Billy explain the science behind all this later. But for now, I'll give you the answers you need."

The woman's touch remained warm on his arm. The soothing

gentleness in her caressing voice had left Robin with his guard down. Be careful, he thought. This is too smooth.

"Our conscious brain waves are connected to the here and now. Call it the local news, if you will. This is the way we know what is happening in our immediate vicinity. Our subconscious memory is in touch with everything in the world, the earth, the weather, tides, even the sun and the moon. Think of this as the global news. Our third memory is connected to everything, everywhere. This deepest level of our third memory is what we call all-seeing vision. Mystics in this time call it the cosmic consciousness. This is the universal news–that we are connected at that deepest level to everything."

MacAllen looked at Billy, then back to the woman who was holding him, and he recoiled like a whip. Still touching his arm was the same eighty-year old he had met the night before!.

"What the heck?" he shouted. "How'd you do that?" He tripped as he instinctively backed away from her and nearly fell over the hot stove. And then, the old woman changed again. Before his eyes, she turned back into the young woman. Robin's eyes widened and his mouth could only gape.

"What you have seen is what I cannot explain in the time we have. Our people learned long ago that all three memories are connected. If you know what to do, you can think at the innermost levels of knowledge. Your thoughts can influence everything, even how you look. It can even guide how others perceive. You may not understand this, but I think now you can see."

Robin blinked, too stunned to move. This was mind-boggling: it surpassed belief. Her transformation was complete. As she spoke, Talking Panther had shifted from a beautiful young woman back to the dried-up old medicine woman he had met the night before, and then back again into the stunning female.

He stammered, "This can't be true, even if I am seeing it." Robin groped for more words, could find none. He swayed unsteadily on his feet. His mouth opened and shut without a sound. He needed time. The best course for now was to apologize. "I'm sorry for being cynical, but…"

His words were interrupted by a loud bang, followed by a crash.

CHAPTER
SEVENTEEN

Robin peered out the front window. A large swamp buggy lay overturned on its side. Just beyond, a sheriff's cruiser sat with a badly dented front end. Steam was rising from its burst radiator. Two Seminole stood anxiously around a prone figure, and two police officers were emerging unsteadily from the wrecked patrol car.

Billy rose. "Let's go. Time for us to hit the road, man," he said. "Don't worry about the little ruckus out there. That's Johnny-Go-Lightly lying on the ground. He used to be a part time movie stunt man. I didn't think he could be hurt so I sent him and a couple of the boys out in the swamp buggy to arrange a little diversion should our friends from the Hendry County Sheriff's Department decide to drop by. Those were the deputies looking for us last night. Should've guessed that if trouble were going to come, it would come from the local law. The sheriff's got his hands in every kind of corruption you can find around here. Johnny arranged that accident. He'll hop around and moan and groan a bit. Might even have some fits, like he has head injuries. Who knows, he might even have taken a balloon filled with cow's blood. Man, Johnny's real good at looking hurt. I don't think these deputies'll bother us for awhile."

They hurried out, loaded into the truck and Billy drove quickly headlong through a stand of palmettos, onto a trail running alongside a swamp.

As the Toyota bounced and lurched forward, Robin's mind raced.

How were we followed again? His dream of the previous few nights flashed before him. And then, Ian's words in the book came like a shock of electricity. "Shadows. Can't see them direct. But I know they're there."

The shadows, he thought. They are there and somehow they're linked to the sheriff! The shadows followed him still. But how? Nonsense, MacAllen, there aren't any mysterious forces. What I'm seeing has to be some comprehensible physical phenomenon that I just can't fathom.

Robin's jaw tightened. But I will. He swayed, disoriented, and his stomach twisted as thoughts of Billy's betrayal whacked a heavy blow in his gut. Watching Talking Panther change to an old woman had swayed and then eroded his very foundations, but now he was convinced it was part of Billy's con. So much I don't understand, he thought.

MacAllen's head began throbbing as he sank deep into a black mood. He tried to reorganize his thoughts to help him spot just how the deceit worked. There is time, he thought. And there is space. I'm a master of timing. That's how I spot frauds. Scams are manipulations of time, space and money. Con artists find targets and put them in a controlled situation. Then they create illusions at an accelerated pace, gaining the sucker's confidence until he's ready to turn loose his money. The formula is simple, so why can't I spot what's going on?

His mind raced as it ran through a checklist. Check the timing. The old man, the book, Ian's call. How could both the old Scot and the book transcend time? The attack in England? The sheriff in Florida. Where and how do they connect? Space, he thought. Miami-England-here? What's the common link? How are they tied in time and space?

The dull throb in his head turned to searing pain as his conclusion brought him back to what he already knew. Billy. It can only be Billy: he's the only common connection. But why is he doing it? And how is he doing all this? He winced from his roaring headache and flashed a glance at Billy and the two women. But no one's asked me for a penny. They've waited too long. Ian's note said billions weren't even spent. It doesn't make sense.

The truck suddenly hit a huge ditch and nearly rolled. Robin instinctively grasped Talking Panther who sat next to him. And at that instant a surge of attraction flashed through his entire being. Robin's mouth went dry and he pulled hastily away, afraid of her very intense, very tantalizing animal presence.

This is a real woman, he thought. The game she's playing right now might be phony, but she's real. Take care, he warned himself. You've seen her transcend every law of nature you know. He tensed at the memory of her transformation. She's all too real, almost too perfect. Everything about her...the silky skin, her radiant beauty, her erotic scent. They all contrived to make him acutely aware of her absolute femininity. She's the type that can pull a man in.

The truck lurched off the trail into a shallow swamp. Robin's head continued to pound as he examined and reexamined the facts. The trickery is extraordinary. Billy and his sisters are up to their necks in it, and I have no idea what it is. All I can do is wait and find the pattern. And I will find it because most frauds tie only three unusual events together to create the illusion. Just three events, are all it takes to change most of our lives. In this hoax, there've been so many more. The answers have to start coming soon.

The Toyota slid and blundered through thick slimy mud. Billy raced out of the swamp onto another road that was little more than two wet ruts covered by several inches of green, algae-filled foam. Familiarity is the key in every sham; the key to people's minds. People live by familiarity, not truth. They believe in things, like electricity, because they're familiar with them, not because they know exactly how electricity works. Electricity to those who've never used it is magic. He glanced across the truck again at Billy and frowned. What's behind the magic that Billy's using on me?

The truck swung and lurched as Billy failed to avoid a large rock. The sudden shock sent Robin crashing into the roof of the cab, but his mind was so absorbed in his thoughts it blocked out the impact. Billy's fraud...my friend...Billy. He grimaced as the invisible band tightened around his head and a bitter taste settled in his mouth. He slouched on the seat. Whatever the scam, there's nothing to do now but play along...wait...relax.

"Robin!" He was torn away from his contemplation as Talking Panther whispered urgently in his ear. "Quit thinking so hard. You are leading them directly to us. Your mind is leaking badly."

"You can even read my mind?" He laughed warily as he looked from side to side. His voice was calm, but his mind spun even faster. I need time to figure them out. Placate and play along. I'll be able to get them when their guard's down.

He steeled himself, forced a half smile at Talking Panther, slowly shook his head and spoke haltingly. "You're right...I've been immune to what's going on. Crazy...I'm sandwiched between two of the most beautiful women I've ever seen, but my mind's somewhere else. I should be enjoying this...at least a little."

He smiled again as he said "It's hard to get into the here and now. I guess I'm like everyone else and get all tied up regretting the past. I worry too much about what's..." The truck slammed across a tree stump, the jolt cutting off his words. He gripped the dash, trying to avoid thrashing the women, but they were being thrown repeatedly by the bumping truck, against him and all over him.   The two Seminoles' instinctual and powerful feline sensuousness bombarded MacAllen. The touch of their tender skin overwhelmed him and clutched at his deepest being. He backed off. Careful, he warned himself again.

Talking Panther leaned close. Her scalding femininity enveloped Robin. Her breath was warm. Jasmine. Rose? And...musk.

She whispered again in his ear, her tender voice overcoming even the roar and whine of the truck. "There are many things I must explain to you. I had planned to begin last night and follow the way of passing the Golden Words. The interference stopped this. We must be alone for me to give these words to you, but even now when we are with others I can hear your thoughts and feel your doubts. This means others can know them and feel them too. This is how they follow. I can feel them following us now."

She went on in her lovely voice. "Billy explained to you earlier that it is special and uncommon to know the Golden Words. Anyone who is given these words must have an extraordinary quality. Even then the Golden Words can only be used when the person touches a golden orb, or special stones which contain gold and rare earth. We call them Huaca Stones, but their essence has been described in many tales over many centuries—the Philosopher's Stone, the Rosetta Stone, Manna, the sword Excalibur—all holding incredible power locked in a stone. The Golden Words make it possible to know and thus affect the present, the past and the future. We touch the stones and we can do this. However, several exceptional people have an even rarer gift. We say they are 'Ones who have Stones in their Head.' Those with this rarest of gifts do not need to touch the stones. They can see and hear without it."

MacAllen leaned closer, lulled by Talking Panther's warm subdued voice. Grabbed by her scent, Robin softened. Watch out, he scolded himself. And dropped a steel gate over his emotions. Don't let your guard down for anything. He toughened his caution and focused on her words.

"Robin, you have the ability to see the future without using a stone or an orb," she said. "I did not realize this when I first felt your vibrations approach us from Miami. Only last night, when I could read your thoughts when you did not have an orb, did I realize who you are and why you were sent to us. All you have to do is learn how to understand what you are feeling. This has been dormant in you and has now been awakened. It will be confusing to you. It also means you are very finely tuned to the vibrations. This is how the Controllers keep finding you. Imagine a radio tuned to the universe. Some radios can only send and others only receive. You both send and receive. You are sending out very strong signals when your emotions run high. Last night, I also learned that I could no longer grasp your vibrations after you grew calm and slept."

The woman continued, even more softly now. "You must be calm. Do whatever you can to relax. I know how you are feeling about me, about Billy and about this whole situation. Your thoughts are so exposed that reading them is quite simple. I promise you,

Robin, we are not trying to trick you. We are not con artists. We are your friends and we are linked for life. We will gladly risk our lives to help you. But right now, you must help us."

Robin did not know what to say. He tightened his jaw to mask his astonishment. The effort of that, coupled with the noise and turmoil in the truck, robbed him of a reply. He just stared vacantly at Talking Panther as she went on.

"Calm yourself, Robin," she said. "Have faith in my words for just a few hours. Then I will have time to tell you all. Until then, do anything you can to diminish your tension. This may save all our lives."

As his equilibrium swung out of control, MacAllen was no longer able to hide how utterly stunned he was and his jaw slacked. "How could you know?"

"Robin, I feel your pain, your doubts, all your confusion." She clutched his arm and pulled him closer. He was taken aback by the strength of her grip. As the heat from her body flowed through him, he abandoned his caution and quieted down.

She whispered, "Everything will be okay, if you relax. And take this as it comes. Please, Robin, believe in our friendship for just a few hours more."

Talking Panther spoke with such earnestness, Robin let go of all the swirling thoughts and his sturdy frame loosened up. Believe? Have faith? But nothing I've seen makes any sense at all and she asks for faith. Yet, Billy has been a good friend. Except for Billy, I wouldn't even be here at all. The least I can give is a few hours of faith. For my life, Billy deserves that much.

Suddenly, he wondered: could Billy and the women be risking their lives trying to save mine? Nothing has any meaning except Billy being smack in the middle of a con. How can I have faith when I have so many doubts?

The question reminded Robin of a chance meeting he'd had over two decades ago while working in the Philippines and traveling throughout Asia's exotic ports. He had discovered a lot about Asian mind-body science, especially three forms ... Yoga, Zen and Kyudo.

At one time or another he had practiced all three.

One evening, while visiting a small unnamed beach near Bangkok, he had hiked from his rickety bamboo hostel into the thick jungle in order to practice Kyudo.

Kyudo was the art of guiding the bow and arrow with the soul. It was often frustrating, but that evening everything had worked perfectly for Robin. After an hour of intense concentration involving just five shots, all bull's eyes, he had felt great. He loved it when the arrows followed his heart's command. Afterwards, he had sat under a huge hardwood to enjoy the feeling of exhilaration this exercise brought him whenever it worked. He was almost dozing when he became aware of an old man sitting next to him. The man was very small and wizened, and dressed like a peasant. His countenance and bearing instantly made plain he was not. Robin hadn't heard the elderly Thai approaching; he had suddenly just been there. "Your arrows flew well," the ancient had said. "How do you feel?"

"Well, uh, very proud!" Robin had replied, trying to keep the surprise from his voice.

"This is your pride," the old man had suggested quietly. "But were the arrows yours or the winds which blew? Whom did the vibrations of the bow-string really belong to? The bow-string sings for us songs of the things we do not know. This is the lesson of the bow. To loose your arrows and forget. To release your burden of pride with the arrow and the doubt which is pride's foundation. Is action not your duty, reward not your concern? You should remain with the only real thing any of us has...the here, the now. Are these archery lessons or a building of faith? When the target jumps for the arrow, are not the target, the arrow, the bow, and even the breath you draw, belonging to some force greater than your own? Is not the faith in that flight a greater force than your pride?"

Robin's eyes had drooped as if he were awakening from a deep sleep. Closing his eyes and shaking his head to clear his mind, he had turned to the old man. He was gone. The incident was so bizarre that it had to have been a dream. He had discussed it at length with Melanie. His thoughts jumped back to the present, and Talking

Panther who sat so close to him now. How can these two look so much like Melanie?

"Robin," Talking Panther whispered sharply. "You must quiet your mind!" MacAllen took a long breath, counted slowly backwards from ten, and allowed his mind to gently drop inward, deeper and deeper. "Breathing in, I calm my whole body..." They have asked for faith. The thought floated lightly between his mantra. I don't, can't understand. Faith? I'll give it my best. "Breathing in, I calm my whole body..." What's going to happen next? Don't know...doesn't matter...don't care.

Now, despite the questions, despite the bouncing truck, Robin drifted into a profound, even more relaxed state. Warmth replaced the icy knot in his stomach and the ache in his head melted away as his mind floated easily on his mantra. Soon, he was as tranquil as a man could be who was riding through a vile swamp in a pickup squeezed between two unbelievably beautiful women, and followed by phantom shadows.

Billy coaxed the truck through the shallow end of the swamp and then slowed it down. "That's it, folks. Don't think they can follow us through this. If you stay calm, Robin, they have no way of knowing where we are. They can search for hours and never catch us now, man. We're ahead of schedule. We don't want to arrive early at the airport." Turning to Talking Panther he said, "Why don't we stop now and we'll fill Robin in on the details."

Talking Panther stared at MacAllen for a moment and a look of comprehension crossed her face. "No, Billy, I want to talk to Robin alone. Stop here."

Billy pulled the beat-up Toyota under an outcrop of palmettos. The truck rolled to a stop and the four of them climbed down on a grass-covered knoll. Wild aromatic fennel filled the air with its acrid spicy scent. The tall plants provided perfect cover, making them all but invisible to anyone who was even a few yards away.

"Come with me." Talking Panther motioned to Robin.

The cool morning reinvigorated Robin as they walked through the brush to a small pond. Sunshine diamonds caught his eye as they skidded and glistened on the mirrored surface of the pool. He turned to speak to Talking Panther and saw that she had sat down. Her entire countenance had changed into a younger form of the woman he had watched at the grave the night before.

All of a sudden, words leapt from her lips. The voice was not hers. "A sign has shown me that it is time to give you your first Golden Word." The chanting tone of the voice was flat, ancient and motherly, caring yet stern. "Your first Golden Word is *Buffalo*. This word will reflect and let you reflect on the spirit of the buffalo, who through his strength is master and walks through the valley with no fear. When the herd of the buffalo moves, no thing living can stand in its way. This is the spirit of strength, of the One and of unity, and of the strength of the whole. Your first word is Buffalo."

Robin was astounded and did not know how to react. The woman who sat before him was surely Talking Panther, but the voice had not been hers. "Talking Panther?"

The Seminole woman opened her eyes, her face transforming yet again. When she spoke, her voice had returned to normal. "It was decided by forces beyond that I should not be the one to give you your first Golden Word. As a simple mortal, I would have needed time to prepare. This time is not ours now. And you needed this word. When we have faith, we unlock strengths beyond our own. We unlock the fathomless strengths of the universe."

"Faith?" he questioned. "You mean like faith in Jesus Christ or in God?"

"Not exactly, Robin," she replied. "When we have faith in any-thing, that thing gains the strength. Then, at best, we can only be illu-minated by reflections of that strength. I do not mean that we should become faithful. I do not mean we should have faith in anything. I mean we should become faith. As faith, we become light, not an object the light reflects upon. We will talk more of this later. Now we must return."

Together, they walked briskly back to the truck.

Billy immediately began to explain their situation. "Okay man, we don't have a lot of time. You have to trust us for a little while. We already know you want to return to England to help Ian. Last night, while you were watching shadows, you exchanged many unspoken thoughts."

Robin found himself locking his face into a mask once more to help conceal his astonishment. His mind spun. They already know what I want!

Billy didn't allow the silence to last. "We are bound to help you and your friend in England as you were bound to help us when we had trouble. We are so connected in ways you can't believe, in ways you just can't see. Eventually you will, but we have to help you right now. We're as much in this as you.

"You're more than a friend, Robin. You're sacred to us beyond friendship, because you see without the stone. This morning I made arrangements. We can't be late. If we keep on schedule, we'll be okay. But you have to stay calm. I know you have more questions, but for now, you have to remain unagitated. Otherwise we'll all be in deep shit."

They climbed back into the Toyota and disappeared back into the swamp.

CHAPTER
EIGHTEEN

Robin saw the airport across the road, one hangar and a couple of tin shacks partially obscured by morning mist that lay in thin sheets across the flat ground.

Immokalee Airport was a perfect place to disappear from. I couldn't have thought of a better plan myself, he whispered under his breath.

Despite his doubts about Billy, he was happy to accept help. MacAllen's mind began to deal with his options once he did disappear. His secretary, Usha, was waiting at the airport when they arrived. He heard the concern and distress in her voice as she spoke.

"Are you all right, Robin? I came an hour early, I've been so anxious. When you didn't show up yesterday I really became worried. You're always so punctual, I just knew something was wrong. I've been on edge since you phoned. By last night I was frantic, I was ready to contact the police but Billy's call last night stopped me."

Robin held Usha close to him for a brief moment. She was the sister he didn't have, the mother he had never known. She was a fine and decent woman who had looked after his business, and him, for years. He trusted her with his life. Now, he was going to put his entire fate in her hands.

He began, his voice low, "Usha, I can't explain everything that's going on right now. We don't have time and I'm not sure I understand everything myself. All I do know is that I've been trying to help Ian Fletcher and in the process I've somehow stumbled onto the biggest case of my life. I can't even comprehend what I have stumbled onto yet, but I know it's big and it's very ugly."

As they walked away from the truck, Robin handed her the copy he had made of the book. "Take this. There's a note in it for you explaining what I know. Don't go back home, Usha. Drive to Tampa instead. I know that it's a hundred and fifty miles out of your way, but please believe me, every precaution I'm giving you makes sense."

Robin's voice was grave as he continued. "In Tampa, find a public library. Make three copies of this. Do not use a photocopy center or any place where anyone can see or even touch it, not even for one second. And make the copies yourself. When you're done, don't let them out of your hands."

His assistant's face was greatly troubled and Robin eased the tone in his voice. "On your way to Tampa get enough cash from our office account at any branch of our bank. Don't get the cash in Tampa, get it before you reach there, and get enough to pay for everything I am going to tell you to do."

He continued rapidly, "Send one copy of the book and the note to Roger Prector, my friend at the FBI and one copy to Bill Moran at the CIA. Also here are the addresses of two hotels overseas. Send the original to one hotel and the copy to the other by DHL, to my attention. Don't read the book and don't keep a copy of it. Don't even look at what you're copying."

MacAllan saw that Usha was listening intently. "When you're finished, don't go back home. Call your husband at his office from a payphone before you get to Tampa. And don't use your phone card. Pay cash. Don't call anyone else, only your husband and tell him to leave work immediately and meet you in Orlando. Tell him not to phone anyone or tell anyone where he's going. When he arrives, drive to another town. Buy tickets to somewhere out of the country. Take a holiday someplace you wouldn't normally go. Don't use credit cards. Pay cash for everything. Don't return to the office and don't say anything to anyone, not a single person. Usha forget the office. You and Narenda just disappear for a week."

MacAllen hesitated when he saw the growing fear and alarm on Usha's face. He loved her, she was very dear to him, and he hated to hurt her in any way. He didn't want her so scared, but knew she was. But there was no time for laxity or second thoughts now.

Robin continued speaking to his assistant in a more temperate voice. "Usha, to survive I've got to act quickly and with severity. My situation is precarious. I could end up dead. So could everyone around me, especially all of us who have come into contact with this book. That old Scot, Clague, who came to my hotel suite, brought us this curse and I suspect he's already dead himself. Please, follow these instructions, Usha. You'll be okay. But do exactly as I say. And tell no one! After a week, check our Canadian address at Dormer Enterprises. Use only a public phone, but not one at the hotel where you're staying."

Dormer Enterprises was a Canadian shell company he maintained for his investigations. Anyone looking would see a successful family-owned investment firm in Toronto. He kept his ownership in Dormer well hidden and had used this firm several times as bait to tip a con artist's hand. It operated from a mail forwarding service and he never communicated directly from his local office there. They never contacted him directly either. The Canadian address would be safe.

"If I haven't left a message for you in Canada, fly to another country and stay another week. Keep using cash. Then call again from a payphone away from your hotel. If I haven't left a message by then, call Roger and Bill and tell them to read the copies."

He frowned as he thought of the shadows. They were so intrusive. He wondered if he could throw them off track to protect her.

Usha's eyes had widened and again MacAllen could see the terror and confusion on her face. "Follow these instructions, Usha, and you'll be okay. Just remember that following them could make the difference between life and death, both yours and mine. Now, go on. If for any reason I don't return, take everything out of the company, it's yours. But don't go back home. Abandon the place. Move out of the country. Don't hesitate either. Doing so could mean your life. There isn't any time for questions." Robin hugged her tightly. "Go now. Hurry!"

She left without a word and MacAllen's stomach sank as he watched her car disappear. The panic Usha must be feeling now. Robin clenched his fist and vowed that someone would pay for the anguish they caused her. His anger swelled to rage until he remembered Talking Panther's warning.

Robin took a deep breath and began repeating his mantra as he walked back to the car. A King Air 90 emerged out of the fog like a phantom and drifted quietly into the wind on the north-south runway. A patch of sun fleetingly broke through the haze and flashed brilliantly off the white and blue striped wing of the aircraft. The sleek, expensive plane had been flying low, below radar, with its engines set for minimum sound. The registration N090KW stood out in bold red letters on its tail, just above a name, Agricultural Enterprises, Inc. The gleaming plane looked out of place at this airport. Immokalee was a poor farming community. The planes were mostly battered crop dusters and there were several for other agricultural uses. There was also a beat-up DC-3 that stood forlornly on the side of the field.

Billy nodded his head towards the aircraft. "Let's go, man. Timing is crucial. Johnny Jay looks after this airport. He's Seminole and can keep this arrival to himself. But this plane can't sit here long without attracting attention. If one person knows in a small town like this, everyone knows and that can mean..."

The thin wail of a siren began in the distance. "Hurry," Billy shouted. "Let's get out of here!"

Billy rushed Robin and his sisters to the plane, even as it was still rolling slowly ahead. The door opened and they were on board. Aircraft King Air November Zero Niner Zero Kilo Whiskey fishtailed as it spun left and started forward again. The pilot did not taxi back to face the wind. Instead, he brought the engines to full power; the plane jumped and lifted back into the low-lying clouds. In less than two minutes, the plane had touched down, collected its passengers and disappeared into the morning clouds.

Robin leaned back into his seat and watched the ground disappear underneath the gossamer fog, trying to shrug off the stress of his meeting with Usha. His spirits lifted as the plane broke above the clouds into the blazing sun.

He was sure no one had seen them. Nor would anyone take notice of the two Indian farmhands who had arrived at the airport in a rusted green van and picked up Billy's old Toyota. No one could have seen Usha either. And I didn't notice any shadows, he thought.

I might be operating for the moment on faith, but what more than faith does one really ever have? Robin's mood lightened and he began to concentrate on the tasks ahead.

I have a chance now. As far as the world is concerned Robin MacAllen is gone.

CHAPTER
NINETEEN

Jimmy Ray Burnett swore as his car, siren still blaring, slid to a stop in the gravel parking lot of Immokalee's airport. He had rushed across the county line without giving a damn about stepping on the Collier County sheriff's toes. Immokalee Airport lay several miles to the west of Hendry County, but as far as he was concerned, this was a pursuit. A mile or two from his county was close enough.

The plane he'd been alerted to was not in sight. All he could see were empty fields and three vacant runways partially obscured by the remainder of the morning fog.

"Cock suckers, mother-fucking cock suckers," he bellowed in a rage. He swore again. In one motion Jimmy Ray kicked the car door open, holstered the large gun that lay on the seat beside him, swung his large body out of the cruiser and switched off the siren.

He had few options. They had either not yet arrived, had already come and gone, or were somewhere around here. I'll know soon enough, he thought, as he jerked his shotgun from its rack in the front of the car and headed for a rusted tin hut with a crookedly hung sign that read Airport Office.

As he pounded swiftly across the parking space, Jimmy Ray felt his anger mount. Goddamn deputies totally screwed up again. Acid bile bit at the back of his tongue as he pictured for the twentieth time in as many minutes the scene he had just viewed–the demolished cruiser, deputies milling around and an Indian who had suddenly jumped up when the ambulance arrived saying he was fine after all.

Burnett almost choked on his fury. "I ain't that mad about those idiot deputies destroying my newest patrol car; when I want new cars I can damn well get them," he muttered under his breath. "I ain't even that mad at how stupid my deputies were, standing round gawking like dumb shitting chickens with their heads twisted off. I don't choose my men cuz a their genius. I want them to do what they're told, not to think. Smartass deputies don't last too long working for me. Bein' fooled by slow-witted stupid damn Indians is what's pissin' me off. Indians, the fucking low lives of the universe, and they fooled my deputies. God dammit! They fooled me too."

Jimmy Ray had stood and stared at the Indian kicking and twitching just like his slut lickin' deputies had. Another spasm of rage shook his frame. "Some son-a-bitch is going to pay for this!" he whispered with vehemence. The sheriff cocked the slide of his shotgun with a vicious jerk, feeding a twelve-gauge, three-inch load of #1 buckshot into the chamber.

He kicked hard at the dented metal door of the building and it clanged open. He stepped inside, looked around and saw a man hunched over an old steel desk. The man was Indian and Jimmy Ray's rage turned into a storm. "Freeze, mother fucker!" he roared. "Assume the position. Put your hands against the wall!"

The man looked at him, bewildered. The Seminole slowly raised his hands, stared down the barrel of the shotgun and timidly asked, "Somethin' the matter, officer?"

"Yeah. Something big is the fucking matter." The sheriff shouted so loudly that spittle ran down his chin. "And you better tell me what the fuck it is. Any planes take off outta here this morning?"

The Indian took a step back and answered quietly, "We don't allow no drug dealing from here, Sheriff. You know that."

Jimmy Ray hollered his reply. "Don't screw with me, Indian. My finger is itchin'. I'd just as soon blow you away as not." The sheriff turned slightly and the shotgun thundered. The blast in the tiny tin shack was enormous, and shocking.

He watched with satisfaction as the unsuspecting Seminole

jumped, tripped and fell backwards over a chair, and lay shaking on the floor. Jimmy Ray looked at the gaping hole he had blown in the side of the desk and growled, "That was a warning, asshole. The next shot'll damn well cut ya in two. Now answer my question! Have any airplanes taken off outta here this mornin'?"

He saw the Indian turn very pale and crawl backwards as if to escape the wrath of the sheriff. "I, I don't know," he stammered. "Honest, uh, I, I just arrived. Johnny Jay was on the night security shift. He, ah, only he would know and he already left. Don't, uh, know where he's goin to. Don't see no record of any flights coming or going. I, I don't imagine... there's no flight."

Jimmy Ray knew then that the Indian wasn't going to tell him anything he needed to know. If that man and Indian woman had been here and were gone, he was screwed. No way he could tell if they had been. They ain't here now. Doubt they will be with my car sittin' out front.

"Shit," he barked. He thought back to the earlier phone call saying the man and Indian woman were now heading for Immokalee Airport. It had been the same deadly calm voice of his supplier. He had not doubted or questioned the information.

Now he wondered if the man had been wrong. He stepped forward, lowered the shotgun and glared at the Indian lying on the floor. He could smell his fear. "You're either a very brave man or a real dumb ass Indian. Lucky for you I don't think anyone's that dumb. You probably don't know if that plane was here. I could find out for sure if I had time, but I don't. So you got a lucky red ass this mornin'. I should just shoot ya, but that'd mean too much red tape, being outta my jurisdiction and all. The law in Collier's all hooty-tooty. Sweet Jesus they'd scream and have me fillin' out forms for weeks."

Suddenly Burnett's stomach started to ache. "I'm gonna let you go. Less trouble for me. But, don't think you're fuckin' smart, wise ass. You ain't heard the end a this." You hear me, boy?" he yelled at the top of his lungs. The Indian crawled back further and nodded. "Don't you let me catch your butt on my side of the county line, Tonto, or I'll skin your red ass but good. You got that?"

Jimmy Ray started to back out of the room. "If I find out about one plane leavin' here this morning, I will personally blow your balls off and see your hide tanned good."

The sheriff turned and walked out the door. Now what should I do, he wondered, as he pushed his bulk over the gravel toward the car. I better call and get someone over here to watch, just in case they come later. I ain't hangin' around here till some damn Collier deputy shows up and wants to get in a pissin' contest over jurisdiction. Got better things to do! He reached his car, yanked the door open and radioed instructions. "Get a plain clothes detective over here to the Immokalee airport right now. Have him check out any plane that comes in or tries to go outta here. Have him stay outta sight. This is strictly unofficial. Call me if he sees anything. I'll be at home."

He dialed his supplier on the car phone. The man had that same tone of voice that had earlier filled Jimmy Ray with great apprehension. These were downright dangerous men, he thought. "The target was not at the farm this morning. Not at the airport either. Folks here say your man never was here." Burnett's voice grew aggressive. "Now listen up, my friend. You've had me runnin' all over this fuckin' county all morning. I don't think these people were anywhere you said. When you got problems, I'm happy to help. but this is gittin' out of hand. I've got things to do, so find yourself somebody else to do your legwork. Remember you ain't the only guys around here with a supply. But I am the only sheriff in Hendry County. I make money from you guys but you need me too, so next time you want some help, think twice before wasting my time."

These men fed on fear and he had let them know he was not afraid. He wiped sweat from his face and quickly disconnected the phone. His legs wobbled and he fingered the big gun in his holster nervously. This was his God-damned county. He was the force to be reckoned with here.

He had just begun to relax a bit when something grabbed him from behind. Jimmy Ray jumped and whirled, half drew his gun and then dropped it to the ground as pain wracked his body. A huge vise-like grip began to crush him.

He looked around. No one, nothing! As the pressure to his body increased, he dropped on his knees and was pounded to the ground. The grip compressed, then smashed and strangled him. And as unexpectedly as it began, it stopped. Jimmy Ray lay on the ground with the gun at his side. His heart raced and his lungs begged for air. Fear clenched his soul as pain raged through him. Sweat saturated his uniform. The cold gravel seeped through and prickled his skin.

Through his haze of agony, Jimmy Ray heard the ringing of the car phone. Pushing back his terror and pain, the sheriff slowly rose, reached inside and answered. His breath was coming easier now, but almost stopped when he heard the same dispassionate voice speaking once again.

"Jimmy Ray, that was just a small example of what my friends do when they feel let down. Right now they feel very, very let down. But I have asked them to give you just one more chance. The man we want is now flying to Tampa. Pick him up there and bring him to us. Alive! Don't fail, Sheriff, or next time our friends will not be so easy with their grip. Am I clear, Jimmy Ray?"

Slumped in the seat and sweating, he was unable to control the tremble in his voice. "They're in Tampa?"

"Yes," said his supplier. "They're in the air now. If you value your life, Jimmy Ray, you will get this man. A friend will be waiting for you at Ft. Myers airport. Meet him at the United Airlines check-in counter. He will have help for you and the target's photo. Do not fail us again. If you do, there is nowhere you can hide. There will be no more second chances. Oh, and Jimmy Ray, one other thing. Wear your belt with the gold buckle at all times. Do not take it off."

Fury lashed through Burnett "What the fuck? Now ya tellin' me how to dress? Who the fuck do you think you are? What the hell's my belt buckle got to do..." The attack was immediate; he gasped for air and dropped the phone, jerking in agony.

As the receiver slipped from his hand, Burnett heard the heartless voice that would ring in his ears again and again. "No more questions, Jimmy Ray. Just wear the belt and bring us the man. Or you die."

CHAPTER TWENTY

Robin leaned back in his seat as the plane reached cruising altitude, leveled and sped smoothly towards Tampa Bay. He looked out the window and watched the ground below shimmer as the rising sun began to melt the thin clouds; he blinked at the brightness. The morning colors danced and flickered, billions of minute gems on the lakes below. The Gulf of Mexico loomed on the horizon, and MacAllen let its motionless blue serenity absorb him. Sighing deeply, he allowed his earlier tensions to dissolve along with the morning haze.

Robin sank deeper into the soft leather seat as his eyes shut. Sun flooded the cabin, helping to erase the abuses of the morning. He was drifting between wakefulness and sleep when Billy lumbered unsteadily across the plane and dropped into the next seat.

Ignoring Robin's closed eyes, Billy began to gab nervously over the drone of the plane. "The plane belongs to our tribe. It's part of our Seminole agriculture enterprises. Like the farms we own. No one knows. The tribe keeps its assets in the background. I hate flying, man. I really hate flying."

Robin sat up, accepted a coffee Silent Panther handed him and sipped the hot, bitter beverage. Billy continued, "I called for the plane last night. Figured we'd need to get out. We're flying to Tampa. I've got seats for all of you flying to New York and then to England."

Robin spilt coffee on his borrowed jeans as he jerked straight up.

"All?" He asked. "Who's all?"

Billy looked uncomfortable. "Uh... well... the three of you. You, Talking Panther and Silent Panther."

"Billy," he said, "I've got to go on my own. I owe you all, and incredibly but I can't let them come. It's too risky and I don't want to drag them any further into this mess. Whoever's following me is dangerous. Besides, I work alone." The warnings Robin had given himself flooded back. The two sisters in England would be a lose-lose proposition. They're either my friends, in which case I can't let them take the risk, or they're in on the con. I can't tell which yet, but either way I lose.

Billy looked over and shrugged as he replied, "I agree, Robin, but the girls have made up their minds. They're tough, man, and they insist."

Robin clenched his jaw and spoke more firmly. "No way, Billy. They can't come. Forget it! They just can't come."

MacAllen shifted in his seat, leaned back and looked away from Billy to end the conversation. He was a loner. Even if Billy and Talking Panther did allay his fears, he was not used to traveling or working with anyone. Having two women with him would add danger, to him and to them. This was a sticky enough mess without that worry. And another feeling persisted, something abstract, that he couldn't quite define. But his gut feeling was, unequivocally, to get away from Billy and his sisters.

He tried a mental checklist to help him grasp why. He was practiced at working in the dark with con artists. He never knew at first who was involved. But... but he always knew their modus operandi. Con artists never have a hidden motive. It's always greed. Greed is always beneath their scams. That's it! That's the problem. Neither Billy nor either of his sisters has shown any hint of greed, any suggestion that this is all about money. I can't figure out what they want.

His thoughts were interrupted as Billy began speaking again. "You can't stop them, Robin. Don't try, man. You're into something bigger than you know. The girls can help more than you'll ever imagine."

But Robin couldn't bend on this. He pointed out his issues. "There's too much at risk, Billy. Your sisters wouldn't be safe. They won't know what to do and one mistake by them could get us all killed. They'll cut down my mobility." He shook his head. "It's too dangerous. I don't want them."

Billy edged closer, but spoke louder, with a more agitated tone. "Robin, they have to come. They know more about the dangers than you do; they can fight them in ways you don't know how. There's no sense arguing, man. You can't stop them. You can't avoid them. They'll just follow you like the others are. They can help. Besides, there's interests here other than your own. The tribe is involved! Talking Panther and Silent Panther might help you but they'll help the tribe too."

What do the Seminole have to do with this? Robin's curiosity rose at the mention of the tribe's involvement. But still, he did not want the women to come. "No, Billy they can't come, period." He turned and glared at the women and barked, "I appreciate your help, but you can't come to England. I'm sorry but you just can't."

Then he returned his gaze to the window, sat in stony silence and watched the plane quickly eat up the ground that lay far below. He sat unmoving, but grew increasingly uncomfortable.

Billy stared in silence at him. The two women remained quiet, steadfast and tranquil.

Robin turned to reason with them, "Listen, I have to do this alone. I really do appreciate your help. You're good friends. That's why I need to go to England by myself." He shifted in his seat and watched warily as Talking Panther got up, motioned for Billy to move and sat down next to him.

She spoke mildly but her words cut through the drone of the engines. "We must come with you, Robin. You know you cannot stop us and it will be hard for you to lose us if we insist on following you. We must come for the tribe but also we must come for you. You are our friend. We can no more abandon you than you can abandon Ian Fletcher. You will face dangers you cannot yet imagine; we already know this. We can be the difference between life and death for you, and for Ian Fletcher. Can you afford not to have our help? Would this be fair to Ian? Already where would you be without us?" Billy started to interject, but Talking Panther cut him short. "You and Billy argue like two crows chattering in the trees and the noise you make accomplishes as much. Billy talks from the fear that he may not return your favors. Your voice carries other fears. Neither of you speak of the things which must be. Robin, you have the strength to walk alone. But now you need us in your shadow. You possess great skills and many more beyond those you have already used. You need all of them now. You have abilities and powers we can help you unlock. If for no other reason than this, you need us."

She touched his hand and MacAllen felt fire pulse through him. "To your hand of iron, Robin, I will be the velvet glove. Without me, your path will be lined with hazards and thorns. We are involved. Your success or your failure will be ours. I must come, for in this time and place, we are bound together, and have been from the moment I entered your mind and you entered my heart. By combining our hearts and minds, we will both gain equilibrium."

She moved even closer to him and lowered her voice as she pressed her warm hand on his. A spark shot through Robin as she spoke again. "There is part of us which is united. It always has been and always shall be. All that has changed is that now our eyes and ears and senses know of it. Our union was destined lifetimes ago. Neither you nor I can change this at all. No more than the leaves can change their union with the wind. I must come with you. Since this is so, so too must Silent Panther, for she and I are one. I could no more travel across these waters without her than I could without my soul. Silent Panther is a part of me and the three of us are linked in chains which have never been... and will never be... broken."

Talking Panther paused and grew pensive. "Silent Panther and I are twins. We have never needed to speak to know each other's thoughts; we are more complete by working in different ways, but always together. I live and work in the outer realm of this consciousness we call life. Silent Panther inhabits and works in the inner realm that is at the roots of our existence. Her silence is not from lack of words, but from lack of need. Her thoughts and her life are more profound... more silent than ours. But my words are hers and her innermost reflections are mine. Now the power of this union is also yours."

A sweet smile formed on Talking Panther's lips. "Words would draw her from life's real power. Speaking would separate her from the dimensions of life where words cannot go. A voice would cost her knowledge of things that the tongue cannot express."

Robin was dazzled by the Seminole woman's words. Connected to a truth he could not express but nonetheless understood, his will rocked between the warnings his mind sirened and the more intense reality his heart felt. This indecision left him without a rebuttal as Talking Panther continued.

"Speech, Robin, is like a thong which binds our thoughts into bundles of meaning through words. These bundles give great strength and security to man, as the bale offers strength to the single straw. But these thongs limit nature's infinite knowledge, just as bound straw can no longer fly with the breeze. Speaking constricts truth to the limits of our minds and freezes the knowing in our hearts.

"Speaking requires great energy. Words are a wonderful bounty but the price of that bounty is high. To speak of love is wondrous, but one can never know love through speech. The energy of speech saps love's true strength, limits its depths. Sound interferes with one's true hearing of love. Words become the noise of the babbling brook that drowns reality — the silence in the woods. Such is the price we pay for the shallowness of speech."

Robin jerked upright in his seat, confused yet captured by Talking Panther's words. He was suddenly aware that the heat from her body was competing with that of the sun.

"Silent Panther listens to waves of nature that are the very source of existence. She does not limit herself with words, does not spare energy for speech, when she can be boundless in knowledge. In this way, we both live connected at a depth beyond any one depth. You need these heightened powers to train and reinforce yours."

Talking Panther touched Robin's hand again, sending a sharp jolt of electricity through him. "We have much to discuss about our trip together and little time to talk."

MacAllan again shifted uneasily in his seat. "Talking Panther, what you say sounds very wonderful, but you just can't come."

Robin looked directly into Talking Panther's eyes and stopped. He could smell the sweetness of her breath and feel her silky tender skin. He was tongue-tied, his arguments buried themselves out of reach and he was unable to go on. Robin slumped back in his seat, suddenly defenseless. He tried again, couldn't access a single contrary thought and sat still, waiting for understanding, or for the strength to continue.

When neither came, he said nothing and crossed his arms self-defensively instead. He was more speechless than he had ever been. The tone in her voice, the glint in her eye, the pounding in his chest told him that any discussion about this was over. Robin had just acquired two new partners. "Damn." As he accepted this, despite all the previous concerns he'd had, his worries gradually melted. A confusing, disconnected sense of peace surrounded him and overwhelmed the alarm bells resonating in his brain.

Talking Panther leaned even closer to him, put her arm through his and whispered, "I still have much to tell about all that is happening, who we are, how we are followed. I can feel your suspicions and I understand them. But we cannot talk of this right now. Not with Billy here, because even he is not allowed these words. At the airport, we will talk. Now, Robin, we must speak of protection. We will need protection soon."

MacAllan leaned forward in his seat, his bemusement turning again to anxiety. He was used to being in charge and spotting risks before anyone else. He had a nose for trouble and prepared for it well before it came along. Now Talking Panther was in charge, was dictating his every move… even his thoughts. Yet Robin couldn't murmur a word of protest. He had dismissed his arguments and couldn't even explain why to himself. An invisible hand had grabbed his thoughts. Now that same hand moved his mind to matters of weaponry.

His thoughts whirled. She's telling me what I need yet I still feel good. She's telling me I need protection and I don't feel trouble ahead at all. Robin decided to try and let his doubts go and uncrossed his arms to affirm that at least he still had command of his own body. He stood up, bent to avoid bumping his head and leaned against the bulkhead as he spoke, trying to regain control. "Whoever we're facing plays rough. They know tricks I haven't even thought of. What do we need protection from? What kind of weapons are you talking about?"

MacAllen desperately wanted a gun. Having grown up in a remote coastal town, he'd had guns from an early age and knew how to use them well. But it would be impossible to carry a weapon on board the upcoming flights. And getting one in England, he thought, would be too much trouble. He sat back down. "Forget guns. We can't fly with them or get them through customs. I'm pretty deadly with a bow and arrow but that's too impractical. Knives are good."

Talking Panther leaned back, waited for his attention and asked, "Have you ever used a knife before, Robin?"

"I've used everything at one time or another," he replied. "I'm not trained, but a knife is better than nothing."

Talking Panther's face became placid and her eyes motioned him to come near. He leaned forward, closer, as she spoke, barely above a whisper. "One of the first transformations you will gain with the Golden Words is a great increase of compassion. The words will teach you that there is unity in all. When a person dies, so does a part of the whole; each death reflects on us all. You won't be able to be violent; you won't have a desire to kill. The knife and the gun are weapons of destructiveness and death. You cannot use them. But, still, we do need protection."

Reflected sunlight spilled onto Talking Panther's ravishing face. She looked more serious. "Many of our Grandfathers made serious errors when the white foreigners invaded the land where we lived. We tried to kill what we feared. We should have protected instead. We did not recognize our need for protection and we mistook aggression for protection. Killing only reduced our power and weak-ened us in ways we should have avoided."

The Seminole woman squeezed Robin's arm as she continued. "Our people have always lived in harmony with nature. And learned much from it. We have found that hunters never see as many seasons as their prey; to hunt and to kill requires enormous energy. Every meal becomes a life and death struggle for the hunter. Over time we learned to avoid extreme struggles but still be protected."

Robin nodded as Talking Panther went on. "When Silent Panther and I travel, we often go places where women should not go, where we must have protection. If we have reasons to be there, we go. We have learned from our friends in nature how to protect ourselves. Look at the porcupine. He does not carry a gun or a knife, but even the greatest aggressor does not bother this friend. From this lesson we have learned to carry fish hooks."

Robin looked bemused and replied with a laugh, "Yeah, fish hooks make great weapons. For when we're attacked by trout."

The woman ignored his sarcasm and waved her hands. "We know that anyone who tries to lay hold of us will always grab our wrist, arm or lower leg. If they want to kill us, they will grab our neck. When you have a few fish hooks bound onto each of these, they will remember the experience for many seasons. They will feel like the panther cub that tries to eat his first prickly friend."

Talking Panther's face calmed as MacAllen motioned that he now understood. "We can carry the fish hooks through customs. They cannot be taken from us as a knife can. Fish hooks are safe, easy and very practical. They protect us but do not bring anyone serious harm. You can dream of guns or knives but we will use fish hooks."

The drone of the plane changed pitch. Robin peered out the window and saw that the aircraft was angling down. Tampa Airport appeared on the horizon and suddenly, unanswered questions or not, Robin was very glad he was seated here next to Talking Panther.

CHAPTER
TWENTY ONE

The King Air floated in on its final descent, flared and touched down with a thump. Robin stared out the window at the sprawling terminal ahead. The plane rocked gently in a cross-wind and rushed on towards the concourse. His mood lifted and he wondered why.

The unfamiliar seat buckle argued for a moment but he fought it open and stood. Tampa was among his favorite airports. For years, he had kept a permanent suite at the Marriott Airport Hotel.

Maybe I feel good because after all the strange and obscure events in the last few days, this place is so familiar to me. But there's something more, beyond what I'm accustomed to, a new inner quietness, a sense of peace. What am I feeling?

Looking forward, Robin watched the plane continue its bumpy roll to the terminal. Mixed memories here, he thought, remembering the years when this airport had been home. Life had been exciting and financially very rewarding during the time he had lived here. But home? An airport, even when packed with people, especially when packed, can be the loneliest of places. Too transient. The many girls, primed for fun, had been too absorbed in the city's glitter and in themselves. They were just passing scenery wrapped in pretty clothes, temporary distractions from the isolation every traveler feels within. And a traveler he was. There was no family awaiting him at journey's end, no mother or father, no relatives. Robin had no roots or place to call home. He knew many people in many places, but lacked close comfortable friends. Ian Fletcher was the only one and Melanie... Melanie had been. He pushed down the thought.

Many admired Robin's rugged good looks, easy personality, and his success, but few really knew him. The real Robin always remained hidden within, always alone. Travel had been his only means of escaping the loneliness. He had loved leaving from this place, but not being here. No, this wasn't home. So why do I feel so good right now?

MacAllen was jarred as the plane lurched. This commonplace impact broke loose a niggling image that had been hiding somewhere in the recesses of his mind. Talking Panther and Silent Panther are the source of my comfort. Even with my concerns, dammit, I like being with them. They feel like family. They feel right. I only met them last night but already I can relax with them. It's like being home. The fact that they were coming to England suddenly made him happy. Even as he enjoyed this bit of contentment, a warning surfaced in his mind. Careful, Robin, there's still too many unanswered questions. The con, how they looked like Melanie. Why... I can't let my guard down. As the plane wheeled to a stop, they all rose and stepped out into the sweltering Florida air.

Billy stopped at the foot of the plane and squeezed Robin's arm. "I'm flying back. Can't make this journey with you. It's beyond my powers. Got lots to do back home. I hate planes anyway, man." He looked embarrassed. "You'll need great spirits on this trip. I'll be with you through them."

Billy looked in Robin's eyes for a moment, then looked down, squeezed his friend's arm again and climbed back into the plane. The aircraft promptly turned and taxied back to the runway.

Robin walked with the two women into the terminal. They hurried outside, hailed a taxi and gave the driver instructions to a nearby shopping mall. He hated malls, and hated shopping even worse. When forced to buy, he would normally be drawn to the quiet elegance of Tampa's older waterfront stores.

Talking Panther had insisted. "Time is important. We have to prepare for the trip."

"We also need a quiet place where we can talk," he had told the sisters. He needed answers to his questions and he wanted those answers now. He decided once they reached the mall to push for them before making another move. As the three of them sped through Tampa in the cab, MacAllen watched closely to make sure they were not being followed. He saw nothing. Makes sense, he thought. I didn't even know where we were coming two hours ago. We have to be in the clear. If someone's following my thoughts... Again, Robin's intuition nagged at him. Despite these new feelings, I have to be careful with these women!

Inside the mall he found a nearly empty fast food restaurant selling cinnamon rolls. He demanded they stop. "I want to talk. Now!"

Robin ordered three cups of coffee that he did not expect to drink, and settled the women into a free booth far from the cashier, a young girl not apparently interested in anything, including the three of them.

MacAllen took command. "Ladies, time to answer some hard questions." He leaned forward, steeling himself to be as tough as he needed to get the answers he wanted.

Talking Panther once again read his thoughts. "Robin," she said, "you still have doubts about Silent Panther and me. I know you want to talk. But we have little time for that now. We need to prepare for a long journey. Our trip will take us to war. We will suffer hardships and must be ready. There are many items to assemble for the battle."

She stopped briefly and frowned. "We must travel to England as fast as we can. Time is short. I feel there is danger here; this is the place where the lion hunts. There is danger everywhere, but for us, safety will be in the den of the lion, not in his hunting ground. He is looking for us here right now."

MacAllen persisted. "We'll go soon, but first we have a talk", he said. He shifted uneasily and raised one arm onto the back of the booth seat in body language that said, "I am not moving."

Robin hoped he looked at lot more confident than he felt right now. He'd waited a long time for these answers, and he wouldn't budge. "I'm tired of waiting and I want to know what's going on. I agreed to have faith in you and to accept that you know what's happening. So I have. I've been patient, but now I need some answers. If we're going to war, I have to understand my allies and recognize my enemies. I also want what I came for in the first place—the Golden Words."

He sat still, thinking how the war analogy was phony, but they started it and I'm not about to allow them their evasiveness. Besides, I'm the professional here. He sat stone-like and tried to stare into their unfathomable eyes. But he couldn't keep it up. They pulled him in, draining his strength.

He blinked and looked away, occupying himself with a sip of the tepid coffee. All of a sudden, Robin wished he wasn't so obstinate. He slumped in the booth. "Christ, I'm losing my grip!"

Neither woman blinked. They only stared back at him placidly, hands folded on their laps.

Talking Panther began to speak. "This is not the place to share the Golden Words, Robin. We must be truly alone. We must prepare before we begin; there are rites of initiation we must follow. Your first Golden Word was given as a great exception, but there will be no more deviations from this ritual."

MacAllen replied sharply, "Okay, let's pass on the Golden Words. How about we start with the enemy. Who's been following us, and how? I know I wasn't tailed from England or from Miami. And I was in the clear in the Everglades. I didn't talk to anyone except Usha and Billy. And I didn't tell Usha I was coming to see you in case her phone was tapped. No one could have known where I was except you and Billy."

His voice had risen and Robin leaned forward, heated now, anger and frustration spilling from his voice. This had no effect at all on Talking Panther. She remained composed, but her eyes panned the restaurant, taking in, examining. She was alert without any sign of nervousness. Her reply was husky, yet collected. "Calm yourself. Your voice and your thoughts can be heard clearly when you lose control. You must remain relaxed, otherwise the Controllers will be able to zero in on our location even sooner. Your anger and fear, its father, are your greatest enemies. You must…"

She stopped. Her words had been harsh but her gaze was quizzical and came through mellow eyes. She hesitated, her face showing compassion. Talking Panther spoke in a voice that soothed like a cool balm. "You are impatient like the panther cub. Such curiosity will bring you great knowledge, but it also can bring great risk. Curiosity is the root of all knowledge, the seed of life. But the curious must be tempered and nurtured."

Her voice turned even softer now and Talking Panther looked down into her lap. "The love of the she-panther rises to great wrath so she can protect her curious cubs. But from this love she also learns to box their ears."

Then Talking Panther looked up and smiled warmly, directly into Robin's eyes. "I can feel that your curiosity must be filled, if for no other reason than your own protection. I can't box your ears, so let me try to explain briefly so that we can soon leave."

She sighed, and continued. "The men who follow you do so from England. You will never see them here. This is why we must go as soon as possible to them. The men who searched for you in the swamp last night, and those who came this morning, are here now. They are nothing but meaningless soldiers." She leaned closer to Robin and a worried look appeared on her face. "These soldiers are dangerous barbs ready to strike, but they know nothing. They are like the fangs of a snake, lethal and poisonous but only as instruments of action, without intellect or thought. These men are just tools of a master who presents a much greater danger."

She moved very close now and whispered, "Robin, we do not bring you this trouble. You must believe this. We are here only to help. Look at me and you will see this."

He sat deathly still now, considering. He stared directly into her black obsidian eyes. And he was swallowed. No chance of staring this one down, he thought.

He took a drink of the watery coffee. He didn't even notice its bitter taste as she continued speaking. "You have seen that not all in this world is as it seems. What we touch is not solid. What we hear is not the only sound. All we see not the only light. There are vibrations at the roots of all being which cannot be seen, felt or heard. This resonance of nature can be known only by those who allow these vibrations to be heard. These waves are the flow in the wind, the beating in the heart, the spark in the lightning bolt."

The Seminole stopped and waited for Robin to absorb her words. She then leaned forward and placed her hand on his arm. "This trembling of the cosmos forms everything. These pulses are infinite and cannot be described. They are the oscillations of all. They form us. They are us. We are shells cast by these echoes. They form even the universe. And through them, we are all connected, and are one."

Talking Panther's impassive delivery helped still MacAllen's growing rage, but her words also confused him. His baffled look prompted her to continue. "We are waves in the cosmos, so we know these vibrations that form us because they are us and we are them. These waves connect everything. They connect the small to the large. They link that which is far to that which is near. When we listen to these cosmic waves, we listen to all. But we cannot get in touch with them unless we learn how to ignore the sounds of our senses. The trembling of the cosmos forms everything, including our senses, and so cannot be understood by them."

Robin saw Talking Panther watching him closely. He was impressed. She can even perceive when I'm puzzled, he thought.

"The forest is connected to the sky, and the heavens to the stars and the suns. They appear separate only because our five senses are limited. The connections are not. The senses cannot perceive their own essence and so they create a false reality."

He watched as Talking Panther slipped her graceful hands off his arm and onto the table. She took a deep breath and spoke again. "Everything is in touch with everything else, but we humans rely on senses that do not perceive this contact. Most have lost the ability to feel beneath our sensual perceptions to the unearthly tremors that connect us at the root of all life and all things."

She now shifted her focus. "This is how they follow you, Robin. They feel you through these vibrations."

Gary A. Scott

He knew the blank look on his face showed how perplexed he was. "I don't understand. What vibrations?" She looked away, attempting to conceal her exasperation. He could see she was trying hard to help him comprehend. An ever-growing part of him wanted to believe her, but his doubts stood firmly in the way.

"Let me explain this in scientific terms." Her voice became more tutorial. "To begin, forget all your concepts of matter, liquid and gas. Imagine they are all the same thing—just vibration—but moving at different speeds and spinning in different ways."

She took a cup and tapped the side, causing ripples to flow across the coffee. "Imagine that everything starts like this ripple. Imagine that all light, sound and matter are the same energy that caused this ripple. All motion, light, sound and matter are just a fluctuation of something–the same something that just moved across the coffee in this cup."

She looked at Silent Panther for direction, then tapped again, harder, spilling coffee over the cup's rim. Her voice rose, becoming more earnest as she delved into the explanation. "Today's science has identified levels of motion that we call sound. Scientists call each of these levels of sound an octave, and they claim that there are sixty-four of them. But there is one octave, Robin, that is different than the others, that is like the warp and the weft of all the others. It's not the weave itself, it's…it's like a glue that causes the weave of all the other octaves to stick together. It is a sixty-fifth octave."

Robin saw how beautiful her eyes were as Talking Panther looked up. "Those who follow you do so through this sixty-fifth octave," she said in a measured voice. "They see your motion much in the same way you just saw this coffee spill out of the cup."

MacAllen watched her face turn solemn as she took a deep breath and handed him a different idea. "Visualize this glue of the sixty-fifth octave as a single sheet of liquid metal, something like mercury, only very sticky. See it permeating everywhere, in everything." He watched the smoothness of her hand as it flicked on a metal ashtray. "This piece of fluid metal saturates everything that exists, and it vibrates whenever anything is touched, like the tinkle you just heard from this ashtray. By striking anything, anywhere, you strike a part of the metal and the whole sheet quivers! Does this make any sense to you?"

Robin shifted uneasily, wrapped his fingers around the coffee mug and said nothing. Talking Panther tried another angle. "Think of it in this way. This metal is the binding of life. And this metal is everywhere, all the time, always has been and always will be, forever. This metal is beyond all dimensions of time and space because it is time and space."

A tiny spark of understanding glimmered in Robin's mind as he sorted through his knowledge of science. He said haltingly, "I've had enough science to know that even when a fly lands on a thick beam of steel it bends the beam. I guess I can see this metal as a very big beam, and I can see each touch as a very small fly." He stopped to think this through, then added with a lopsided grin, "The idea works better for me though if the metal is jello." He almost laughed aloud. "Everything in the universe, then, is encapsulated in some kind of invisible jello. Any time anything touches anything else, the jello wobbles a little bit. Right?"

His words kindled further explanation from Talking Panther. She reached with her long delicate fingers and pulled the ashtray across the table to her. "Yes, but we cannot describe this jello. Cannot truly understand it. This is because we cannot truly understand infinity. Our intellect jams at the possibility. All we can do is nibble around the edges with analogies like comparing it to metal or jello."

She tapped the metal tray against her coffee cup. "No one can feel this jello because it is beyond feeling. The jello is feeling. Most also cannot feel the vibrations when the jello moves. But a few people can. You're one who can feel those vibrations, Robin."

Instantly, Robin became aware of a surge of warning rising in him, alerting him. "Why is that?" he asked evenly.

"I do not know." Talking Panther touched the gold ring on his hand. "Imagine that gold has more of this jello in it than most objects. This is why gold is timeless. If you drop a piece of gold in the ocean and leave it there for ten thousand years, " she explained, tapping his ring again, "that gold remains undisturbed and comes out as clean as when it went in. This is not because gold is impervious only to corrosion. Gold is also impervious to time! Gold is filled with, and amplifies, the vibrations of the sixty-fifth octave. And these vibrations are time. Because gold is rooted in the sixty-fifth octave, parts of it are timeless."

Talking Panther leaned back, looking drained. "The Golden Words are sounds which have a known impact on the sixty-fifth octave. Those instructed in the Golden Words learn how to amplify these vibrations of the sixty-fifth octave as they flow through gold. Through these vibrations, they can connect with the sixty-fifth octave. Through these vibrations they can understand the past, the present and the future, because these three dimensions are all connected. Through these vibrations they can change all things, because all things are these vibrations."

She groped for a way to clarify this concept further. She looked again to Silent Panther. "Let me give you another idea, Robin. You heard voices come from within me two nights ago. Those voices belonged to people who long ago lived together as brother and sister, before mankind spread apart."

MacAllen nodded and shivered slightly as he remembered that spiritless voice. "I wanted to ask about that," he said, trying to still the prickle that rushed along his spine. "Why did your voice change?"

A frown strayed across Talking Panther's features. "The voices will be explained later. They were not mine," she said. "For now we must discuss only the sixty-fifth octave. You must understand it."

She scratched a circle across the surface of the table. "Imagine, Robin, that this is the world. At one time, there was just one landmass on earth. Then this landmass was broken and spread apart by what scientists now call the continental drift."

Robin nodded as she continued. "That was the beginning of mankind's separation. Before the drift, life among man was total harmony. This drift destroyed the unity. And man's only real civilization ended.

"There is a very ancient account of a civilization some call Atlantis."

"The myth of the continent that sank into the sea? You're not going to try to get me to believe that one are you?"

She nodded. "Yes, I am. All the tales of our grandfathers are true—the many stories of the floods, the saviors, of the sinking continents. They are allegories, Robin. Earth's one landmass did split, became separate continents, and these continents did drift slowly apart. But it was the civilization that sank, not the continents. The spirit of man's original and only real civilization is demonstrated in the concepts of Atlantis—not just that a mass of land dropped into the sea, but that the true spirit of cooperation among man was lost."

A startled look crossed MacAllen's face. "I've never heard it explained that way, Talking Panther."

"I imagine, Robin, that it seemed very much like a continent was sinking to those who originally saw the land split, and saw parts of their homeland drift slowly into the sea. That is how these tales begin, but imagine how the history changes over the thousands of years it is told and retold, and retold again."

She leaned closer. Robin could smell the sweetness of her breath as she spoke again. "The continental drift added a new dimension to human society—the dimension of distance. But mankind's inexperience with this distance created fear. Man began to fear man. This fear bore with it the desire to control. And that desire created the Controllers."

She paused. Robin digested these notions as he lifted the cup of cold coffee to his lips Talking Panther went on. "When the first Controllers developed their skills, man was still very intuitive. Emphasis was not placed only on the sense of sight, but equal focus was put on what was felt and heard as well. Then, over the millenniums, as we learned to create symbols, our logical brain and sense of sight began to dominate the other senses. We lost touch with our heart's attunement to sound vibrations, and to our feelings. Today man needs to see in order to believe. In times long past, man believed more in what they heard and felt."

The medicine woman pricked Robin's wrist with her fingernail. A flood of warmth rushed up his spine. He leaned closer as she lowered her voice almost to a whisper. "The Controllers discovered that gold helped enhance their intuitive powers. Gold amplified the vibrations of the sixty-fifth octave and so the Controllers were able to feel anything they wanted to know. They perfected this skill to such a degree that they could sort out differences in the most minute vibrations anywhere in the world."

Again, Talking Panther poked his arm hard, and Robin started at the unexpected jab. She stopped and stared deep into his eyes. "When you move, the sixty-fifth octave vibrates differently than when I move. Every person and every thing creates a unique vibration in the waves. These are so slight most Controllers cannot feel them unless they are touching a mass of gold. Gold amplifies our vibration."

She touched his arm with tenderness and traced her finger down to his ring. "Do you know why it is a popular custom to wear gold rings?" she asked.

MacAllen was puzzled but answered, "Because gold is so malleable and wears so well. And it's also a symbol of eternity."

She shook her head. "That's what the scientists and jewelers say, but long ago the Controllers started this custom for very different reasons. If one wears gold, it amplifies the vibration and makes it easier for a Controller to follow it. They knew that whoever wore gold could be more easily followed. The gold wedding band gave men a way to follow their wives! Ancient Pharaohs, advised by wise counsels who were Controllers, honored their generals with great necklaces of gold. The generals thought gold was a reward. They did not realize that the necklace allowed the Pharaohs to track their every move. The Pharaohs then knew where their generals were, who they were with and could even tell if they were being plotting against."

Talking Panther pointed a finger at Robin as she emphasized what she meant. "At the least, most Controllers need gold to be able to follow. Many need gold to be touching the one they follow as well. You, however, do not need the gold. You feel these vibrations without gold. And now you'll learn how to be in tune with these."

She touched his arm very gently and lowered her voice. "You are special, Robin. I cannot explain how or why, but you can feel the vibrations of the sixty-fifth octave without gold. We know because you also send vibrations without any gold. This is a wonderful gift. And is sacred to our people.

"But this also allows Controllers to follow you. Your actions create a unique resonance, like shining beacons rippling through every corner of the universe. Those who know how can watch every step you take. This is why we must take such care." Talking Panther looked at her sister again. "Silent Panther is in the waves always. She feels you. When you are angry or afraid, your signals are very clear." With a smile, she added, "Your cup spilleth over, you might say."

The smile helped Robin ward off the chill that her talk of the Controllers had brought. "When you're calm, your vibrations are more quiet, almost hidden. Only the most sensitive can follow you then. But your abilities are untamed as yet."

She suddenly looked brighter. "Fortunately, we can train you to hide your vibrations in the maze. Then no one, not even the best Controllers, can follow."

MacAllen placed his hand on Talking Panther's as she continued. "But your training will take time, Robin. Until then we are in great danger! So please let us handle these vibrations. We can protect you if you remain unagitated and give us your full trust."

Robin sat still and absorbed the ramifications of her words. This makes some sense, he thought. But so do all scams. More and more of him wanted to believe this captivating woman, but he remained wary. *Everything I've ever known still points to these women being in on a con. How much can I believe? I must take care.*

Talking Panther's face melted with compassion; once again, she had understood his thoughts. She continued in a lighter tone of voice. "These are bewildering changes you face. There will be even more turmoil ahead. Our path will not be easy. Your trust and your belief, though, will help. Can we have them for just a few days more?"

Robin's face softened. "Sure, I have to give you the benefit of my doubts. We're here and what you're saying makes sense." But still his vigilance did not abate. And if you are in on the con, he thought, I want to stay close to the action. But his face was transparent and Talking Panther intuitively responded with words as soothing as she could make them. "I know what we have shared is small, like the babbling brook, and your desire is to swim far in the deep river that runs to the sea. But time is short. Give me your trust and your faith just for now. Soon, when we are alone, I will give you the Golden Words. Faith is power, Robin, the most powerful essence in the universe. If I can have your faith just for now, we will all be strong."

She brushed his hand with great gentleness. "Robin, I must give you the Golden Words in the right way. Believe in me for just a while longer." Then she looked directly into his eyes. "Besides, if I am in on a con, wouldn't the best way to get to the bottom of it be to follow me there?"

Talking Panther's eyes were like ebony stones and they seemed to be staring directly into his very essence. Her hand on his was more intimate than the touch of all the beautiful women he'd ever known.

How can Talking Panther know, he wondered. Robin tried to retreat from the gaze she had locked him in, but instead could only sit frozen, lost in her eyes. His heart beat wildly in his chest and his nerves, normally like steel, jumped like fish out of water.

MacAllen stammered. "I-I really don't have a choice. We've come this far. Where do we go next?" Yet his mind still echoed beware... Beware. BEWARE!.

She leaned back, smiled brilliantly and teased, "Robin, we may be Indians and seem to have many strange ways to you, but we are still women. Where do we always want to go?"

He looked at her blankly. "Pardon?" he asked. She smiled again. "Let's go shopping!"

He learned quickly that both Talking Panther and Silent Panther did not shop. They bought. They knew exactly what they needed, and moved quickly, buying a variety of clothes ranging from smart to rough. More than once, Robin became exasperated. What they wanted, and what he thought they needed, often differed. But he found himself giving in repeatedly to sweet but steady insistence. The sporting goods store, where they purchased binoculars, a compass and hiking boots, brought him great aggravation. They wanted fishing hooks and a sharpening stone, and were fiddling around testing for the best ones.

His patience finally gave way. "Ladies, come on—we're not going on a fishing trip! Let's stop wasting time." But the women knew what they wanted. Talking Panther's black eyes danced and she jokingly chided him, "For once let someone else do part of the work. We're in this together, Robin. Relax. Let your impatience run away like the melting snow."

To his amazement he did.

Several hours later, a rusting yellow taxi scraped the curb as it dropped them at the airport terminal. Robin's senses were immediately grabbed by the energy surrounding the place. People were heading all over the world, were excited and lively. Many adventures and memories would begin here this day. And even though MacAllen's mood also became animated, his muscles tensed automatically as he scanned the crowd seeking any dangers ahead.

While looking, Robin's mind flashed with the realization that tension, anger, fright and joy are all catching! Emotions spread out, expand and are sensed at levels beyond sight and sound. Is this the kind of connection Talking Panther was trying to explain?

Now tension mounted in MacAllen. Returning to England won't be easy, he thought. I don't know exactly what lies ahead but I do know that very probably it won't be very agreeable. Yet despite everything, Robin surprised himself by feeling lighthearted, oddly content. He realized that for the first time in days he wanted a good meal.

"Girls..." He encircled the two sisters, one in each arm, and squeezed them close. "I have a treat for you. We have time to eat, and I have a friend here who is going to cook us a meal you don't want to miss. By the way, do the Seminole eat oysters?"

CHAPTER
TWENTY TWO

James Seafood Grill and Bar was just a short walk from where they were. He knew that their meal here would be extremely satisfying, a real pleasure for all of them. At first appearance, it looked like any other airport restaurant, but Robin knew better. The difference would come in the form of the owner, Mr. Sean E. O'Flannigan. Sean was proprietor of the place, but a chef at heart. He loved to cook memorable meals for his regular, special, customers. Robin and now the two women because they were with him, were fortunate to be on Sean O'Flannigan's list.

The food at James was usually good enough, but when an order was cooked by the Irishman himself it became a feast. Sean loved to make Appalachicola oyster stew, Robin's favorite. The oysters were from the Big Bend of Florida, an area not far north of Tampa. When fresh, anyone could make these oysters taste good but few chefs could make them into a dish as impossibly fabulous as O'Flannigan's stew.

Robin directed the women through the crowd, not watching for a tracker now. Such a familiar place had to be safe. He stopped and looked into the grill, then waved as he spotted Sean. O'Flannigan shouted in a thick Irish brogue, "Robin, me lad, how are ya be doin'? Tis so nice to be seein' ya again, especially when ya be bringin' along such good lookin' lassies. And I see that ya be bringin' them by the pair as well."

He ignored Sean's blarney and his brogue. Robin knew that O'Flannigan had been raised in Portland, Oregon, a third generation Irish-American. He spoke in a flat northwestern accent and had never even been to Ireland. He had picked up the brogue as a gimmick when adding Irish stew to his menu years ago. MacAllen wasn't sure Sean knew which manner of speaking was really his any more, but whichever way, it was always fun.

He led the women to the counter. "Sean, how about the oyster stew?" O'Flannigan set down the steaming cup of inky, impenetrable coffee he had just begun to drink. Always one to show off in front of pretty women, he began telling them about his stew as if it were a love story. "Ahh, me lassies, ya are in great luck today, for your friend Robin has known to bring ya to this place."

Sean eyed the two Seminole women. Talking Panther, who had introduced herself as Tippy Peng, looked far more Asian than Native American. Her transformation was perfect. The clothes she had changed into while shopping were exactly the right accent for the illusion. She would make a good con artist. Too good, Robin thought.

Sean had immediately bought the deception. As far as he could tell, they were from the East and he talked accordingly. "Lassies, your Chinese food is indeed very good, but we Irish have learned a trick or two ourselves about how we should be cookin'. So you'll be wantin' the stew is it? Or would a good Irishman be a wee bit more to your liken?"

Talking Panther had a gleam in her eye. "Perhaps both an Irishman and his stew, if we knew more about them."

Silent Panther had not spoken at all and had shrunk into the corner. Talking Panther had a way of taking over for her sister and worked through situations like this. Talking Panther, Tippy Peng now, always seemed to be in the fore; she drew all the remarks. For some reason, O'Flannigan talked only to Tippy. He never asked Silent Panther a question. Is it body language or some indiscernible power of suggestion? Whatever it is, it works well, Robin mused. Sean doesn't even seem to see Silent Panther.

Sean gabbed happily about how he would prepare their meal. He loved to talk but was also a craftsman and he explained exactly how he would make their stew special. "First me lassies, I'll be mixen large pots of fresh steamin' oysters that have arrived this very day. Freshness is the key to good food. I'll be givin' ya only the best. I'll add the finest ingredients–sweet cream, French marsh salt, ground Florida pepper and me own secret touch. I'll thicken this mixture with pure pureed turnips rather than flour. And they'll be turnips grown organic and picked at dawn after a full moon so they'll have been properly coated with leprechaun's dew. Flour dampens the taste but the fresh vegetable base will make the flavor spring ta life. Plus, wouldn't ya be thinkin' these vegetables must be healthy too. Then I'll fill three large crockery bowls, properly warmed, until they drip over. And only then at the last minute add just a touch of sweet butter, not salted, which a course I'll have churned meself, that will melt slowly into an exquisite sauce."

Sean was waving his arms in merry enthusiasm by now, and turned to go. "I'll be bringin' ya these special morsels right away me friends, and would ya be wantin' a spot of brew with the meal? I know Robin's not much one for the drink, but I have a true, Irish stout on the menu that gives blessin' when it touches your palate. In fact your Uncle Jimmy McRay, the sheriff, ordered it and said it was the best he'd ever had. He said it reminded him o' home. By the way, did he find you? He was in here lookin' for ya not more than half an hour ago. A fine gentleman he is too, and a fine tipper at that. How is it ya never mentioned before Robin you had a proper Irish uncle in your family. Ahhhh—havin' an uncle who is Irish is such a blessing. I was surprised ya had not been lettin' me know your uncle is a lawman. Bless us Irish. We are always so good at the law."

Robin was perplexed. He had no uncle and was about to tell Sean, who was now walking towards the kitchen. But Talking Panther poked him hard in the ribs and whispered fiercely, "Be quiet, Robin. We must leave now. The man who spoke to Sean was not Jimmy McRay. He was Jimmy Ray Burnett, the sheriff of Hendry County. He's the man who's been following us since last night."

He started to protest as Talking Panther dragged him out of his seat. "What will Sean think if we're gone when he brings the food?"

"If we stay here, we might never taste good food again. Explain to your friend later. Sheriff Burnett must have help from the Controllers to have picked up our trail so soon. He'll be very dangerous. . . We have to get out of here now. I need to make some calls to get the sheriff off our track."

Talking Panther's voice softened and Robin saw a grin start across her face as they walked from the restaurant. "I think I might just find some ways to see just how smart Uncle Jimmy McRay might be!"

CHAPTER
TWENTY THREE

Talking Panther had rented a green Ford Taurus using a driver's license and credit card in the name of Tippy Peng. She really is a con artist and a damn good one too, Robin thought as he drove west, heading to the I-4.

As she was outlining how they might help each other, Talking Panther had asked Robin if he could tell her about Ian and his problems. "We can work best if we recognize each of our talents," she had said. "And let them work together. I understand my existence mostly through my heart. You understand yours through matters of the mind. If we can combine these powers of mind and heart, our knowledge will have greater equilibrium. The heart's deepest awareness of truth touches our spirit and reaches even heaven, but because we live as an outer part of this earth, we must know its outer ways too."

Robin had laughed. "You mean we have to keep our heads in the sky but make sure our feet are planted firmly on the ground?"

"Yes," she had replied. "All things stem from a thought, but that thought is only half of existence. We live on an earthly plane, and our thoughts need a physical half to be whole. Matter and action disconnected from thought are unstable, like wings that have no direction to fly. But thoughts that don't lead to a more physical creation are imbalanced as well, like a bird without wings. You understand what I have shared. This makes my heart sing," she had said.

He had nodded, reflected on where to start and was now ready to talk about Ian. Robin began slowly to make sure he had Talking Panther on the right path. "A lot of what you've told me can help me explain Ian Fletcher and the trouble he's in. I can't tell yet about his specific problems, but if we look thoroughly enough, I think we'll be able to make a good guess about what kind of mess he's in."

Robin set the Taurus' cruise control at 70mph, pausing a moment to gather his thoughts. "I think Ian has stumbled onto a scam of incredible proportions. That's how the situation looks to me. But this is supposition. We've got to look deeper to understand the roots of the problem. Then we can build a possible scenario from that."

He removed a hand from the steering wheel and waved for emphasis. "Money!" Robin exclaimed. "Money's always in the middle of a con. I think that's where we should start. The money will give us a valuable clue as to what Ian's trouble might be. I'm disturbed that none of the money seems to have been spent. This means the scam isn't typical. But I'll get back to that.

"First, let's understand the money. To spot most cons, all I have to do is follow the money. But to understand a con artist, man or woman, I have to look deeper. Sure they're after money, but that isn't always what they really want. Sometimes they want prestige, or a feeling of conquest or security. Other times, the key is lust or luxury or maybe a high-rolling spouse. Some con artists are looking for revenge or just a thrill and challenge. Money's like a scent when following game, but it's not the prey itself. It can't be because money's not real. It's only an idea, a social contract. Money's just energy stored in a thought. It's like these vibrations you keep telling me about. Money is society's way of turning thoughts into a thing or an action."

MacAllen suddenly clutched the wheel with both hands as a red Porsche Boxer driven by a young blonde switched lanes and nearly drove him off the road. The Controllers? The Porsche lurched forward and rushed away, weaving through the dense traffic ahead. Robin looked briefly at Talking Panther and went on talking. "Take that girl who just passed us. Understanding why she needs such a fast car and why she drives so aggressively would help me under-stand her needs beyond the car. If I knew what those were, I could predict her actions. In the same way, if I understand a con artist's need for money, I can understand how and why they might plan their scams. But we've got to have knowledge of money before we can look beyond it.

"What word do you think best describes money?" he asked. Then he answered without waiting for a reply. "The best word is disci-pline. Real money is just a representation of real goods and the abil-ity to produce goods and services. You've been telling me about gold and its connection to the sixty-fifth octave. Well, gold has a connec-tion to money, too. Always has, since the idea of money began. Real money has to be durable, divisible, desirable, but most of all it has to be rare. And gold is rare.

"That's why there are always problems when governments con-trol money. They're the biggest con artists of all. Governments gen-erate money when they want it, not just when real productivity has been created. This brings about all types of imbalances. The biggest problem is…"

Talking Panther abruptly cut Robin off. "Here! We need to turn. Get over, quickly." He was startled to see where they were going, but quickly changed into the exit lane. Nothing but surprises with this lot, he thought as he left the off ramp, hit the brakes hard and turned left. He drove towards their new destination, wondering why and what would happen next.

CHAPTER
TWENTY FOUR

Jimmy Ray Burnett was watching. He had seen the man and two Indian girls the minute they had disembarked from the plane. "There they are," he warned the men with him. "The bastards can't escape now."

The three had tried hard not to be found. The sheriff had trailed them from Tampa to Cleveland, then on to Cincinnati. From there Delta 1448 had flown them into New York's John F. Kennedy Airport. Now the man and two women were just in time to make British Airways' evening flight 116 to London. His supplier had traced the reservations made for Robin MacAllen. How'd he do that, Jimmy Ray wondered.

"Finally gonna get these shits," he muttered. "We got the edge," he reassured his men. "They ain't 'spectin' us here. They'll feel safe and they'll be worn out. Look, you can see they're tired." The damp, the dirt and the gloomy decor of the airport matched the rank weather outside. And all of it matched Jimmy Ray's foul mood. Burnett edged closer, motioning his men to be ready as he saw the man his supplier had said was MacAllen walk away from the two Seminoles and approach a Delta agent.

Jimmy Ray could see fatigue in the man's eyes and hear weariness in his voice as he asked a ticket agent for directions to the British Air flight. Jimmy Ray had five New York policemen to help him capture MacAllen and the two women. That he'd never met the five cops before bothered him. He toyed with the idea of sending them on a wild goose chase and then collaring the Indians and the man on his own. Better not. My supplier sent those cops. He might not like it, and anyhow, they could be a way out if anything goes wrong. I'll blame any screw-ups we have on them.

The sheriff decided to act on the spot instead. "Okay, you guys," he said quickly. "They'll be easy to take. They're beat and shouldn't resist much. Let's wrap this up fast." He started to move as he continued speaking. "Remember, we want the man alive. I don't give a shit 'bout the Indians, but if you lose the man your asses will be grass!"

"Stop! Police!" Burnett aimed his huge revolver directly at the trio. "You are all under arrest." Looking more startled than anything, all three froze as the five officers surrounded them.

A woman walking by shrieked at the sight of the huge gun and several nearby passengers flung themselves to the floor and began to crawl away. Everyone else stood paralyzed for a moment, then scattered in every direction with much yelling and crying, plunging the area into great confusion. Jimmy Ray took advantage of the panic around him, and of his captives' bewilderment. He grabbed and roughly handcuffed all three. "Now, let's get them the fuck out of here," he said quietly to the other policemen.

As he rushed the three handcuffed prisoners through the crowd, one of the New York officers loudly began reading them their rights. "You have the right to remain silent, any…"

Those goddamn idiot police thought Jimmy Ray. Watchin' too much goddamn TV. A Florida sheriff grabbin' people in a New York airport? And they just gawk. Shit… Dread stabbed him in the gut as he thought how risky this was. Damn, he thought. It's gotta work. Has to.

He shuddered again. He appreciated full well what would happen to him if he failed. That supplier has power like I never seen. More damn connections than I care to think about. How'd he know the reservations for these three to here and to London when he called me in Tampa? And a private fucking jet to get me here! This's not a guy who screws around!

Adrenaline beat through him and he pushed his three captives harder towards the security gate. This was Jimmy Ray's area of greatest concern. He mentally ran through the situation ahead. My supplier's got connections. He's got muscle too. Had these five cops waitin' when I arrived. But they can't be here officially. Might not even be New York cops. Burnett had a lifetime of experience with the law; he knew law men and he knew muscle. These guys're good. They know what to do. So they're cops. But definitely not cops on duty. Means a big risk at the security gate – those cops there are on duty. Jimmy Ray was close to panic at the thought.

"Get ready," he urged the five men, his voice shaking with an apprehension he didn't want them to hear. "This's where things could fuck up. Shoot anyone who gets in your way. Just don't lose the guy!"

Burnett's thoughts jumbled as he ran towards the security gate. How'd his supplier get cops and cop cars so fast? Hope to hell they bribed the right someone at security. His stomach grumbled and turned. Suddenly he didn't want to know anything. Jimmy Ray just wanted to deliver the man to them, get on a plane and get the hell back to Florida, to his own territory where he was boss.

Exertion, mingled with a piercing anxiety, drenched his shirt with perspiration. The security gate was straight ahead, the last damn barrier. He trembled at what could go wrong, and his stomach turned again. Mother a shit, I'm dead meat if this screws up. But the very significant risk of retribution from his supplier if he failed, and his dread of the deadly voice on the phone, drove Burnett on.

One of the five policemen rushed ahead and shouted, "Police, police! Out of the way. Careful. Got dangerous criminals here. Careful." Jimmy Ray edged his hand toward the gun at his side as the cops rushed forward and continued to shout. "Bombers! Gotta get'em outta here. They got friends in here somewhere. Gotta go on alert. Careful! Danger!"

"Hey," one of the guards at security confirmed, "I just got a call... Get those mothers outta the airport. No shooting's gonna go on here!"

Hot damn it worked! Them bribes'll work every time! Jimmy Ray smirked inwardly. Past security, he moved his three prisoners out the door and slammed them into the back of one of the waiting patrol cars, threw himself into the front seat and roared at the man who drove, "Go! Go! Go! Get the fuck outta here. Now!"

Once on the road, his fright turned to rage. He looked back and glared at the man and two Indian women sitting in the back seat of the car. "Thought you were all slippery cocks, huh?"

The three of them, were clearly terrified and it fueled a hard, cruel surge of loathing in Jimmy Ray. "Ya fuckin' Indians and Indian lovers are all jest the same. Think yer so friggin' smart. Yer not. Just goddamn trouble! Well, look at who's smart now."

Their horror and his absolute power over their destiny rose to sweep away his own previous fear. He was back in control. "Nothin's gonna go wrong now," he muttered absentmindedly as he rubbed sweat from the back of his neck. He was bringing them in.

He turned and looked again at the trio. "Plenty's gonna go wrong for you though." Burnett looked more closely at the two women. He undressed them with his eyes and whispered to the one nearest him, "Pretty. Nice tits. Nice legs, too."

The woman had banged her head when the sheriff pushed her into the car. A thin trickle of blood ran from her lip, down her chin and onto her dress. She was slumped deeply into the car seat, hand-cuffed from behind, her dress bunched up to her waist.

Burnett spoke harshly. "Good lookin' for an Indian though. Umm-hum. Got a name, sweetie pie?" She stared up at him but didn't say a word.

Instead, the man replied. He was clearly intimidated, his voice nervous and too loud. "Officer, you've made a mistake here, a horrible mistake. I don't know who you're looking for but it's not us; we haven't done anything wrong. You have the wrong people. It's not us. You can't do this. You're violating our rights doing this."

Jimmy Ray's emotions, now well risen, surged beyond fury. He reached back and maliciously slapped MacAllen, the full force catching him squarely on the side of the face. He jerked from the shock of the unexpected attack. And then Jimmy Ray struck again, and the man's head snapped and smashed against the window of the car from the brutal vehemence of the blow.

"Shut the fuck up, MacAllen," roared the sheriff. "Shut up you mealy mouthed mother fucking asshole. If ya speak again until ya been spokin' to, I'll rip yer goddamn tongue outta yer goddamn mouth. You hear me, boy? The man's eyes glazed. He was too stunned for more words.

Jimmy Ray snorted a tiny mean laugh, turned back again and placed his rough hand just above the knee of the Seminole woman, feeling its smoothness. He reached further up her leg. "I asked ya kinda nice, honey, what's your name?" He moved his hand higher and still the woman remained motionless and silent. He reached higher now, feeling her thigh.

Heat rose in his groin and Burnett stiffened. "You a sly one, babe doll? Well, let me show ya somethin'." The sheriff smacked her viciously on her cheek and then dug his fingers deep into the flesh of her thigh and twisted hard. Jimmy Ray sneered at her widened eyes and her gasp at the unanticipated, startling pain.

The woman tried to shift away, but there was nowhere to go. Again, Burnett thrust his fingers powerfully into the flesh on her thigh and growled at her; his voice was gravely and filled with malice. "Let me tell you somethin', honey doll. I ain't never screwed no Indian girl before. But I might soon. Don't know what my man wants, but I think he just wants him and I 'spect he'll just blow you girls away like the worthless trash you are. Get the idea? But if yer really nice to old Jimmy Ray, I might just let your red hide go. Might, might not, but either way, I bet I get to have ya anyways. And when I do, I can do it nice or I can do it not nice. You hear me?" He squeezed hard, savagely sinking his fingers deeper into the girl's skin.

She shrank back, her eyes large, but still the woman didn't say a word. Jimmy Ray laughed unpleasantly and let go, turned and sank back into his seat. "Have it your way, honey. But I'm telling ya, I'm gonna have me some fun."

The scenery flashed by. They had left the heavy traffic behind and were heading through an area that was treed, but gray and depressing in the rain. He spoke loudly, not looking back. "You three have well and truly fucked my day. Now I am gonna fuck yours."

He turned to the driver. "We got much further to go?" The driver, who had remained impassive, shrugged "Five minutes." Jimmy Ray turned again and smiled. "Five minutes, honey. That's all the time you got left. Yeah, just a few minutes more, honey, and we're gonna have some fun."

The car turned off the main road onto the grounds of a large estate. A huge Tudor house set back from the road and surrounded by trees stood, silhouetted in the dark. Forbidding metal security gates swung back in a jerky motion, allowing the car through. The house loomed ahead. As they approached, a garage door yawned opened. The car pulled in and rolled to a stop.

Jimmy Ray roughly pulled the three out of the cruiser, slammed MacAllen against the car, and waited. Two burly men, both in suits, arrived. The larger of them stepped forward and motioned Jimmy Ray to follow, leading them down a flight of stairs along the inside of the garage. Jimmy Ray smelled the damp concrete and felt a chill from the stairwell as they stepped down into a barely lit basement.

"Where we goin'?" Jimmy Ray asked. The thickset man did not reply. Jimmy Ray's knees suddenly felt more like soft rubber than cartilage. The hair rose on the nape of his neck and a spooky sense of misgiving and apprehension crawled up his spine. Burnett's cutting uncertainty threatened to overwhelm him. He had once again lost control and did not like the feeling one bit.

The sheriff held back slightly, keeping the three captives in front of him as if for protection. He touched the gun still on his hip, for reassurance, and tried to peer into the almost black room before entering.

"Come in, Sheriff Burnett. You have done well." Jimmy Ray had just heard the same heartless, deadly, metallic voice that had spoken to him on the phone many times. Sweat popped on his brow despite the cold dankness of the basement. He did not feel good about this at all.

"Come along, Sheriff." The voice was louder now. "You have nothing to fear; you have helped us. We're very generous with our friends, Jimmy Ray."

The officer who had driven the car stepped over and spoke inaudibly to the man sitting in the gloom. Jimmy Ray watched intently, walked slowly in, making sure his hand was close to his gun. His eyes strained to see in the weak light, but the man sitting in the shadows was only a blur.

"Really, Sheriff. You will be well rewarded. Our mutual friends who work with you in Florida will be sending you an extra shipment of goods this month. The street value will be about the same as usual. As a token of our appreciation for your help there will be no charge."

At this, relief immediately began to spread from far within Jimmy Ray's ample belly. He stammered, "Thanks... uh thanks a lot, Mr. Uhh..."

"Names are not important, Sheriff. But our gratitude is," the man replied quickly.

Jimmy Ray relaxed as he heard the man's mellow tone of voice. He stepped into the middle of the room and replied, "Goddamn, that's a big load of stuff. I really do appreciate that, sir."

Holy shit, he thought. Those shipments are worth a million bucks. These dummies are givin' it away.

"We are very friendly when we are pleased, Sheriff. We are equally hard with those who fail us." Burnett could just barely make out the figure shifting slightly in the shadows. He tried to see more through the dark, but still could only see a dim outline.

The voice continued. "I understand you like these young women, Sheriff." Word sure travels fast, Jimmy Ray thought. What do I say? He decided that in these unusual circumstances honesty might be the best way to proceed. "They're Indians, sir. Can't like 'em too much, but one of 'em might be some quick fun."

Burnett noticed that the three captives were now talking quietly among themselves. "Yeah, I wouldn't mind taking the slim one off your hands for a bit."

The opaque figure leaned back. Jimmy Ray realized now that he was not meant to see the man, or to hear his real voice. Careful sons of bitches, he thought. He did not like this situation much, but inwardly had easily warmed to the million bucks. And having the Indian.

The voice spoke again. "Sheriff, I think you can have your choice of women, or take them both if you'd like. Use them as you please. But first there is one more job we have to ask of you."

Instantly, Jimmy Ray was on guard. What the hell they want now? "Sure, anything," he said. "What can I do?"

The voice in the shadows was even more ominous sounding now. "We have a few questions to ask of Mr. MacAllen. If he does not care to answer, we would like you to very slowly kill one of the girls."

"Yes sir, I can do that. Sure 'nuff." Jimmy Ray grinned, grabbed the heavier of the two women, and dragged her into the center of the room where he threw her fiercely to the ground. "Never kilt me an Indian girl before."

The voice directed itself to the handcuffed man. "Of course, Mr. MacAllen, you can save this young woman's life by merely telling us where the rest of the book is. If you do, I promise that both women will live. They may spend a few unpleasant moments with the sheriff, but I promise you they'll live. This is a simple request. All three of you will be allowed to go on your way, just as soon as..."

Jimmy Ray had just flung MacAllen onto the floor at the center of the room and was reaching over to grab one of the Indians when the voice stopped abruptly.

A moment later, the voice whispered as flat as death, "This is not MacAllen. You have brought us the wrong man!" Terror raced through Jimmy Ray. His stomach turned over as he heard the words.

The sheriff's bowels shuddered, then let loose and Jimmy Ray knew utter and unbridled terror for the first time in his life. "Cain't be, n-no it cain't. I... I g-gottem just like you said." He looked at the man lying handcuffed on the floor. "They cain't have screwed us again."

Burnett's horror converted to blind frenzy as he glared at the man. Then he heard sirens screaming in the distance. He looked into the shadows as he spoke. "MacAllen screwed us both but I'll get him sir. I will bring him to you even if it is the last thing I ever do!"

"Yes, Sheriff. You do that. "And Sheriff. If you don't get MacAllen, it will indeed be the last thing you ever do. Now get out of here. Dump these three on the roadside. Do not harm them. They're probably some kind of police and we do not want that type of trouble. Don't worry about them. You'll be safe as long as you are under our protection. But if you lose our favor, Mr. Burnett, there's nothing they can do to you anyway. Dead is dead, Sheriff. "Now go!"

CHAPTER
TWENTY FIVE

MacAllen lay back, enjoyed the smell of the fresh cut grass and relaxed in the warmth of the sun. They were alone in a roadside parkway just off I-75, not far from Fort Myers. Cars rushed by in the distance, but the rarely used rest area was isolated, a tiny strip of asphalt running through a lush patch of grass. A few paint-flaked picnic tables stood almost hidden among stands of melaleuca, pepper bush and palmetto.

Talking Panther sat nearby, her eyes closed, seemingly far away. She was preparing herself for the sacred task of sharing another Golden Word with Robin.

He looked at the intensely azure sky again. Robin's mind, eased now by his rest in this wonderfully balmy day, wandered over the events of their hectic trip. Was it really just this morning that we started? After leaving Tampa they had headed towards Orlando, but had turned off I-4 near Kissimmee and had driven to the enormous, bizarrely decorated building where Disney World hired its employees, and where some of them worked.

A friend of Talking Panther's was a makeup artist. She had transformed the three of them into entirely different people, complete with new identities and passports. Con artist, he thought. She could run a school for them!

They had dropped off the green Taurus rental at Orlando Airport and then hailed a cab and had driven into downtown Orlando. They had left the cab and walked ten blocks to a small car rental company where Talking Panther, now a Chilean named Elvita Ortega, rented a blue Chevrolet Caprice. They had then doubled back, driving south on I-75. Right now, they were only 50 miles from Immokalee.

He recalled Talking Panther's explanation. "The Controllers knew where we were almost as soon as we reached Tampa. They have been able to follow you too well. Silent Panther has now moved very far within and is masking your thoughts. We've had to have a total change of plans. We're going to Miami International Airport. I don't think they will be able to find us."

Talking Panther had been reassuring. "We can see many distinct signals in the way the Controllers look for you. They are using conventional methods, like talking to that restaurant owner. This means they are able to discern only glimpses of your vibrations. This is good for us. Had they known for sure where you were, they would have ambushed us at the airport."

She had waited several seconds then, to allow the gravity of her words to sink in. "Your vibrations fluctuate often, Robin, and grow too loud, but now we are prepared. They will not find us easily."

She looked at him. "You are frustrating them. They are like children listening to a radio station fading in and out during a solar storm. Your signal continually breaks up. They keep fine-tuning their dial but they can never quite get a lock on you or clearly receive your thoughts."

They're amazing, MacAllen thought. Or are they just clever? This could all be manufactured. That makes a lot more sense than what they're telling me.

Their plan had seemed almost too complex for him to believe. Friends–three special agents in a secret investigative branch of the Bureau of Indian Affairs–had flown on their tickets to New York, posing as him and the two women.

Robin had been half convinced by Talking Panther's simple explanation. "The forces of nature teach us many ways. We learn much from our brothers in the wild." A gleam had appeared in her eyes as she spoke of the plan. "From the wild turkey we have learned to watch after one another."

He had laughed aloud at this. "Turkeys? What do turkeys have to do with sending federal undercover agents on our flight pretending to be us?"

He remembered how a fleeting sunbeam had caught her hair and how very beautiful she had been as she softly spoke. "The spirit of the wild turkey is caution, deception, and the ability to avoid trouble. If you stumble upon their flock, an old hen always flies suddenly into the open. As you watch, the flock runs quietly in the opposite direction. One sacrifices itself for the sake of the entire flock.

Thinking back to many of his turkey hunts this did indeed appear to be true. He had warmed to the pure simplicity of it. And then had laughed aloud at the thought of his pursuers eagerly chasing a trio of decoys through the streets of New York.

Robin decided to take no chances. This has to be a scam; there has to be illusion here. This happens all through vibrations? I don't think so. But I do think that I have to go along with Talking Panther and her sister. Friends or not, they're still my only lead to Ian.

They had driven hard for nearly two hours and had just made a feast of dried mango and papaya. At this deserted rest area he waited, lying in the grass, warmed by the sun, relaxed. He was feeling very peaceful inside and started when Talking Panther unexpectedly began to speak, her voice composed, delicate. "The second Golden Word is *Silence*." She was so beautiful, sitting there perfectly still, her eyes closed. She seemed lost inside of herself, and completely serene at the same time.

Her words flowed like a melody. "In the beginning of civilization, silence was the most favored sound because silence is the sound of the present. One cannot be truly alive when involved in the making of sound. Silence is here. Silence is now."

Her skin radiated a warm inner glow. "Words are bows bending into the past to shoot arrows into the future. Words that slip like the arrow through the air are the weapons of man, but they are only potential. Words can never truly strike their target for their striking changes the very target at which they are aimed. With words, we can anticipate the moons that will be full and count the suns that will rise. We can know the minutes of love and the seconds that count our lives. With words we can lament sorrows, hearts broken, arrows that went astray and paths that were steep."

Robin closed his eyes, listening to the velvet cadence of her voice. "But words carry a great price. They can be used only at the forfeit of truth. Our sounds and sights can only reflect distortions of that which is real. Words can never be real and the very use of them destroys the things they describe."

Talking Panther's speech was unhurried, her voice hushed. "We are blinded by illusions of our words and these illusions can replace us. We can become nothing but words, nothing but futures and pasts, nothing but hopes and regrets, nothing but illusions. When the words take us, we cease to be."

Then she became silent. The sun emerged from behind a passing cloud and the drone of katydids rose with the warming air.

Robin's eyes were heavy as she continued her litany. "With words we can scatter like the winds to four corners of the earth. Words have no bounds, and like the wind can drift with the currents. But we can never be an ocean with words. Words can sigh through the treetops but words cannot be the trees. We can race through the peaks and soar into the clouds with words but we can never be the mountain tops or the valleys that lie below."

He heard a car approach, looked up and watched a park security guard drive slowly by. Trouble? He grew alert, but the car passed by without stopping. MacAllen looked back at Talking Panther. She showed no signs of fear and sat tranquilly, unmoving, unbelievably lovely. He relaxed again and waited silently for her to continue.

"There is great wisdom in those who are mute and those who labor only for the reward of the day. To take thought of the morrow, we must walk from the garden where all is harmony and at peace. When out of this garden, words remind us of hunger when even our stomachs are full. Our thoughts, clouded with the hopes for the day, cease to know the dawn. Our hearts cannot be in the sunset if our mind plays with words that hold regrets from the day.

Gary A. Scott

"When our thoughts are only words, they become like ghosts that are only pale casts of worry. These ghosts of the past and spirits of the future are mists casting darkness where light should be. Words absorb our true meaning. They magnify our illusions. They sharpen greed. Possession seems real. The solace of nature and the now are lost."

Talking Panther stopped speaking again. Peacefulness and harmony flowed through Robin. His mind suddenly stilled. The Seminole's simple words were more than just words. The intensity of her delivery transcended his logic and impressed upon his feelings. He felt Talking Panther's emotions, was touched by them, even though he didn't understand the meaning of all she had said.

She opened her eyes. "Silence is the second Golden Word. Truth is the quality you can gain from this word. Now you know."

Robin waited. He had been enormously moved but didn't really understand why. At least his feelings had brightened, though. Not resisting, he closed his mind and let it drift into nothingness.

"Robin, we must go." Talking Panther touched his arm gently and he opened his eyes. "You have been using the word already. You have been in a profound silence," she said. "When you are with the Golden Words, time stops." She rose as she spoke.

"How many minutes did I sleep?" he asked, his mind still not fully awake.

"About twenty," she replied. "But you were not asleep. You were in the silence, and in those minutes many lifetimes passed. I will explain later. Now we must go or we'll miss our flight. Airlines do not realize the illusions of time. Though our spirits can climb with the clouds, our bodies cannot. They have to adapt to the same illusions as those who fly the planes. To be all in the silence is as bad as being all in the world. In either case, you can't fly."

"Talking Panther," he said. "Thank you. I feel now that I have the answer to a question that has plagued me for years–why so many good business people and investors fail. Why informed, totally up-to-date-people make bad investment after bad investment.

"Maybe it's because they never have any silence. They fill their minds with clutter, with so much noise they can't make any sense.

They are so busy studying facts, figures, hype and statistics that they never take time to see truth, to use their common sense. Being busy all the time actually becomes a form of laziness. They fill their minds with day-to-day, useless financial information so they never have to face real cold, hard economic truths. Being a good investor requires investing in what you know. And what you know has to be truth, truth that comes only from contemplation and silence. Now all of their failures finally have some meaning for me."

Robin brightened even more as he added a final thought. "Money in the bank is like words. It only reflects reality but never brings it. People feel rich when they have a lot of money, but in reality, they aren't. Most money, especially today, can disappear in a myriad of ways—bank failures, inflation, currency devaluation. Any of these can wipe out money in the bank overnight. Money also promises happiness, but never really brings it. It can bring sorrow more often than not. Money—like words—is just an illusion, not real wealth."

Talking Panther grabbed his arm and pulled him towards the car. "Don't think too much on this now. Just let the word settle in. There is a time to think, and also a time to be silent, and a time for action. I'll explain more when it's time to think. But now it's time to act."

"Okay, but I have something important to say, before we go," Robin said. "We shouldn't fly directly to England. If the Controllers can get help from local law authorities here, they might also have insiders at British Immigration. I know a back door into England. It's a small island in the Irish Sea–the Isle of Man. Flights from Dublin to the island are domestic. But so are flights from the Isle of Man to England. We can clear Irish Immigration and then get into England without any further checks."

Years ago, he had learned the trick from a London con artist who had been cheating on British tax for years. Her Majesty's government had relentlessly looked for the guy, yet he seemed to move freely in and out of the country whenever he wished. Robin had followed him and found this crack in Britain's immigration armor to help capture the man.

He raised his knee and laughed. "You women might have intuition, but maybe you need my experience in these things."

"I know we do," she replied. "That's why we've already booked our flights to the Isle of Man." Talking Panther and Silent Panther were already in the car and Robin forced himself to push down his bewilderment as he climbed in. How'd they know?

He worked his way into traffic and put the car on cruise control. Then, as he often did on journeys, he let his mind sort out the events that lay ahead. "I wonder where we'll be this time tomorrow?"

The sisters did not reply. The new Golden Word came to him again. Silence. He realized that tomorrow didn't matter. All that mattered was right now. Silence. Silence brings truth. He liked that concept. Truth. All he ever wanted.

Robin drove faster. He was smiling, but without thought. There was just silence and in this silence he felt strangely content.

CHAPTER
TWENTY SIX

The plane levelled and Robin tried to recline his seat as he looked out the window into the deep blackness of the night. The seat refused to budge. An uncomfortable feeling surfaced as he thought about this plane. They were on Aeroflot Flight 326, Miami to Shannon, and he wondered about the quality of this Russian-built aircraft. If the seat doesn't even work, what about the engines?

He watched Miami's skyline fade into distant dots of lights twinkling on the horizon. I'm at the mercy of Russian technology and workmanship for 5,000 miles, he thought uncomfortably. But why am I afraid of the Russians? Because they lack familiarity? God! My whole life...so much uncertainty...and I've never really known.

His uneasiness continued. Robin made a mental checklist of the benefits he'd gained by taking this flight. First, he thought, Aeroflot is an airline I've never used or even considered using. This'll make following me a little harder. My past efforts to stop being tailed sure haven't accomplished much. He grimaced at the thought.

Second, this Aeroflot flight to Moscow began in Santiago, Chile. Talking Panther had planned this all along. Talk about cons! Our phony Chilean ID's, my dark complexion, makeup and black hair fit in perfectly with the other passengers. We look like any other Chileans headed for Russia. And we bought tickets all the way to Moscow, even though we'll get off early in Ireland.

Third, boarding the flight separately broke our trio profile. We took different taxis to the airport and I hung around a coffee shop while the two sisters stayed in the first class lounge until the plane was ready to roll from its gate an hour ago, at 8:25 p.m.

Fourth, departure was an hour later than the Delta flight I'd normally take. It gave us extra time to shop and replace the items we left in Tampa. He suddenly grinned to himself. Surprised I survived shopping again, but watching them try to find fish hooks in downtown Miami was almost fun. This flight's nearly empty... a big plus, he reminded himself as he slung his feet onto the two seats beside him, lay back and smiled again. Leg room. An unexpected bonus!

The empty plane gave him what he needed most, time and space to lie back, wrapped in the darkness, and sleep. He listened to the repetitive sounds of the machinery. Clicks, whines and the grumbling rhythm of the jets surrounded him. A particularly noisy plane, this Ilyushin. The noises were soothing, comforting. He drifted... and then slept.

But drifting in sleep did not bring Robin serenity. His mind was restless and troubled, and he tossed in his seat. After some time, he surfaced from sleep with his mind spinning.

The Seminole women were sitting in first class. Silent Panther looked like the elegant Chilean wife of some jet-setting businessman. Talking Panther looked about eighty years old, and could have been Silent Panther's doting grandmother. Isolated from their influence, Robin's mind wrestled with all his old doubts again.

How can Talking Panther change her looks? Why does she have so many tools of the scam trade, the false ID's... changing appearances on the spot... phony names, makeup... so many sets of clothes? She's too good. He rolled over and tried to reassure himself by remembering why he had allowed them to come and everything he'd done. They're my only lead to Ian and the Controllers...

The thought of the Controllers brought with it a twinge of fear. Everywhere I've been, someone has always been waiting, watching. Could they be here... on the flight? I've been in tighter spots. I'll never run. Maybe I can stop them or maybe I can't, but I won't make it easy for them. I'll screw up their lives every way I can. Shake them up. Show up where I'm not expected. Worry them. I'll watch and try to survive. But who? Talking Panther, Silent Panther, someone else? Who should I watch?

Robin pushed these negative thoughts down and began his mantra. "Breathing in, I calm my whole body." Still Robin's mind refused to settle down. His concerns returned. He tried to think his potential problems through. The women's real intentions defied his logic. His heart told him the women would help, yet he still worried. Then, a disturbing realization hit him. I'm feeling much more than friendship for Talking Panther. It's more than respect. Love? Lust? I've been infatuated before. Can't this time. There's too much at stake. It's too dangerous, and it'll cloud my thinking. Have to put Ian first. I'll deal with feelings later. She looks so much like Melanie… He shifted his thinking as fast as he could, away from his past, and his pain, away from Melanie.

Robin slipped deep into a semi-dream state. Everything became clear. The Seminole had engineered these unbelievable events. Ian Fletcher was their friend and they had hatched this elaborate scheme together. Ian, Billy, Silent Panther and Talking Panther rose from a misty field, tomahawks in hand. They smiled in evil unison and crept a deadly cadence, closer and closer. Robin cringed. Their tomahawks became oily snakes spewing out foul odors, smoke, fire. His throat tightened and he choked.

There was no other answer. Only these circumstances fit! His heart resisted this truth. Turbulence tossed him against the seat's hard edge and Robin moaned softly. Now, he watched his heart and mind jump into a canvas ring and wrestle, his logical mind screaming, "It's a con! It's a con!" His heart spilled blood, but fought back, trying to understand. There's more here than you can see. "Hold on, just hold on," it cried. He tried to wake up.

Something was reaching for him and he had to move, had to escape. But something else held him solidly, his limbs were paralyzed and useless, trapped. He tried crying out but the sounds froze in his throat. The something approached, it was coming closer, nearer and nearer.

Robin started to jump as terror seized him, but he was immediately soothed instead. A tender voice filled him and allayed his panic. "Calm yourself, Robin." It was Talking Panther. "You are leaking badly into the vibrations again. Silent Panther and I have been sensing you strongly for at least twenty minutes. We do not want the Controllers to know more than they already do."

Talking Panther's gentle touch and soft whispers woke Robin. "We are not the ones. You know this in your heart already. Let your fright go. Feel your inner forces. Understand what you already know. These new realizations are to be embraced, not feared. Hold them in awe. Such growth is a sacred path. They are your awakening. Your past is over, but you cannot ascend to your higher existence until you release these fears. Now I wish to give you other Golden Words. Be silent and listen to these truths."

Calmed, MacAllen slipped into semi-sleep listening to Talking Panther's voice. He floated, embraced by the night's cocoon. Was it really Talking Panther's voice? *She's not here, yet I sense that she is.*

Her words began to float through the haze of his sleep. "The third Golden Word is *Goose*. This spirit is of the snow goose who flies day or night to lands that are far and unknown. His spirit is guided by the polestar that aims him, like nature's perfect arrow, to a place where abundance, peace, happiness and fulfillment will always be. The third word is Goose."

Talking Panther paused a moment. "The fourth Golden Word is *Cat*. This fourth spirit is of the cat whose inner light gives it the night. With this innermost reflection, all that is hidden and subtle to our eyes of the day becomes known through the spirit of the cat. The fourth word is Cat."

Goose... Cat, Robin's thoughts drifted. *I travel. I search without, but I have not looked within. My outer wandering is just a reflection of this thirst to delve within. Look. Listen, here, inside. The girls... Ian... Melanie. I know! I really do know.*

Hours passed but Robin did not notice them. He was suspended within the immeasurable cradle of timelessness and sleep. He woke with a start. He was alone and the noises he heard told him the crew was preparing to land. Did I dream her voice last night? The Golden Words? Was her touch just part of a dream?

He pushed his thoughts inside, felt for the dream, but could not find the door to its memory. There's a truth here but I can't reach it. I only have vague feelings, no words, no logic at all.

Robin sat up feeling stiff, and he tightened his seat belt for landing. The plane shuddered and began a shallow descent. He looked out and saw a thin salmon patina glowing faintly at the edge of the sea. He watched it burst against the eastern horizon, casting vibrant glorious colors across the blue morning sky. He watched in awe, trying to identify them separately, orange, pink, red. Words failed him. He tried sunrise, but it was wrong. Dawn, daybreak, morning, sunup, beginning. None of these were right. He saw, and understood what he saw, but couldn't describe it.

Then, in an instant, Robin knew. Words are illusions. I'm using words and they aren't real. I've used words to create my fears. I've wandered all over the world looking for something that's always been right here within me. I've been looking for answers so I can find Ian, but I already have them. She did send me more Golden Words.

My thoughts really are illusions! But if I can't trust my own thoughts, what can I trust? His mind began to jam; his thoughts scrambled as his confusion grew.

Robin shook his head and rubbed his brow to help clear his mind. I have to stop this. He began his mantra. "Breathing in..." His mantra changed to the Golden Words – Buffalo... Silence... Goose... Cat. Again and again the words flowed and his thoughts drifted gently between them.

Return to the basics, MacAllen. The plane is about to land. When it does, whatever my dreams have been, whatever the truth is, when I step off this plane my life will never be the same.

The Golden Words returned. Buffalo... Silence... Goose... Cat. I'm here, his thoughts wandered. I might not be ready, but I'm here to help Ian. I can't think what to do. I don't need to. My inner intelligence already knows what needs to happen next!

Buffalo... Silence... Goose... Cat.

CHAPTER
TWENTY SEVEN

Robin walked far behind Talking Panther and Silent Panther, off the plane and into Ireland. The brisk Irish air immediately felt damp and not welcoming. Below dull high clouds, the morning was as barren of color as the sunrise was from the plane. A raw southwest wind rushed off the Atlantic, and the slate sky indicated that this day would probably not improve.

At least it probably won't rain. This cheered Robin some as he thought of the long drive to Dublin that loomed ahead. He looked around and wondered how this airport could even exist, an international airport operating hundreds of miles from the capital! What a dinosaur.

Robin collected his car rental papers and walked slowly toward the coffee shop, lost in thought. Shannon had made sense twenty years ago when it was Europe's first landfall. Then, it had given airplanes a much needed refueling station. But now, planes flew easily from the U.S. to Europe, except for a few inefficient planes, like that Ilyushin he'd been on. Perhaps this airport is like the struggle in my mind, trying to keep going but totally out-of-date?

He considered this idea. Are my doubts about vibrations and Controllers as obsolete as Shannon is? Am I automatically suspicious of them because I can't see or touch or hear them? Maybe my perceptions are dated by forty years. The theory of relativity says we can't believe anything we see.

We are in a new millennium. How many institutions still use fifties thinking? Is the fabric of mankind so outmoded it's worse than useless, just because it's always been that way? Perhaps the whole world's minds, including my own, just run on inertia? MacAllen remembered Talking Panther's warning about creating waves and he tried to stop thinking.

Damned if I can believe it, but for now I'd better. There's so much I simply don't understand. Trying to clear my mind only seems to make it worse. Okay, now I'm thinking about not thinking. I have to quit thinking about this.

Think about coffee instead! He had slept through breakfast on the flight and though the bracing morning air had jolted his body awake, his brain remained foggy. Coffee will help, he thought. And I could use some food too.

Robin knew Shannon Airport well and liked its modern continental feel of polished stone, smoked glass and chrome. But walking into the coffee shop he wondered why this part of the airport was always so dirty and drab. He filled his tray, paid an exorbitant amount to a dour young girl and went to sit in a forlorn corner trying to extract some enjoyment from the bitter coffee and dry stale rolls.

He saw Talking Panther and Silent Panther enter shortly after he sat down. His mind began to roam. Do so many airport coffee shops have such bad food because it's too small a problem for anyone to bother with? He wondered if this might also be true of his thoughts. Maybe my thinking is so hard to change because it's just too much of a bother to do it. Again, Robin caught his thoughts drifting and he tried to focus on silence, half-fearing that his every thought was now being transmitted somewhere in the vibrations, putting the three of them at risk.

"This is ridiculous," he growled beneath his breath. "Just drink your coffee." He was so caught up in his musing, he barely heard the announcement over the loudspeaker. "Attention. Attention. There has been a bomb threat to the airport. Please walk calmly and quietly from the building. Please leave the building immediately." As the tinny, impassive voice began to repeat this, Robin's mind received the alert, but his body did not act on it. The message sank in, yet he continued to eat, bolting down his coffee and roll. He was hurrying to finish his meal when there was a sudden jerk on his arm.

Talking Panther had grabbed him by the sleeve. "Come on, let's get out of here," she whispered. She pulled him from his chair with surprising strength and half dragged him across the restaurant. Even then he continued to devour his roll. Talking Panther spoke quietly but with great force. "Robin, forget breakfast! We must leave."

His deeply ingrained habits controlled him even during this bomb threat. Old words and ideas are just habits, his mind flashed; maybe that's why we stick so stubbornly to them. Maybe the whole darn planet runs on habit!

Talking Panther pulled him towards the exit. "Robin, this isn't the time to stand around thinking! We have to get out of here!"

The crowd's exodus out of the terminal was casual. After many alarms, few regulars believed the threat was real.

The parking lot filled with people. MacAllen and the women huddled among the group as they assessed their situation. "Think the bomb might have anything to do with us?" Robin asked. Talking Panther closed her eyes and paused. "No," she replied quietly. "There is no bomb. But there is no such thing as coincidence either. We cannot feel any Controller's presence, but everything in life is connected. This may just be a warning from the forces of nature. Or it may have been caused by the Controllers to create turmoil. Maybe it's something entirely different. We cannot tell but it does not matter. Our destiny is sealed. We must go on regardless of events here. This only warns us to take extra care."

Robin made an instant decision, "Okay, then let's get out of here," he said, taking control. "You both wait here and get the bags if you can. If not, we'll leave them. I'll get the car. Be ready to jump in when I drive by. We won't be hanging around."

He pushed ahead of the crowd and hurried towards the car rental lot far from the terminal. Walking vigorously in the sharp air helped his mind clear. We have to get out of here. Something's wrong; I feel it. He broke into a steady trot, repeatedly looking back to check on the two Seminole.

The terminal was now a fair distance away but Robin could see the people milling about. Soldiers and policemen were everywhere, roping buildings, bringing in dogs, restoring order and directing traffic. He was so absorbed in the scene he ignored the fact that he was now entirely alone. This, and his worry for the women, prevented him from spotting the two men until it was too late... far, far, too late.

The men closed in fast. Only when MacAllen saw them did he realize how isolated he was. They know exactly what they're doing, he thought. They were too close for him to escape. He was boxed in.

He watched the man on the left, who despite a considerable bulk moved easily toward him. He was massive and he looked extremely confident, strong. His size won't slow him, Robin surmised. The small guy looks like a rat; he's compact, well put together. He'll move fast. He won't let me escape either.

Robin slowed as he assessed the two further. I don't believe they'll make any stupid mistakes like the green-haired gang in London did, he thought. Are they official or just hired muscle? Can't tell, but I see in their eyes they mean business!

He considered his options. I don't have much time. Yelling won't help... too far to the terminal. Too much distraction with the bomb alert. The alert was planned!

He tried shifting to the left, past the huge man, but both shifted with him, boxing him tighter into their net.

In his mind Robin measured the distance to the car lot. They've maneuvered it so that I can't reach it. Too far... too far to the exit. He quickly reassessed his position. They're calculating whether I'll run or fight. Probably know my next move better than I do. They've got to be pros.

Ice ran through his veins. And a bolt of fear forced its way from his stomach. At least they think they know what I'll do, he thought, as he abruptly stopped. He had felt frightened before; it strengthened him, gave him the power he needed to act. His adrenaline surged.

Robin stood totally still and recalled one of his discussions with Talking Panther. "The unexpected always wins the war," she had said. And this, Robin thought, is not what they'll expect.

He relaxed despite the terror that rose in his gut and worked its way up to his throat. He forced down the urge to vomit. "Breathing in, I calm my whole body..." he repeated, over and over. The two men slowed and looked at one another, but continued their advance. Robin began to shiver, from panic or perhaps from rage. He didn't know which.

Can I pull this off? He remained motionless. Out of the blue, a Golden Word flashed through his mind. Silence. Silence is the power behind all. Silence... silence.

Confused, both Robin's pursuers stopped. They had seemed ready for trouble, either his fleeing or his fighting, but now they looked puzzled, not knowing what to do.

An urge to run overwhelmed Robin, but he compelled himself to stand where he was. Silence. He watched, and to keep his mind absorbed gave names to these aggressors. "Little" and "Large", he thought, just like that team of British comedians. The notion brought a short burst of laughter with it. He saw perplexity deepen in their eyes. Large, looking bewildered, glanced at Little. First break. Go for Little first. He's the boss. Little's face also showed uncertainty but mixed with a trace of cunning as well.

Just like a rat, Robin thought. He may not like what he's seeing but he won't stop.

And Little did not pause. He motioned Large and they both began to close in on him. Robin's heart raced. He fought back the urge to clench his fists and move. Silence. Sweat trickled down his spine. He shuddered as they came nearer. Silence... silence. They walked to within ten yards of Robin and then raced forward.

He still did not move as they grabbed him, one on each arm. They were strong, their grips like steel. His heart pounded but still he stood impassively as they began to drag him down. Perfect. Now! Robin went totally limp.

He pictured himself dead and dropped heavily, like a stone. His two assailants almost lost their grip but managed to tighten their holds. This, and Robin's sudden drop, drove the razor-sharp Eagle Claw No. 2 treble prong fish hooks savagely into their hands.

Eagle Claw hooks can be dangerous. Even the most careful fisherman eventually cuts himself on one. When sharpened further with a diamond hone, they are lethal. They slashed immediately through their protective corks. Neither Little's nor Large's hands offered any resistance to the hooks Silent Panther had sewn into the arms of Robin's jacket.

Both men looked stunned as the vicious hooks penetrated to the bone. Both men jerked back, away from the unexpected shock. This move set the hooks deeper still. Their steel construction was more than a match for both men. They collided with each other as they were yanked back into Robin's jacket, which he had abandoned. He dashed towards the car.

He looked back. The faces of both his attackers betrayed shock, but now each had started to roar. Large bellowed like an outraged bull, and Little cursed, his eyes growing wide as he struggled to free himself from both Large and the coat. Large looked panicky and thrashed about, setting the hooks even deeper. "Hold still you fucking dumb shit," Little swore at Large.

Robin climbed quickly into his car and fumbled with the keys. The engine roared into life and he was gone before the two men figured out what had happened. And before they could decide how they were going to explain their predicament to the doctor who would eventually have to cut them free.

Robin sped to the terminal and found the two women. "Get in. Let's move. We have to leave. They're here!"

He maneuvered as speedily as he could through the crowd, watching all the way for other pursuers. "You won't believe what happened." He spoke excitedly as he drove. "We have to re-plan our trip."

His emotions brightened. "But that's okay. I think luck's on our side now. I can feel it. We can beat them. The Controllers know we're here but we're still ahead and I'm beginning to like the score."

CHAPTER
TWENTY EIGHT

Robin pushed the rented Renault hard. The rear end fishtailed as he raced through a bend in the road. As he saw the women reach over for support, he swore and eased off the gas a bit. Though an excellent driver, he knew rental cars of this type could be driven only so aggressively. The last thing they needed was a crash. Besides, it didn't make sense for him to vent his frustration on the road.

"How'd they know?" he asked, even as his mind answered its own question. Either there are Controllers and vibrations and magic, or Billy and the women are doing something so monstrous it's beyond my comprehension.

He didn't like either answer. The women said nothing. The exhilaration of surprising Little and Large waned, and he settled into the task of driving through the dreary Irish countryside.

A road sign, written in English and Gaelic, showed that they were now on the N7 heading northeast to Dublin. On previous trips, he had been lifted by Ireland's landscape, a lime green so rich it almost glowed. Everything, even the verge of the motorway right up to the pavement, had been lined with grass.

Now the scenery was brown and melancholy. He watched this bleak winter's view and felt his ire grow. Then his anger turned to irritation over the jumpy roughness of the road reverberating through the car. This B road was so rough he couldn't even hear the radio. "How can a civilized country have such awful roads leading to an international airport?" he griped.

There was no reply. He looked at them in the rearview mirror and saw that both had their eyes closed. They appeared serene in their contemplation. He started to ask again but decided that complaining accomplished nothing. He left them alone and drove on in silence, smoldering.

Finally, the road smoothed. Yet his fury escalated. He knew he had to calm down and he tried the radio again but there was nothing worth listening to. He spoke to the sisters once again. "Over a hundred miles to go."

He saw Talking Panther look up but she did not comment. His irritation had transmuted into moroseness, and he grumbled, "Talkative bunch this morning, aren't we?"

Robin's thoughts wandered as he looked at the passing countryside. Shouldn't blame my gloom on the girls. I'm not sure what depresses me the most, the cheerless Irish villages or the lousy Irish weather.

He drove by dull pebbledash and brown winter grass, always the same, for mile after dismal mile. The dark weather had turned to a fine mist. It always seems ready to rain here, but never does. No honest, hard pouring rain, like Florida thunderstorms. Just drab mist and heavy leaden clouds hanging low in lifeless skies.

Now, MacAllen's thoughts drifted back to the Controllers. He was increasingly accepting that Controllers could, and did, exist. Incredible. Could all these conspirator theorists be right? No, it just can't be. The book is the key, then. If that's real then there actually is some kind of collusion happening that's huge. But the money's never been spent. What does that mean?

An impression started to take shape in Robin's mind. "Ladies, I have an idea that I'd like to discuss. I think I'm beginning to understand how the Controllers work," he said without taking his eyes off the road. "This whole thing has never made sense because of the money. Ian's notes in the book said that he found billions of dollars and that none of it had ever been spent.

"Money's only a social contract, a promise of future delivery of someone else's energy. Before currency, things represented money. If you were a baker, you baked enough bread to feed yourself, then you baked more to trade with others. Bread was your money. But bread isn't very good as money. It's desirable, but not too portable and not durable at all. Bakers needed a way to sell extra bread in exchange for a promise of something to trade in the future.

"Rare, precious metals, especially gold, took over this role. With metallic coins, the baker could trade his bread for the coins and then trade the coins for something he needed later on. But even metallic coins, though durable, desirable and rare, have a hitch. They aren't portable enough; a chunk of gold is heavy. So paper currency was created. At the start, jewelers and silversmiths created this currency because they had vaults as part of their business. They would issue notes that represented the gold or silver stored in their vaults. This was fully backed currency; a person could trade the notes for the gold or silver anytime they desired."

He glanced back in the mirror. The two women remained tranquil, their eyes closed. However, they nodded in agreement, so Robin knew they were listening. "Money changes when governments take control of a currency because they invariably produce notes that aren't backed by gold or silver, or the production of anything. This causes problems with the money supply, because the money just becomes paper and loses its desirability. This creates inflation, which is too much money but not enough products or services available to buy."

Just then, Robin looked back and at that moment, Talking Panther looked up at him. In her glance, he knew she understood that speaking helped him reason things out.

"But this whole thing– amassing billions and not spending any of it–could be about deflation. Planned deflation, where there are too many goods available and not enough money to spend. Deflation is harder on a nation because it affects business and that affects everyone. Businesses can adapt to inflation by simply raising prices. Businesses can keep going during inflation. But deflation destroys businesses because they can't continuously lower their prices."

Again, MacAllen looked back at the women; they still had not moved. "Here's the point," he said. "If I wanted to produce real havoc in the world, I wouldn't try creating more and more money. Inflation only hurts those few on fixed incomes. I'd want to take money out of circulation, and cause deflation. That creates recessions that affect almost everyone. Maybe that's why they've been building up all this money. They are going to create a major deflation!"

There was no response, and so Robin stopped talking and ended this speculation. He pushed back the driver's seat, stretched his legs and immediately started mulling over Little and Large. Somebody knew when we would be arriving, he thought. Those guys were waiting even before we touched down in Ireland. But neither Talking Panther nor Silent Panther had anticipated them. Are there really Controllers out there? Robin grew restless with his own continual questions and started twitching in his seat.

He spoke to the two women again, trying to release his aggravation. "They found me again, didn't they. How do they react so fast?"

Talking Panther shifted in her seat and replied coolly, "Robin, we are feeling this now. Let us have silence." He drove on, struggling to steady both his overflowing indignation and his depression. "Breathing in, I calm my whole body..." *"Buffalo... Silence... Goose... Cat."*

MacAllen watched Talking Panther sitting passively with her eyes closed, and was struck afresh by her tremendous beauty. Something deep within him stirred, an ancient memory, powerful emotions. Melanie... her face floated briefly in his mind but left too quickly to grasp. Talking Panther's loveliness, her grace, the smooth coppery richness of her skin, and now, his intense feelings for this woman were something he had not expected. He had never felt this way about anyone before. It's the memories of Melanie, I'm not really falling for her. Yet, this was different. He had never felt like this, even with Melanie.

"Now's not the time," he grumbled to himself, and he pushed the thoughts away. As the miles rushed by, the endless stretches of road and tiresome colorless landscape made Robin's mind lethargic. In this mesmerized state, he did not notice the truck.

Robin had been driving fast, but carefully. The dual carriageway was like a freeway but much more dangerous. Speed limits were high and there were intersections where cars could cross. Signs reading "Surface Dressing" and "Loose Chippings" warned of construction and gravel on the road, among the other dangers.

He was surprised at how rapidly the tan and burgundy truck marked "Cappoque Chickens" was moving as it tried to rush by the Renault. He was speeding himself, but the truck was going at a much greater speed. Robin tensed as he heard Talking Panther say in a subdued voice, "They are after you, Robin. Stop now!" Just then the truck swerved and headed towards the car. He slammed on the brakes and swerved hard left, shouting, "Hold on!"

The Renault stopped just in time and dropped behind the truck. It skid on gravel, the brakes locking, and began to slide out of control. Robin pumped the brakes as he glanced quickly at the women in the backseat. They both looked as collected as before, and still hadn't opened their eyes.

"How can they do that?" Robin muttered as he wrestled with the steering wheel. The car veered onto the grass verge in the middle of the road and ground to an abrupt halt. He heard the muffler ticking and smelled scorched grass.

The truck ahead had stopped as well and had now spun into reverse. It was heading directly for the Renault.

Talking Panther spoke again, her voice still self-controlled. "The panther knows when to fight and when to run. Now it is time to run."

The right door of the truck opened and a man stepped to the ground. He saw the bleached wooden stock of a shotgun and Robin instantly slammed his foot on the accelerator. The car's thrust pushed Robin back in his seat and they surged forward, tearing across the grass median.

An instantaneous feeling of timelessness and of functioning in slow motion swept over MacAllen. Silence, he thought, as he heard tires screaming as they bit pavement on the other side of the road. He heard the shotgun resound and the tinny clatter of pellets slamming the surface of the car. But these noises were somehow distant, removed...he was completely detached from them. And he understood. Silence...and its unmoving unexcitable calming power.

The Renault's engine screamed as he raced down the wrong side of the road. Thank God no cars are coming, he thought. The scenery hardly seemed to move; seconds seemed like hours. And all the while MacAllen remained cool, self-possessed. "We're out of range," he said, surprised at the casual tone in his voice. Is silence starting to change me?

Robin gripped the steering wheel tightly as the car continued to roar down the wrong side of the empty road, still heading for Dublin. A large berm of dirt in the median prevented him from crossing back to the left, but also hid the Renault from the truck.

Robin watched in the mirror as the van pulled across the verge some distance back. A sharp bend loomed ahead, and he prayed no cars were coming. But there were and MacAllen was forced to make a sharp swerve into the dirt-filled verge to avoid a head-on crash. The car slid in the mud, nearly bogged and it was barely able to push back onto the road.

The truck roared into view. "Turn right, Robin." He heard Talking Panther's controlled voice just as a small road running below a railway bridge exited the highway just ahead of them. Her eyes were still shut. How'd she see it? He hesitated. "I can't see the exit. What if it's a dead end?"

He saw the van gaining on them.

Robin gunned the Renault. "We're not going to make it," he yelled. "The truck's got too much speed!" The short-barreled shotgun exploded again and pellets clanged solidly against the car.

"They're trying for the tires," he shouted, his voice rising and his heart pumping strenuously. The exit was his only option. He turned a hard right at the last minute, hoping the truck would miss it and would not be able to follow.

His head slammed into the roof as they bounced heavily onto the dirt surface. He continued to build speed and the car flashed under the low bridge and continued down the dirt farm road, bucking wildly. "We're in trouble if that truck makes the exit," he warned. "The truck's got heavier springs… higher clearance. It'll catch us for sure on this bumpy road."

Robin looked in the rearview mirror and saw the truck make the turn. The truck driver had ignored the caution sign. It was about to clear the bridge when he heard the mighty crunch of wrenching metal. The shock of crashing into the bridge tore the truck's box from the frame and catapulted both men through the windshield onto the hood, where they lay, dazed and bleeding. The remains of the vehicle rolled hesitantly onto a field beside the road.

Taking a deep breath, Robin slowed the car, turned and smiled. "Luck is with us. It's you two! You bring good luck." He pulled easily away. A short distance later found an entrance back onto the N7. Only then did Robin realize how much he was sweating. And how his hands were trembling.

He pulled the Renault to the side of the road and looked at the two women, ready to speak. He abruptly changed his mind. They were still silent, eyes still closed, expressions still calm, unworried. He saw on both their faces the hint of a smile. Silence… He grinned.

Right away MacAllen relaxed but he was unable to conceal the tremor in his voice. "We've escaped again. Thank you. I can't believe it. Don't you two know the meaning of fear?"

Talking Panther opened her eyes, and at once they swallowed him, two deep, black pools looking directly into his own eyes. She spoke mildly, her manner serene, voice sweet. Her face was remarkably beautiful. Robin sank in the softness. "We were doing more than it appeared, Robin. We could feel everything; we knew all and all was as it should be. We were where fear does not exist. When just being, there is no fear. Fear lives only in the imagination. And what would fear have accomplished? Is it not fear that causes deflation and the issues of money that you spoke about? Money is really only an agreement to eliminate fear."

She smiled as she continued speaking. "As you would say, Robin, we knew the Controllers would be down two. You're still in the lead. We knew this, and we were this, so we did not need to imagine fear. We chose the power of silence instead."

"Great," he said. "Next time we're going to be so lucky, could you let me know in advance. You may be calm but my nerves have worked enough for all three of us!"

Another shiver raced down his spine. They had a long way to go. These men knew exactly where they were. He spoke again, this time more softly, "If you can really bring good luck, use your magic, ladies. We're going to need it." He drove again, in silence.

CHAPTER
TWENTY NINE

Robin turned off the road and stopped by a white food van marked Dan Dooley Snacks. "I'm ready to eat. What about you?"

They stopped, ordered syrupy dark coffee and hot, flat rolls called baps, which were smothered in clotted cream and fresh strawberry jam. "These baps," the man had proclaimed, "are the best you'll ever find. They be a Scot invention, but we Irish'll be forgiven 'em for that. I make 'em meself, fresh every mornin'. You'll not be findin' nothin' like 'em anywhere else in this country!

"Me and Mick here like 'em better'n anything." The vendor reached down to pet his large golden-hued Labrador. "You'll find 'em delicious."

Robin was finishing his third bap when the man's dog nosed into the three of them searching for a bite of Robin's roll. He stroked the dog and gave him a piece, then leaned back and began contemplating the dignity of this simple life he was witnessing. Just a man and a dog…modest work in the countryside, not much money…but such pride and care. And they seemed so content.

His thoughts were interrupted by Talking Panther's words. "Robin, your thoughts are leaking again. This cannot be helped for now and we cannot stop the Controllers from feeling where you are. Silent Panther and I have listened and felt this. We can help slow the Controllers and maybe divert them by teaching you more Golden Words."

He asked without hesitation, "When can I learn?"

"Before the Golden Words are given, I must become one with the forces and discern the correct words to share with you. But at certain times, the forces of nature speak suddenly… and very clearly. They have just given me a sign that it is time to share a word."

As she stood, MacAllen saw the swirl of her long, glossy black hair. "We can start at once, but we must be alone. Come."

They walked away from the table and down a steep bank into a grass-lined gully below the road. They sat on a mound of matted brown grass that was sheltered from the wind. A small creek bubbled beside a field of overgrown hay. The sun broke through the clouds, beaming thinly, fighting against the breezy winter air. With closed eyes, they let the sun embrace them.

A wave of tranquility swept over Robin. "Your fifth Golden Word is *Dog*. This fifth word is the spirit of the dog, who through the day and into the night has pure loyalty and love, and gives only friendship and happiness and asks for nothing in return. With this spirit the dog can sleep, always free from care and pain. The fifth Golden Word is Dog."

Robin continued to sit in the warm sun, protected… absorbed by the word until Talking Panther spoke, "Robin, we should go."

He looked at his watch and was surprised to see that twenty minutes had passed. As they climbed from the creek, Talking Panther proclaimed softly. "I must prepare to give you more Golden Words. This will take me several hours. And we must also change our plans; the Controllers know where you plan to go. Silent Panther can give your thoughts temporary protection. But we must hide. I need to give you more words, and we must create a new plan."

Back in the car after they finished eating, Robin headed northeast away from Dublin, back towards the sea. He drove in silence and watched intermittent patches of brightness break through the clouds. Rays of sunlight filtered thinly through the dreariness and lifted his spirits. He relaxed behind the wheel and worked the gears, driving smoothly over the twisting roads. Dog. How can dog be a Golden Word?

And then realization. He said to Talking Panther, "Loyalty and giving is what this word is about, isn't it? I've been thinking so much about what you and Billy might take from me that the fear of it has been completely engulfing me."

Talking Panther and Silent Panther sat, eyes shut. Yet Robin felt compelled to continue speaking. "Shouldn't we just live like the dog does and stop worrying about what we have and what we don't? Most people spend a good part of their lives worrying about how to accumulate wealth, losing sleep over it, and the other half anxious about how to keep it. If we learn how to give, though, how to be loyal to some method of sharing our wealth, our money can help us sleep! Dog." Robin laughed out the word. "Maybe the idea of having a dog's life has more wisdom than I thought."

When he reached the river Moy, MacAllen turned off the main road and followed a narrow winding path that ran into Lough Conn, a pristine clear lake now forbidding in the winter light. At the lough, he turned again and followed a secluded side road overlooking the water, and stopped the car. The three sat in silence.

Wan rays of afternoon sun shone through broken clouds and began to heat the inside of the car. Talking Panther appeared to be in deep meditation, and her sister Silent Panther sat unmoving in the back seat. Rather than break their silence, MacAllen surveyed the rugged landscape that was gradually being darkened by a bleak afternoon storm blustering in from the sea. He watched the squall line approach. Low clouds skidded through the sky and obscured the mountains around the lake, and gusts of raw wind buffeted the white tops on the lough. The Renault shuddered in the bitter wind that howled and shrieked and surrounded them.

Robin leaned back, sheltered in the warm car. Protected and secure, he let the rough patterns of the wild storm relax him. Talking Panther had sensed that Robin was reposed and she was ready to share her knowledge again. She spoke, and her voice sounded very far away, not her own.

"The sixth Golden Word is *Action*. He sat up straight as she continued. "All action begins in silence. Life is silence in action. In the beginning of time there was only silence. Then, on the first day, silence became action. Our Grandfathers saw silence and action as everything, and they gave us this Golden Word."

Robin turned slightly left to look at Talking Panther clearly, and a tingling sensation rushed up his spine and he flushed with peacefulness. "Silence is of the bowstring drawn taut, action the motion of the arrow, always graceful in flight. Silence is the acorn buried in soil, action the oak standing proud and mocking the wind."

Rain was coming down hard against the car, its rhythms harmonizing with the softness in Talking Panther's voice. "The Eagle forever soars high, floats in warm currents, silent, waiting. Silence is the beginning. Its swift fall is the pure potential of action bringing silence to its prey once more."

When the squall passed by, winter's early dusk masked the car and cloaked it in shades of gray. Talking Panther's face shimmered in the fading light. She whispered, "We are but pools of action upon which the universe can express its silence. When we have the most silence, we can have the most action. No silence exists that is not born of action."

Her voice turned husky as she shifted slightly in her seat, and continued speaking. "As a storm cannot be without wind and rain, we cannot be without thoughts. Silence cannot sing and we cannot think silence. Our thoughts, which are fullness, come from the silence. Silence is the first word and the way to this word is not through emptiness but through action."

The Seminole opened her eyes and looked directly at MacAllen. "Without action, there can be no silence. Silence is the womb of all action. The sixth Golden Word is Action."

Then she closed her eyes again, and spoke, more loudly now. "We must keep moving. Head for the sea, we can rest and eat there. Tonight I will explain more and I'll give you more Golden Words."

He sat for a moment in the half-light, mulling over what she had said and then spoke. "What you have given me, Talking Panther, is very profound wisdom. I've been battling to have an empty mind but it can't be any emptier than a pitcher, can it? Both have to be full of something. Meditation isn't about having an empty mind; it's about focusing on the right things. Money works this way, too. Money is just silence waiting to become action. Money gives us permission to take action. But cash can't be silent. It has to be used.

"This means we've got real trouble. If these Controllers understand this about money and have been storing up so much cash, it can only mean one thing. Big silence for a big action. And we can be sure the action they are planning won't be good action!" He stared at Talking Panther. She possessed an odd tranquillity, a peacefulness that did not, at the same time, suggest passivity. It suggested, instead, an extraordinary power. Her quiet nature, her moderation, spoke boldly of great strength.

"Is this the power you describe when you say silence creates action?" he whispered. He recognized right then that Talking Panther could never be involved in any wrongdoing, could only be a friend. She and Silent Panther were there to help.

"This means I have to stop pushing thoughts down and concentrate on which thoughts to have?" he asked. "I think I understand action." He spoke softly to Talking Panther as he ground the car into first gear and turned carefully around on the slick, wet road.

His countenance had changed. It had lightened, and had become enlivened, more heartened than a few minutes ago. I always think I'm facing problems, but the only real problem I have is my fear. He smiled, shook his head and laughed. Who would believe I could feel so joyous hearing just one word! Okay then, if Action is a Golden Word, I am ready to use it. I'm ready to act!

CHAPTER THIRTY

The Victorian Manor House where they were staying, with its long oak-lined entrance and heavily wooded grounds was genteel and elegant. The firelight in the empty bar flickered and danced, snug in the room's dim mahogany corners. Yellow-orange reflected on the rich deep patina of the wood and cast and recast the fire's almost mystical message; its lively illumination mellowed winter's melancholy.

A light supper of steaming barley soup, an assortment of cheese, pickles and fresh Irish soda bread sat waiting for Talking Panther and Silent Panther to come down from their rooms.

Robin heard footsteps, and saw Talking Panther descend the ornately carved staircase, walking past a line of seascapes framed in heavy gilt. Each hung perfectly on the oak-paneled walls along with objects of seafaring memorabilia.

She joined him at his table and began to eat without saying a word. Unaccustomed to seeing them separated, he asked if something was wrong with Silent Panther.

She put a small piece of cheese in her mouth and continued to chew slowly. When she finished it, she replied, "Everything is fine. Silent Panther is protecting your thoughts. She must be very much in the spirit world to do this. The physical world, this food and drink, is not for her right now."

She reached for another piece of bread. "But I am hungry, and in hunger we should always eat. We have not been alone when we have

179

eaten before; we have always been with other people, or have had to talk. Now that we are alone we can simply feel one another. There is no need to speak." She placed her bread on a plate and continued speaking. "When alone, we always eat slowly and in silence. In this way we honor the spirit of our food. You could not have known this. But you will learn more about it from the Golden Words. The words will help you know how to live in the present so you can tap into the unbounded intelligence of nature. Our Grandfathers will share all of this through me. But first let's eat."

The soft rhythm of Vivaldi's Four Seasons echoed faintly from a distant room. The two ate in tranquil silence. Listening to the crackle of the fire and enveloped by the warmth of the flames, the connection between them strengthened and they found an intimacy that hadn't been there before, and knew would never leave.

Talking Panther finished eating and shifted her chair to face the fireplace. He could barely see in the now dark room but realized her eyes were closed. He waited. When she said nothing he rose and poured himself a snifter of brandy.

Talking Panther suddenly spoke up. "Robin, the need for alcohol will pass shortly. To understand the Golden Words, your mind must be clear and sharp. I will explain later what eating and drinking have to do with the Golden Words. It really would be better to not drink this now.

"The only difference between an illiterate man and a scholar is education. Not all scholars are wise, though. The difference between a scholar and a wise man is truth. But not even scholars who have heard truth are wise. The difference between a fool and a wise man is action. The key to action is knowledge, knowing. Our silence needs to rest in truth. This leads to action harmonious with the forces of nature. Many men hear truth but fail to understand it or know it."

The blank look on Robin's face prompted Talking Panther to continue. "The Golden Words will give you an education in truth and the laws of nature. The key to using this truth is understanding, and it is understanding that leads to action. You will gain truth, but will have to act to apply that truth to your own existence."

She closed her eyes again as she spoke. "If I tell you how to ride a bicycle, you can learn all about it. You could learn all the truths of how to ride that bicycle, the details, the techniques, what to say, do, wear. But will you then know how to ride the bicycle?"

"I could still break my neck trying to ride," he replied.

She opened her eyes, looking directly at him and asked, "What must you do to know how to ride?"

He thought for a moment. "Ride," he said.

She leaned closer to him now and her voice lowered to almost a whisper. "Exactly! You have to ride, to have the action of riding. You have to act so you can combine your thoughts and your actions. Until you do this, all you have are thoughts. Thoughts are like a rudder without a boat, a compass without stars.

"Thoughts are the source of action, but in our present world they are rarely united with action. What we call knowledge is just speculation. We speculate about the panther's roar, but until we meet him face to face and feel his hot breath and experience his malignant claws, we do not know the panther. Knowledge that has never been turned into action through experience is just speculation. Have you ever thought about the truths of the past, such as who really discovered America?"

"I, uh, I don't think so. I've been a history buff for years," he said. "But no. Columbus, wasn't it?"

Talking Panther's face grew vibrant and animated. Her reply was immediate. "How do you know? Or are you speculating because others have told you that Columbus discovered America? How do you know they know?"

"I guess I've never thought about it," he said.

He saw her smile. "That is exactly wrong, Robin. All you have done is to think about it. You've never experienced it. This is what I mean when I say most of our thought is only speculation. We mistake familiarity for truth. If an idea is familiar, most often we accept it as truth.

"Most people live entirely in their heads. They fill their minds with random thoughts they never use; information that is little more than a useless burden to them. They never connect these thoughts and they accumulate like junk in an attic. A few speculations that they accept as truth guide people's daily lives. They never use their thoughts at all! Many do not even carefully choose the information they pass to their sons and daughters."

Talking Panther's voice took on a soft, husky quality as she spoke again. "The seventh Golden Word is *Union*.

"Our Grandfathers saw that all life is a union of silence and action. Nature is never-ending vibration. Each living creature, every rise and fall of the breast, are a tiny burst of vibration. These vibrations are the sway of the treetops, the ripples in the pond, the threads of the wind, every dew drop on morning leaves, just innocent sunrises that eventually set. These tiny movements create much larger vibrations, giving rise to even larger suns rising even brighter in even higher skies."

The pale firelight reflected off her high copper-colored cheekbones as she continued. "Nature is creation. Creation is union. Nature's eternal quest is seeking union of all things. All her creations follow this path. The lover's kiss, the call of the dove, these are songs for union that bring forth the newly born.

"Hunger's eternal pang is life's love, a kiss that unites life with its food. Life and food, united, become their tomorrow. The breaths of sweet air filling the breast and the water, wet on the lips of life, are unions and nothing more."

Talking Panther leaned forward and rocked slowly and her words and turned more melodious. "But silence and action are not life. They are but the shells, discarded like the butterfly's chrysalis. Union is not life but just its beginning spark. Life and the nature of life's creation lay hidden in the gaps between the silence and the action and in the act of union itself. This reality cannot be described in words. You must learn to feel in these gaps.

"These three Golden Words work together: Silence, Action, Union. Now these and the other words are yours, but they will only be thoughts until you act and let your mind, body and soul know them. When you know them, then you will know what to do. First, be silent. Listen for the gaps between this silence and the thoughts that come. You will gain knowledge from what you hear. Then unite this knowledge with action."

Talking Panther then returned to her other self. Smiling, she said, "Robin, would you please get me a drink of water and more food."

He brought her a large pitcher of water and a bowl of fruit, and watched her eat daintily for several minutes. She drank three glasses of water before speaking again. "Now I can explain what eating has to do with the Golden Words, and why drinking alcohol will stop you from using the Golden Words."

Again, she rose from her chair and touched his arm. "Please walk with me outside. When I give you Golden Words I have to give myself to the world of the Grandfathers' spirits. I have to surrender my link with this life and this earth. In the normal way, these three words would be shared over many moons or even many seasons. I have given you more than just the speaking of the words. When I give the words, I must walk with my spirits so that we can touch yours."

As she walked, Talking Panther's body sagged and she almost slumped forward. Her voice dropped to barely a whisper "Giving you so many words in two days has left me far removed from my earthly existence. Eating and drinking, feeling the earth on my feet and the rain on my face will bring me back to this outer world."

"You're exhausted. What can I do for you?"

A gentle but very discernable power emanated from her eyes, and she replied, "No, Robin, not exhausted, not tired—on the contrary, I'm exhilarated. My body appears weak because part of me doesn't want to return. Usually, the Golden Words are given by one ready to return to the Spirit Realm. Being with the spirits is so very beautiful; one does not always want to come back."

"You have to return," he said, shocked at the thought of losing her now.

She squeezed his arm tenderly and moved closer to him. "I know, Robin."

He picked up their coats and they walked out the door into the Irish night.

Chapter
THIRTY ONE

Gravel on the pea stone path crunched beneath Robin and Talking Panther's feet. A damp sea fog filled the valley where they now walked. Emerging from the darkness of the woods, they broke through the mist into a crisp, resplendent night. Countless stars winked and danced in the sky, flashes of brilliance above them.

The evening's chill cut deeply, but their shared warmth shielded them from its bite. Robin was becoming increasingly aware of Talking Panther's lithe firmness against him. Her scent was sweet balm, pure... inviting... animal. He shook his thoughts back to the Golden Words and snuggled deeper in his coat. And pulled Talking Panther closer.

MacAllen spoke mildly, not wanting to disturb her calm. "Talking Panther, I've been skeptical, worried you were involved in these deceptions. You've proven yourself, been of enormous help, and have taken many risks. Now I know you're not, yet it's hard to accept the alternative. I want to thank you for the Golden Words and what you have done to give them to me. I know they are extremely important, but what good are they for what's going on now? How can I use them to find Ian Fletcher?"

Talking Panther put both her arms through his, and moved closer. "Robin, there are many things you will come to know through the Golden Words but one of the most important is knowing how every part of this universe is connected. I have given you these words to help you see the connections in nature."

She slipped on an icy patch. MacAllen gripped her and helped her regain her footing. "I'm not used to ice," she said with a faint smile.

She added, "As you are not used to listening to your feelings in the infinite connections that unite us all. You have these feelings. You always have. To avoid feeling pain you have blocked and ignored them. These feelings are strong within you. If you learn to accept and heed them, you will be able to feel Ian Fletcher. You will be able to sense his thoughts, know what he is seeing, even know what he feels and hears. The Golden Words will help you unlock this power that you have inside of you."

This time Robin thought before he spoke. "Talking Panther, I have never met anyone like you. You have shared profound insights with me, and I can perceive the power in the Golden Words. But their use seems so far away. I need to find Ian now."

He followed as she moved to a bench and sat. Her words floated to him on the wind. "You will be able to use the Golden Words tonight. We will find your friend soon; we have an easy trail to follow. The Controllers have made the way clear for us. The path they are using to follow you, like all trails, runs two ways. We can track them as they follow you. Silent Panther and I can do this already. Tonight you will possess this ability too."

She shifted nearer to Robin, leaning against him. "The Golden Words—*Silence, Action, Union*—will unlock much knowledge so you can use the other Golden Words you learn. The words work through the connections of nature because everything in this universe is connected. Everything is linked, and even the smallest thought, once formed from the silence, becomes an action uniting and affecting everything else in the universe in some subtle way. Your power, Robin, allows you to tap into this process at its finest levels.

"Because all things are connected, all things affect your thoughts. And your thoughts affect everything. With the Golden Words you can also increase your influence over the universe at these most refined and purest stages."

She laughed lightly. "Comparing your thoughts to the tail of a dog may help you comprehend what I mean. That tail can wag the dog if it's wagged correctly. And if you possess the ability to focus and concentrate your thoughts, you can know everything that has ever happened and everything that will ever happen. By concentrating on the Golden Words, you can also increase your influence over what has occurred and what will occur."

She continued speaking, whispering so quietly MacAllen could barely hear. "I will teach you how to do these things tonight. Now, I will help you learn what to do. The process we use is a type of focused thinking based on our sense of sound. This is only one of the many ways to become one with the universe. Since the beginning of time, our Grandfathers knew of our universal connection."

She paused and Robin felt Talking Panther move even closer to him. "Though there are many paths, I will teach you our way of using the Golden Words to reach nature's true reality. These paths to truth and freedom are called many different names: meditation, prayer, Zen concentration, chant, enlightenment, contemplation, yagyas, the eight limbs of yoga, and others. But whatever the name, the process to attain truth is the same. We will use the sense of sound to journey into the reality of nature, but any sense can be used. All lead to the same destination – Unity."

Talking Panther's voice changed, grew strong and full of purpose. "Any of the five senses can be followed from their highest level to their deepest, where they reach their finest state. At this point, we find the place where the senses unite. This is the most profound level of universal being. This point is the gap between the union of our senses and nature. It contains the essence of existence—the seeds of all creation. At this level, you can use the Golden Words."

Robin could see the how much effort it took Talking Panther to explain all this to him and he was overwhelmed with compassion for her. "Should we discuss this tomorrow?"

Her reply was strong. "No, tomorrow you must know the technique. You will learn other Golden Words that will allow you to hide in the vibrations so you cannot be followed. You will learn words that will show you how to follow others through the vibrations. This knowledge will let you find Ian Fletcher.

"You have learned that thoughts come from silence. You found that when you wished to be silent, you could not clear your mind because your mind is thought. You learned that the only way to gain silence is through action; that the mind becomes full when filled with a single action. A full mind is silent, just as a water bag that is full does not slosh. Now you will learn how to unite silence and action, not to control your mind, but to guide it to the source of all truth."

The tempo of Talking Panther's words quickened and she gestured expansively in the dark. "This technique is as old as man and has been used in many nations, by many masters. Tonight you will learn to infuse your mind with a thought and to alternate that thought with silence. Each time the thought and the silence unite, there will be a gap. As your mind settles down, that gap will grow deeper and deeper, until it breaches the finest levels of existence. When you cast your Golden Words into that deepest gap, anything can be done."

The hair rose on the back of MacAllen's neck as the Seminole continued. "This technique will allow an animal spirit to pick you. That animal spirit will be yours forever and you will be his. Once you have been chosen, never speak your spirit's name. To do so will offend your spirit."

Finally Robin spoke. "Is this something like the meditation technique I learned from a Vietnamese monk?"

Talking Panther reached down, lifted a pebble from beneath the bench, and tossed it into the blackness in front of them. She answered rapidly, "This is good, Robin. You see that the techniques are similar. They are because they are connected, they came from the same place. We are all connected.

"When the Grandfathers escaped from the Controllers, they took the technique with them. The Controllers tried to hide this knowledge; they know these techniques give them power. And this is why they try to destroy us now. They fear us because we also know how to use the Golden Words."

She paused. "Have you ever wondered why we are called Indians, Robin?"

This unexpected change of focus roused his curiosity. "I, uh… Columbus discovered America while seeking India. He thought he was in India," he said.

Her laugh startled him. "Yes, you're familiar with that answer, I see. All humanity did come from a common source eons ago. When the first people escaped the Controllers, they journeyed to a land we now called India, and also to numerous other places. From that time onward, all those who escaped from the power of the Controllers were called Indians. Our forefathers were among those who escaped. The Controllers looked for us for many centuries. They knew we had the Golden Words and they knew we had gold. The Controllers delegated the task of looking for us to Christopher Columbus. Your modern educational system is ruled by the Controllers, and they will not let the world know this truth."

She sat up straight. "Their plan, Robin, is to obliterate us," she added with force. "And they have almost succeeded, too!

"Our return to fight these Controllers was told by our Grandfathers. Their prophecy is very old and says we will return and repel the attack that has rained upon our people, and that we will reverse the forces that have led man to ignore his unity. But we will stop this war with love, not weapons. This is the reason I came with you."

Talking Panther relaxed and lay her head on Robin's shoulder. "But I'm here now for a very different reason."

"Yes?" he asked in an almost imperceptible voice. Talking Panther's sweet captivating scent encompassed Robin. He experienced the soft silkiness of her hair caress his arm and his heartbeat sped up at her touch.

"I am here to be with you."

The trace of her fingernail across the back of his hand was like burning coal. "This we will speak of later. Now you must use the technique to find your friend, Ian.

Talking Panther continued her explanation, her voice joyless.

"Indians in the Americas and Indians in India do use similar techniques to be at one with nature. Over many centuries the Controllers have guided education to focus on the differences between man, rather than the similarities. They have stressed how our skin is red and yours is white. They have let it be forgotten that we all have hearts that beat with love, sweat that comes with toil, eyes that see grand visions, and babies who cry in the night. The Controllers have distorted the truth to make different cultures fear one another."

MacAllen could almost experience her sadness. "The Controllers have created such immense pain for their own brief pleasures and material gains. I am so happy your vision sees beyond this and recognizes the bonds. With the Golden Words, you will see many more connections. Now it is time for you to know your animal spirit and permit him to guide you. I will help you find him and he will help you find Ian Fletcher. But first, we must go back inside. The wind is too high, and we must be warm so we are peaceful and still."

Robin held Talking Panther close as they walked along the path to the hotel. The walk was steep and the wind pulled severely at them. Yet he found his steps more buoyant than previously. In fact, he felt more buoyant than ever before in his life.

CHAPTER
THIRTY TWO

The room they were in now felt comfortable, secure, protected from the sharp winds outside. The blaze in the fireplace erased the chill from their walk; its flames cast ivory shadows on the polished oak paneled walls. Talking Panther sat on a worn leather Chesterfield sofa, sipping a hot chicory drink she had made for both of them from herbs she always carried with her.

She set the cup on a tray next to her and spoke in a voice that barely carried above the crackle of the flames. "Now I'll help you learn how to use the Golden Words. First I'll explain why you must beware of drinking alcohol."

She came and sat beside him on the hearth, and once again her alluring scent enveloped Robin.

"Alcohol is a drug that separates a person's spirit from the whole; its use is caused by an imbalance in thought. Incomplete thinking separates sickness from the whole and concentrates only on overt symptoms rather than the causes of the sickness. When people experience stress, sometimes they have a drink and the alcohol masks the stress. But the cause is not removed, and the drinking usually only complicates the stress.

"This type of thinking permeates western society. For example, western medicine focuses on eliminating symptoms and ignores the roots of the discomfort. Drugs are overused, clearing the obvious side effects but not touching the real causes and problems. These drugs separate a person's spirit from the body, and actually encourage illness rather than health."

Talking Panther's hands gestured gracefully and her voice turned mellifluous. "To our people medicine is considered a part of our soul. But since you are more familiar with dealing at the material level of your body I will focus on that.

"Think of the brain for a moment as a muscle. Using the Golden Words is an exercise that strengthens the brain and enhances your body's entire information processing system."

MacAllen set his hot drink down. "You mean the Golden Words are mental exercises."

"No, the words themselves are not the technique, they exercise your brain and other information handling components, not your thoughts. Much the same as weights are not the exercise. When you exercise a muscle, you don't exercise the bio-electric signals that make the muscles work. You are developing the muscle fibers themselves and their related parts such as blood vessels, nerve connections, bones and sinews. As these different parts strengthen, the bio-electric impulses sent to the muscles become more effective.

"With the Golden Words, you train your neural pathways, cerebral blood supply, brain hemispheres and coordinating channels, so your entire thinking mechanism can process greater amounts of data."

Robin was listening intently, trying to understand Talking Panther's complex explanation. He took another sip of the bitter chicory brew and asked, "So I think of my brain as separate from my mind or thoughts?"

She said, "Picture the brain as a machine in which your mind and thoughts work. They affect each other, they're connected, but they are not one.

"Beta waves can be looked at like the local news, alpha waves global and theta waves the ones that tap into universal news. When you increase your brain's capability, it becomes able not only to receive but integrate these waves as well. All of the data that your brain processes can be connected. Can you imagine what this means?"

Robin couldn't think of a reply and nodded for Talking Panther to explain. "By conditioning your brain, you can access and integrate all the information, all the data, in the universe."

She grew animated. "Take your growth process as an example. Your body knows how to grow arms."

"Grow arms? No, I don't know how to grow arms. What do you mean?"

"What is this?" she asked with a smile, tugging his arm. "Didn't your body grow this arm? This arm is proof that your body has the knowledge to grow arms. Your intellect may not be able to explain how, but your mind and body, working together, grew your two arms for you."

She squeezed his arm again, harder. "Imagine what happens, Robin, when you integrate your brain. You gain the power to grow another arm, if that is what you wish to do! You can learn to think at this unbounded, universal level. And your intellect can influence this vast universal knowledge."

Robin set down his cup and sat back. With a caustic voice he said, "Come on, Talking Panther, you're not trying to tell me I can learn how to grow another arm."

"No, Robin, I am saying that you can condition your brain to focus your thoughts. And do far more than just grow an extra arm."

Talking Panther stared directly into his eyes, and MacAllen was again swallowed by their utter blackness. "With this you can unleash the very power of creation itself, in every part of your life. You will not gain this power overnight, nor can you tell how much power you will acquire over time. For example, I cannot grow arms, but as you have seen I can alter my image. If you'd like, I can make myself look like an animal or something else to convince you."

The implications of what she was saying set in and Robin replied, "Yes, yes, I know. I've seen you change. But can I attain such powers?" Then something else occurred to him. "I've heard of yogis with incredible strength or the ability to never eat, or to live for days buried in the earth. Is this the technique they use to be able to do these things?"

"Yes, Robin," she replied softly, "this is how they perform such acts. But that is nothing compared to what some people can do.

"The very powers of creation await anyone who wishes to use them. You must learn them, however, because these powers carry extraordinary responsibility. They must be used only with wisdom. This is why those who have learned how to tap these powers of infinity do not display themselves in foolish exhibitions."

Talking Panther rose and stretched. Her easy litheness distracted him. "Enough theory for now. This exercise is like any other, the technique works whether you understand how or not. Just like jogging—if you run, your legs get stronger; you don't have to understand why. What you learn now will give your thought processes enormous power, a little at a time, just like any exercise." Again, she sat down near him by the hearth. "The exercises will integrate your brain, but alcohol disintegrates it. Alcohol makes you feel strengthened when in reality you are diminished. If your muscles are weak and painful, alcohol stops you from feeling the pain, but it does not make the muscles stronger. Alcohol separates you from your spirit. That is why you should not drink it."

Talking Panther poked Robin's leg. "Using the Golden Words expands your view. For example, if your leg is weak, your expanded view will help you see why the weakness exists. Your expanded view will help you know whether you should make the muscles strong with exercise or if you should rest and stop using the leg."

MacAllen reached, caught her hand and held it lightly as he asked, "I rarely drink alcohol so that's not a problem for me. But what does eating have to do with Golden Words? Are you going to tell me eating disintegrates the brain too?" The moment he said this he wished he could grab his words back, realizing how they must sound.

The Seminole caught him once again with her piercing eyes and the hard edge in her whisper bore through him. "Robin, I feel your turmoil, I feel your fear. But you can no longer hide from the ability you have. It is a gift you will be compelled to use. I can easily help you hone and understand this gift or you can learn it on your own. I will give my life to help you, but you must want me to. If you are not ready, I will stop now. Just tell me what you wish me to do."

Robin apologized as quickly as he could. "Please forgive me, Talking Panther. I... I'm sorry. I didn't mean... I'm overwhelmed and confused. Yes, I want to learn. I'll shut up and listen."

Talking Panther continued. "Actually you are partly right. If the food you eat is incorrect or if too much is eaten improperly or consumed in the wrong combinations, yes, food can cause the brain to disintegrate. Most people eat too much and too fast. My people have learned to avoid eating salt and sugar at the same time, or two types of fat together. Doing so causes fermentation in the stomach, and fermentation results in alcohol. Eating slowly, and in silence, helps us eat less. But this is not really the reason we eat in silence."

Robin could see Talking Panther's hesitation; she was weighing her words as if undecided about how to say what she wanted to.

"There are many ways to connect with nature's universal power. Any number of paths can lead you there. Joggers often obtain this bond through long runs; they call it a runner's high. Athletes call it being in the zone. Great musicians acquire this union through their art.

"To maximize this power we must focus every connection we have with the universe. And eating is one of our closest. We actually gain information from our food. If we concentrate on that, we gain knowledge far beyond taste. Eating slowly and in silence puts us in touch with this wholeness."

She squeezed Robin's hand tenderly then stood and continued speaking. "Now I must help you start.

"Sit with your spirit. Every day think of him at dawn and at dusk. Think of him with the emotions of gratitude, of thanks, love and compassion. Fill your mind with thoughts of him and nothing more. Just as you fill your mind with thoughts of your food as you eat. Let his name drift gently into the recesses of your mind."

The fire's glow shimmered against Talking Panther's face. Robin leaned against the mantle and listened.

"As your spirit drifts, it will begin to roam in and out of your mind in a symphony with silence. As that spirit and the silence unite, your mind will drop into the gap that harbors the roots of all existence. From this gap will come a great knowing, and that knowing will be passed to you through your animal spirit. That knowing will sometimes be in words. Other times it will be in the form of visions or sounds, or perhaps come only as feelings. Sometimes a knowing that words cannot speak will come. In this place you can learn anything. Here is where you will find Ian Fletcher."

MacAllen rose from the couch, poured himself some more tea and walked back to the fireplace. He stood a moment and looked at the exquisite woman, then asked, "Will Ian speak to me while I am in this gap?"

"You may see visions of him. You may hear his words. Or you may see a map, hear a sound, or in an indefinable way just know. Do not look for signals. Do not look for Ian Fletcher. Walk with your spirit only for the purpose of being with him. This infinite intelligence will know what information to pass to you. Do not try to tell the universe what you want. Instead, let the universe tell you what you truly need. And accept what is sent. It may be, Robin, that you are not meant to find your friend."

He interrupted. "I have to find him. I have to help. I've already made my mind up about that."

"I know he is your friend, Robin," Talking Panther replied in a voice that was subdued and caring. "And I know you must try to help him. Only the forces of nature know your fate and Ian's fate. We follow a path, and lean when the winds blow. But it is the wind that decides our final directions as we travel that path.

"Listen to your spirit, Robin. Let him be your guide. Trying to tell him what to do and ignoring his lead creates great danger. You can alter the existence of nature with this technique, but doing so without wisdom can bring you great harm. This power is so great I can change my appearance. I know you have wondered about how I do this."

She walked gracefully to the hearth and stood by him, smiling slightly. "Would you like me to explain how?"

He nodded his reply.

"Every thought and action in the universe has an impact on everything else, for all time. These endless actions and reactions mix and meld, push, pull, attract and repel, and the sum total of this all-encompassing flux is the universe. We have defined the actions in this pattern and call them laws. So we have the law of gravity, the law of thermodynamics and many others. But these actions are not absolute laws. They are the laws of statistics."

Talking Panther picked up a small piece of wood that had fallen from the fire, tossed it back onto the flames and continued. "The laws of statistics are laws that determine the flip of the coin–half the time heads, half the time tails. But this is not an absolute law. Half of the forces in the universe aim to push the coin towards heads. Half aim to push it towards tails. Nothing says the coin cannot come up heads every time; the universe has no particular intention about how that coin should fall. If you think about that coin at the deepest level of creation, your intention can influence how the coin falls."

She picked up another piece of wood and flipped it into the fire. "This is why some people appear to be so lucky. Somehow, usually unknowingly, they learn to place intentions in the universe that no one counteracts."

A spark danced out onto the hearth. "This explains the stories of the ancient Sufis on flying carpets or yogis levitating. Many generations ago our Grandfathers discovered that gravity is not an absolute law. For instance, you probably have noticed that when your emotions are high your feet feel light. Those days when the work is heavy and your disposition is low, gravity pulls more heavily, like wet clay under your feet. Your intentions affect the impact of gravity! The ancients concentrated their intent at the finest level of the cosmos, and in doing so, they reduced the effects of gravity!"

Just then, Talking Panther's skin began to wrinkle and her face filled out. Her beauty dissolved and an old woman stood in front of Robin. Then almost immediately she changed back to herself.

"What you saw was only an illusion. I was always right here and did not change, but my intentions were focused at the roots of reali-

ty and it changed the way the light reacted to me. I used my intention to influence the light around me and so I altered the image of
me that you perceived.

"Everything we sense is an illusion. I have learned to influence
just one of the illusions we rely upon. Anyone can do this by finding
a spirit to lead him to light. That spirit can be invoked very simply
by thinking the right word. That word is one of many Golden Words.
Everything you do depends on the words you know and upon your
concentration on those words, and your practice and dedication to
them. If I use the correct word, I can change my weight or my skin.
If you know the right words and practice regularly, you can change
many things within yourself and without.

"At the same time, for every intention you invoke, you must take
responsibility for it. There is also a law affecting thoughts not in pure
harmony with the roots of nature."

"Is this the law that says that for every action there's an opposite
and equal reaction?"

"Yes, and no one escapes this law." Talking Panther's voice had
hardened. "If a person's thoughts are not in tune with nature's
desires, nature will comply, but her price will be very high. When in
contact with the laws of nature, only our real needs should be our
desires. When you listen to your animal spirit, you will always stay
in tune with nature. And so there will be no mistakes and then no
negative consequences. The Controllers use the words for their own
corrupt ends and try to deny this responsibility."

MacAllen jumped as she slapped her hand on the stone hearth.
"In the end, they will use the laws of nature to destroy themselves.
They cannot avoid the consequences of their actions! This is why
their progress is slow. Perhaps we are meant to help the universe in
this way. If so, we will be protected. If we are meant to die doing
this, then so be it. If this is what the infinite intelligence of our
Grandfathers chooses, there is no reason for us to fear dying now."

Then once again her voice mellowed. "But we have strayed far.
Before you can speak with the forces of nature you must first learn
to listen to your spirit. In this way you can reap nothing but good

from the universe and for the universe. You are thus bound. Your animal spirit will always protect you if your heart is innocent. But only when it is."

Talking Panther pulled Robin onto the couch. "Sit here with me," she said. She closed her eyes and began speaking. "It is time for me to help you find your animal spirit. Sit here while I call forward the words of our Grandfathers."

Her voice dropped into a toneless resonant chant. Robin glided deeper and deeper into sleep.

He awoke in confusion. He couldn't see. Where am I? Am I awake or dreaming? His ears were buzzing; the sound was far away but somehow near. What is that?

As he tried to rise a hand on his shoulder held him down. He jumped and grabbed at the hand. But it wasn't a hand, it was something much larger and softer, stronger, covered with hair! He screamed but no sound came. I must be dreaming; but no, this is real.

An enormous paw seized him. A paw, was it a paw? Yes! I'm sure. It's a large golden paw. How did I know this was a paw? I just know!

A rolling rumbling sound vibrated with sublime force. It grew louder and bolder and filled him with joy. The sound of a purr exploded, radiating contentment. Yes! It is the purr of a cat – immense and powerful, majestic and fearless! Robin shouted out its name.

Incandescent light crowded out the darkness, then closed in and narrowed to form a tunnel. Colors spiraled and hovered, ivory that flickered to yellow, white, blue and then to white again. The tunnel pulsed and brightened. Surrounded by pure light MacAllen slid, slowly at first, then faster and faster down the tunnel that kept lengthening and stretching in front of him.

At the end was his animal spirit, splendid, tawny and golden, with an glorious, regal mane. This creature's power was Robin's power. When he tried to speak its name, his lips would not move. He tried to shout it, but his jaw was frozen.

He woke at a touch. "Robin, you have your spirit now. I can feel it."

He tried to stand up, but his head was reeling and he quickly sat back down. "How long have I been asleep?" he asked.

The response came through his blurred senses, "I was with my spirit and I did not watch to see. But it has been long and it is late now."

This time MacAllen rose unsteadily. "My dream was wild. I met an animal spirit for sure. It was…"

She put her finger to his lips. "Shh," she whispered. "Never speak your animal spirit's name. This would offend him. The image of your spirit animal is to be thought at only the finest levels of your mind. To speak the word pulls it to a grosser plane far from the roots of creation. You must use his name only in the silence of the gap."

Talking Panther kissed Robin lightly on the cheek. "We are united now in the spirit world. It is time to sleep. Go to bed. But before you lie down, sit for twenty minutes and just think the name of your animal spirit. Think it easily. Take any thoughts that come. Then allow yourself to drift off to sleep. Do this, and if it is meant to be, you will find Ian Fletcher. When you wake up, think again of your spirit for twenty minutes. If the spirit so chooses, you will know what you are meant to know, and what you are meant to do."

He held her hand for several moments, silently inviting her to come with him to his room. "Go do this, Robin. This is what you must do for Ian. We will discuss our own destiny at another time."

They walked together up the stairs. In bed, Robin lay thinking of the animal spirit he had seen. Then he fell asleep.

He floated… ascending higher and higher… his body passing through the roof of the inn. Catching a breeze, he drifted out over the sea. There was a ship below, and the moon blazed so vividly he could see the ship's captain standing on deck reading a map.

All of a sudden, the captain, his boat and the water melted and lines formed around them. The lines wandered and took on the shape of a large map, pale white, with lines of yellow, green and red. Its contours floated, moved, shrank and then rose again. They moved once more and then dissolved into massive fields that appeared below.

The fields turned from white to yellow to gray, progressing and spilling into empty voids and wide spaces. They grew larger still, wheat- and corn-colored. Then Robin floated over acres of endless yellow, to a great castle constructed out of large tawny rock. Ramparts escalated sharply into the sky and its bright flags waved proudly. Lions of stone stood, dark gargoyles staring savagely into space.

Then these lions of granite came alive. They all smiled broadly and began a strange but familiar tune: "We are you. And you are one. And we are everyone. You are our son."

MacAllen had heard the melody before, but could not remember where. The song faded. The castle grew smaller and dimmer.

Now he slipped away on the wind, the ramparts fading from view. Indistinct figures gathered on the receding castle wall. Robin could barely make out two men, one dressed in black, the other in white. He knew the man in white.

He also knew the man in black. Everything he despised within himself was in that man, every part his opposite. He was a rich man right from birth where Robin had been poor. He was a selfish man, arrogant and soulless. An aristocrat by birth, he had shed everything that was good in the upper class. Cruel and manipulative, black was his only color.

This was a vulture feeding on the weakness of others. Then Robin saw himself, the man in white. A conflict between them grew. And he himself called the man's name... His voice swelled, amplified but quite distorted, reverberating... Ce... dr... ic, CE... DR... IC!

The dream shattered. The men and the castle waned and disappeared.

"Cedric. I know Cedric."

Robin woke with a start. Sunlight illuminated the room and turned the floral wallpaper into a vibrant tangle of color. Lying on the bed, disoriented and stunned, he recalled his dream. Flying... water... castles... lions... this man, Cedric. Everything about it seemed a blur. Then he remembered Talking Panther's instructions and he sat up, closed his eyes and thought again of his animal spirit.

When he opened his eyes twenty minutes later, the meaning of his dream had crystallized. He dressed in a hurry and rushed from the room to find Talking Panther and Silent Panther sitting by the fire. Oblivious of whoever else might hear, he shouted. "Ladies, let's go. Make it quick. We have a plane to catch."

CHAPTER
THIRTY THREE

Robin paid the bill and rushed the sisters from the inn. In silence, through the ice-cold dawn, he twisted and turned the car through winding roads. The sun soon rose over craggy, barren hills. They sped through valleys, past flawlessly clear lakes and glinting streams.

Finally, when they reached a straightaway, Robin spoke with great animation. "I know where Ian is. I can't describe the exact spot to you. We'll get a lead at the post office in a village called Dowdeswell. But this isn't as urgent as getting out of Ireland is."

He banged the steering wheel with the palm of his hand. "The Controllers have set a trap for us. We've got to get out of the country now, today. It might already be too late. If we don't move fast, we'll never make it. I've trusted you both so far, now you'll have to trust me.

"There's a one o'clock flight on Manx Air, Dublin to Ronaldsway on the Isle of Man. We have to be on that flight. We'll make it out if we take that flight."

Talking Panther and Silent Panther smiled delightedly at one another. Then Talking Panther said, "We are happy your spirit has spoken so wisely and strongly to you. We always trust words of the spirits."

Robin pushed the accelerator hard and concentrated on the road. The Irish countryside flashed by.

When they reached the outskirts of Dublin, MacAllen pulled

over to the curb. His voice was determined as he leaned back and said, "I don't know if you can feel it. We're riding into the den of the lion. The hair's standing up on the back of my neck."

Talking Panther looked at her sister who was holding a gold chain in her hands. "Yes, Robin, Silent Panther feels the danger too. One point is very evident to her. We must avoid confrontation with any type of authority. There will be danger if we do."

Robin pulled back onto the road and drove ahead slowly, watching for speed limit signs. He followed an avenue lined with lime trees that led into the city. Rows of Edwardian houses in drab red brick lined up despondently next to shops of all kinds. A beautiful and imposing stone church stood in striking contrast next to a car dealership whose merchandise spilled over onto the pavement. Corrugated tin shacks housed fruit vendors displaying their winter fruit and flowers wilted miserably in the cold.

In the distance, a soccer field loomed brightly, its lights poking like giant skeletons in the sky. A police car marked "Guarda" in bold letters sat by the curb in front of the stadium. As they passed, it pulled away and joined the traffic behind them.

Robin again slowed down. "Watch the police car in back of us. I'll concentrate on the driving. Check to see if they're following us."

The traffic grew denser. Street signs pointed chaotically every which way. At a row of shops, one marked "Gents Hairstyles," another "News Agent," he turned onto Ipsbourgh Road. The Guarda's car headed in the opposite direction.

Approaching Dublin Airport now, MacAllen remembered that it had one of the toughest security systems in the world. The hair rose on the back of his neck again, and he spoke sharply. "We have to turn around now! There is a security check ahead! We need to avoid going through it at all costs."

Talking Panther leaned forward looking for their obstacle. "I can't see it, Robin."

Robin turned left and pulled the car over to the curb. "You can't see it because it's a block ahead. I forgot all about the security here. It's so intense because of the situation in from Northern Ireland;

they're always on guard for bombs and terrorists.

"I don't think we can avoid an inspection," he said. "But we can reduce our risk if we walk in with only carry-on bags. If a trap has been set, it will probably be at this checkpoint. The men in the truck yesterday probably passed on the details about our car. Let's leave the car here with most of our clothes in it. Put sweaters on beneath your coats. Just bring warm clothes with you. I'll call the car rental agent when we get to England to tell them where the car is, and we can buy more clothes there. Even if no one is watching out for us," Robin warned, "the last thing we want to do is drive up to a security check in a car riddled with shotgun pellets."

Once they had each packed a small bag Robin said, "You two go in separately, one at a time. Go through different checkpoints if you can, so you don't attract attention. They are less likely to be looking for you than for me. If you see any danger, come back out and wait for me. I'll follow in five minutes."

Talking Panther and Silent Panther stepped out of the Renault, one looking like a slender and very chic young Italian and the other a much older, overweight mother.

When another chill hit Robin, he knew without doubt that they were indeed walking into a trap. Yet he forced himself to wait the five minutes before he went through. Each minute dragged, seemed endless to him. Don't be a fool. They can take better care of themselves than I can. "Breathing in, I calm my whole body…"

The biting wind hit him as he abandoned the Renault. When he turned the corner a short time later, MacAllen could see the sentry ahead. The hair on the back of his neck bristled again. The entrance to the airport terminal was about fifty yards in front of him.

A police car pulled to the side of the road near him. Ignoring its proximity, he quickly pulled up his coat collar and walked away from the car and into the building. He immediately passed through the security check, without incident.

Robin checked at the Manx Air ticket counter to make sure there were seats available on the flight they wanted, but he didn't purchase any.

It was all so easy. Yet something was wrong. Then he saw the two men standing near the car rental stations. They knew I had a rental car!

He swiftly stepped behind a column out of their view and started to work his way back to Manx Air. Then two police officers burst out of a side door and headed directly to the Manx Air counter. MacAllen froze.

They spoke briefly to the ticket agent and positioned themselves on either side of her. "Damn," he muttered.

An arm grabbed him from behind. He twisted around, prepared to act. As he swung around, he found himself looking into Silent Panther's dark eyes. She motioned him to be silent as she placed something in his hand. It was an airplane ticket, Manx Air 216 at 13:05—just 20 minutes from now.

Silent Panther indicated that she wanted Robin to follow and she placed her arm through his. He leaned down and whispered, "Where's Talking Panther?"

She said nothing and continued casually towards the departure lounge. He walked with her, then stopped abruptly. Two men he hadn't seen before stood by the door they had to enter. "They're part of the trap," he murmured to Silent Panther. But the Seminole urged him to continue. Putting his trust in her, Robin complied, and proceeded on.

He heard his name over the public address system, the bland voice continuously repeating the same message. "Mr. Robin MacAllen. Please come to the Aer Lingus ticket counter immediately. Mr. Robin MacAllen…"

Again, Silent Panther urged him along gently by the arm, walking steadily straight to the two men.

With her arm hooked through his, she nonchalantly led him to the gate. The men left where they were standing and started towards the Aer Lingus counter. Another man who had just walked from the departure lounge directly to the Aer Lingus counter was being surrounded by the two men from the gate, as well as the four he had seen earlier. All six converged at once on the lone man. MacAllen leaned over and started to ask Silent Panther who it was that had responded to his name, but she continued to steer him forward, their pace increasing.

He heard the scream of a woman. "Help me! These men are attacking me, help!" The voice was familiar. Robin began to turn to see who it was, but was prevented with a forceful and unyielding jerk. Silent Panther pulled him through the departure door.

As he quickly glanced over his shoulder, he saw the six men standing at the Aer Lingus counter holding an old woman who yelled again as a crowd surrounded her and several policemen rushed the desk.

Silent Panther pulled Robin yet again and they passed through the door.

The flight was half full. MacAllen checked his watch. Ten minutes...

He looked for Talking Panther and asked, "What's going on? Where's your sister?" Silent Panther had closed her eyes, appearing quite composed. It was a look that by now he knew well.

He looked at his watch, again. "Three minutes..."

His fear changed into agitation. Silent Panther glanced up at him, squeezed his arm slightly and said, "Relax, Robin. Our sister will be with us soon. She is fine. We are all safe. Calm down, before you lead them directly to us."

Robin was stunned. He had never heard Silent Panther speak before. But as his surprise wore off, MacAllen realized that he had heard her speak but had not seen her lips move. What can be happening, he wondered? Was she actually speaking or did I just hear?

Silent Panther cast a brief look at him again and Robin knew that she had spoken to him. But her words had no sound, were mute. She had spoken directly into his mind. "Remarkable," he mumbled to himself. "It's incredible.

"One minute..." Just as he was about to shake himself from Silent Panther's grip and leave his seat, an old woman stepped on the plane. The door was immediately closed behind her and the plane began to taxi away from the ramp.

The old woman bumped into Robin. She looked directly at him, and her penetrating eyes once again swallowed him. She kept on, walking slowly to a seat at the rear of the plane.

Robin was unaware of the plane rolling to the runway, then shuddering and lifting easily into the air. Before the plane hurtled skyward and out over the Irish Sea, Robin had already lifted into his spirits.

CHAPTER
THIRTY FOUR

The barren winter landscape passed by. Robin listened to the throaty rattle of the diesel taxi that carried them over a narrow, winding road from Ronaldsway Airport into Douglas, the largest town on the Isle of Man. "I'm surprised we found this London-style taxi. They're uncommon here," he said, attempting to break the silence. "I'm glad though. They have great heaters and lots of extra leg room."

A gale's dying rage lashed brief curtains of rain across the long plains. The car rocked, buffeted by a sudden furious wind, but the steady hum of the heater coddled them with its ceaseless currents of warm air.

"Look at this beautiful land. I love the way the farmland contrasts with those rocky cliffs." Crags jutted ahead of them, razor-sharp from the impact of the never ending crashing of the Irish Sea. In the distance, clouds parted above heather-carpeted moorland. A pallid winter sun broke through mist that hung over the distant South Barrule Mountains that ran like a spine along the middle of the Isle. "I love this place, it's so peaceful and pastoral but at the same time it's filled with mystery. You know, the Isle of Man Parliament has been in existence for over 1,000 years. It's the oldest free democracy in the world."

The taxi headed down a steep hill, driving past sheltered glens, old crofter cottages, and tiny brick row houses. An ancient mansion of slate stone flashed by, its plaque declaring it "The Nunnery". They were just about to reach Douglas Harbour at the south end of town.

"Money first brought me to this place, and I'll bet the Controllers use it too. Lots of small islands like this are involved with money. Being a financial center is the only way many of these islands can prosper."

Talking Panther looked away from the passing scenery and asked, "Didn't your friend Ian say that the Controllers were using financial centers to store their money in?"

"Yes," he replied. "But they don't really store money in a financial center. Money actually can't be stockpiled; it has to be continually circulated. Financial centers just make sure that its re-circulation is a little less severed by taxation.

"There's two parts to having wealth – making money and keeping it. Money has to be protected from all types of theft. And the biggest swindlers of all can be governments when politicians try to buy votes. These politicians make so many promises trying to get elected that when they win they need more and more money to fulfill their mandates and they increase taxation. These governments pass layer upon layer of tax regulations, year after year. I don't think they intentionally plan to steal but that's the effect. At one time the top tax rate in England for people with as little as $60,000 income was 98%!"

Talking Panther replied coolly, "Yes, Robin, our people are aware of just how governments can have insatiable appetites. The United States Government took all of our wealth. They took our land, our rivers, and our skies. They even tried to take our culture. This is exactly why Silent Panther and I remain hidden."

"This robbery wouldn't be quite so bad if the taxed money was efficiently used," Robin continued. "But it's not. Governments are inefficient in everything they do. But if the authorities who are supposed to protect us are always trying to take money and waste it, who can protect wealth?"

Talking Panther didn't answer and Robin continued, "You hire another government to protect you from your own. It's the ultimate protection racket. Governments of financial centers promise no tax or very low tax to non-residents who bank their money in their financial centers. The Isle of Man is a perfect example. If an American citizen banks here, he doesn't pay any tax on interest earned here. Isle of Man residents, though, have to pay Isle of Man tax. But at the same time the Manx can bank in America tax free."

Talking Panther paused a moment and then asked, "The Controllers store their dollars in financial centers so they don't have to pay U.S. tax?"

"It's more complex than that," he replied. "First, the Controllers don't store dollars here. There is only one place where dollars can be used, America. Most dollars sent to financial centers eventually end up deposited back in the U.S. The money never moves. All that changes is the account name."

He stopped to watch as the taxi driver slowed behind a flock of sheep crossing the road. When they were done their leisurely parade, the car sped up and Robin continued his explanation. "The Controllers have billions hidden. So we know they must be up to something big. They'll have spread the money around because almost every financial center in the world has signed treaties to help stop money laundering and terrorism. If anyone moves too much money, suspicions arise, and someone will inevitably report it to the authorities."

A sudden change in the scenery quieted Robin. A burst of color had broken through the clouds and shone its thin light over the harbor at North Quay. Green, brown and red were splashed on old wooden fishing boats. Masts and rigging stuck and spun like spider webs amid flags. And the old Victorian and Tudor buildings with their gingerbread trim stacked like crooked dominos along the wharf created a wonderful old-world feeling.

MacAllen leaned over towards the two women, and keeping his tone conversational, said, "The fishing fleet isn't what it used to be, but the remaining boats are still active. This is what my father and grandfather used to do. This scene here has changed little over hundreds of years."

He spoke louder to the taxi driver. "Driver, stop here at the English Hotel." The man nodded and said, "Up to you, sir." He stopped outside a small Tudor-style building sitting on the wharf, white and ribbed with ancient oak beams.

As the car pulled away, Robin spoke again. "We're not staying here. Business people don't stay here. That's why the driver was surprised. I don't think we're being tracked. I can't explain why, but I'm just pretty sure we're not. I feel safe, but let's not take any chances."

The three of them began walking briskly as Robin talked. "The facts should be obvious to those men who were waiting for us at Dublin Airport. If they've lost us in the vibrations, they'll figure we've flown somewhere. Several flights went to England so they may be looking for us there instead. But we know they're thorough. Since they're so well connected, they might look for us here. I usually stay in Douglas. That's where they'll probably look first, so let's cover our trail."

MacAllen stopped at the end of the wharf and turned to face Talking Panther and Silent Panther. "We'll separate. I'll send you two to Ramsey, a small village on the north end of the island. There's an old hotel where you can stay tonight. I doubt if anyone will look for you out there. The hotel might even be closed, but I have friends who know the owner and they'll get you in. I'll stay at a small cottage I know away from the towns. Right now, though, let's keep moving. There's an excellent Indian restaurant around the corner. We can talk about what happened in Dublin."

Turning a corner, they stopped and Robin looked up Douglas' main road.

"This is the promenade," he said.

It ran next to the sea alongside a wide beach that was covered with mounds of kelp. Overlooking the bay was a succession of grand old Victorian apartments, hotels and shops, built one against the other, and in various states of repair. Tram lines ran down the center of the street.

"Horses pull the trams during the summer," Robin pointed out.

"You have to turn your watch back about a century when you come here. The Manx are an ancient race, very insular. Conservative and slow to change. This used to be a famous and very popular tourist resort in Victorian times. This part of the town has remained much the same. Not because they've tried preserving it, they just keep using the buildings as they are. Tourism's pretty well died though, but not the financial business. Investors want places that don't change. Old conservative Manx values—thrift, hard work, slow to change—makes this a solid financial center.

At the Indian restaurant, Robin led the women to a corner table and remarked, "You see, Manx virtues affect everyone on the island. Even those who have immigrated here never change. This place is exactly like it was when I was here 10 years ago."

As soon as they had ordered their food and the waiter left, Robin said, "Okay, what happened at the airport?"

Talking Panther looked over at her sister and smiled before replying, "There are forms of defense that are stronger than attack. This is why the meek shall inherit the earth. Nature's reflection of this truth is camouflage. We used camouflage in Dublin to avoid conflict."

The waiter arrived with their tea. Robin leaned closer to Talking Panther as she continued speaking. "Silent Panther felt danger at the airport just as you did. When we walked inside the terminal, we immediately saw the men waiting for you. We also felt your spiritual change. Your animal guide has led you on to a different path, one that is new for you and lacks aggression. But it does alter the signal in the vibrations so the Controllers can still feel you. Yet they don't know precisely who you are.

"You have not yet learned how to defend yourself without the use of aggression. Avoiding conflict rather than using it will make you safer, but now you are like the molting crab, vulnerable until his new shell hardens. We expected you would have trouble getting past the men without using force so we used a little camouflage to help you."

Despite the pungent Indian aromas drifting from the kitchen that were fighting for his attention, Robin focused on Talking Panther.

"When Silent Panther and I saw men at the Manx Air desk, I purchased a ticket in your Chilean name. Then we saw you come in and paged you to draw them away. I transformed myself to appear as you."

He asked, "You mean you can change your shape to look like anyone?"

"I never change my shape, Robin. I simply let nature choose a different way for light to reflect on me. Others choose how they interpret the reflection they see."

The waiter arrived with steaming curries, hot basmati rice, warm naan bread, spiced vegetables and cool raitas. "Were you the man, uh, I mean the person I saw walk to the Aer Lingus counter after I was paged?"

Talking Panther grinned. "Indeed I was. I looked like a man to those who wanted me to look that way. You must have expected me to look like you just as your pursuers did."

"You mean you can look differently to different people at the same time?"

Her reply was very soft. "All vision is a matter of interpretation. If one child has been punished with a Ping-Pong paddle and another has used it only to play happy games, do you think that each sees the same paddle? One sees a toy and is filled with laughter and joy; the other sees only an instrument of pain and begins to cry. But isn't the paddle the same? Sight is an illusion. Our eyes alter reality every time we open them. We distort reality so we can see what we expect to see."

"That's just like making money," he said. "Every time there is change in the world, most people see it as a problem. A few, however, see it as opportunity and make even more money. Good investors are those who see things in different ways. But how do you actually change the way people see you?"

Talking Panther stopped and looked down at her plate. When she spoke, it was almost in a whisper. "Concentrated thoughts can alter the most basic statistical laws affecting light. All the sensory stimuli –sight, taste, sound, touch and smell–are produced by variations of vibrations in molecules. These molecular vibrations are in turn regulated by trillions and trillions of vibrational threads that are finer than atoms. The weave of these threads is reality. You could call them the sutures that tie together the laws of the universe."

MacAllen had to lean closer to Talking Panther as her voice grew even more muted. "With practice and the dedication of meditating on a Golden Word, you can tune your thoughts to vibrate at the level of these universal threads. Each Golden Word is a different vibration affecting a different thread. By focusing on a particular Golden Word you shift the weave of these threads."

Now, she spoke with more emphasis. "Thoughts, like everything else in the universe, are vibrations. Just like singers who can hit certain notes which shatter glass, you can focus a correct thought, such as a Golden Word, and alter the threads of creation."

"Do you mean that with the Golden Words I will have the ability to shift even the smallest parts of creation?" Robin asked.

"There is no smallest part of creation, Robin. Since nature is infinite, it is both large and small. If there were a smallest point, what would lie beyond? Nature is a never ending process of smaller and smaller vibrations and larger and larger cycles continuing forever."

Robin hesitated then said, "What I really meant is will I have the power to change how I look?"

She touched his hand. "Robin, you must be very careful with these powers. The lesson of the Golden Words is that we have no power and never will. Power over others is a concept born from misunderstanding our individual relationship to the universe. Power is a word that implies we are separate from the rest of the universe.

"We cannot use the Golden Words to gain or to use power. This would only emphasize the tricks our senses play upon us. We use the Golden Words to see beyond the illusions of our mind and see the connections among everything. We use the words only to attune ourselves with nature. When we are one with nature, we are power. When we use the Golden Words, we place an intent in the universe, then prepare to accept whatever happens. The only power that comes from the Golden Words is our ability to recognize, accept and adapt to the ultimate desires of the forces of nature.

"The Controllers try to use the Words to gain power, to dominate. This is what will destroy them in the end!" She banged her fist on the table with surprising severity. "You will gain happiness through the Golden Words, Robin, if you listen and act as your spirit tells you. At the airport this morning, I used the words that I know affect light. I then let nature decide what others saw. I have no power and I never will. Nor will you. We cannot even understand what power is, let alone use it.

"However, if we use the Golden Words regularly, perhaps one day we can obtain complete humility. Then perhaps we can speak the word 'power' and begin to comprehend its meaning. Our food is growing cold. Let's eat."

They ate slowly and in perfect silence.

After the plates had been removed, MacAllen spoke. "What you said earlier explains why I find Indian food so satisfying. Now, I can look at food as a weave of six vibrational patterns we call sweet, sour, pungent, salty, astringent and bitter. In order to remain balanced, we need a combination of these six. My hunger could be a search for vibrational balance.

"But why do I have a hunger for power? Was this why you said I have to learn humility before I can have power?"

Talking Panther folded her hands in her lap and beamed. "You are a good student and have learned one of the most important lessons from the Golden Words. We know every action has an opposite and equal reaction. Every thought, idea, trait, and vibration must have an opposite balance. Yes, humility is the balance of power. Total humility must be attained before one can have absolute power. You are ready for more Golden Words. I will give them to you as quickly as I can."

"I should have known this," he replied, "because it's the same with money. The people who invest or set up a business just to get rich always fail, even if they do make money. The ones who truly prosper run businesses that serve and are concerned with others."

As the day faded into winter's early dusk, and daylight weak-ened, Robin's even mood did not blur as it usually did when this season's bitter nights were setting in. He knew now that there was a balance for the dark and the cold. MacAllen's breath caught at his unexpected embracing sense of euphoria.

"Talking Panther, Silent Panther," he said, "let's go. I feel unbelievably about what I've learned, but some things unfortunately haven't changed. Ian's still missing and the Controllers are still waiting for us, somewhere, anywhere."

CHAPTER
THIRTY FIVE

Once outside, Robin hailed a taxi. "Both of you will be going to a suburb north of Douglas called Onchan. Stop there and get another cab. Have it take you to the Grand Isle Hotel in Ramsey, a town further north at the end of the island. I'll call ahead. If the hotel is closed, I'll alert them to open for you."

After they were gone, MacAllen walked further into town and caught a taxi for himself. He rode across the island to Lhoob Dhoo Cottage near Peele where he booked into a rental unit. Though the group of cabins was quite luxurious, few people knew of them.

That night he meditated on his animal spirit before going to sleep and once again wild dreams filled his awareness. Again, when he awoke, he meditated on his animal spirit as Talking Panther had instructed. He rose in the early morning darkness and called the two Seminole women. "Get ready. I'm coming early. I've had more insights and we need to move on."

After picking them up in Ramsey, he directed the taxi to take them to Maughold, an area near a ring of Neolithic stones called Cashtal-yn-Ard.

The cabdriver was a talker. "There are not many people ta come out 'ere this time of year," he said.

"We've been to the island on business," Robin replied. "We have to leave today but wanted to see the sunrise over the castle before we go."

The driver looked back, evidently seeing one young woman and one old. He zeroed in on Silent Panther and addressed Talking Panther as "Ma'm." Each woman looked exactly the same to Robin. He wondered if he was now seeing the illusion of light differently.

Eyeing Silent Panther's legs in the rear view mirror, the driver barely managed to keep the taxi on the road as he spoke. "You ladies ever been to the castle afore? Tis a wonderful place. When the sun rises, tis glorious, but draughty and chilling this time a year. Cashtal-yn-Ard is an old Celtic name, you know. Means 'castle on the height. Our isle's an ancient and magical place. The Celts regarded it as holy. There were people here even before the Celts and they were a mystical lot. They were the original settlers coming from the north by boat 4,000 years before Christ. Farmers and hunters. Many of their arrows and spears and farming tools are in our museum now."

Robin grabbed hold of the steering wheel as the driver nearly ran off the road, but the man just kept right on talking. "These ancients built huge graves and monuments, like the Meayll Circle down south of the island near Cregneish. Gigantic stones this circle is, up to eight feet high. Tis an extremely large burial mound, one of the most unique in Britain. Real mystical these people were. Then they disappeared. No one knows what happened to em. Vanished like mists off the sea!"

The car bounced and rocked mightily as they turned onto an even rougher road. The driver droned on, keeping his monologue going effortlessly, with barely a pause. "This castle we're headin' for now is a burial place standing on the top of a headland near Port Cornaa. It's one of the largest gallery graves in all of the British Isles. Has a huge semicircle of stones."

Finally, the road ended and the three passengers left the taxi and walked to the site of the ruins. Last night's storm had ended; the sky was cloudless, the sea air bracing and very cold. They stood in the wind, shivering lightly and watching the stars' last glimmers.

The sky transformed into intense shades of salmon and orange, and the sun climbed out of the black mists spread across the horizon like a dark blanket. The sea turned blood red while they stood among the colossal stones jutting everywhere from the ground.

Robin whispered to the women, "What do these stones have to do with us? And why did my animal spirit guide me here?"

Neither replied. Again, he looked back at the heather-covered moor barren in its winter garb. Robin pulled both women close to him and whispered again, "This is a place of enormous beauty. It has such balance and peace. I've been here before, but my animal spirit brought me here to share this with you."

Talking Panther looked up, capturing him with her jet-black eyes. She spoke quietly. "You have been here before. So have I. But not my body. I have visited here many times in spirit. Now I know why.

"There is more you feel than just peace, Robin. Come sit. It is time to receive the Golden Words that are for you now. I do not have to prepare. I have been preparing for this moment in my dreams since I was a young girl."

All three sat sheltered from the wind in a small indentation in a rock, their eyes closed. Talking Panther began speaking in a sweet lilting chant. "The Golden Words are of the spirits and we are here with the spirits of so many suns and sons. Here are the spirits for you and here are your Golden Words."

Robin opened his eyes for a moment and saw Talking Panther unbutton her coat. Rays of sunlight flickered like jewels on her copper skin. He sank back into tranquility as Talking Panther began to speak again.

"The eighth Golden Word is *Opossum*. This spirit engenders compassion for even the most violent predator. By being willing to bare its throat to any threat, the opossum can live among ferocious beasts without use of claw, and walk among the most savage without fang. The eighth Golden Word is Opossum."

Talking Panther turned and faced the sun that was full in the sky and continued. "The ninth word is *Alligator* who lies for hours absorbing the strength of the sun. Alligators store in them the very nature of the cosmos. Even when the sun sets, they are sustained in its boundless wisdom. The ninth word is Alligator."

Talking Panther radiated a passion that spread through his body to the depths of his soul. "The tenth Golden Word is *Coyote*. The coyote sings his song in harmony with the spirit of the moon. He sings to its ivory light and through his song always knows where he is in relation to the moon and the stars. The coyote can range far and spread wide yet always knows where to go. Through this wisdom, the coyote survives and grows even through the greatest obstacles, when all wish that he were no more. The tenth word is Coyote."

A whiff of smoke from a farmer's cottage briefly caught Robin's attention. And then he continued to listen, and absorb Talking Panther's words. "The eleventh Golden Word is *Tortoise*. This spirit is of the tortoise who returns to his shell upon danger or for rest. There, he concentrates on his inner being which is the center of his universe, and he stays warm, safe and calm. Thus he lives without hurry or fear and in this way he lives long. The eleventh word is Tortoise.

"The twelfth Golden Word is *Elk*. The elk lives well in harsh highlands and dense forest where he cannot easily be seen. Through his long hollow throat he sings the shrill song that echoes a love that is nature itself. Through this song he sows his seeds of creation that burst forth between his hunger and thirst and thus allows the herd to grow. The twelfth word is Elk."

Talking Panther paused very briefly and Robin opened his eyes.

"The thirteenth Golden Word is *Porpoise*. The porpoise is a sleek creature of the water that draws the spirit of life deep into the tubes of its chest and can remain without breath. This stilled pulse of the deep is at peace and in nature's grace as it sings its tune with the cosmos and is delivered the bounties of the sea. The thirteenth word is Porpoise."

As Talking Panther's chant went on, Robin shut his eyes once more. "The fourteenth word is of the *Eagle* who soars high above the land. His spirit of sight allows him to speak with the clouds and soar with the highest winds, yet still see his smallest prey below. With this spirit of sight, the eagle's heart can rise to the gods and be free, yet his stomach remains full. The fourteenth word is Eagle."

Robin opened his eyes and saw that Talking Panther was walking to him. She sat close and the marvelous warmth she radiated pulsed through him. She took his hand in hers and spoke gently.

"The fifteenth word is *Deer* with his keen senses of hearing, touch and smell. His spirit of alertness guides him to food and away from danger. In this spirit he remains hidden, even when his enemy is near. Thus his life is long and his family grows. The fifteenth word is Deer."

She moved even nearer and whispered, "Robin, you now have fifteen Golden Words. In this number there is great balance and through these spirits you can know all there is to know, the harmony of creation and the balance of the cosmos. Through them you can free yourself from your pride. With these words you can take your place as the lowest creature on earth and at the same time, the highest god. And with these words, you can know nature's true spirit, humility. And from humility you can know true freedom. I bless upon you these spirits."

As they sat side by side in silence, they each allowed the spirits to float in and out of their minds.

A car horn sounded. It was time to head for the ferry.

CHAPTER
THIRTY SIX

The ferry rocked as it plowed into a wave. Robin stood and steadied himself against the slow roll of the boat. They didn't speak in the taxi that had taken them from Maughold to the Palace Hotel. From there they had taken separate taxis to the pier in Douglas. Then as soon as they boarded, Talking Panther and Silent Panther had disappeared below.

Now, as he looked into the clear indigo sea and smelled the salt on the fresh breeze, Robin let the Golden Words run over and over in his mind.

Talking Panther came on deck. "Where's Silent Panther?" he asked. She pulled her coat tight around her neck and shivered. He moved closer and she placed her arm in his. He looked around to make sure no one was near. Talking Panther spoke first, her reply only just cutting above the wind and the waves breaking on the bow.

"She is feeling the vibrations."

"I'm confused," Robin said. "I see how Golden Words can help in my business. My job is to help people see through illusion, to understand fundamental economic truths. Investors shouldn't concentrate on knowing stocks and markets but should be looking at deeper fundamentals. The deeper the better. Instead of watching share prices, they must study the needs of people and how to fill them. With the Golden Words, I can help them look below the obvious needs to the roots of what makes mankind work."

They turned and walked out of the wind as he continued. "But how do I actually use them to invest better or find Ian or do whatever I'm trying to do? Suppose I can learn to modify my shape with these Words. How does that help me in practical life?"

Talking Panther looked back at the horizon where the Isle of Man had faded from view. "Thinking about the Words means nothing. Look at the wake of this boat," she said. "Do you know what it represents?"

MacAllen looked back. "Motion?" he asked. "Doesn't it represent the opposite reaction to the motion of the boat?"

"You are correct on one level, Robin," she said, "but on another level that wake is wasted energy. The engine is forcing this boat to go where it does not wish to be. The wake is a sign of the effort needed to make this ferry go. Imagine yourself paddling up a stream. You must row hard, and you leave a wide trail in the water. You spend great effort, and still your speed is slow. If you travel down the stream, you don't have to paddle. You only have to steer and you leave no trail. With little effort, you travel far.

"If you think about the Golden Words, you are not opening your heart, you are opening your mind. Just think the Word, not about it. Just focus your thoughts on the Words and unite them with the heart."

"But if an engine didn't push the ferry we couldn't get where we wanted to go."

She had led him perfectly to this point. "You are right, Robin. We often think we know where we want to go, when really we don't. Day in and day out, we paddle up streams we do not even know. We are caught in illusions and are blind to brighter, easier paths. Better lives are always there for us if we just let them speak to us. When you think the Golden Words, they will speak to you."

"You mean we should just let life lead us wherever?"

Talking Panther smiled and answered, "If you cruised in nature's stream at least a little, wouldn't you have more silence to hear? Wouldn't you have more time and energy to enjoy the journey? What a struggle it is to paddle upstream!"

Before Robin could answer, Talking Panther reached up and kissed him lightly on the cheek, stood back and smiled affectionately at him. "You deserve the Golden Words, Robin. You have realized more already than most understand in a lifetime. But there is more for you to understand now.

"When the spirits of the Golden Words become you and you become them, you are one with the spirit. You do not become strong when you know the spirit of the buffalo. You become strength! If you travel effortlessly with the stream of life, after a while you are the stream. Then you not only travel without effort, you also know where you're going."

The ferry changed course slightly and Robin and Talking Panther fell into shade. They were immediately chilled. They walked across the deck and were again warmed by the slender rays of the winter sun. MacAllen leaned on the rail and looked out at the sea as Talking Panther asked him another question. "What do you think of when you think of a river?"

Without delay he replied, "Water."

"This is precisely why we need the Golden Words. We usually only think of what we sense. This is why it is important to become one with the spirits. This is why you are strength when you think of the buffalo and are not just trying to become strong. We fool ourselves with our senses. A river means water to our senses, but water is just a small part of the river. Think about the many spirits that guide the river."

Robin shook his head. "I think I'm missing the point," he replied.

"The true nature of the river is emptiness, Robin. Isn't the spirit of emptiness the creation of all that which is full? Isn't a river an empty channel without it? Without motion a river is only a long narrow lake. Aren't lives and deaths of fish, birds, plants, animals, even the births of great nations part of rivers? Yet all we see is water."

Talking Panther plucked a bubble of water off the railing. "Water can be the rain or the dew or sweet nectar on the songbird's tongue. Water is not the river. If we wish to know the river but think of water, we fail. In order to know water's reality, we must become vacuums.

Then we can become the river."

Robin replied, "I still don't get how just thinking can help me change shape or color like you do. I don't see how thoughts can change physical parts of my body."

She smiled. "How do you think the chameleon changes color, Robin, or a larva grows wings and becomes a butterfly? All these beautiful things begin with a thought."

"Sure," he replied. "They have some spirit that allows them to change, but they don't actually think these changes. Their genetic makeup makes the changes happen without thought."

"Are we so proud that our intellect has to take credit for every-thing?" she asked. "The thoughts from our intellect come from the same source as our genetic thoughts; they're all part of this same bundle of opinions we call ourselves. Using the Golden Words can change both these processes which we call our intellect and our genetics."

The intense cold had grabbed them once again and they walked towards the ferry's stern searching for a more pleasant place to talk.

Talking Panther continued to speak. "The Golden Words connect your existence from the tiniest glimmerings of your subconscious to truth. Thinking your animal spirit with an open heart integrates your brain spheres. Your three levels of thought—local, global and uni-versal—become united. Your mind and body become integrated. Your desires become your real needs. You'll only want to go where nature will provide the most support for you."

Robin looked out, watching the ferry's wake boil and swirl in protest to the sea. "Should I think about the Golden Words twice a day, just like my animal spirit?"

Talking Panther leaned her head against his shoulder. They stood at the rail looking to where the blue of the sky slipped into the water. "Yes, to begin. This will unite your mind with the Words, in silence and action, at the gap. The other side of the gap is the spiritual side of the material reality. Nature accepts your thought in the gap and gives you positive truths in return. You rid yourself of illusions by replacing them with nature's truths. Over time, these are solidified within you. You slowly fill yourself with truth. This is how, with regular practice, you can change anything, mental or physical.

"Eventually you will think only truth even when you are awake and active. At this point, you no longer acquire power, you are power! By becoming truth in this way, at the same time you also become wisdom. This is nature's assurance that you will not misuse the true power of the universe. If you are disciplined, you will know how to act. The Words will help you find your own unique path to being one with the universe."

"Let's get out of this cold," Robin said. "We'll be in England soon, and the lion's den will appear. We'll need to be alert. You've said so much, my mind is tired. I need a rest."

They strolled, arm and arm toward the cabin and looked out over the sea. The clear sky and white tendrils of high cloud appeared frozen. The marine blue water frothed with whitecaps, whipped by the growing wind. A storm was creating itself farther out to sea, and the day was turning even more frigid and numbing.

Before stepping inside, Robin said, "What you said applies to everything. It certainly applies to wealth. Most investors study investing so much but don't make any money because they never gain any experience. They're so worried about safety they never act."

Talking Panther nodded in agreement. "And it applies to our situation right now. We're heading into the unexpected. We've been studying in silence through the Words. Hopefully we'll help Ian... maybe not, I can't tell. But I do know that nothing will happen if we don't act." She added in a voice that hardly carried over the wind, "Soon enough though, I think, we will."

CHAPTER
THIRTY SEVEN

Robin drove slowly as the women navigated through the early morning traffic of Cheltenham. Thick haze lay over the road and the acrid taste of fear bit at MacAllan's lips. The English drove in the fog like madmen. The fact that they could barely see did not seem to matter. His car had nearly been hit twice since leaving the Queens Hotel where they had stayed the night. He struggled with the car as he slowed and entered a roundabout. He was thoroughly lost, the pavement was slick, and he had to concentrate on driving on the left side of the road.

He spoke haltingly as he drove. "The plan is simple. We'll go to the post office Ian Fletcher described in his note and get directions to the cottage he found. There's got to be clues there that'll lead us to him. Somehow, searching for that cottage is the key to finding the fields and castle from my vision." He struck his fist against the steering wheel in excitement, almost lost control of the car and swerved sharply to regain his hold on the road.

He became quiet then and concentrated on making it out of town without incident. Once on the A40 London road, he drove past the village of Charlton Kings, up a road ascending steep chalky cliffs, and then turned right onto the narrow thoroughfare posted for the village of Dowdeswell.

Within minutes they reached the village—several old stone Cotswold cottages bunched against each other on a narrow strip of asphalt. Up a hill rising behind the village, several stately houses stood haughtily peering down over the cottages and fields below.

Not seeing the post office, he stopped to ask a milkman sitting in his electric truck. The man replied, "Err, the post office be three miles on. In the village of Andoversford it be."

Robin drove through Upper Dowdeswell, turned left on the A436 and saw the village he wanted. Andoversford was not a quaint sleepy Cotswold village, but was modern and built at the intersection of two busier country roads.

Shoppers already lined the streets and a crowd milled in front of the white pebbledash building housing the post office. There had been a fire there. People were talking among themselves as they looked on curiously.

After parking the car on a side street, they entered the building, a typical English post office with a small shop selling sweets, cards and nothing more. The postmaster had probably lived in back and would have made a small but steady income providing the postal service.

The fire had been severe. The walls were heavily stained and streaked charcoal and brown. The distasteful smell of burnt grease hung thickly in the air.

An elderly woman came out of the back and spoke to them in a thick Gloucestershire accent. "I'm ever so sorry, Sir, but we'rr closed. I don't know when, if ever, we'll get this shop opened. There was a terrible terrible fire 'ere last night."

Again MacAllen surveyed the mess. He felt that something was wrong and didn't want to miss any clues. He looked at Silent Panther and Talking Panther, could see nothing in their faces, and spoke to the woman. "We aren't here to buy anything. We just need to speak with Mr. Quinn."

The woman's face melted with sympathy. "Oh, was ee a friend? I'm so sorry but ee passed on last night. I'm so sorry. Such a good man. Dear, dear poor Mr. Quinn, such a shame. I just can't bring myself to believe it. 'Ere ee was so well liked and seeming so healthy too. Been 'ere thirty years 'en now 'ee's gone. Such a shame.

'Ee'll be missed. Died just last night and started that fire out back as 'ee died. Had an attack or somethin while fixen his dinner. Must've knocked some grease on the burner. Wasn't a big fire, just lots of smoke.

"They know the fire didn't kill 'im nor did the smoke. Don't know the cause of death, but you can call Dr. Barnes down in the village. 'Ee might know and 'ee'll know about the funeral. Just can't imagine. So healthy, not that old. Started 'ere as just a lad. Don't think 'ee was even pushing sixty, was 'ee?"

Bumps shot up Robin's neck. "Thanks, ma'm, you have my condolences but I didn't know Mr. Quinn. I just had a postal inquiry. I won't keep you any longer. Could you tell me where I could get some postal information?"

The woman brightened, puffed up and took an officious look as she replied, "Oh, I'm the one's in charge o' postal records now. That's why I'm 'ere, luv. Didn't really know Mr. Quinn meself. Post Office just sent me up to keep watch. But I may take over, and I'll be more efficient too."

She leaned closer and lowered her voice as she spoke again. "You're me first person who didn't know Mr. Quinn, so I should put ye straight. Not that I would speak ill of the dead, but there's been trouble 'ere. Mr. Quinn was not as reliable as he should've been. I might take over now. Won't be any more trouble if I do."

Quinn's death roused Robin's suspicions. The Controllers must be back on his trail. Things were closing in. He spoke rapidly, feeling time was running out. "Can you tell me where in Cheltenham I can find the postal records?"

The woman brightened even more. She had apparently been bored and now had something to do. "Oh, dear, you won't find any records in Cheltenham. No, they wouldn't be there."

His concern and sense of urgency were mounting steadily. He asked, "Where? Where can I find them?"

The woman looked as if she were surprised he did not already know. "But luv, they're still 'ere. That's why I'm 'ere—to guard the records. Must get them back in shape if I can."

Relief rushed over MacAllen. "Perhaps you can help me then," he said. "Mr. Quinn directed a friend of ours to a Thaxton Cottage, which received its mail here. I'm looking for this friend. Could you look in your records for directions on how to get to the cottage?"

The woman motioned for him to follow as she walked into the back of the house. "All the records will be back 'ere. If we deliver mail to that cottage, there'll be a note. Hmmm, dear, dear, this is strange, the files seem to be missing. I know Mr. Quinn kept them 'ere. Can't see them. Maybe the firemen picked them up. You know, keep 'em safe. 'Ere, I'll call the fire department."

He clipped off a quick reply as he headed toward the door. "Thanks, but don't bother. The records won't be there."

Robin returned to the car and updated Talking Panther and Silent Panther as he drove away. "The Controllers have already been here. They must've killed Quinn and taken the records. They know we're here. Innocent people are being killed! We've got to do something to stop them and we need to do it right away!"

He glanced at Talking Panther and saw her eyes were shut. She said, "Yes, Robin, they know. They gain glimpses of us, though they do not know exactly where we are. For some reason they become aware of us just once in awhile. Silent Panther and I cannot understand, but we sense that some special event takes place occasionally which gives them sight of you."

MacAllen sped towards Cheltenham. "I can't understand how they know we're here. But there's an even bigger question. Why do they treat me with such care? They've had several chances to kill me. We know they have no hesitation killing. They proved it last night. Yet every time they find me they try to take me alive. Those men in Ireland shot at our tires, not at me. I must have something they want. What could it be?"

Driving down a hill Robin saw a reservoir and Dowdeswell Wood on the right. He knew that Cheltenham would appear just around the bend.

"Let's get back to the hotel," he said. "I'm not sure where to go from here. But I know we're going to get a break. We're close to Ian

Fletcher. I can sense it."

He had been positive the post office would have the information that could lead them to Ian. Now he had no idea where to turn next. His spirits dove, forming a thick lump in the pit of his stomach. He was lost for clues and an innocent man had died. The Controllers had found him, but where were the Controllers?

Approaching the Queens Hotel where they had stayed the night, a man walking in caught Robin's eye. For the briefest moment their eyes met. The man's profile, the way he stood, seemed familiar. There was something furtive and sly about him. He was small, tough yet nimble. The man's hands were wrapped in bandages.

"Little, that was Little," he burst out.

Talking Panther and Silent Panther look at him, surprised by his outburst. "That man going into the hotel tried to grab me at Shannon Airport. He saw us drive by. We have to get out of town now!"

He stomped heavily on the gas pedal and the car lurched forward. Through the rearview mirror he saw three men rush out the hotel's entrance. A moment later a red sedan jumped out from among the parked cars and tore up the road after them.

Just then their car entered a bank of dense, blinding fog. Robin slammed the brakes, sending the car into a skid, its wheels striking the curb mercilessly. The ashen face of a woman standing on the sidewalk dissolved into terror as they streaked by.

"The road splits somewhere ahead," he shouted. "Look for it! It's a one way grid and I don't know which way to go!" MacAllen looked back. He could just make out the red car in the fog. It was nearly on them now.

And then the road divided. The women did not speak. Robin held his breath, hesitated just a second, then tore to the right. Taking a hard left, he drove on, but when he looked back the red car was still behind, and closing in on them.

He rushed through traffic, oblivious of speed or danger. Cars swerved off the road as he raced by them. He sideswiped a blue van, twisted out of control, then regained control of his steering and darted forward again. More pedestrians scrambled to get out of their way. He drove off the road and along the sidewalk.

He hit a street sign, came to a stop and glanced for an instant at the women. They were holding on for support but still appeared calm. There was grim satisfaction for Robin in the fact that these men could not unsettle either sister. Then the red car emerged out of the haze once again.

MacAllen made a hard left. Out of the fog three cars promptly shot straight at him. "We're going the wrong way!" Reacting virtually in a fraction of a second, Robin slammed on the brakes and spun down an alley so narrow and tight the car scraped the walls on both its sides.

There was a loud bang behind him. Brakes were screeching and a crash echoed in the distance. The red car, having half missed the turn, knocked solidly against the side of the building and bounced back into the road where it was suddenly slammed into by a huge truck. Little and Large had failed again.

The alley ended. Robin turned right onto another road. He stopped, checked to see which way the traffic flowed, and drove on slowly. Only then did he look at Talking Panther and Silent Panther. Both sat motionless, eyes closed, faces passive and untroubled. They said nothing. Robin shook his head, smiled and drove out of town into the countryside. Seven miles later, an old whitewashed building with a faded sign appeared. It was the White Swan.

"We'll stop here. I don't know why, but we should. Besides it's time for lunch. We may be lost, but that doesn't mean we have to starve."

They entered a room with low ceilings supported by a patchwork of ancient smoke-stained oak beams. Seats of worn velvet flanked the booths next to the walls. Two battered round tables sat in the center opposite a wide-mouth fireplace in which a coal fire now sputtered and burned.

MacAllen looked at the modern mock-Tudor bar across the room, standing among the time worn furniture like a poorly fitting toupee. Two men in dirty overalls lounged at the bar drinking pints of bitter ale. The rest of the room was empty.

Robin coughed at the smoke hanging in the stale air and heard floorboards creak as he approached a thickset woman standing behind the bar. "Could I have three ploughmans and three cups of coffee?"

"Ta, love," she said. "Anything else?"

An inner compulsion made him ask, "Ever heard of Thaxton Cottage?"

The woman stood quietly for a moment and then asked the men, "Stan, Colin, ya know Thaxton Cottage?"

They shook their heads.

"Sorry, love, that's not a name standin' out in our minds, but there be so many little places scattered about 'ere. I've a map though. If you could look and point out the place I might be able to help you more." She reached below the bar and handed him a map. Like many things in this room, it too looked well used, its creases torn and held together with tape.

"Thanks," he said. "Let me study this and see."

"Ta," she replied.

Robin and the two women sat around a scarred table, allowing the blaze in the fireplace to lessen the cold inside them. Talking Panther carefully unfolded the map. Robin had to force himself not to shout out, "That's the map I saw in my dream!"

It was an Ordinance Survey Map, a Landranger 1-1/4 inch per mile. It provided amazing detail of the lay of the land, showing almost every building and landmark that existed. They pored over it.

Suddenly Talking Panther said, "Silent Panther has a theory, Robin. This may seem wild, but look at these Roman burial mounds, they're called tumuli, and other forts and castles marked here on the map. See how they all lie in straight lines. For example, those that start at Cleeve Hill run all the way to Cirencester and beyond to Ashton Keynes. Silent Panther sees an association here, a very significant link."

She spread the map, reached over for a magazine and used it as a straight edge to run along a line of ancient sites.

"When our original civilization fell, the keepers of wisdom went far and wide and started many new great civilizations. One of these civilizations was Egypt, another was a great tribe in the Andes of South America. Others were in India and China."

Talking Panther stopped speaking as the stout woman brought lunch and put more coal in the fire. As she walked away, Talking Panther continued.

"There is a story not often told of ley–lines in the earth that would speak to us if we listened. We know ancient civilizations used these lines to communicate with one another. Silent Panther thinks the Romans and other ancient civilizations knew of these lines and used them for communication. That is why they built so many sites along these straight lines."

Robin regarded her daintily taking a bite of her lunch. She stopped talking and became silent as she ate. He ate as well until she began speaking again.

"If there is a connection between the Romans and the American Indians it may be through Egypt. Much of Roman culture actually began in Egypt. There is a connection that few know about, that has been handed down only by the Carriers of the Word. But if you look at Egyptian art and much of that from the Americas, you can quickly see similarities.

"There was communion between them. But no one knows how, or how much knowledge was shared. Part of that knowledge was how to follow and use the ley lines. Silent Panther and I have known of this but have never used their force. These are subtle lines of energy that cross the lands. Part of this must have been learned by the Romans. This is why they built such linear, direct long roads. They believed building on the ley gave Roman travelers extra strength and energy. They also used the lines for communication. Similar sciences still exist in much of the world. The Chinese science of Feng Shui acknowledges these lines and measures their energy and flow."

Talking Panther's enthusiasm heightened and she made sweeping gestures with her arms and showed him points on the map as she spoke.

"See how the Romans used straight lines. Look at the roads on this map. See how the roads from Cirencester branch straight out like spokes from the hub of a wheel. Cirencester is at the beginning of a huge power source and those roads follow ley lines, every one of them. The Romans used these lines in other lesser-known ways, as well. Understanding this could explain how you have been followed all over the world. Ley lines are everywhere. They are connected in a global energy grid."

She stopped talking as a man entered the room and looked around him. When the man joined the other two at the bar and ordered a bottle of ale, Robin's tension relaxed. He returned his attention to Talking Panther.

"Every person is an electromagnetic device and generates a unique electrical signal. This signal is very subtle, but every time we cross a ley line, our electrical signal disturbs that line's energy. The disturbance creates unique signals, and these can be tuned into like a radio broadcast. If someone has the right equipment and knows how, he could tune into your frequency when you pass through a ley line. These signals work like directional indicators and are as fast as radio waves. Whoever is seeking us has communication stations along the major lines.

"This explains what Ian Fletcher found in that cabin and how they locked in on him. This explains how you were gripped and paralyzed by an unseen force and how you have been followed since. And how they follow us even when you block your thoughts. They catch your signal when you cross a ley. There are many of these lines; that's why they pick you up again and again. They are looking for us right now."

Hearing this MacAllen stood to leave immediately, but was pulled back down by Talking Panther. "We are safe here. Everything depends on the ley lines. The map shows us this. I believe if we had passed a ley lines, they would already have sent someone here. Let's wait. Moving around will increase our risk. A ley line might be just ahead. Also, we should stay because now I know how to show you where Thaxton Cottage must be."

Talking Panther pointed to the map as she spoke. "We can't see ley lines, but we can see the communication lines the Romans and

Gary A. Scott

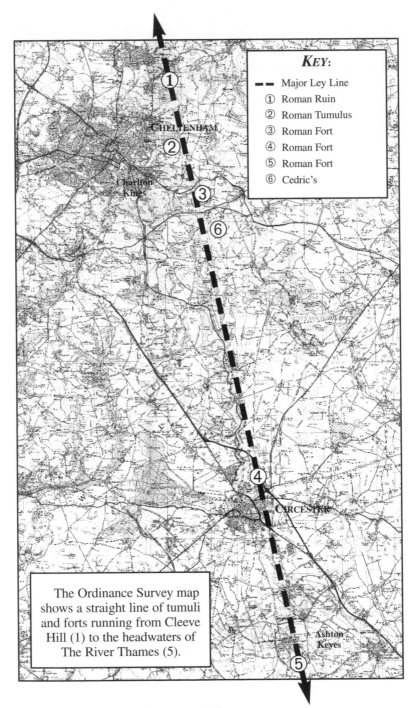

KEY:

- **– –** Major Ley Line
- ① Roman Ruin
- ② Roman Tumulus
- ③ Roman Fort
- ④ Roman Fort
- ⑤ Roman Fort
- ⑥ Cedric's

The Ordinance Survey map shows a straight line of tumuli and forts running from Cleeve Hill (1) to the headwaters of The River Thames (5).

other ancient civilizations used. They follow the ley lines. Look at this ancient Roman tumulus located just to the northwest of Cheltenham on Cleeve Hill. It shows on the map as a viewpoint, just as this burial mound at St. Paul's Epistle to the southwest of Cheltenham does. Now look what happens if we draw a straight line from one tumulus to the next, and then continue south. Look at these other forts on the map that were not Roman. They were built along the lines. Older cultures understood this power too."

A straight line ran directly to yet a third tumulus in Cirencester.

"Cirencester was Roman and is a central city," Talking Panther said. "Notice how roads spoke throughout the area from Cirencester. The tumuli were used to communicate from one mound to the next. This line extending from Cirencester is a vital one. See what happens when we extend the line a little further. It reaches two special termini that sit where Derry Brook and Swill Brook come together and form the River Thames. This is the most important river in the country. Ley lines often follow or run under large lines of water. These lines could run all the way to London."

Talking Panther's exquisite face grew hard and her voice became severe. "Now that we know how they follow us, all we have to do is backtrack to find them. We can follow the ley lines right to their home. Thaxton Cottage must sit on one of these termini. That's why the golden orb that Ian Fletcher found was there."

Robin grinned. A keen sense of satisfaction was beginning to build. "Best we've been able to do up till now is run... hide from the Controllers. Now it's time for us to attack."

CHAPTER
THIRTY EIGHT

The three of them stood on a hilltop. Robin focused his binoculars on Cheltenham and watched the city awaken. He glimpsed slender, curled tendrils of smoke escape from chimney tops. Their sooty webs smudged the unclouded early morning sky. Automobile headlights cut through the gray half-light of dawn. A steady hum of traffic grew and announced that the town was waking.

They had walked across a golf course frosted white in the morning chill. The icy blanket crunched beneath their feet and dampened their shoes. Robin shrugged deeper into his thick wool sweater, reviewing his situation and the moves that lay ahead.

"This is Cleeve Hill, the northern edge of a great geological fault that forms part of the Cotswold Way. Millions of years ago this fault created huge cliffs and rifts that rise sharply and dominate the Severn Valley."

MacAllen now moved to the crest of the rift, looked to the west and pointed as he spoke again. "That's Cheltenham. From here it's approximately four miles away. Further on, you can see the motorway and the whole of the Vale of Gloucestershire. That flat valley slides right into the River Severn. You'll see it, with the Malvern Hills behind, as the day gets lighter. The ley lines we have plotted runs right along this rift. The lines must be related to this broken geology."

Robin lowered the binoculars and listened to Talking Panther's reply. "Everything in the universe is related, Robin. We cannot say ley lines are related to geology because ley lines are geology. Geology does not affect ley. The lines create patterns in the land we see and have named mountains, rifts and crests. To look at rock formations as separate from the energy of the earth is like medicine that studies the body while ignoring the soul. Ley lines are the earth's thoughts."

The woman walked towards him, stopped and looked over the cliffs as she continued to speak. "Ley lines are vibrations or energy of the earth. They are its heart pulsing deep within, ringing from its mantle and singing its songs. Mountains and rifts, cataracts, valleys, rivers and plains are only the stirrings of the earth's soul that swell to the sweet music of this tune. Yet modern science dwells on words like 'rock formation' and 'crystalline structure' and thinks this tells of the earth."

"Music of the earth is a beautiful way to describe geology," Robin said. "You speak as if the earth's alive."

The morning's first hints of sunlight streamed across Talking Panther's face as she said, "What is life, Robin? Some people so separate themselves from the rocks and the stones they believe humans are animate and stones are not. These people have lost the real meaning of life. Animate comes from the Latin word animatus, which means life force, spirit. Instead of understanding how minerals have spirits or a life force exactly like ours, people misunderstand. They see only one small part of the bigger picture and believe stones do not have intelligence and are not connected with mankind.

"These stones may not have a life force that moves them like ours, but they certainly are not still. They vibrate with intelligence and with great spirit. Look how long they remember to remain what they are."

"Is this how my second sight works? Does it work through the vibrations?" Robin asked.

She replied with enthusiasm, "Yes, Robin, just like the gold, or a dowsing rod. Some part of you tunes in and magnifies vibrations. Everything is affected by many different kinds of earth vibrations. For example, pigeons sense the earth vibrations we call magnetism and are able to fly to their home. Scientists would say the pigeon

becomes a conductor moving through a magnetic field. This movement induces a voltage difference within the bird. The pigeon needs
only to fly in the direction that brings it to the magnetic intensity that
sings 'You are home.' Our people would say that the bird feels the
spirit of the earth and follows.

"You, however, do not need the gold or the rod. Your sensitivity
feels the vibrations change within your head. When you listen to
your animal spirit, you let strong spirits within feel the vibration and
guide you. Your animal spirit visions are a translation of what you
cannot say and what your mind cannot comprehend. That is how we
are here now. This is why I know we will find your friend."

MacAllen's confidence in the search for Ian strengthened.
Regardless he would have persisted. Despite the continued resistance of his logic, he preferred following spirits over a futile chase.
As the light heightened, Robin observed the landscape to the south
and spoke to the women. "I agree. We'll find Ian soon. We'll find
that cottage. And the clues we need."

As he moved his field glasses in a slow arc, Robin remembered
how they had spent yesterday afternoon plotting the ley lines on the
map. They had not returned to the Queens Hotel, but had chosen a
small inn near the village of Chedworth so they could stay east of the
main ley line that appeared so evident on the map. We remained
invisible to the Controllers by not crossing those lines, he thought.

Robin said, "No one seems to have picked up our trail. But what
happens if we stumble across another ley line here?"

He gazed over the valley as Talking Panther replied, "There are
many lines of energy, some minor, others major. The line we have
plotted is strong. The only time the Controllers can feel is when we
cross over strong lines. If they did not limit their listening to major
vibrations, they would be overwhelmed."

As they started down the trail, Robin reviewed his plan. "Okay,
we'll walk this ley line right to Dowdeswell. If we haven't found
Thaxton Cottage we'll keep going on to the Andoversford post
office, looking for the cottage as we go. We know from Ian's letter
that this cottage isn't far from the post office. The area is covered

with footpaths, so we'll just keep hiking in the area until we find what we're looking for."

MacAllen walked and looked around as the sunlight intensified. Then he stopped and used his field glasses to scope the land below. After a careful search they hiked south on the Cotswold Way, a large well-maintained path running east of the ley line for about two miles. They stopped at each high point and carefully looked through binoculars at the countryside below.

Upon reaching a small road, they turned west on a smaller path leading out over a plateau that ended in a sharp cliff. From there they had an expansive view with vistas of the many valleys below. He pointed Andoversford out in the distance, almost due south. "The village on the right of it is Dowdeswell. The cottage could be any-where here. We should…"

He abruptly stopped speaking and focused his field glasses on the valley below. The sun rose behind him now, the fields just turn-ing from white to the ochre and browns of dried wheat and corn. At the end of the field, an ancient manor house loomed, an immense castle of tawny stone. Monumental ramparts cut into the sky. Bright flags whipped proudly in the wind. The gates were shut and by them stood two animals. They were lions sculpted out of rock, staring savagely ahead. He surveyed the castle and the lions. Then after a moment he spoke. "We won't need to find the cottage after all. We found the castle… the castle I dreamed and… Ian's in there. I know it." The anger, frustration and tension of the preceding days pinched his mouth into a grimace.

"Now it's our turn. Let's get down there. We're going to find Ian."

CHAPTER
THIRTY NINE

Alternately, Robin was bombarded with seething waves of fury and dread. His rented Mercedes rolled through the massive iron gates that protected the estate. As he entered the drive, an ominous-looking cloud suddenly obscured the sun and the sky turned forbidding. The wind shrieked and lashed icy tendrils at the trees. An omen? But it didn't matter. He was going in anyway. He drove ahead.

They had to walk into the unknown. He was ready and single-mindedly determined to find his friend, despite the surges of pent-up rage he was experiencing, could almost taste.

The car's tires crunched over thick gravel, sounding like small explosions. He spoke to the two sisters, attempting to ease his tension. "I'm ready for whatever's in this castle, but I'm wound tighter than a piano string."

"We are, too," Talking Panther replied. "There are times when tension is good. The panther is tense before she strikes her prey."

The gravel entrance, edged with alternating rows of trees and thick hedges, looked a mile long; it spiraled and twisted like a coiled snake. The castle revealed itself, then disappeared again behind the shrubs.

MacAllen drove slowly, moving closer and closer to the very considerable manor house that sprang again into view. Reflecting the morning sun, at a distance the house's tawny stone appeared quite beautiful. Now, as the sky turned gray, Robin saw that the stone was damp, smudged and black. The surroundings grew foreboding, malignant, as the Mercedes continued its slow approach. Then the house disappeared behind another thick hedgerow.

Robin followed the gravel road as it turned left and saw the mansion through a break in the hedge. Near the house was a rusted fence of heavy metal, charcoal-colored and spiked. Ancient gargoyles and two tremendous carved lions stood, icy stone cloaked in a weighty blanket of mold. Robin shuddered as the vacant granite eyes of the lions bore into him, profane faces contorted into malevolent grins. They spoke to him as guardians of the darkness.

"I'll get out near the house and work my way through the shrubs to the rear," he said. "Talking Panther, you inquire at the front door. Ask to see the head of the house. Say you're on an urgent matter that can only be discussed with the owner. Try to get inside, see whatever you can. Keep the owner busy claiming to be a photographer wanting to do a photographic essay of the manor. Silent Panther, you stay here and feel the vibrations while I try to get in from the rear and find Ian."

They turned one more bend and he saw the house directly ahead of them. He stopped just before the gate. "Okay, I'll get out here and work my way through these bushes to the back. Talking Panther, be careful. If you feel any trouble, get out and go back to the hotel. Silent Panther, if you feel any trouble at all, honk the car horn. If I hear you honking, I'll come back, but don't wait if you're at risk. Leave and send the police. I'll take care of myself."

He stepped out of the Mercedes and was about to walk into the thick tall cedar bushes when he was stopped by a man's voice calling his name.

"Mr. MacAllen! There is no need to use the service entrance. Please come in and do bring those beautiful, enchanting native women with you. I have waited such a long while to meet you again. Tea is ready. We can sit and chat—you, me, the young ladies and Mr. Fletcher!"

Robin was so stunned that for a moment he could not move. He was elated at the mention of Ian's name. An enormous wave rocked him at the same time. He glanced at Silent Panther and Talking Panther. For the first time since they had started this journey, he saw that they were truly startled.

He heard the crunch of footsteps on the gravel. Someone was walking towards the car. The man who had just spoken approached. He was tall and slim, elegantly dressed in black silk shirt, dark corduroy trousers and high-topped leather riding boots. He appeared to be middle-aged. He had high cheekbones and was cleanly shaven, had a ruddy complexion and well-oiled black hair slicked away from a deep widow's peak. Cedric!

The man spoke again, his voice unctuous and smooth. "Come, now, Mr. MacAllen, you have traveled so far. You must be exhausted. And we have much to discuss. Please, do come in. The weather is appalling out here. You will enjoy the fire. You are quite safe you know; nothing to bother about here. Mr. Fletcher and I can explain everything."

Robin looked at both women. Their eyes were closed and they looked calm, steady. Talking Panther whispered, "We can't feel anything here, Robin. We cannot sense a thing! Do we have a choice?"

This was Cedric. This was the man in his vision. His dream had warned him that Cedric was a treacherous man who would do anything to get his way. He was self-centered, evil, wanting everything and willing to do whatever was required to procure it, regardless of the rights of others, or their pain. Actually, the man liked to watch pain. He wanted others to suffer. Cedric would kill without a second thought. And he had.

Robin knew the two women were with him totally, as far as death. Now the decision was his. His mind reeled. Their lives and Ian's life could well depend on his next move.

All this raced through Robin's heart as Cedric offered his hand to shake Robin's. "Pine-Coufie is my name, Cedric Pine-Coufie. We met once, long ago. I'm so pleased you are here. Come, follow me." Pine-Coufie spoke in a high-pitched dead voice that indicated he was anything but pleased.

"We've met?" Robin replied, his mind trying to sort the face and the voice. He searched his memory and then recalled Pine-Coufie. He suddenly understood why the man had seemed so familiar in his dream.

"Yes," Pine-Coufie replied. "About twenty years ago."

Robin had been operating from the Philippines and was consulting for a British client named Royce whose ill health had forced him to retire and sell his manufacturing firm. The buyer was Cedric Pine-Coufie, the second son of one of England's oldest families, one that had influenced England for centuries. With a history of ruthless but self-serving support for the Royal Family, the Pine-Coufies had prospered, especially during colonial times. Mainly they had grown vastly wealthy at the expense of the East Indians.

Stories of immense fortunes built from factories run by near-slaves brutalized by unimaginable atrocities had been told all too frequently not to be true. There had been a family secret concerning Pine-Coufie's elder brother who should have inherited the estate. He had died early... mysteriously, in India, as had the senior Pine-Coufie's second wife.

Robin recalled the meeting where he and Cedric had met. The Pine-Coufies' large house had overlooked Manila Bay. They had met in an oppressive cavernous hall. The walls were covered with tiger skins and mounts of elephant. There were many other treasures, all memorabilia of the stains left on colonial lands.

He remembered Cedric, a man refined by generations of unchecked exploitative families, and the tragedy that had occurred. His client, Royce, had been a good person. He came from a wealthy family of the old school—proud, responsible, honest and loyal to the core. His word had been his bond; he and Robin had naturally accepted Cedric's word.

"Every employee will be kept on," Cedric had promised. "Plans will be developed to build an even larger business to benefit the community." On a handshake the deal had been made.

Cedric had immediately moved the business from the Philippines to India and had terminated the entire workforce. Simultaneously, a trustee of the company had embezzled the entire pension fund and mysteriously disappeared. The small village that Royce's business almost exclusively employed had been destroyed.

Disgraced and in shock, Royce had hung himself. Royce's death had ended the monthly endowment for life Cedric was to have paid for the business, leaving Royce's wife of fifty years destitute. Robin had given her money just to return home. He remembered how Melanie had tried to help the poor woman. That had been when Melanie had disappeared!

Blood pounded in his Robin's head. A red haze filled his line of sight.

Robin had never believed Royce's death had been a suicide. Nor had he believed that the company's trustee had stolen the pension. He had always felt that both men had been killed, leaving Cedric the business and pension funds at no cost.

MacAllen's mind exploded with comprehension. Melanie had been helping Royce's wife pack and was cleaning up Royce's papers. Suppose she had stumbled across information that implicated Cedric! Rage hammered and tore through him, and his body prepared to strike out.

Talking Panther's hand was suddenly on his arm. "Good Morning, Mr. Pine-Coufie. My name is Talon Osceola. This is my sister, Wing. We are friends of Mr. MacAllen's."

Her gentle touch helped Robin catch himself. There's enough terrible danger here without losing my cool. That bastard.

Somehow Melanie... He knew he had to calm down. He's leading us into a trap. But we have to go through with this. It's the only way to find Ian.

Cedric motioned them to follow. Robin watched Pine-Coufie's stiff, short steps. He let Pine-Coufie enter the house first and went in next to block the two women from any immediate danger there might be. He scrutinized the large entrance hall. Only a butler was waiting nearby.

The hall, paved with massive flagstones, led to two wide stone staircases rising on opposite sides of the room. Two enormous bouquets of long-stemmed red roses stood in pedestal vases across the hall near an arch. Beyond the arch he could see a sitting room with high ceiling and framed windows overlooking a huge, very well manicured lawn. The crack and roar of a fireplace came from that room.

The three of them followed Pine-Coufie through the entrance hall and past the fire in the sitting room, where they turned left into a large study with walls covered in mahogany and leather panels. Here another fire was burning. In the center of the room, sitting before the hearth in a chair of cracked leather, was Ian Fletcher.

"Ian, for God's sake! Are you all right?" Robin blurted out as he rushed into the room.

Ian glanced at him briefly and then turned without reply and stared vacantly into the flames. Robin searched Ian's blank face, spun around and asked Pine-Coufie, "What have you done to him?"

Hearing no answer, he turned and saw Pine-Coufie locking the door. He turned to face Robin. A sudden, baleful expression had transformed the man's face. Cedric's look of urbanity had changed into an evil malevolent glare—the look of a death mask was reflected eerily at Robin in the glow of the firelight.

Pine-Coufie spoke, the oily tone gone. It was replaced by a brusque ugly voice. "No, Mr. MacAllen, Mr. Fletcher is not quite salubrious. We have had to use some measures that have been, shall I say, harsh. In the last few days we have used influential drugs. He is recovering and should be able to speak coherently in a few moments. For the time being, you and I, and these beautiful ladies shall have a chat. I trust you will be more, shall I say, accommodating than Mr. Fletcher. Would you care for some tea or coffee?"

Robin scanned the grim room. They were trapped. "What kind?" he asked stalling for time, his mind searching for a path of escape. The only light, a small lamp sitting on a large mahogany desk, was aided by the flickering of the blaze. It had become foreboding as it danced its ghostlike reflections across Pine-Coufie's stony face. There were no windows, nor any doors other than the one that had just been locked.

Pine-Coufie's reply was snide, his voice cruel. "Yes, Mr. MacAllen, you are trapped. This was so effortless. You avoided all the idiots who were supposed to bring you to me. Finding the proper help these days is tedious. Please don't get any ideas about either escaping or hurting me. The door is locked from the outside as well as from within, and my man out there is well armed. He would be highly unpleasant to meet right now. Believe me, I am far more pleasant than he, and my needs are ever so humble."

Then Pine-Coufie's face turned red and his voice shook as he ferociously smashed his fist on the door "What I want, Mr. MacAllen, is the rest of that bloody, damn book." Robin instinctively placed himself between Pine-Coufie and the women as he replied, "Rest of the book? Rest of what book? I don't know what you're talking about."

Pine-Coufie stood by the door, composed himself and spoke again, his voice low and deadly sounding. "Come now, Mr. MacAllen. Don't be covert. We know Mr. Fletcher gave the book to an old man we had been following in London for months. We know the man gave the book to Clague and we know Clague passed the book to you before we were able to attend to him." His blank face suddenly twisted into a malefic smile. "I enjoyed watching Clague dealt with. He went down with such a pleasing thump. Killing can be that way, you know, the ultimate control. You understand I want the rest of that book very much and I'm willing to be quite lenient if you will help. You don't have to die."

"How about Melanie and Royce?" Robin asked as he stepped towards him. Cedric reached into the drawer of a table that stood by the door, retrieved a small stainless steel pistol and pointed it directly at Robin.

"Not one more step, Mr. MacAllen. I assure you I'm an excellent shot. I have a military background, you know. The Royal Guards. It wasn't the best part of my life. Too much exertion and, as you can imagine, I don't fit well in a chain of command, except at the top. Damned peons trying to tell me, the son of our oldest family, what to do. But I did learn to use guns. Don't let this one's size misguide you. The bullets are glazers. They explode upon impact so I won't have to hit a vital organ to tear you apart!"

Cedric stepped closer as he continued speaking. "Royce? I almost forgot him. So many bodies ago. That's how you and I originally met, isn't it? You were as foolish as that bloody old stuffed shirt. The Royce family, always so imperious. Thought they were better than we were, just because they had served the Royals in the colonies for a little longer than our family had. Well, look who controlled their business in the end. Our families had grappled for generations. I enjoyed the denouement. I assume Melanie was that interfering little tart who called herself an accountant. We sent her fishing. She made excellent bait, if you get my drift. Now I think we have talked enough. I want the rest of that book."

Cedric stepped closer and raised the pistol level to Robin's eyes. "We took the first half from you at the Bear Inn. Do you remember? Or do I need to remind you. But you had removed the second half. I want it back... Now!" The man's voice had gotten progressively louder and was sounding more disturbed than ever.

Pine-Coufie's face turned a deep scarlet. "I am trying to keep my composure, Mr. MacAllen. I know you have communed with the book. Otherwise you would never have been able to do what you have this past week. You must be quite clever to perceive the concepts so expeditiously."

Robin was overwhelmed. His breath was taken away and he couldn't reply for a moment. "Melanie's dead?" he asked after a minute. He was still looking down the barrel of the gun that was ready to carry him to oblivion. A sense of closure began to engulf him. After all this time, after so many years of questions and uncertainty, he finally knew.

"Of course, she's dead. I shot her myself, you ass, with this very gun. Twice in the back of the head. My men dumped her in Manila Bay. She pried in places she should not have. Just like Mr. Fletcher here. She was a pestilent, righteous bitch, Mr. MacAllen. She kept insisting that Mrs. Royce should have her money. These damned accountants shouldn't snoop so much. They should keep their place, do their jobs, and keep their mouths shut."

Robin's eyes teared. All these years. I knew you didn't run, Melanie. I knew you were good. Now I can say goodbye. Then he looked into the threatening gun barrel again. Or maybe it's hello, he thought. Maybe we're about to be together.

MacAllen took a step back and asked, "She didn't suffer?"

Cedric looked blank, paused and then laughed. "Suffer... Suffer? The girl? You must be demented. You don't know the meaning of the word. But unless you tell me where to get the book, you will understand the word all too well. The girl? She was too busy on the phone trying to inform the police even after I warned her not to. I had to stop that. She never knew what hit her. She denied me the pleasure of watching her cry and beg."

He aimed the gun again, directly at Robin's head. "But I said this is enough talk. Tell me where the rest of the book is!"

"She wouldn't have, you know," Robin replied, his voice steady as he kept his eyes riveted on the gun.

Cedric's look shifted from annoyed to puzzled. "Who wouldn't what?" he demanded.

Robin's gaze remained steady as he replied, "Melanie would not have begged. Not for you, not for all your men. You might have beat her, you might have tormented her, but you couldn't have broken her. She'd never fear the likes of you."

Cedric laughed. "Oh, come now, Mr. MacAllen. You really don't understand, do you? Everyone has something they fear, especially women. Have you no understanding of culture at all? Women are so sentimental, so... messy. Even my mother." Cedric's eyes took on a far away, almost dazed, look, as if he were seeing something clearly in his memory.

"Father should have known when he dipped into common blood. Damned commoner sneaking back to her own. Returning to the natives. But I took care of her too—and my brother, the bastard!" Cedric spit the words out.

"Claiming I was not his equal. But I am not a half breed!" By now Pine-Coufie was shouting. "Nor do I desire women, especially half breeds. What is it about you, Mr. MacAllen? Why are you always dallying with the natives? It's so like you commoners, always rutting with anything you encounter. You're barbaric, uncouth. No culture. You're uncivilized. Not like myself with my pure blood. My blood runs pure from my father, and his father before him, and back for generations."

The man's insane, Robin thought. I must stay in control. He wouldn't be speaking like this if he planned to let us live.

He watched Pine-Coufie move his slender, angular frame towards the fire and heard him speak again. "Come, come, Mr. MacAllen. I have played enough games with Mr. Fletcher. My patience has expired. Perhaps I should remind you of the last meeting we had at the Bear Inn, so you will not forget with whom you deliberate."

Robin was about to speak when he saw Pine-Coufie reaching for a small golden orb hanging from a chain around his neck. Cedric's eyes suddenly rolled back into his head. The whites stared at him lifelessly, like a ghost's eyes, loathsome and forbidding and soulless.

The attack came without warning, snatching him like a vise, wrapping around and crushing him, even though nothing was there. The force was instant, and then just as suddenly, it stopped. The onslaught hit again and increased in intensity. Robin reeled. He stumbled backwards, numb from it.

Robin first dropped down to his knees and then crashed to the floor. The force on his body immediately lessened. He lay there a moment, then crawled to his knees and stood to face Pine-Coufie.

A stunned look appeared on Pine-Coufie's face. "How? How can you stand against the force?"

Talking Panther spoke, her voice hoarse, but somehow still composed. "There will be no more of this. You cannot use the force while we are here. We return it to the universe. If you try this again, we will return it to you. Like this."

Pine-Coufie's skin blanched and he jumped back. He caught his breath and Robin could see a flash of fear crossing his face.

A hateful smile creased Cedric's face and he spoke again. "Well,

well. What do we have here? We certainly did not learn that by reading bits of our book, did we? So this is your little secret, Mr. MacAllen. You have brought along your own little rogue Controllers. How absolutely charming."

Pine-Coufie's voice was just a little short of a hiss. "Your little red native here is quite impressive. She seems to know the vibrations quite well. Not that it will do you any good. You are quite ingenious to have hidden them from us for so long. We thought we had wiped out these Indian devils centuries ago. You must..."

Robin cut Pine-Coufie short. "I don't think we must do anything. I think what you must do is let the four of us out of here right now." Talking Panther spoke to Pine-Coufie again. "Robin is right. Your powers are useless here. You have learned how to become one with the universe, but your intentions are not full. Your spirits are harnessed and directed for personal use rather than for all. A harnessed spirit can never run as strongly as those free to act in total accord with natural law. Your power is limited by your desire. Unlimited power is attained only by following your spirits and hearing the wisdom which only the free spirits of the cosmos can sing."

She was cut short as Pine-Coufie spat, "It's so charming to see that you are such a righteous red Indian bitch. But don't you dare threaten me!" Pine-Coufie was beginning to lose control. The tremor in Cedric's voice was now from terror, not rage. He's weak, Robin thought. His power comes from inflicting punishment, from a position of surprise and absolute control. Now he doubts his powers. I can hear it in his voice.

Robin struggled to hold his emotions in check. An impulse that was so strong he felt rather than thought it swept through his mind. It was Melanie! "You are the strength of the buffalo, Robin. I'll always be with you in this strength. We are united always. We are all of us, one in the spirit. Let the rest of me go."

MacAllen knew he did not need to attack Pine-Coufie. His own power was in this feeling of peace he now had and the quiet inside of him. Melanie was gone, but she was fine. His suffering and doubts had been wasted. The doubts he had had for so many years about Melanie's fate, and the anguish of not knowing were gone. My suffering over Dad, too, he thought. They've been forced from me, but they continue to live in me. There's nothing to regret. This physical existence is just a blink in eternity. We've never been apart and we'll never be apart.

"I won't die today, Pine-Coufie," Robin said quietly. Cedric raised an eyebrow.

"Ian, Talking Panther and Silent Panther are staying with me," Robin continued. "You have no power over them."

Talking Panther interrupted. "I do not threaten you. I will not even try to thwart your attempts at misusing the universal power. I lay the lives of my friends into the hands of my spirits instead, and I will accept this fate. But, be warned, Mr. Pine-Coufie, that my friends are guarded by these spirits now. If you use your power against them, you will suffer whatever fate the spirits choose. My life and my friends' lives are now in their hands."

Robin stepped forward and Pine-Coufie whirled. "Stop right there." His voice was higher than ever, almost soprano. "You might try to obstruct my power, but I've still got the gun in my possession."

Robin cut him short. "Pine-Coufie, you can't imagine the power these spirits have. I don't think you want to see it. You don't even want to know."

Pine-Coufie stood deadly still, appearing confused and nervous. He looked at the four of them, only his eyes, black hard stones, slowly moving from one to the other.

He regained his composure somewhat and spoke again. "Oh, yes, I think I can imagine what power you have. But you are only partially correct, Mr. MacAllen. I would indeed rather not see that power used against me, but it might be quite useful added to my collected forces. We could perhaps make some sort of an arrangement that would be attractive to you and these charming ladies."

Then Robin heard Ian Fletcher's voice, very weak and unsteady. He was laboring to articulate his words. "Jesus, Robin, I knew you'd show up. Don't believe him. He doesn't intend to give you anything. He just wants the rest of that book and is too damn stupid to understand neither you nor I have it. The minute he has the book, or the minute he believes I don't really know where it is, he means to kill us all. I'm just so sorry to have dragged you into this mess. I had no idea what would happen when I called."

Ian suddenly arched back, in obvious agony. Virtually at the same instant Pine-Coufie gasped. His attack on Ian had been rebounded by the spirits.

Talking Panther spoke again. "I warned you. You cannot use that force on us. We will not harm you, but our spirits will allow the vibrations to return to their source. If you direct your vibrations toward any of us, you will reap their destiny, not us."

Eagle flashed through Robin's mind. The sight of the eagle, he thought as he looked again at Pine-Coufie. Now he unquestionably saw the man's terror. Here was a corrupt image suddenly exposed by light. Pine-Coufie's power without their fright and anguish was powerless. Robin's vision became acute. He saw a tremor in Pine-Coufie's hand he had not seen before. He saw his sweat and a nervous tic twitching at the corner of one eye. He saw that Pine-Coufie was simply afraid, and always had been. But he had unceasingly hidden behind his power.

Then the spirit of the deer suddenly came to MacAllen. His hearing and sense of smell deepened. He heard the raggedness of Pine-Coufie's breath and smelled the sour stench of dread in his sweat.

Robin was about to take advantage of this fear and attack Cedric when another Golden Word seized his mind and shook his being. Opossum. Use the spirit of the opossum, he thought, and he was wrapped in compassion for Pine-Coufie. This man's terrified, alone. What he's done is part of us too. Can I condemn that? What's within him must be within me too. I can't kill him just because he has killed. Even Melanie. Isn't there some way I can help?

He spoke gently. "Cedric, you're right. We should join forces, but for the good of humanity. I promise you I haven't seen the portion of the book you claim is missing. I don't know what has happened here with Ian, but obviously he is hurt and you are afraid. Put down the gun and let's see if there isn't some way we can resolve this."

Ian spoke again, his speech, as previously, strained and unstable. Robin kept his eyes on Pine-Coufie and could see him stiffen at his friend's voice. "Robin, I've read the book. What a mess this is. I had no idea when I started investigating Smythe and the missing money at the stockbrokers and found that damn cottage and took the book. I read the first part, the part that explained all about the origins of mankind. How there was just one civilization that ran on the laws of nature and how they all knew that what they did for others they did for themselves and that they all felt the connection and felt a part of the whole. There's no way out of this you know. There's no way out."

Ian's voice had become barely audible and Robin spoke softly to him. "Ian, it's okay. Take it easy."

Clearly upset, Ian replied, "No, you must understand why he cannot let us live. I read the second part of the book, Robin. It explained about civilization and how when it grew it became too large. Then no one felt the connection any more. Parts no longer knew the other. And then fear came out of this, and it was something that there had never been before. A group of men infected with fear turned to greed. The fear blinded them. They learned how to use fear to manipulate others and they thought that this was good. The second part tells all the techniques to use to control others."

Ian slumped back in his chair. His eyes closed and his head fell. Speaking had drained what little strength he'd had. Robin walked slowly over to his friend, sat next to him and felt his pulse. It was shallow and very faint. He spoke quickly. "He needs help or he's going to go into shock."

Summoning inner resources, Ian fought back into full consciousness, opened his eyes and said, "He won't help, Robin. As far as he's concerned I have to die." His friend's breath was labored and was coming with great difficulty. "The book explains how Pine-Coufie and his family joined with sixty-four other families. Each has learned how to use one part of the vibrations to create fear. Only for the purpose of controlling others. They've wreaked havoc on society for their own bloody gain."

Ian slumped further but kept talking. "They cannot let us go because we know how they're using fear to manipulate the whole goddamn world. The book tells how to illuminate fear. That's why they're hoarding so many shares. They plan to dump everything on the market at once and create a global economic stampede to generate even more fear. They'll use it to grab even more control.

"Cedric has to kill us because the other Controllers don't know he let their secret out. He was too damn lazy to deal with the stockbroker himself. Used a Carrier instead, who was killed by lightning. The man's death led me to their damnable secret. If the other Controllers knew, they'd kill him for sure."

"Stop!" Pine-Coufie screamed. "You have said quite enough, Mr. Fletcher. You and your snoopy high-held opinions. Where do you think the world would be without our stabilizing influences? It was us who took on the responsibility to make sure mankind doesn't destroy itself through ignorance. We have kept the order. Someone has to. Humanity does not have the sense to lead itself. You need us."

Now Ian laughed despite his fragility, and he was racked by a fit of coughing as he spoke. "That comes right out of the book. This is the first seed of fear. They plant fear of the unknown, the fear of disorder."

Suddenly MacAllen's friend shook violently, suffering a dreadful seizure. "I must tell you where the rest of the book is." Robin could barely hear him. "It contains their whole plan. I've hidden it…" This time Ian coughed blood. He shuddered terribly, doubled over, and then went still. His eyes stared vacantly.

"Ian?" Robin whispered. "Ian…"

Talking Panther moved over and felt for Ian's pulse. She looked up. "Robin. He is at peace now. He's joined the Grandfathers."

Robin turned and looked at Pine-Coufie. His face now looked like a madman's; he had clearly crossed over from sanity to insanity. He laughed wickedly and spoke. "Well done, Mr. Fletcher. Thank you for letting me know that you really did hide the book. He's right, Mr. MacAllen, you must die. Now that I know you do not have the book, it might as well be now."

Cedric aimed the gun at Robin. "In the hands of the general public, that book poses no danger at all. It isn't easy to read and has no naked women in it. Should it be found, most people wouldn't even take the time to read it. I have been very lucky today. Mr. Fletcher soothed my concern about the book. He led you and these two rogue Controllers to me. And saved me a bullet as well. I'll tip my hat to you at your grave, Mr. Fletcher."

Robin watched Pine-Coufie turn, unlock the door and call, "Samuelson, come in. Bring your shotgun. Now."

Pine-Coufie turned and bowed his head. "Goodbye, Mr. MacAllen, ladies. I'm so sorry I cannot stay longer but I have important things to attend to. My man will take you outside. We wouldn't want to ruin these fine carpets, now would we?"

Cedric put his gun in his pocket, opened the door and then suddenly stopped. An overweight man, his shirt stretched to its limits, fat belly hanging over a large gold buckle, was facing him at the door.

The man pointed a huge pistol at Pine-Coufie and spoke very loudly to him. "Stop right there. I don't know where the hell you think you're goin', but right now it ain't gonna be nowhere."

Pine-Coufie was immobilized at this, his drawn face a mask of confusion. "I say, who are you? Where is my man, Samuelson?"

Without a word, the heavy man shoved Pine-Coufie back into the room, stepped in himself, and looked around. He grinned malevolently before he spoke to Pine-Coufie.

"Curiosity killed that cat. I guess Samuelson is the son-of-a-bitch that tried to stop me comin' in here. It'll be a long hard time before he tries to fuck with me again."

Robin watched the big man stop and look directly at him as he spoke again. "Well, I'll be damned. What do we have here? Mr. MacAllen and the lovely Indian twins. What a fuckin' surprise. Let me introduce myself. Jimmy Ray Burnett, sheriff of Hendry County in the sunny state of Floreeda. We haven't met before, but I have been wantin' to make your acquaintance for quite some time. Y'all are under arrest."

Robin was bewildered. Pine-Coufie said, "Listen, Sheriff, you must be under some terrible misconception. You have no jurisdiction here. There has been no crime. You can't just stroll into my home and maltreat me in this manner."

The sheriff strutted closer to Pine-Coufie, pointing his weapon at him as he said, "Sure I can, fella, cuz I got the gun and you're lookin' at it.

"Now listen up, folks. I got lucky this time." Looking at MacAllen, Jimmy Ray said, "Night before last, seems some dumb ass decided to rob your room over at that fancy Queens Hotel. The police caught him after he crashed his car a little later, driving like a lunatic down the wrong side of the street. Sure nuff the police found your stuff including a letter that guy stole from you. And ya know what that letter was about? It introduced these two foxy Indian girls here to the Prime Minister of England. Told him to give them every assistance."

Robin stared at Silent Panther and Talking Panther. "You had a letter to the Prime Minister?"

Talking Panther replied blandly, "The Seminole are an independent nation. We never surrendered to the U.S. government, ever. We keep it quiet, but we have our own diplomacy around the world."

Jimmy Ray bellowed, "Shut up, bitch! I'm doin' the talkin' here. However you got that fuckin' letter, it damn well got those English polleece hoppin'. They got on the phone to find out more about such important folk who were missin'. Them cops must have been plenty worried cuz sure 'nuff they called the sheriff in the county where you live. That's me by the way, good ole Jimmy Ray Burnett." He bowed slightly. They called me clear across the ocean. Course I flew over right away. Just to help out, understand. I knew this meant you were here. They even let me talk to the little guy who broke into your room. He sent me here. Seems my interrogation on that asshole was better than what those wimp English constables could do."

Jimmy Ray regarded the study; his eyes were menacing, ruthless and ice-cold. "Now you folks think you're real smart, I know. Ya felt damn smart foolin' me back there in New York like that with those look-alikes and all. That cost me a bunch. It screwed my reputation with my suppliers but good."

Burnett's face turned scarlet. He shouted, "You really fucked me, ya hear? You made me look a fool! Now it's my turn to screw you." The sheriff's timbre became subdued now, his voice filled with contempt. "And when I screw, I screw hard. Unnerstan'? Iff'n you move, when I deliver you to my friends in New York, it will be in pieces. I'd rather cut you in two than as not, so don't think a movin'."

Jimmy Ray walked towards Pine-Coufie. "Wait!" the Englishman said. "Now I understand. You are the sheriff my acquaintances in New York hired. You were supposed to detain them for me. Regrettably you didn't. You are in error, we don't need you now."

Burnett looked at Pine-Coufie and spit on the floor in front of him. "Sure, bub. Sure. Now listen up, asshole. I've been fooled once already. Won't happen again. Get in my way and you're double dipped screwed. Unnerstan'?" Jimmy Ray's face became more heavily crimson as he yelled, "Hear me?"

Pine-Coufie reached for his necklace. Almost instantly, his eyes became vacant and rolled up to the left. At the same time Jimmy Ray's eyes bulged gruesomely and he staggered back, collapsed against the wall and grasped his chest.

He roared, "What the fuck?" Then he looked at Pine-Coufie and understood. "You bastard you." He aimed his gun and pulled the trigger.

Robin's ears rang from the large gun's burst in the enclosed room. Pine-Coufie's head had just exploded. Most of it was now coating the fine paneling on the wall.

Within seconds, Silent Panther jumped up out of her chair and scrambled for Jimmy Ray's gun. Jimmy Ray's hand went his chest and he reeled. Somehow though, he sensed the woman's movement. He leveled the gun and one shot tore out.

"No!" Robin raved. The gun had discharged not more than a foot from Silent Panther's chest. The sound was muffled by how close she was but the force of the bullet slammed her against the wall. He heard a sickening thump as her head smashed on the wall. Her body sank to the floor and rolled partway under the massive desk. It lay there motionless, unbearably contorted.

"No!" he exploded again, jumping towards Burnett. Before he could lay his hands on the gun, the sheriff released it. He coughed up an immense jet of blood and dropped like a stone. He was dead before he hit the floor.

Robin was beside himself, wild with rage. His anguish was painful. Talking Panther spoke to him in an unwavering voice, urgently and firmly. "She is no longer here, Robin. We must leave her and Ian Fletcher and go. We must not be apprehended by the authorities."

His eyes widened with shock. "Silent Panther was shot. And Ian's dead. We can't go anywhere. We can't just leave them here. We need to..." MacAllen was losing control.

Talking Panther clutched him by the hand. Her words were deliberate. "They are no longer here. What's left is a husk. But they are still with us. Please believe me; all is well. Don't let your heart ache, Robin. We must leave now."

He could not move. MacAllan tried to convey the enormity of the dismay he felt. All he could say was, "But, but... he shot her, Ian's gone..."

With sublime compassion, Talking Panther touched her finger to his lips and whispered, "Death is just one more illusion in life, Robin, and is as natural as birth. Do not be a prisoner to this illusion."

MacAllen let out a great sob.

Now the word Tortoise swelled in his mind... the spirit of the Tortoise, a place of balance where whatever is outside, there is peace within. He drew himself into that. Peace washed over him.

Hours later they were on the outskirts of Manchester. From there, they planned to catch the next morning's flight home. They pulled into an inn to stay the night. Robin opened the car door, started to get out and stopped. When he spoke his voice was so low he could barely hear his own words. "Silent Panther?"

Silent Panther beamed at him from the back seat of the car. Still she did not speak.

CHAPTER FORTY

Tears welling in his eyes, Robin looked at Talking Panther. He asked in wonder, "How... What? Do you have even this power?"

He stopped and choked, unable to trust his voice further. He just listened as Talking Panther said, "I have no power, Robin. I have told you this before."

MacAllen stared at the horizon. The sun was shining over a distant creek, glinting like a silver thread running through brown winter landscape. He tried to speak, but wasn't able. Words were more than he could manage; he couldn't even think of any that might be right. He stopped trying and just pointed instead. He smiled a glorious smile, pushed back his tears and concentrated on what Talking Panther was saying to him.

The three of them walked down a gently sloping path that led into a wood. They stood there lashed by the gusting wind, looking at the valley spread out below. When she began speaking, Talking Panther spoke quietly, her words sweet like a song.

"When I was young I dedicated my life to my tribe and to the Golden Words. I learned there is more to life than appears. I also learned what the hardest challenge is — to see the reality that is beyond our illusions. The senses are extremely convincing, and we are easily fooled. I learned a technique using the Golden Words that allows my spirit to be with the most profound forces of nature. Few have known this absolute liberation, but I was privileged to learn it from one of the old keepers of wisdom."

Both women sat down on a mound with a soft covering of sepia-colored grass, and Robin sat beside them.

"The whole of the cosmos is a thought of the Creator. This mammoth earth upon which we live is only a dream of the forces of nature. The earth first formed as an idea, then turned to atomic energy and then turned from energy into matter itself. All the molecules, the atoms, the earth are really just a dream, a spirit, bound by nature's will.

"That spirit is within all of us. We too quicken our dreams into flesh. We are all a cosmos within as well as without. When I made a vow to free myself from the oppressions of the flesh, I dreamed of Silent Panther, one who never speaks but is ever present, working always beyond the illusions of this world. She has been my balance, my alter ego, my tie to the gods. Right now Silent Panther is no longer needed in this world."

MacAllen watched Silent Panther as she began to glow and shimmer; she transformed into a subtle violet vibration, a faint aura, and gradually she merged with Talking Panther. For a moment they were two, then one, connected, glinting gentle blue-white beams. Then Silent Panther was gone.

Robin's mouth opened once, twice. Nothing came out. He was truly speechless. His animal spirit sprang into his thoughts and brought with it a surge of strength and understanding. Warmth flooded through him.

He reached out, clasped Talking Panther's hand and said, "Why has Silent Panther's time come to an end?"

"Silent Panther was my balance. She was my inner being, my closest companion and my friend. She was my wholeness when I walked this path alone. She is with me forever but her presence on this earth is not needed. You, Robin, have replaced her. You are my other half and now you can share this responsibility once again, as you know you have in the past. You can no longer hide from what you have always known."

CHAPTER
FORTY ONE

British newspapers reported that Pine-Coufie and his butler Samuelson had gone missing, nothing more. There was no sense trying to explain what had happened in Cedric's study to the police, especially since all the records had been missing. Someone else could deal with the manor house. How could they have convinced anyone of the truth? And all the bodies had disappeared.

Ian's body had been found on a Gloucestershire Common. The obituary said he had died of a stroke. The rumor in Hendry County was that Jimmy Ray Burnett had absconded just ahead of a drug dealing indictment. No one knew where he was.

Usha was back from her overseas trip that she said she hadn't enjoyed for a second for the worry. Everything seemed fine now. But was it really? Someone had removed Pine-Coufie and Burnett and the butler from sight. Someone knew what had happened to them and was saying nothing. And just who was that someone?

John Thurlow's pocket scanner was already handed to Robin's biggest electronics client. John was thrilled. So was the client.

Melanie's fate had been determined after so long a time.

The messes had been cleaned up, hotel rooms paid for, and rental cars returned.

Robin rolled over, propped himself on one elbow and looked down the short, white sandy beach of Caya Costa Island. He scanned the Florida mainland in the distance. The isolation suited him well; he felt protected here. Waves of comfort rushed over him as the sun broke from behind a cloud.

It was only days since they had returned from England yet it seemed as if it had been an eternity. Billions of shares are still sitting out there, Robin thought. Hidden, somewhere... they're a deadly economic time bomb. And where's the rest of the book?

Robin thought a Golden Word. *Alligator... I lay in wait.* His body instantly relaxed and he became aware of a lazy bird song swelling from the pines at the edge of the beach.

He looked around. He and Talking Panther were still alone and he took a quick guess at how long they had before the sun set. Then he collapsed back into the inviting sand.

Golden Words quelled his anxiety. *I don't have to fear the future,* he thought. *There's excitement in the unexpected. It's the key to life, however long it might last.*

Will the Controllers come after us? He thought the risks through. *I doubt it. Cedric lost the book and was trying to hide the fact. The last ones who he wanted to know were the other Controllers. I have to look for them. Talking Panther and I have to let the secret out.*

Talking Panther had returned from England earlier than him and they had been apart until today. There was so much he wanted to say to her. But did he dare?

His mind gave in to exhaustion and he slept.

When he woke later, he checked the sun. It was a massive fiery globe, hanging low over the horizon, descending lazily toward the sea. *I've avoided it all day. I have to deal with it sometime,* he thought.

He propped himself up and looked out once more at the water. His heart pounded. *How can I,* he wondered for the hundredth time, *with the path so full of danger?*

Then he saw a dolphin break in rhythmic precision from the waters beyond, reflecting like a million crystals in the afternoon sun, and then gliding gently back into the sea. *Such beauty and grace.* He recalled the Porpoise and the spirit of the Golden Word that Talking Panther had given him. "This stilled pulse of the deep is at peace. In nature's grace it sings its tune with the cosmos and is delivered the bounties of the sea."

A sign for me, he thought. Tranquility sprung up in him, and he watched the sun lower itself gently from the sky.

Fortified by this calm, he rolled over and looked at Talking Panther lying peacefully asleep next to him. Robin watched her murmur some lost word, perhaps a fantasy of her dreams, perhaps as real as this world.

The gentle swell of her breasts rose and fell as he ran his hand softly down her arm and said quietly, "Are there any remarkably exquisite women here who need to wake for the sunset?"

Her slim form rose from the blanket as she blinked herself awake. He admired the soft curves of her swimsuit. "I needed this rest badly and slept with the spirits. This beach is perfect. Do you come here often?"

"No," he replied. "Only when I'm worried or need to think."

She looked deeply into his eyes. "Did you bring me here to worry with you or did you want to think?"

"No," he laughed. "I certainly don't want to think. I've had enough thinking to last a lifetime. I told myself I brought you here because it's an enchanting place to watch the sunset. But I guess really I'm worried."

Talking Panther caressed the back of his neck and shifted closer as she whispered, "Do you not have to think to worry? There certainly are many better things for us to do than think now."

His hand had slipped off her arm and now rested on her thigh. Her skin was satin. God that feels good, he thought.

"Just fill your mind with beautiful action. Worries cannot exist there. Fill your mind with Golden Words."

Together they watched night come over their island. The sky filled with shades of burnt orange and rose; the sun was sinking, as it always had here, into the pink and gray waters of the ocean. Reflected light spread from behind the horizon and painted the clouds.

Robin spoke very softly. "It's hard to think beautiful thoughts when I am so worried for you, and about us."

Talking Panther reached over and rested her hand on the nape of his neck and she leaned close to Robin. He was captivated by her delicate scent. The expression in her voice changed imperceptibly. "Do you mean my being here brings you worry?"

He turned to face her, his hand falling again to her leg, her skin sending a shock up his arm and spine. He laughed with a great deal of delight and replied, "God, no! Just the opposite. I'm worried because I want to be with you. More than I can say."

Talking Panther's hands moved from his neck and roamed his chest. He was drowning in her black eyes. She grinned and said, "Is it so bad to be with me that you must worry?"

Then her smile faded. Her lips brushed his face and she breathed into his ear, "Worry? Robin, have you not yet learned to live without fear?"

She shifted closer, her hip resting cozily against his leg. MacAllen's hand, still resting on her thigh, began to burn.

"I can't forget the Controllers," he said. "Or forgive them. Ian said there are sixty-four other families. I have to find them and stop what they're doing. This sense, the second sight, I've realized it's a unique gift and I have to use it to do something good. But we found nothing about them at the manor house, no records, no clues, nothing about them at all. They could be anywhere. They could be looking for us right now! I need your help, but I can't ask you for it. I don't know how to protect you."

He caught a wisp of her sweet breath as she whispered again, "Remember the Eagle, Robin, the eleventh spirit. Be of the Eagle who soars high above the land. This spirit of sight allows you to speak with the clouds and soar in the highest winds but still see the smallest distortions below. With this spirit of sight, your heart can rise to the gods and be free. Trust this spirit, Robin, to protect you, me, and the world."

He rolled onto his side. "Talking Panther," he said. "I haven't been able to feel deeply for anyone since losing my father and then Melanie. You're so much like her, you know."

Talking Panther squeezed his arm affectionately. "I know that, Robin. Destiny has meant for us to be together again. When lives are bound again and again, kinship grows so strong that when we meet we remember the times of the past when we were together. Thoughts can't recall those times, but our spirits know of them. You've seen my similarity to Melanie, but what really drew you to her years ago was your quest to find me again. Our unity is one from many times past. This attraction people call 'love at first sight' is really memories of lives together in the past. We have fought the Controllers before, Robin, and we shouldn't be afraid of struggling against them once more. This is a conflict of the material world that will never end."

MacAllen paused, not actually comprehending what Talking Panther had told him, but not really caring any more either. "I've never been able to give myself freely for fear of..."

Talking Panther put her finger tenderly to his lips. "Robin, you have given up so much of your life because of your fearfulness. It's time to let these fears go. Fear is only an illusion, a false notion. But now you can speak with the spirits and you can see that there is real beauty right here, right at this moment."

Talking Panther's lips briefly touched Robin's. His voice was hoarse as he said, "I have other fears that are not just illusions, Talking Panther. I want to be with you, but I have to find and stop the Controllers, and I don't want to put you at risk. And you have so many spiritual commitments to your tribe."

She leaned over and again delicately touched her lips to his. Another breath of her alluring scent. She whispered, "My commitment is to the cosmos and following its path of truth. I do not limit my journeys of tomorrow by the imaginations of the past."

As Talking Panther caressed his chest with her hand shivers of joy charged through him with each stroke. His heart was hammering and his hand trembled as it moved across her slim, taut leg.

He controlled his voice with an effort. "Yes, but there is something about our being together that transcends the physical. I don't want anything to interfere!"

"Trust the guidance of our spirits, Robin. These spirits are Wisdom itself. We are committed together for the spirits, but it is they who have brought our bodies together with our desires. They have brought us here together now. Would they do this if it meant harm? The desires of a woman and a man are life's desire to fulfill itself."

Her caresses moved lower and her whisper became even more hushed. "I cannot control the world's fears, but I know my spirits will not lead me astray. We—you and I, the tribe, the rest of mankind—all began as one. We have always been connected and are all still connected. The universe expands, blends, folds and unfolds again and again; it never remains still. Our being together will not take from the spirits, but will fulfill them. Our physical union can only bring our bodies and spirits closer to reality."

Robin pressed his lips on hers. The effect was devastating. Talking Panther stifled a groan as his hand explored the gentle curves of her body. It was firm but yet so supple and so very seductive. His breath was coming harder, and any resistance he might have had disappeared.

He pulled her to him. She was soft and warm. Robin caught a glimpse just beyond the tall pines that stood behind them. The moon was rising, round and ivory and radiant, over the trees. Suddenly he was filled with the words he had heard for the first time only a few days ago, they had changed him for life. They were the words Talking Panther had given him on an island far away, but words that remained and infused his heart and soul.

"The spirit of the Coyote sings his song in harmony with the spirit of the moon. This melody of ivory light watches and knows always its relation to the moon and the stars. Through this spirit, the coyote can range far and spread wide yet always knows where to go. Through this wisdom, the coyote survives and grows even through the greatest obstacles and when all wish he were no more."

That's it, he thought. Silence... Action... Union... all in tune with the moon and the stars. That's everything.

MacAllen pulled Talking Panther even nearer and held her. "You're right. Our guides have brought us here and we should journey together. I was reluctant and afraid. There always will be obstacles but they're just stepping stones to fulfillment."

This woman next to him was all that beauty could be. All that ever was and ever would be. Robin's heart drummed furiously as he removed Talking Panther's bathing suit. He trembled with every touch and every blissful caress.

Their naked bodies embracing each other sent pulsations of the earth's heartbeat through them. They were brought to a distant place of peace, tranquillity, of absolute contentment. Their beings explored and sang while the spirits sealed their destiny. The spirits fulfilled them as the seed of their eternal union was planted.

He received... she gave...

She received... he gave...

The two of them lay on the sand, entwined in the fading light. The breath of the earth blessed them. Their fate was pledged and their journey was just beginning.

Robin heard Talking Panther sigh and whisper, "You understand the Golden Words you have been given. And now you understand the true power of Union.

"Yes, Robin, yes!"

An Excerpt From...

THE 64TH TREATY

The Next Robin MacAllen & Talking Panther Story

GARY A. SCOTT

Sunstar
PUBLISHING LTD.

64TH TREATY

An amber moon cast ivory beams that floated lightly on the water like a film of thick cream. There were no lights here, far from the small Costa Rican village. The stars were radiant and danced their way through the darkness shattering into splinters and reflecting eerily on an unusually smooth Caribbean Sea. The balmy breeze was from the south, ripe with the smells of the tropics and so richly damp that had anyone been with the old fisherman they could have rubbed the air between their fingers.

But no one was with him. Nor was there any sound save the ocean's gentle lapping against the hull of the ancient boat. The fisherman was alone with a sea so familiar he would have drifted into sleep had it not been for his troubled thoughts.

He had always been in the village and everyone just called him "Vida"—Life. The name may have been shortened from a longer one, but no one in the village knew for sure. Or maybe the name just described the man's extraordinarily long life. Many said there was another meaning. Rumors persisted that he was a shaman, descended directly from the indigenous people that had been there so long ago. The rumors said he could give life even to those who had died.

But Vida was not thinking of this now. He shifted uneasily on the boat's hard wooden seat, struggling with an oppressiveness he could not describe, an unknown pain with a source he didn't understand.

The fisherman was small and bent, with skin brown and thickened from decades of tropical sun. His fingers were gnarled from

years of sea-born dampness and hauling laden nets. The gray in his
black hair was spotted just enough to avoid comment about its color
for a man his age.

It was his eyes that were wrong. There was incredible life in
these eyes. Pristine and black as jet, they were obsidian disks that
danced when he smiled—the eyes of a young man or maybe an
eagle. And he smiled a lot, like a youth, not a centenarian. Many
swore those eyes had seen hundreds of years. Perhaps they had started the whispers.

Vida just laughed when confronted with these rumors. "I'm a
simple fisherman, Señor," he would reply. Always polite, he called
everyone "Señor" or "Señora" and then would say nothing more
except, "The only life I bring is from the sea. I was even born of the
sea." He would smile and his eyes would twinkle, but he would say
no more.

Tonight, though, he was not smiling. A worry bore at him that
even the impassiveness of an old man who had seen it all could not
quell. "The spirits are upset," he said aloud. He often talked to the
wind and the sea. "The Gods are angry. They…" His words were
clipped short by an unexpected pull at his nets. "This strain is too
heavy," he said, again to the wind. "The pull too dead. This does not
feel like the fish I have known… And I know them all."

Vida began to sweat with dread. "Give me comfort, Dios," he
whispered into the breeze. "Lay your blessings upon me. Release me
from this tiredness that presses worry into my soul."

Yet this was not to be, for beneath him tiredness even greater than
his own was about to end. Far within the earth's crust, below the sea,
were two tectonic plates that had struggled one against the other for
endless millenia. They at that moment finally gave way. The rocks
suddenly liquified with a force that registered on seismographs
around the world.

In just seconds, gigantic blasts of volcanic pressure broke the
crumbling rock, melting granite, ripping loose with a violence that
split the seabed. The plates cracked apart, lava raced up and water
roared down simultaneously. Incredible forces met in a raging

explosion that pushed an energy wave at hurricane speed toward the Caribbean's surface and the old fisherman's ancient craft.

The first swell of water hit Vida's boat and nearly threw him into the sea. He grabbed instinctively at the gunwale and only his fisherman's instincts, honed from a lifetime at sea, saved him.

He felt an even stronger wave slap the hull and shouted in surprise to no one, "Why is the boat rocking?" His thoughts raced. My nets are out and they are full. This should steady my boat. There is no wind. "Why should the boat rock?" he asked the wind. The boat suddenly pitched furiously and then just as quickly was calm. Vida silently prayed. "I must return quickly to shore," he muttered, again overwhelmed with dread. "There is evil here. I feel it in my bones." He reached out to pull in his nets.

He was bending over the bow when an even larger wave hit and spent its fury on his boat. The impact of mud and steam that belched from the heaving seabed below hurled the fisherman over and immediately tangled him in his nets. Stunned, Vida hardly registered the wet, the warmth of the sea or the pain; his mind was shutting down.

The next surge smashed his head hideously against the boat and his consciousness faded so quickly he barely had time for one last thought before the blackness became all. His last reflection, a remnant of what had been a simple fisherman's creed was Vida... Life.

Waves boiled, spitting fish and seabed thousands of feet into the air. Huge rollers tossed at the boat and nets, sweeping upon Costa Rica's slumbering coast and the villages in its path.

Giant rifts beneath the sea widened. Rock formations sank and others rose. Suddenly freed, they pushed upwards and thrust rock bed like steam pistons with such force that the entire ocean floor rose 40 feet for a mile or more.

Then, the ageless frenzy was spent, its energy released, the trembling stopped and the rocks slept once more. The night became quiet almost as quickly as the rage had started and the moon once again cast its glow on a silent sea. But the shoreline that received this rich amber light was new and the coastline was a mile further out to sea.

At sunrise, the shoreline had already begun to rot with despoiled villages and millions of stinking fish. There was also the ancient boat, its old nets wrapped around a body. And there was Vida, barely alive and telling a story that almost no one believed. He talked about a dead body in the nets. "Dios spoke to me through this body," he said. "I must deliver God's message to a special person who needs to hear this tale."

"I must deliver it," he said again and again. "Dios has given me this message to deliver only to the one who knows how to hear."

Most, upon hearing the old fisherman's tale, believed shock had destroyed his mind. However, not all took his words in that way. To some, Vida was a man who could bring life from death. "Perhaps there is life in his message," they thought. They questioned Vida. "Tell us about those who know how to hear." After his reply they quietly slipped away, inquired, then returned and talked with Vida some more.

He listened to what they had found out and then handed them something. "Deliver this," he said, "but swear to me, speak of this to no one and do not open this packet for it can bring great evil upon you. Deliver it for a man called MacAllen and then disappear. Do not approach me or return here."

They solemnly agreed, slipped quietly once more into the rain forest, and were never seen in Vida's village again.

Readers interested in more information are invited to write:
The Secretary, Sunstar Publishing, Ltd.
204 South 20th Street, Fairfield, Iowa 52556
For more Sunstar Books, please visit our website:
www.sunstarpub.com

AUTHOR'S NOTE

The Golden Words in this book, with its concept of mankind's unity, are complete figments of my imagination.

Yet consider these facts. Upon completion, this book immediately ran into trouble when our beloved agent, Phyllis Luxem, unexpectedly died. Neither my wife nor I knew the name of the editor at St. Martin's Press who Phyllis had told us had a contract for the book as well as an option for the 64th Treaty, my next book.

We spent six months of fruitless effort trying to find the editor in New York, but finally gave up. "St. Martin's is obviously not meant to publish this book," we both said. Leaving the manuscript with our new agent and best friend, Joe Cox, we put it on the back shelves of our mind and headed south for a new project on a book about the pioneer financial markets of Ecuador.

There we learned about an obscure Ecuadorean valley, Vilcabamba, and how its residents lived extraordinarily long and healthy lives. It's one of three valleys (the others are in Georgia, Russia and Hunza, Pakistan) featured for longevity by National Geographic. "Good health is a big part of wealth," we said. "We have to see this place." This began a journey that forever changed our lives.

The trip to this isolated valley caused us to meet a great Andean Yatchak, Alberto Taxco, a direct descendant of the Incans. He is one of South America's most famous philosophers and healers. In training since he was three, Don Alberto studied under the masters throughout the Americas and was given the impressive honor "Force of Great Light" by the Shamanic Council of South America. With this honor came a lifelong responsibility to unveil Incan secrets which had been cloistered for 500 years. The governments in power did not want this knowledge given out. In fact, practice of Incan traditions was against the law until recently. Ceremonies before that time had to be conducted in secret at night. This knowledge so frightened the governments at one time Don Alberto was forced to live and hide in caves to avoid arrest. Talk about Controllers!

When we met Don Alberto, he expressed something we thought odd. "It's so good to see you again," he told us. "Again?" we asked. We had never met this great man before. Over the months, as we worked more and more with him and his village, events began to unfold that in retrospect were eerily similar to the 65th Octave.

We were helping Don Alberto's village create its own supply of running water and became enmeshed—me, a global economist and Don Alberto, an indiginous medicine man, fighting organized oppression together. I missed the similarities. The book was a year out of my head and I had forgotten.

Then one day Don Alberto visited us in Florida. We met him at the Ft. Myers Airport and were driving him to our home in Naples. As we passed the roadside rest area that was one of the settings in the 65th Octave, Don Alberto suddenly blurted, "I want to teach you a Golden Word." I nearly drove off the road! Of course he knew nothing about this book.

He gave us a Golden Word for prosperity and we used it. Did it work? At that point over two years had passed since the 65th Octave had been completed. Our new agent had bravely worked through dozens of rejections. (I suspect he even held some back to save my feelings.) Less than a week after receiving and using the "Golden Word" Don Alberto shared, I was introduced to Rodney Charles, President of Sunstar Publishing. He readily agreed to publish this book.

There is a final twist that suggests that reality is connected with fiction. I spoke with Don Alberto about his native Incan language,

Quichua. "Where did your grandfathers begin?" I asked. He answered in his usual unassuming way. "No one can see through the mists of time," he quietly told me. "But draw conclusions for yourself. The root of this ancient language is Sanskrit, the golden language of India. Or perhaps Sanskrit comes from our native tongue!"

We really are all one.

About Gary Scott

Gary began writing and speaking about international investing 30 years ago when he moved from the U.S. to Hong Kong. He currently writes an economic newsletter and financial columns for numerous financial and health oriented magazines.

While living in Asia and Europe he was introduced to Eastern philosophical thought. When researching his investment report, "Ecuador–Opportunity in the Land of the Sun," Gary learned that one of three valleys featured for the longevity of its residents by National Geographic was in Ecuador. Through the process of visiting this valley, Vilcabamba, Gary and his wife, Merri have met some of South America's greatest healers and philosophers.

The Scotts, who have four daughters and one son, share their lives between Naples, Florida, North Carolina and Rosaspamba, an Incan monastery in Ecuador. They are both experienced yogis and have studied philosophies of the ancients worldwide.

Gary is a trustee of Land of the Sun Foundation, a publicly funded charity that helps the native people of Ecuador. The Scotts offer programs based on ancient Incan traditions. For more information contact: www.garyascott.com